DES DILLON was born and brought up in Coatbridge, Lanarkshire, and read English at Strathclyde University. A former teacher, he is now a poet, short story writer, novelist and dramatist writing for radio, stage, television and film, and has been a scriptwriter for High Road and River City. He has taught Creative Writing at the Arvon Foundation, and was Writer in Residence at Castlemilk, Glasgow, between 1998 and 2000. Des now lives in Galloway.

To date he is the author of eight novels and one poetry collection. His novel, *Me and Ma Gal*, was shortlisted for the Saltire Society Scottish First Book of the Year Award and won the 2003 World Book Day 'We Are What We Read' poll for the novel that best describes Scotland today. It was broadcast as a drama on Radio 4 in 2004. A short film of *Duck* was premiered at Edinburgh Film Festival in 1998 and in 2003 his play *Lockerbie 103* went on national tour. Des has adapted *Six Black Candles* into a play which won the International Festival of Playwriting Award in 2001, and in 2004 played at the Royal Lyceum Theatre in Edinburgh.

Also by Des Dillon:

Fiction
Me and Ma Gal (1995)
The Big Empty: A Collection of Short Stories (1996)
Duck (1998)
Itchycooblue (1999)
Return of the Busby Babes (2000)
The Big Q (2001)
Six Black Candles (2002)
The Blue Hen (2004)

Poetry
Picking Brambles (2003)

The Glasgow Dragon

DES DILLON

Luath Press Limited

EDINBURGH

www.luath.co.uk

First published 2004

Des Dillon has asserted his rights
under the Copyright, Designs and Patents Act 1988
to be identified as the author of this work.

The paper used in this book is recyclable.
It is made from low-chlorine pulps produced in a low-energy,
low-emission manner from renewable forests.

The publisher acknowledges subsidy from the Scottish Arts Council

 Scottish
Arts Council

towards the publication of this volume.

Printed and bound by
Bell & Bain Ltd., Glasgow

Typeset in 10.5 point Sabon

Actu 2007

This book is dedicated to Julie 'The Razor' Fraser.
Last known whereabouts: masquerading
as a florist somewhere in Glasgow.

To Kirsty

Best Wishes

Des Dillon

Acknowledgements

To be well thanked: Jennie Renton for doing a life-saving job on this book. Also Gavin MacDougall, Suzanne Kennedy and Amanda Palmer at Luath, and Julian Ward of the Department of Asian Studies at Edinburgh University for verifying Chinese characters.

Others to be thanked in chronological order are Eileen Quinn. Tessa Ross. Lucy Richer. Junior. Jonathan Curling.

Where were you born?
Under a peach tree
Do you have a mother?
I have five
Don't you owe me money?
I paid you, I recall
I don't recall that – where did you pay me?
In the market in the City of Willows

God I offer myself to thee to build with me
and to do with me as thou wilt.
Relieve me of the bondage of self,
that I may better do thy will.

Take away my difficulties
that victory over them may bear witness
to those I would help of thy power,
Thy love and Thy way of life.

May I do Thy will always.

膽識
courage

Behind an able man there are always other able men.

THERE'S NOTHING THE Devil hates more than his best soldier going over to the other side. If one man tries to cross over, six-hundred three score and six Demons rise up to bar his way. Today's Demons don't have teeth and claws and spiky red tails. Nor do they breathe sulphur and spit out flames. No. Look about you. Try telling the Demons from the good guys. Today's Demons do their work through people. They are everywhere and they are legion. But if the Devil works through people then so does God. There are Angels but they don't have fluffy wings and halos. Nor do they breathe in sunlight and sigh out stars. Angels could be anywhere. Angels could be anybody. Christie Devlin doesn't know it, but he's already begun his journey to the other side. He is about to flee his Demons.

Our story begins at the Chinese New Year. Imagine yourself staring into the eye of the Dragon as it dances to the beating of the drums. The streets are reflected in its eyes, its face washed with red and violet lights. The Dragon is red, green and gold. It's hard to tell which is dominant. Now it's red, now it's green, now it's gold. Here, nothing is as simple as it seems.

And the Dragon dances for you: its eyes are two dark circles embedded in red as it jerks from

side

to side

up

and down

in time with the music.
Underneath its undulating bamboo and silk sinews, Kung Fu boxers step out intricate rituals. The Dragon glides through the neon streets thanks to their long nights of sweating practice on wooden floors. Because of their sacrifice, the Dragon lives.

The Dragon dances through waterfalls of banners, under

4

archways, past shop fronts spelling out their esoteric wares in Cantonese. Beautiful young Chinese girls walking like their feet are one inch above ground hand out leaflets: Eat all you can, £4.99. And even if they don't know it themselves, they are bobbing up and down to the clash of cymbals and the beat, beating of the drums.

—*Tsoi kin*, they're saying: Good bye. Or more accurately: Again see.

The Dragon grins the sinister beauty of the Orient into the souls of dark-eyed children. Yellow flags of silk flow in the wind, thin as bird skin. Chinese of all ages, shapes and sizes dance, spin and jump behind its tail. Behind them, lines of marching men in San Yee On T-shirts move in perfect step. These are the Forty-Nines, the foot-soldiers of the San Yee On Triads.

The Dragon pushes into the face of a screaming child in her mother's arms. The child twists away, terrified. The mother comforts her baby, laughing the Dragon away. The Dragon turns to threaten some young boys. They stand erect. Impassive. Advertising bravado to the Triad gang.

Four pairs of black patent leather shoes stride along the street. People shuffle sideways, bowing respect. The four men, detached from the jubilation, make for where Ming Fung waits alongside a black Mercedes. She's tall, slim, stands with such poise she's got to be a dancer or a martial artist. Has the grace to walk on snow and leave no trace. Tai Lo is first there. Ming Fung gives him an imperceptible bow and opens the back door. The respect is partly because he's boss of the San Yee On but he's also her father. Heung Chu gets in beside Tai Lo. He's the spiritual leader of the Triad gang. Hung Kwan gets in and I Lo, a prospective new lieutenant, gives Ming Fung a glance he shouldn't, before squashing in beside the heavy Hung Kwan.

The engine purrs like money. Fireworks explode, casting instamatic shadows. Firecrackers crackle. Junkies slump in doorways. A boy carries a large goldfish in a bowl. It might be a pet or it might be someone's dinner. You never know. Two prostitutes in short skirts and curveless buttocks ignore two nuns who say hello.

WHOOSH

a tube of flame shoots up into the sky. The prostitutes' faces are lit up in rapture. The firework explodes softly into an umbrella of stars.

—Ahh! says the crowd.

The black Mercedes inches along. Suddenly Heung Chu whips his head round, looking across the street to the Golden Moon Restaurant. Tai Lo asks what's wrong.

—*Mat-ye shi*?

—*Ngoh m chi*, says Heung Chu.

He doesn't know what's wrong. But there is something. Heung Chu closes his eyes to meditate. Tai Lo scrutinises the Golden Moon until the car is consumed in the tail of the dancing Dragon.

Steam cascades from the Golden Moon onto the street and creeps along the ground, diffusing the flashes of fireworks to a milky light. Constant streams of Chinese shuttle in and out, laughing, singing and chattering. An old man with white hair stares up through folds of skin at the cold light of the stars. His head doesn't move. It's hard to tell if he's blind or wise.

Inside there's a stainless steel counter and chipped Formica tables. Christie Devlin watches figures moving through the steam. The chef seems to be taking orders for meals on the telephone, but it's bets he's taking. He writes the bets on soluble rice paper, memorises them and flings them in a pot of boiling water. Then he passes the information orally on to a one-armed man who disappears through the back. Now and then someone trips on the torn linoleum and swears in Chinese. Devlin laughs and some Chinese laugh back. Some shout and joke. Some read Chinese papers silently. Plates clatter. A fat woman stuffs her mouth with roast duck. Devlin watches flames shoot up in woks and disappear leaving a hollow behind, a hole in the world that takes a second to reconstitute itself before – whoosh, up go the flames again. The hollow returns with a feeling something is missing. Not right. The meat hisses as it hits the hot fat. Blood seeps into the fat. Devlin's head tilts as rice is tossed up and

falls

back into pans where it's scooped into rows of dinky Chinese bowls and thumped onto trays with savoury dishes and pots of green tea. Shabby waiters weave through the tables like a military operation. Plates bump in front of customers. Some have noticed Devlin watching. Some haven't. Others openly point at the Gwai Lo. Comment on his shiny black shoes and white socks. His immaculate suit shirt and tie. Who is he, sitting in their restaurant with his three whiter than white pigs?

The Chinese love gold and Devlin's ring hasn't gone unnoticed. It's a golden Triangle made with three words:

UNITY
SERVICE
RECOVERY

Even though Devlin's thoughts are somewhere else, part of him listens to his men's conversation. Sam, small and dark-haired – he could be a TV repair man – tries to explain a credit card fraud to Bonzo and Sholtz. Sholtz is bald and beer-bellied. Bonzo is just under six feet, compact, with broad shoulders. Devlin trusts Bonzo with his life.

Sam holds his hands up in exasperation.

—They're all blank!

He shows Bonzo and Sholtz a blank credit card.

—You record somebody else's information on the magnetic strip. Like printing money.

—Show us then, says Bonzo.

—I can't. I need my laptop and the machine to download the data, says Sam.

Bonzo and Sholtz take the piss. Their Scottish accents draw attention.

—I'm serious, says Sam, frustration on his face.

Bonzo's noticed Devlin's miles away and is about to ask him what's up when the waiter, thumbs in the bowls, bumps down four noodle soups.

—Thanks, china, quips Sholtz.

—Hey! I chink I know him, says Bonzo.

That gets a wee smile from Devlin. As his men eat, Devlin takes a Mother's Pride bread wrapper from his pocket. He carefully opens it, revealing an outsider. He halves it, sits one half on the wrapper and dips the other in his noodle soup. The men say nothing. They've been with him too long. But the chef screams in Cantonese.

—*Hey, no food to be brought into the restaurant.*

Even though it's Cantonese, Devlin knows the chef's shouting at him. He ignores it. The chef repeats, miming dipping bread. Bonzo, Sholtz and Sam can't contain their laughter.

—*No food to be brought into the restaurant.*

The Golden Moon falls silent. Reflected in a hundred Chinese eyes, the chef shouts into Devlin's face.

—*No food. No food.*

This world has ground to a halt. Devlin's men know anything could happen. The Chinese hope something will. Devlin looks the chef in the eye and hoists his outsider over the bowl. The entire restaurant pauses on Devlin's outsider poised over the soup. Devlin grins at the chef and

Whoom!

dunks it into the soup. Eats it at the chef, biting chunks and letting wet bits of dough slide down his face. The Chinese burst out laughing and return to meals and pandemonium.

The angry chef walks back behind the counter and lifts a cleaver, thinks about jamming it in Devlin's head. But Devlin's looking at him hard. Thump! The chef chops the head off a large fish.

Devlin rubs a hole in the silver screen of steam and presses his head to the window. Here comes the Dragon. Bonzo, Sholtz and Sam are too engrossed in credit card fraud to notice. The Dragon's eyes flick to Devlin. The giant yellow head turns. It's coming towards him, dancing two steps forwards, one back. At the window of the Golden Moon the Dragon falls still except for the wind in its ribbons. It stares at Devlin. Devlin stares back. The Dragon tilts its head left. Devlin tilts his. Insulted, it tilts right. The crowd cheers. Devlin tilts his head to the exact angle of the Dragon's.

—*Ooh*, says the crowd.

The Dragon shudders like a peacock. Devlin shakes his head so his skin wobbles.

—*Ooh*, say the crowd.

The Dragon presses its face up to the window. So does Devlin. His nose spreads on the glass. Half pig, half man.

—*Gwai Lo*, shouts an old woman and laughter rings out.

The Dragon's motionless. Devlin immobile. Eyeball to eyeball through the glass.

Slowly, deliberate as a Tai Chi master, the Dragon withdraws. The crowd breathes out one long breath.

The old man with white hair draws his eyes away from his cold field of stars. He sees the Dragon's head, lit by neon, mirrored in Devlin's eyes. Watches it recede like a fearsome red and yellow fish sinking into dark waters.

兄弟

brother

Of all the thirty-six alternatives, running away is best.

FOUR CAR DOORS thump. The Triads leave the black Mercedes. Ming Fung takes her father's arm as they enter the Silver Seas Casino. Their car is on a double yellow but they'll pay the tickets. They always obey the laws of the land. When they can. Heung Chu is last through the spinning glass door. He peers along the street before entering. In the distance the Dragon twists to look at him. It rises up, then bows to the spiritual master. Heung Chu bows back.

The festival is reflected in the hearse-like panels of Devlin's black Mitsubishi Shogun. Got an appointment with the Triads. Can't be late. Has to make a good impression. In this business the less left to chance the better.

—*Siu-sam*, Be careful, says a woman's voice.

—*Siu-sam*, replies Devlin.

His adrenaline rises an infinitesimal drip every time the crowds force him to stop. He looks out through the black-tinted windows: six upside-down chickens pass, some flapping. A startling young woman carries them by their feet; three in each hand. Three have given up struggling and watch the ground go past beneath then. Two, in her left hand, flutter now and then, but to no avail. The other lifts and pecks her, drawing blood. She whines. Gives the five birds to a boy at her side. Wrings its neck. One squawk and it's relaxed as a bunch of rags. She takes the rest of the chickens back. The boy with the dead chicken over his shoulder and they walk on. They could be mother and son, Devlin's thinking, or brother and sister. They could be anything.

—*Yap lai*. Come in, says the *Teach Yourself Cantonese* tape.

—*Yap lai*, replies Devlin.

A horn toots behind. The road in front is clear again. Devlin shunts another six feet, stopping beside a wooden cage. Four ducks gaze out with bewildered resignation. The Chinese kid carrying the goldfish bowl stops and stares at the car window, expressionless. Devlin can't tell if he's inquisitive, hostile or puzzled. There's a feeling rising in him that this kid knows something he doesn't. As the boy walks away his mouth lifts to a smile and water slips over the lip of the bowl. The fish's eyes bulge in terror.

—*M ho.* Not good, says the tape.

—*M ho,* says Devlin.

A man drags a screaming monkey into an alley. The whites of its eyes glimmer in ultraviolet light.

Bonzo nudges Devlin.

—Boss, we're clear!

The parade is disappearing. Stragglers wander like they've been invited to a party they can't find.

—*Ho-la.* Alright, okay.

—*Ho-la,* says Devlin.

The two nuns help a junkie from the ground and walk off with him.

—*M-koi.* Thank you.

—*M-koi,* says Devlin.

Bonzo turns the volume down.

—You wishy speaky Chinkee in five minutes?

—Yessy, says Sholtz, —Wa Shing Ka!

—He is washing his automobile, replies Bonzo.

Devlin snorts, turning the volume up again.

—*M-hai.* No, it is not, says the tape.

—*M-hai.* Devlin says.

—Wai Yu Mun Ching? asks Bonzo patting Devlin on the belly, —I thought ye were on a diet?

Sholtz farts.

—Good arse, he says.

—Ah fuck it!

Devlin's had enough. He slides the tape out, slips in another one and turns to Sholtz.

—Yu stin – ki pu. Means you are fuckin bogging. Somebody roll a window down.

Bonzo rolls the window down. Talking Heads starts drum-diddy-drumming on the door panel speakers. Bonzo and

Sholtz beat the rhythm out on the dashboard and back seat. They sing at the top of their voices as they cruise ultra-slowly through the alternating lurid lights and macabre gloom of Chinatown. Devlin joins in.

♪♪ We're on the road to paradise… here we go, here we go…

The car and the Chinese festival all reflect on the river surface. Up ahead is the Silver Seas Casino. Inside the Triads wait: Tai Lo the boss, Heung Chu the spiritual master, Hung Kwan the general of the foot-soldiers and I Lo the new lieutenant.

Chinese chatter and shout, leaning into blackjack tables and spinning roulette wheels. Apart from some Pakistanis, Indians and a couple of Jamaicans it's wall to wall Oriental. Bets are placed. Punters are pushed back. The croupier is a white-skinned Scottish girl with long, brown hair and straight shoulders. She spins the ball in the opposite direction to the wheel. It clicks and bounces.

—No more bets, she says.

The table is a quiet black-hole in a chaotic universe of folding notes, clicking chips, stacking coins and notes stuffed into the boxes below the tables. The epicentre of chaos is the Punto table. Punto: from a distance it looks like a cock fight. A hundred men and women leaning over the table screaming. One croupier deals and hits a groping Chinaman a back-kick with her heel. She gets him in the balls and he tumbles down laughing in pain. The table laughs and she continues to deal, count and play without pause. If any game is a microcosm of Hong Kong, Punto is it.

Devlin enters with his men. No one turns. But they all see. He moves through the mayhem. Searches over the blackjack, poker and roulette tables. In the doorway of another immense hall, Tai Lo waits with his men. Behind them is the colossal sound of thunder. Tai Lo nods and disappears into the room of thunder. Devlin glances sideways at Bonzo.

—Lose the grin, he says.

Bonzo loses the grin. I Lo and Hung Kwan watch from the Mah Jong room.

—*Look at them, they look like white pigs*, says I Lo.

Tai Lo reproaches I Lo with one look. Devlin strides over. He's been waiting for this moment. And he's been practising Cantonese to make an impression.

—*Nei ho ma?* asks Devlin: How are you?

It works. Caught off guard by unexpected Cantonese from this tough Gwai Lo, Tai Lo smiles with a slight bow of the head.

—*Ho yau-sam*, he replies.

Devlin's guanxi has already started to build and I Lo doesn't like it.

Guanxi has an abstract but definite value. You can't sell it but you can hoard it. It can be inherited, shared or given away. Some Chinese carry little books recording the favours they've done for others and the favours they've received. Who owes them how much guanxi and how much they owe. Utilitarian karma: what you do for others is returned on request, not by cosmic bequest. They also list who they are connected to. These connections can be approached for help. No modern Chinese business operates without guanxi coming into play. Even I Lo has come to join Tai Lo's gang by dint of his guanxi, this time acting as a reference. I Lo has a *curriculum vitae* of violence.

As I Lo whispers venom to Hung Kwan, Tai Lo sweeps his hand low past his hips.

—Come, we have much to discuss, he says.

They are led through the Mah Jong room. Bonzo mutters a joke to Sholtz.

—I took my chicken curry back to the Chinkee's last night, This chicken's rubbery, I goes. He says, Fank you velly much, I make it myself.

Bonzo and Sholtz hold in their laughter. Just.

—This chicken's rubbery! says Bonzo.

Tai Lo seats them in a far corner. They are served green tea by Heung Chu. Hung Kwan orders a Forty-Nine to fetch something. Forty-Nines, sometimes knows as the *sze kau,* are under the direct command of Hung Kwan. They are at the bottom of the Triad ladder, the rank and file – the criminal workforce.

Nothing is said. Devlin and his men stare at the Triads. The Triads stare back. The Forty-Nine returns and tosses a bag of powder on the table. Tai Lo shows it to Devlin.

—Every war has a silver lining, is it? No heroin coming from out Afghanistan more. The Mericanoes clamping in Bekaar valley... Iraq, the Middle East, tied up by military. We free to bring much heroin from China. Flood the city. Rule the city.

He tosses the bag to Devlin.

—Number four heroin, says Tai Lo.

—China White, Devlin says.

He passes the bag to Bonzo. Bonzo inspects it and nudges Sam.

—We have the merchandise. You have the infera... Infor...

—Infrastructure, I Lo corrects.

—Inerfastructure, says Tai Lo.

And he throws a tiny glower at I Lo. With the Chinese everything is face. In the uneasy quiet Bonzo makes up a hit and pops a vein in his arm. Devlin breathes long and slow before speaking.

—We've got the infrastructure all right. I can have this whole city tied up in a week if you can guarantee...

Devlin taps the bag just as Bonzo shoots up a tiny amount of heroin. Before the syringe is fully compressed Bonzo's jaw drops open. All eyes are on him. This is quality control. Bonzo floats in infinity for one second, closes his eyes, draws himself together and gives his professional opinion.

—Wow. Flying. Soft and spongy land, clear and white.

Sam removes the syringe, picks up the spoon, the lighter, and clears everything away like nothing's happened. Bonzo, slumped in his chair, assures Devlin that this is the bee's knees this stuff, the bee's knees.

—You have in... Infer... network. We have infinite supply, says Tai Lo.

—I've got dealers in clubs, pubs, schemes and brothels. If you're white and you take smack in this city, it's mine.

Tai Lo smiles. One of those smiles where you don't know if you'll be kissed or killed.

—What about your competitors?

—Competitors, Devlin snorts, —Ye mad?

—No?

Quick change of tone. The little guanxi Devlin had has vanished. The Forty-Nines take one step closer.

—None, Devlin says, —I've no competitors.

Wrong answer. Devlin sees that in the instinctive narrowing of Tai Lo's eyes. He asks Devlin again.

—None?

Devlin shakes his head. Tai Lo signals Hung Kwan to read a list of names from a sheet of yellow paper.

—Brolly, Donnelly, Riley, Malky, Garrett.

Dread! The Forty-Nines are bristling. Bonzo senses danger. He's pushing the effects of the smack away. Sholtz has pulled his feet under the chair ready to tilt the table as he stands. Whip out his gun. Bonzo's hand is on his gun. Sam has a grenade in his pocket with his thumb through the pin. He hopes he can work it loose in time.

Devlin's thinking is clear. This moment is where it all lies. This one moment with Tai Lo staring in his eyes.

—I've already took care of them.

Tai Lo looks to Hung Kwan who shakes his head. Devlin changes tack. Talk is ice on the cold waters of brutality. He could fall through any second.

—I said I can have the whole city tied up in a week. I've already arranged to deal with the names you've got there.

Tai Lo hadn't expected this. His information is Brolly, Donnelly, Riley, Malky and Garrett are still dealing. Devlin promised at their first meeting he'd take them out. One nod to the left, Devlin's dead. One nod to the right, he gets another chance. Devlin holds his palms out and laughs.

—Everything's in place. It's all set up. I wouldn't be so daft as to come here if it wasn't, would I?

That makes sense to Tai Lo. What white man would come into the Dragon's lair bearing unfulfilled promises? Tai Lo coughs. The Mah Jong tiles fall silent.

—You can assure us?

—On my life, says Devlin.

—Your life?

Tai Lo and Devlin's eyes are locked for a microsecond.

—Aye, my life, Devlin says.

The room breathes out. The tiles rattle like applause. Tai Lo leans to shake but Devlin shoves his palm up. The tiles fall silent again. The room floods with paranoia. Devlin clicks his fingers at Sam. Did the Chinkees think he was fuckin daft? Did they think he was strolling in here to be at their mercy? Did they think he rose to the top without realising the value of information? Devlin has a maxim: it's not what you know, it's not even who you know: it's what you know about who you know!

—Here, boss.

Sam hands Devlin a piece of paper. Devlin makes a ceremony of folding it flat on the table. So everybody's got to lean in to read it.

—What about *your* competitors?

Tai Lo laughs.

—What competitors?

—The Jamaicans, the Thais, the Indians and Pakis?

Tai Lo's head goes this way and that. Hung Kwan shrugs his shoulders. Heung Chu doesn't know where Devlin got that information. I Lo's only new and still to get up to speed with this city. Devlin just got his guanxi back in spades. Tai Lo stares hard at him.

—Don't look at me. They don't sell to the white man, says Devlin.

Devlin's business has been the white population. The

Jamaicans, the Thais, the Indians and Pakistanis, Tai Lo knows, sell mainly to their own. Considering the opposition, it's little wonder. The Chinese have been seen as dealers on the same level. Up until now the Triads have just been dabbling in the drugs market, building business interests in a myriad of other places. Electronics, extortion, forged airplane parts. But now they're going big in drugs. Now they're going to take over. Tai Lo knows, for the time being anyway, he can't do that without Devlin. Devlin's guanxi rises again.

—Okay. We to be taking cares of our competitors. You take care of Gwai Lo.

—Done, says Devlin, —You sort the ethnic minorities. We sort out the white man.

—What about policeman?

—Billy? Don't worry about him.

Devlin has Billy Pitt, Chief of Police, where he wants him.

—We have agreement? asks Tai Lo.

Devlin walks round and shakes his hand. Chinese smiles flicker around the room.

—Definitely, he says, —Definitely have agreement. My men'll take care of that… consolidation… and we can meet again say…

—Thursday night okay dokay?

Tai Lo asks his men. They all nod that it is okay dokay.

Tai Lo shakes Devlin's hand again. Heung Chu, the spiritual master, zooms in on the golden triangle.

UNITY

SERVICE

RECOVERY

Devlin notices and nods. Heung Chu nods back. Tai Lo thrusts a glass into Devlin's hand. A waiter watches from a distance.

—Drink?

—I'm driving, Devlin says.

Tai Lo offers Devlin's men a drink but they all refuse.

—Anyway we have to go, says Devlin, —Business! Goodbye.

They leave in a farce of goodbyes.

—Goodbye, says Heung Chu.

—Goodbye, says Sholtz.

—Goodbye, says Heung Chu again.

—Good buy – best ever, says Bonzo laughing.

—Goodbye, says Devlin again.

—Goodbye, says Tai Lo.

Sam joins in. I Lo has to be encouraged by Tai Lo. He needs close watching, this I Lo new person. Good references and guanxi but bad attitude for good business. Eventually Devlin and his men break away. As the Triads watch them leave, Hung Kwan cracks a joke.

—*It's hard to tell one from the other.*

—*What?* asks I Lo.

—*They all look the same to me.*

I Lo laughs, folding over. Tai Lo and Hung Kwan want to know what's so funny. Through his laughter I Lo relates the joke. Once they get it they fall about. Ming Fung smiles from the other end of the room. As he leaves, Bonzo has a good look at her.

Yes, Devlin did have plans to take out Brolly, Donnelly, Riley and Malky. But Garrett? He's never heard of him. That's bad news in this business. An interloper. A newcomer. An unknown quantity. He's holding it in. But he wants to explode. He wants to really really explode. When he gets to the Silver Seas foyer he turns on his men.

—Who the fuck is Garrett?

—Let's go and see our grasses, says Bonzo.

Devlin grogs up a load of saliva and spits on the floor.

—I hate grasses. You go. I don't want to catch something.

The waiter stands by the revolving glass door watching

them leave. When they drive off he discards the white jacket and bow tie. Goes out into the city.

Devlin and his men head north. The Silver Seas is a distant reflection on the river. As they drive along Sauchiehall Street, Bonzo asks Sholtz questions from a spoof Mafia application form. They're suppressing their laughter because they know their boss is irritated. Devlin's hands grip the wheel and it dents so you'd think it was clay. The more his men talk the harder he clenches.

—Whatsa your namea? asks Bonzo.

—Sholtz. Mister Sholtz.

—Isa u a girl or boy? Just chuzza one.

—A man.

—Wasa u ever inna biga ouse?

Yes to that one.

—For whatta wazza you inna bigga ouse for?

Devlin slams on the brakes. They flip forwards. Cars behind toot. They're under one of the M8 bridges. Above, night time cars go past.

—Shut fuckin up! Have yees found out where this Garrett cunt is?

The answer is two blank faces and Sam knowing he should speak but afraid to.

—No! Have yees fuck!

Devlin turns to the front and sighs. Up ahead are Maryhill, Ruchill and Possil, the places he made his name a legend before he was twenty-one.

—Sorry, Christie. Sam's on the case, says Bonzo.

Sam swallows hard and speaks, tapping the keys on his laptop.

—Contacted all our grasses, boss. Could get something any minute.

Devlin starts the car and drives off through a red light. Doesn't even look at the traffic coming down the M8 off-ramp braking, swerving, blaring horns and flashing lights. They head towards the junction between Maryhill Road and the canal bridge, a gaping mouth into Possil. High above the road a freezing fog hangs over the canal. As they stop at the lights Sam's phone rings.

—That'll be it now, boss. Mm mm. Right. Okay… no, just text it. Are you sure? Good. Good work.

—Well? says Devlin.

—Got Garrett's number, boss.

—Bonzo, sort it.

—On it.

Devlin's shoulders drop. He leans back, taking a life-size breath. The lights change. As they drive into the gaping mouth the icicles light up in his headlights. Devlin shivers. It's a long time since they had a winter so cold.

Sholtz reads one of the questions from the Mafia application form to Devlin.

—U wanna be de bigga shotza someday?

—I already am de bigga shotza!

Bonzo joins in.

—Okay. Iffa u application is approved u will aget dessa benefits: One pair darka glasses.

Devlin puts a pair of dark glasses on. He might be angry but your men are your men. Life depends on them. Aye, like brothers that's what they are. He's allowed to get angry. Somebody's got to keep order in this fucked up world. They have to stay together. Be a unit. Especially now they're going to merge with the Triads. Take over Glasgow. Stay on their toes. Keep it tight. Why shouldn't he join in with a bit of fun?

—One appy face button. One pair pointed shooz.

Devlin grins and wiggles one of his pointed shoes at Bonzo.

—One blacka shirt with a white collar. One kilo mozzarella cheese.

Sholtz leans over the seat and slaps Devlin's belly.

—One pair ciment shooz. Free burial and an eight by ten photograph of Frank Sinatra.

—Let me see that fuckin thing.

Devlin grabs the form and reads it as they wait at the lights outside the Possil Bar.

—You like a salami? No? Yes?

The lights change.

Way over to the south of the river, high up in the Glasgow Tower, Tai Lo and Heung Chu look down over the shimmering nightscape. Devlin's Shogun is no more than a dot moving through the back streets of Possil.

爸

father

Married couples tell each other a thousand things without speech.

RIPPLES OF LIGHT shimmer on the cover of a book: four Chinese symbols flicker on a cream background. There's the echoic sound of someone swimming. The rhythmic splash and displacement of water. In a reclining chair, beside a massive kidney-shaped pool, Devlin studies *Teach Yourself Cantonese*.

His wife, Wendy, swims up and down, now and then glimpsing up to catch his eye. But he's engrossed in the book. Wendy's thirty-four and blonde with a trim figure. She's from a desperately upwardly mobile, working-class Manchester family. She met Devlin in a club when she was at St Andrews Roman Catholic College in Bearsden. Back then he was a young, sharp-suited gangster. He swept her off her feet.

She swims over with a graceful breast-stroke. Standing upright, she pulls her hair back. Then she remembers her stretch marks. Like a map of the bloody world. Sinks into the water that little bit.

Devlin looks up.

—Coming in? she asks.

—Funny cunt!

—What's the point in building a pool if you never use it?

He shakes his head. Mouths some Chinese words.

—*M-ho haak-hei.*

Wendy splashes into the claustrophobic silence of water. They don't talk the rest of the afternoon.

Later, at dinner, no one notices Finnegan, the black cat, trying to fish the goldfish from its bowl, his black paw distorted into a giant claw. Wendy, Devlin and Nicole eat. Nobody talks. Nicole is wearing a The Darkness T-shirt and a tutting face. Toying with her food. Wendy watches Devlin place his chicken, cooked in garlic and scattered with pine nuts, on an outsider of plain bread and fold it over. As he pushes it into his mouth she wants to say something. But she won't. She'll hold it in.

She'll bite her tongue. But he's reading that book. He's reading that book and mouthing Chinese words in repulsive whispers as chewed bread and chicken rolls about his mouth. It's a washing machine, his mouth. The tumble of the food. A pine nut falls over his bottom lip and

CLICKS

onto the table. Bread spreads up and down his mouth like stalactites and stalagmites. Wendy's nauseated. The bread. The word. The fleshy lips. She snaps.

—Nicole, don't play with your food!

—That's what the cannibal said to his daughters, says Devlin. —Don't play with your food. Get it?

But they don't.

—They were out playing and he looks out the window and... never mind!

Nicole empties the remains of her dinner onto Devlin's plate. Like she's done that a million times.

—Eat this, scofosaurus.

Wendy's temperature rises.

—Can't we go for a burger just once in our lives, Mummy?

Wendy glares at Nicole. It's not the time. This is not the time. She wishes Nicole would just shut up. But she won't.

—I mean, like, just because *he* doesn't allow it.

Wendy snubs Nicole. When Devlin licks his plate Nicole screws her face up. Wendy turns on him.

—Is that all you're capable of – reading that stupid book?

He stands up and walks away muttering Chinese for her benefit.

—Don't dare walk away from me while I am speaking!

He keeps walking, muttering the single-syllable words. Nicole spectates them out of the room onto the staircase. Devlin leaps two steps at a time. There's a pause, like a still photograph, then Wendy goes up one at a time but at twice the speed. Nicole slips Devlin's wallet from his jacket, takes a twenty pound note and slides it down her bra. She can hear her mother shouting.

—When you take over the responsibility of cleaning and cooking and shopping and running this house, then – then you can undermine my authority with our daughter, mister. Are you listening to me? Do you hear me?

—I'm listening, but all I can hear is your fuckin snobby English accent!

—That's it!

Wendy rushes after him. Devlin stops outside his room, lifts a leg, farts and goes in closing the door. The handle has barely clicked up and it's down again. Wendy bursts in screaming.

—Look at me. Take your nose out of that book and look at me.

—*Yap lai. Tso shan. Tseng ts oh. M-Koi. Yau-sam.*

She grabs the book and tries to tear it. It's not as easy as she thought. She bends over, elbows out grunting and twisting the spine, but it won't even bend.

—Nice arse, says Devlin.

He grabs the book, flings it up into the open loft hatch, jumps and hangs by his hands. As he's about to heave up he's surprised by a sudden weight gain. He's gained exactly a Wendy. She's wrapped round his legs, hanging like they're on a cliff edge. (And they are on a cliff edge, if they could only see it.) He could swing there all night. And so would Wendy if she wasn't losing her grip. Slipping down his legs.

—You bastard. I preferred you when you were drinking.

She lands with a thump on the floor, sprawled like lost dignity. Devlin hoists into the loft. His face is framed in darkness, pink and isolated. He sings to Wendy.

♪♪ Ying tong ting yong. Ying tong ting yong… can ye not let a man read his book in peace.

—Books? Is it books you want?

Wendy's eyes flit from book to book in Devlin's bookshelves. She hunches down, gathers a bundle and propels them, one at a time, through the black rectangle. They fly into

the loft, flapping like birds in an unexpected catastrophe. He says in an English accent,
    —Missed. Sorry, darling.
    Up goes *The Thirty-Nine Steps*.
    —Missed, dear.
    Whoosh, and *Les Miserables* is swallowed by gloom.
    —Oops, missed again. Crumbs, golly gosh, gee whizz. Fling another one, Bunty.
    Wendy listens to locate the exact attic coordinates of his voice. Certain of pinpoint accuracy, she takes aim and...
    Whizzzzzzzzzzzzzzzzzzzzzzzzzzzzzzzzzzzzzzzzzzzzzzzzzzzzzzzzzzzzzzzzzzzzz

BUMP

Moby Dick scuds him on the side of the head.
    —Ya bastard!
    She can hear his rough hand rasping up and down the side of his head. Now she knows exactly where he is. She showers him with books. The classics do the best damage. One splat flat on the forehead. A corner into his temple. A spine on the bridge of his nose. Two or three on the forearms before the volley is over. The cow must be away for more books. It'll be the heavy ones. That's what she's going for. The literary tomes. He can hear her sliding book after book from the shelves. What to do? What to do?
    He spots a big cardboard box.

ZANUSSI

THE APPLIANCE OF SCIENCE

He pulls the box over his head and sniggers. Finds the wee torch that sits beside the loft hatch. Opens *Teach Yourself Cantonese* and reads out loud.
    —*Yap lai. Tso shan. Tseng ts oh. M-Koi. Yau-sam.*

A shower of books thunder the outside of the box. Devlin sniggers quietly.

—Yap lai. Tso shan. Tseng ts oh. M-Koi. Yau-sam.

Wendy's sure she's hit him. Many times. Positive. So how is he still reading? Why did he not yell? She manoeuvres to see what the problem might be. Aha! She can make out the big

Z

Right! She leans back, thinking. One hand on her chin, one on Devlin's prized ironing board. What to do? What to do?

—Yap lai. Tso shan. Tseng ts oh. M-Koi. Yau-sam.

That's what Devlin's shouting into the suspicious hush when

!!CRACK!!

a white light. The abrupt snap of pain. The torch falls through the loft hatch. An illuminated slash of blood hits the floor, splashing into the darkness beneath the now static beam of the torch.

—Ooh my fuckin head, ya bastard!

In the expanding pain Devlin feels the silky texture of blood.

—Right. That's it!

She knew it was a steam iron too far when she picked it up. She knew it was big trouble when she launched it up on an exact trajectory, a scientific parabola in through the folds on top of the box. One second after Devlin's head was steam-ironed Wendy was in the hall. If she had glanced behind – she didn't – she'd have seen Devlin plunging feet first from the loft, blood smearing his face, the iron in his right hand glinting silver like some crazy outsize knuckle duster.

—Here's Johnny! he says.

But Wendy's down the stairs, not looking back. He leaps onto the middle landing. Loses his footing. Falls. Gets up and bounces down the last ten steps. He's so fast he's nearly ahead of her; that's the quantum physics of anger.

Nicole curls her lip as Wendy swivels out the front door slamming it so he slaps into it. He fiddles with the Yale, opens it, explodes through his giant black gates.

—Come back here, ya English hoor.

Nicole takes out her diary and writes. *I am going to end up totally dysfunctional*. She takes two more twenty pound notes from Devlin's wallet. And why not? At this rate she'll be needing therapy. Good therapy doesn't come cheap.

In the ultra-posh, gated estate, Donald and Laura are in their garden clipping winter flowers. They watch Wendy race away from Christie Devlin. Potter in their shrubs pretending not to notice the iron raised above his head. As he passes they tut tut at the blood on his face. And his language? Oh my God!

—I'm gonni fuckin kill ye, ya cow!

A soon as he's out the gate, Donald turns to Laura.

—B&Q's doing azaleas for £3.99.

—£3.99?

—And begonias.

Devlin rugby tackles Wendy and they tumble down a slope towards a burn. The odd jutting rock presses into their ribs as they go. The iron rolls and clunks into a tree. Its casing flies off. They crash to a stop on a bed of grass scattered with frost. Devlin's on top of Wendy. A knee on each elbow. She's looking up at his crotch wondering if she could raise her head enough to sink the teeth in. But her glare softens and becomes a certain look. He lets her lean up and engulf his mouth. Suck his lips and his tongue. Drag him down on top of her. She wraps her legs round him. Feels him getting hard. He's pushed right up to her bone. He lifts the front of her skirt. She's unzipped him and took his cock out. Thoughts of Chinese books, irons and blood disappear like whispers. He thumbs her thong to the side, looks in her eyes and thrusts it deep. Her mouth opens and a fog escapes.

—D'you like that, ya wee English slut? he says in her ear.

—Yes, she whispers, —Yes.

The frantic rhythm evens out so she's pushing her hips up as he's withdrawing. He's pressing her down with each stroke. They breathe as if everything above and below them is a marvel.

Wendy's breath gets faster and shallower. Devlin's beyond thinking about her as he thrust, thrust, thrusts for himself. Everything for the man. And that's what Wendy wants. A real hard fuck by a real hard man. It's sometimes as simple as that. Beneath her political correctness is the animal. And beneath that? The Demon or the Angel. Devlin pumps and the orgasm builds. And his thoughts are rising from far below his animal. Or beyond his animal. Beyond the blood. Beyond the bone, beyond the brain that pulses in mad Morse, beyond his spirit, the essence or whatever the fuck they call it, beyond all that as his spunk pumps out he can see a tiny light, a bright light that doesn't hurt his eyes, and he realises everything he is, has been and will be, is designed to carry that tiny light. Then, as the sinews in his neck strain like tree roots, there's a tiny voice.

—*Christie*, it whispers, *that light is you.*

It sounds like a mother. He flops panting on top of a pink and powerful Wendy. Blinded by the light of orgasm, they sink into the frosted grass. Their fight long forgotten. Steam rising. Skin shining.

—What are you grinning at? says Wendy.

—Every time I come I laugh.

—I hope it's because you like it.

She wonders whether to tell him the news or not. She will. She will tell him. There's no time like now beside the stream and the beautiful bite of winter. And the smell of sex.

—I'm pregnant.

—That was quick.

—Seriously, I'm three months.

Devlin's eyes are two quick stars.

—No! You're serious! Ye are, int ye?

Wendy nods. She falls sideways through his gasp, into his

arms. She hadn't known how he would take it.

—Ya wee fuckin beauty. Hope it's a boy. Doesn't matter if it's not but it'd be good if it was, know what I mean!

—So you're okay about it?

—I'm over the moon, hen. Over the fuckin moon, so I am.

He rocks her gently. They meditate on the future. The sound of the river sometimes far away, sometimes engulfing.

—Guess what?

—You're still hard?

—I'm buying us a house in Galloway. Beside the sea.

—You're only saying that because I told you I'm pregnant.

—No, no I must be psychic. Jarkness it's called. I decided to buy it so that we could get out.

—What, retire?

—If that's what ye want to call it.

Wendy sits up.

—You decided you wanted to retire?

—Aye. Just fade into oblivion. This deal with the Chinkees, that'll make us enough to leave this city forever.

—Oh, Christie.

She kisses him.

Donald and Laura can't believe it when Devlin and Wendy come up the street laughing and joking. When they pass Donald is first to notice Wendy's dress tucked into the back of her thong. A nice arse she's got, a lovely wee arse he's thinking, when his erect hose unintentionally wets his wife.

—Donald, what are you doing! That's bloody freezing!

Nicole is suffering life alone in the living-room when her parents return. She can't understand why they're so light-hearted. She's going to end up totally dysfunctional now for sure. The more they speak the more she wishes she was born to normal parents. Like her friends at school. The Snoberatti, Daddy calls them. I mean, Daddy's a Glasgow pauper that's for sure. And Mummy... she tries to be proper but she's not got the *je ne sais quoi,* now has she? She's a working-class girl trying to posh it up. And it shows. It really won't do. Soon as she's able, like sixteen, duh! She'll be out of there.

Wendy impersonates a Devlin from the olden days. Her best Glasgow accent twists Nicole's face with such torque you'd think her skin would fall off.

—Get your hands off my woman, says a Glasgow Wendy.

Devlin says, —I was nineteen!

—Anybody touches my bird they've got me to deal with, goes Wendy.

As they pass the living-room door Nicole sees Wendy's skirt tucked into her thong and silent-screams in revulsion. Looks out of the window and simply knows Donald and Laura Mackenzie-Smyth are discussing the very same tucked-in skirt. Nicole stuffs a cushion in her mouth and bites on it.

Wendy kisses him on the forehead. Nicole sees Daddy's hand squeeze Mummy's bottom. Yeuch!

Devlin and Wendy are in the living-room. Nicole comes in done up in a little black dress and looking sexy. Devlin's aware for the first time that she's a woman.

—Nicole! he says.

Nicole puts her hand on the hip.

—Papa! she says.

Devlin laughs. Wendy decides now's as good a time as any.

—Nicole darling, we're going to have a baby!

—Gross!

—I thought you'd be happy, Wendy says.

—I get ignored in this house as it is.

Nicole stomps off.

—I want you in for eleven. D'ye hear me? Devlin shouts.

—I'm staying with a friend tonight.

—Which friend? asks Wendy.

Nicole answers by slamming the door. Devlin goes to move after her and Wendy stops him.

—She's nearly sixteen.

He watches his daughter sashay off down the garden path.

我愛你

I love you

It is the beautiful bird which gets caged.

DEVLIN'S MEN HAVE gone to the casino to collect guns from Hung Kwan and I Lo. They're putting them together with weapons from Devlin and giving the bundle to Billy Pitt, Chief of Police, for his gun amnesty. They are led through the Mah Jong room into another giant hall where the Lau Gar Kung Fu club are practising. The Kung Fu club covers as a training ground for prospective Triad members. All the pupils are Chinese. To Bonzo's surprise, Ming Fung is the instructor. She's dressed in red silk with a black sash. Sholtz nudges him.

—Whoo. Some bit of fanny, that funky Ming thing.

Hung Kwan welcomes Bonzo, Sholtz and Sam. Bonzo shakes hands wordlessly, fascinated by Ming Fung's moves. I Lo breaks his line of vision, delivering a few Kung Fu moves with more aggression than grace. A strike. A kick. Bonzo isn't impressed. I Lo stares a moment then

SLAM!

Kicks the bag.

Hung Kwan leads Devlin's men to another room in this labyrinthine building. Bonzo asks if he could join the Kung Fu club. He's always wanted to learn and there's never been a better time. Hung Kwan sends a Forty-Nine to ask Tai Lo's permission. I Lo knows what Bonzo's game is. Ming Fung. This room is green. Even the doors. The Dragon is being put away at the back. Hung Kwan crashes some guns on the table.

—The Glasgow polis'll love these, says Bonzo.

Sholtz lifts a handgun and points it, unaware he's pointing at Hung Kwan. Hung Kwan pushes the muzzle of the gun down.

—No point!

—Sorry, big fullah!

—Come from London. We get more you need.

—Don't give all your guns away, says Bonzo. —Never know

when you might need them.

A voice comes from behind them.

—No need guns.

Bonzo turns. I Lo's grin is reflected in the flat expanse of a massive cleaver.

Bonzo says, —I'd like to see ye taking on five gun-toting Pakis with that thing.

—I would like you also see me, says I Lo.

The Forty-Nine comes back. Speaks in Cantonese. Tai Lo says, yes, Bonzo should join the Kung Fu club. They can gather intelligence on Devlin's operation. Feed misinformation through Bonzo.

Keep your friends close but your enemies closer still.

Sholtz and Sam leave with the guns but Bonzo stays behind for his first Kung Fu class. Try as she might to avoid his gaze, Ming Fung is drawn to it. She claps her hands. The students rush to the edges of the gym where they sit cross-legged. Ming Fung picks up a square wooden board and holds it in the air between thumb and index finger.

—I Lo!

I Lo swaggers forward. Takes aim, spins and cracks the board in two with a reverse turning kick. There's applause as Hung Kwan whispers to Bonzo.

—I Lo crack skulls!

—No half, says Bonzo.

Ming Fung holds up another board.

—*Knife hand strike*, says I Lo.

He wants to break this one with a chop. Ming Fung talks him through it.

—*There are no obstacles. All is illusion. Breathe…*

I Lo takes a long breath through his nostrils.

—*And strike!*

WHOOSH!

he spins, breaking the board. The class applauds. I Lo bows.

Ming Fung reciprocates. Bonzo makes a note to take great care if he ever gets into a fight with I Lo. Next I Lo performs a series of intricate kicks, blocks and sliding moves under Ming Fung's careful eye. He ends by going through a slow Tai Chi form. When he's done, the students applaud again. Ming Fung produces a black sash and ties it round I Lo's waist. He has passed his first degree black belt. I Lo takes his place at the front of the class. Ming Fung claps three times. The members spring to attention and line up. She indicates for Bonzo to join in at the back. The lesson begins. Bonzo mimics the yellow belts in front of him.

—*Yat.*

Ming Fung performs a high front kick and the class copy.

—*I.*

Double punch. The class copy.

—*Saam.*

Into a spinning kick striking with the heel.

—*Sei.*

She jumps and lands moving into a low sweep. The class copy but Bonzo falls and they laugh.

Half an hour later the class is put on bag work. Bonzo lays some neat combinations into the heavy bag. I Lo swaggers over.

—You boxer?

—Done a bit.

Bonzo lays a heavy hook in. Ming Fung comes over and strikes the bag with as much power but infinitely more grace.

—You're no bad at that, hen.

He reaches out to touch her with the intention of demon-strating western boxing techniques.

—Have you ever tried...

She locks his wrist. Sweeps him so fast that he's
> up in the air
> > where he hangs
> > > then

THUMPS

onto the floor, winded. Looking up at I Lo's grin. Hearing the laughter of the club. But is that a wink he catches from Ming Fung as she claps the class back to order?

In a Glasgow night-club filled with under-age girls and over-aged married men, Nicole is up on the dance floor drinking Aftershock as Uncle Jack play live on stage.

Gerry could be anything from twenty-five to forty. He's got a face like a boy. He grabs her breasts from behind and they dance. And they sing. And they grind. He's got blue eyes and a smile to melt gold.

Gerry transfers an E from his tongue to hers. He rolls it to the tip of his tongue. She opens her mouth and his tongue goes in. He drags it back against her top teeth so the E falls in. He fills his mouth with Aftershock and kisses her, letting the drink flow into her mouth. She swallows and downs the E. Shrieks and shakes her hair. Gerry's face is ghostly red in the glow from the giant spliff he's just lit up. He holds his hands together near Nicole's face, opens them revealing a gold credit card.

—Where did you get that? she asks.

Gerry nods at a Armani-clad young man patting his pockets at the bar. Nicole laughs with delight.

—Let's spend spend spend!

Gerry puts his mouth against her ear.

—Is it not about time you told your father about us?

Devlin's lost in the sleepy murmur of holy small talk between Father Boyle and Wendy. She pours another cup of tea. Devlin surveys the arctic surface of a meringue.

—Another meringue father?

—I really shouldn't. I'm on a diet.

But he takes it anyway.

Devlin puffs out his cheeks behind Boyle's back. Wendy ignores him and gets to the point.

—Father, tell Christie about the youth.

Devlin unpuffs his cheeks as Boyle turns.

—He's stealing money from the Saint Vincent de Paul.

—Can ye not keep the doors locked?

Father Boyle shakes his head. Churches and chapels in Glasgow have to lock their doors. If they don't, their collections, candles and silverware are turned into smack.

—After Mass on a Saturday morning we have weddings to set up so we usually leave the doors open, says Boyle.

—Get one of them oul women to watch out for him.

—I did, and caught him last Saturday.

—I hope you battered his cu... gave him a few slaps.

—He kicked me.

—He kicked ye? A priest?

—In the...

Father Boyle can't bring himself to say balls.

—In the groin, says Wendy. —He kicked Father in the groin. He had to go to the hospital didn't you, Father?

—Kicked a priest in the balls! Who kicks a priest on the ba...

—More tea, Father?

Wendy mouths to Devlin to watch his language.

—Yes. Thank you. Those meringues were good, says Boyle.

—I'll fetch some more.

Wendy moves off to get the meringues but she stops in the doorway.

—I told Father you might be able to help him, Christie.

—I thought... I was hoping, mutters Boyle, —You could give him a little fright.

—I could do that for you, Father. No problem.

If Father Boyle had looked in Devlin's eyes he'd have seen them darken.

—More meringue, anyone? says Wendy.

On the dance floor Nicole lets the E take effect. Gerry rehearses in his head what he's going to do with her. How he's going to use her.

In the morning sun, Low Moss looks like an old army barracks.

A few miles to the north of Glasgow, it consists of rows of wooden huts, painted pale blue and surrounded by high fences topped off with razor wire. It's a low security prison used to house non payment of fines, shoplifting, theft. All the short jail sentences.

There's a woman with a limp and a patch over her eye. Marie Devlin's been there many times. Many, many times. To visit her son David. How many days has she lined up with other mothers, wives and girlfriends? How many days has she stood at the giant wire gate and watched as prisoners march to the visiting block, waving to relatives?

How many visits has Marie crushed her tears down and small-talked with David for an hour, over a knee-high table? Cans of coke and bags of crisps. She knows he's still on the smack. Sorted for visits, but mothers have a sense. She knew he was spending his nights curled up on a bunk with a mouthful of prison air and a bloodstream stuffed with clouds and angels. Every time he comes out he owes some dealer somewhere a wad of money. So then he's got to double shoplift to pay the dealer and keep his habit going. If he could only get clean in jail he'd come out debt free. Start all over again. Maybe go back to Uni.

Marie pulls herself out of that dream. She'd settle just for him not dying in her arms. Or worse, dying somewhere else, not in her arms. There's nothing more heartbreaking than a mother burying her child. Glasgow's seen plenty of that. Smack.

Before David went into decline his Uncle Christie put him through Uni. Gave him two hundred pounds a week. So David started his Psychology degree with new clothes and scores of fair-weather friends. But smart as he was, he blew it. Yes, he was taking drugs, but so was everybody. A bit of blow and E at night. Speed sometimes. David drifted away from lectures and tutorials. He took Devlin's money for a year after he'd been asked to leave the university. By the time Devlin found out it was too late. He was already on the smack. Not an out and out junkie, but on the edge of the abyss. When Devlin found out, he waited for David outside Marie's close one night and slapped him about. Then washed his hands of his nephew.

Marie's breath comes out in plumes in the frosty air. A metallic click echoes somewhere in the prison. Voices. Then she can see David coming towards her, as fellow inmates shout their goodbyes through gaps in the windows. He's thin and pale. He smiles. She smiles back, though she's crying inside. He waves and she waves back, her arm the weight of every times she's been there. The Prison Officer turns at the gate.

—See ye, mate, says David.

—Hope not son, he says, —Hope not!

David pats him on the shoulder and walks to Marie. Her one eye flicks up and down making sure he's all still there. All in one bit.

—My wee maw!

He sits his possessions down and hugs her. Even though the Prison Officer has seen this thousands of times, it moves him. That turned the numbers into names for him.

Marie limps towards David and gives him a big hug. She's on the roller coaster again.

—Are ye aff the drugs, son?

—Aye, Maw, clean as a tin of Vim.

教化
enlightenment

The poorer one is, the more Devils one meets.

DEVLIN'S ALONE IN his wee room, thinking. Pondering Wendy's news. She's pregnant. That's fine, that's great. A boy. A wee boy. He'd like that.

He's told Wendy he's getting out. Doesn't know if it's the truth himself. Aye, he's buying the house in Galloway for the family. The new wean. The new future. Where's the lie in that?

Power and money hasn't changed the way he feels. Every morning the dread's there. Same as growing up in Possil. Like an icicle's been driven through his body. Right where the ribs join at the solar plexus. And a craving, a constant craving. For what? He never can quite figure that out. Action's always been the only thing that the dulls down the dread. He forgets so long as his mind is occupied. Like meditation in reverse. Devlin's meditation is to absorb himself in life and ignore his emotions. He traps his fear in a lead box in his chest.

—To the degree we think we're special is the distance we are from repair. We're all special, Christie, we're all unique. That's what Cooney said at the AA meeting. Here comes the dread again. Find something. Find something to rest the eyes on. Aha! The big window at the top of that landing.

The light floods in
The light floods in
The light floods in
The light floods in
The light floods in
The light floods in
The light floods in
The light floods in

It looks out over the garden to the monkey-puzzle tree with its dark branches sweeping down like monkeys' tails. Monkeys reputedly thought these trees were full of friends, or even enemies, who knows? Devlin reckons that's daft. A monkey could tell the difference. Otherwise it would reach for a branch and fall, clutching its own tail. The jungle floor would be full of dead monkeys. Like the city is full of dead junkies.

the tree is beautiful
    the city is full of dead junkies

        the tree is beautiful
            the city is full of dead junkies

            the tree is beautiful
              full of dead junkies

Sometimes he stares at that tree for hours. Doesn't know why. There'd been one at the convent his mother took him to once when Da had battered them both. He'd been too messed up to go to school. Teeth right through his lips, eyes swollen almost closed. Since the convent, he'd wanted a monkey-puzzle tree.

Bonzo turned him on to classical music in the jail when they were dubbed up together for two years.

Devlin shoves a CD in the Bang and Olafsen. With the door closed and the music playing, he does something nobody has ever seen him do. Devlin weeps. He feels weak when he cries. But better afterwards. Sometimes it's sad crying, sometimes happy crying. Fauré's *Sanctus* started it off. That high, lamenting violin came in and his eyes welled. He put the track on repeat. Slept a deep, deep sleep for three hours. Dreamed his funeral. His coffin going down the aisle. Everybody singing. And the air was clear. He'd done nothing wrong. Nothing to be forgiven. It was a great way to die. He woke feeling like he'd slept a hundred years. Something had changed. And although he didn't know it at the time, he'd never be the same again. It's been working on him almost a year now.

But where was that convent? It was his only time out of

Glasgow. Unbroken fields, birds singing. Nuns chanting.

Make me the apple of your eye.

♪♪ That's what they used to sing.

Devlin's got a good lie going about how he took the only way out of poverty he could. Could he play football? No. Could he box? Too angry. They threw him out the boxing club after he attacked his sparring partner in the street. Drugs was easy money for a young guy with aggression and a wee bit of brains.

Okay, so he might not have done many good things in his life. But he's made sure Nicole's stayed on course at her posh school. Nicole speaks differently from Devlin. He's made sure of that. There's no place like Scotland for judging people by their accent. He's giving Nicole the chances he never got. She's on her way.

An hour later he's ironing his trousers into a razor-sharp crease. He's got the Pogues on. *Thousands are Sailing* – his anthem. It suits his Irish blood and his philosophy of sacrificing his own life to spring his family into something better. He's happy and he's singing, sweeping the taped-together iron over the trousers.

Nicole and Wendy are at the dining table. Nicole flicks through her school books.

Wendy's writing on a birthday card.

Happy Birthday, darling – Proud of you. Love, Wendy.
XXX

Above, the music thumps and Devlin sings. Nicole sighs, squinting one disgusted eye at the high ceiling. He's at it again. Embarrassment. He's so – argh!

Wendy slides the card and pen over to her. Nicole throws her a look, sliding it back. Devlin sings and thumps on. Wendy pushes the card to Nicole with some energy. Nicole pushes it back.

—Do you want me to tell him you didn't come in until four in the morning? threatens Wendy.

—Tell him if you want.

—I'll tell you what to write.

—I am perfectly capable, Mummy, of composing my own greeting, thank you – supposing I had the inclination to do so.

—Nicole! Wendy pleads.

—After last night? You have to be joking, Mummy!

—What about last night?

Wendy holds her gaze until Nicole looks away. Wendy's not letting her off.

—Well?

Nicole stares like it's an effrontery to mankind that Wendy doesn't know the what about last night.

—I'm waiting.

—A thong. I mean… Mummy!

Wendy's face turns red.

—Gross! A little string that was…

Nicole plucks at an imaginary thong stuck between an imaginary pair of buttocks.

—…stuck. The whole estate must have seen it.

—Go to your room. Now!

Nicole doesn't move. Waits until Wendy's about to utter the same words again.

—Okay. I'll sign it.

—Say something nice.

Nicole poises the pen above the card.

—This is stupid. He's forty-two!

Devlin's eyes are closed. He's dancing frenetically, singing his favourite line.

If he's done anything, he's broke the chains. The chains of poverty.

—Daddy!

Devlin stops. Opens his eyes. Turns the music down. She's been watching him.

—Just dancing, he says, like he'd been caught pissing on the trolleys outside ASDA.

—I thought you were having an epileptic fit. Here!

Hands him the birthday card.

HAPPY BIRTHDAY
YOU ARE ONE

Devlin stares at the card. Opens it. Reads. Nicole forces out a compliment.

—Well done, she says.

That, from her, is a lot. Devlin is moved.

—Ta muchly. You're a great wean.

She strikes an indignant pose.

—I'm not a wean. Dhuu!

Devlin tries to kiss her but she puts her hands up, backing out of the room.

—I'd rather kiss a folded over fish, she says.

He lets some saliva run down his chin and lunges, arms outstretched, like Frankenstein.

—Daddy want a ki—iss. Daddy want a ki—iss.

Nicole moves like lightening out the door. But she trips and slams it on her own head.

Wendy dashes up the stairs to find her doubled over, holding her head. Devlin, saliva still on his chin, is stuck in the pause before you ask someone of they're alright.

—Did you hit her? Tell me you didn't!

—Shut up! I'd never hit a wean!

—What happened then?

Now that he can see Nicole's alright he bursts out laughing.

—She slammed the door on her own head.

—No I did not!

—She did, she went like that...

Devlin rushes out the door backwards. Demonstrating. Wendy can't help cracking into a smile. Devlin does it again. Wendy descends into hysterical laughter. Devlin joins in. Nicole sits on the floor in gothic glum.

—Oh God, I'm going to pee myself, says Wendy.

She jogs into the bathroom. Nicole draws Devlin a black look and heads after her, looking for sympathy.

Devlin pretends to close his door but spies on Nicole.
She tap tap taps on the bathroom door.

—Mummy, my head…

Nothing.

—I think it may be bleeding, Mummy.

A pause, then light floods out and Wendy is in the doorway. Nicole presents her head.

—Have a look, Mummy. Is it bleeding?

Wendy doesn't get a chance to look. Nicole pulls her out, closes the door, locks it and laughs.

—You are such a silly fool, Mummy, such a silly, silly fool.

The silly, silly fool bangs on the door.

Devlin appreciates Nicole's wiliness. She's inherited his streetwise smarts.

—Nicole, let me in right now, Wendy shouts, —Christie!

Christie's not listening. Fatherly pride lets him, for one tiny moment, be ordinary.

Sunday. Devlin, Wendy and Nicole are at Mass in St Theresa's. Father Boyle's reminded Wendy and Devlin of the Ned Devlin is going to frighten.

♪♪ Oh Lord my God, when I in awesome wonder, consider all, the universe you made, then sings my soul…

Father Boyle gives out the Body of Christ. Wendy and Nicole prepare to join the lines for communion. Devlin never goes. Hasn't been since he left the altar boys. One day he was an altar boy. Next it was soured. Tainted forever. Never went back. And nobody came to see why he had left.

The Saint Vincent de Paul pass keepers usher the line out with a reverence you'd use guiding souls into heaven. Wendy twists her legs to let Nicole past. Two old women to the right of Devlin get up pressuring him to stand too. He stares like there's something on the altar that interests him.

Wendy whispers —Will you run Nicole to school tomorrow?

—The morra? I've got important business.

Wendy waits for the correct answer. The two old women

have started climbing over him to get to communion.

—Will you drive Nicole to school?

—I've got business to take care of!

The old women can't get past Wendy, so they're waiting for an answer too. Nicole's disappearing towards the altar. She's looking round now and then feeling self-conscious. The gap between Wendy and Nicole is growing. For a moment Wendy feels what it would be like to lose her daughter. The old women stare, rosary beads swinging and clicking.

Swinging

and clicking.

Swinging

and clicking.

—Right. Okay! Right! I'll run her.

The old women smile. He's a such good man. A good, good man. They pass into the aisle behind Wendy. Pressure off. The choirs sing another song. Devlin watches the babes go past. A nice arse in tight jeans. The bottom of a Sunday dress swinging left, left, then right, like an ocean wave. Smooth legs all the way down to the Sunday shoes and all the way back up. Whoa! He's getting too carried away. Already his cock's begun to swell and that wouldn't do. A hard-on in a chapel. He looks away trying to find something less tempting. High above the altar, Jesus hangs at an impossible angle. Devlin bows his head and speaks too low for anybody to hear.

—Sorry, Big Man. Can't resist a nice arse.

忠心
loyalty

Who am I to criticise?

DEVLIN CONSTRUCTION AND Demolition has its yard on the Forth and Clyde canal. Devlin's legitimate business is concrete. Construction of bridges, office towers, anything involving shuttering and pouring concrete. It's something of a cliché that there are bodies entombed in concrete bridges and civil engineering structures all over the world. A cliché because it's true.

Devlin's looking out over the canal. Away to the south, Glasgow Tower watches over the city. Devlin inspects a mangle of firearms on his desk. Two fifty calibre tripod-mounted machine guns. Five machine pistols. A sawn-off shotgun. A rocket launcher. Three grenades and the handguns the Triads gave to his men.

He turns to Sam.

—Sighthill. Usual arrangement.

Sam and two Devlinites load the weapons into bags. Devlin doesn't even know the names of his periphery workers. But he knows Bonzo will have carefully vetted them. Their whole criminal history will be known. Associates, family and friends. How much bottle they've got.

And they know if they ever double-cross Devlin – goodnight.

—That's us, boss, says Sam.

—Tell Billy I was asking for him.

—Will do.

—Tell Bonzo and Sholtz to come in.

Seconds later, in come Bonzo and Sholtz. Bonzo unzips a holdall and Devlin takes five ASDA bags from a locked drawer. Lines them up.

—Brolly, Donnelly, Riley, Malky.

Bonzo repeats the names as he drops the money in the holdall.

—Brolly, Donnelly, Riley, Malky.

Devlin has one more wad of notes on the table. Bonzo

goes to lift it. Devlin's hand lands on his.

—And this guy Garrett. D'ye talk to him?

—Arranged meetings face to face with them all, except...
except Garrett. Got him on the phone but.

Devlin goes ballistic. They've met all the dealers face to
face and told them what's going to happen, but they've only
spoken to Garrett on the phone.

—Yees talked to Garrett, the cunt we don't know, the
fuckin wildcard, *on the phone*!

—Sholtz's seeing him the night boss, says Bonzo.

—This guy can fuck up the whole operation and you chat
to him on the phone like he's your wee cousin?

—I phoned him boss, Sholtz interrupts, —I've set up a
meeting. It's all coosty.

Bonzo cuts in.

—Fifty grand and a job for life, or a bullet in the head? He
knows the score... Here!

Bonzo flings Sholtz a handgun as much as to convince
Devlin they've got it under control as anything.

—Go to your meeting, Christie, says Bonzo, —When you're
finished so will we be.

Through a flicker of doubt, Devlin nods.

—You're worryin too much about one guy, Sholtz says.

—Ach, you're right. When my meeting's finished I want
yees to be finished an all.

—We will be, says Bonzo, —Away ye go.

As soon as Devlin leaves the room Bonzo and Sholtz burst
into song. *Tiny Bubbles.*

Devlin smiles.

The song's still in his head an hour later when he's sitting
in a smoke-filled room staring at his gold triangle ring.

On a community centre fold up table are rows of birthday
cards with You Are One, or Happy First Birthday or One! on
them. The card Nicole gave him takes pride of place dead
centre.

Hanging each side of him are two enormous posters.

The Twelve Steps

1. We admit we were powerless over alcohol – that our lives have become unmanageable.

2. Came to believe that a Power greater than ourselves could restore us to sanity.

3. Made a decision to turn our will and our lives over to the care of God as we understand Him.

4. Made a searching and fearless moral inventory of ourselves.

5. Admitted to God, to ourselves and to another human being the exact nature of our wrongs.

6. Were entirely ready to have God remove all these defects of character.

7. Humbly asked Him to remove our shortcomings.

8. Made a list of all persons we had harmed, and became willing to make amends to them all.

9. Made direct amends to such people wherever possible, except when to do so would injure them or others.

10. Continued to take personal inventory and when we were wrong promptly admitted it.

11. Sought through prayer and meditation to improve our conscious contact with God as we understood Him, praying only for knowledge of His will for us and the power to carry that out.

12. Having had a spiritual awakening as the result of these steps, we tried to carry this message to alcoholics and to practise the principles in all our affairs.

The Twelve Traditions

1. Our common welfare should come first; personal recovery depends upon AA unity.

2. For our group purpose, there is but one ultimate authority – a loving God as He may express Himself in our group conscience. Our leaders are but trusted servants; they do not govern.

3. The only requirement for AA membership is a desire to stop drinking.

4. Each group should be autonomous except in matters affecting other groups of AA as a whole.

5. Each group has but one primary purpose – to carry its message to the alcoholic who still suffers.

6. An AA group ought never endorse, finance or lend the AA name to any related facility or outside enterprise lest problems of money, property and prestige divert us from our primary purpose.

7. Every AA group ought to be fully self-supporting, declining outside contributions.

8. Alcoholics Anonymous should remain forever non-professional, but our service centres may employ special workers.

9. AA as such, ought never be organised; but we may create service boards or committees directly responsible to those they serve.

10. Alcoholics Anonymous has no opinion on outside issues; hence the AA name ought never be drawn into   public controversy.

11. Our public relations policy is based on attraction rather than promotion; we need always maintain personal anonymity at the level of press, radio and films.

12. Anonymity is the spiritual foundation of all our traditions, ever reminding us to place principles before personalities.

Draped over the table is a deep purple velvet cloth with large golden lettering.

ALCOHOLICS ANONYMOUS

WELCOME YOU TO

POSSILPARK SUNDAY NIGHT

Twenty-five people in rickety school chairs stare at Devlin. He's been more nervous than this before, but not many times. Fags are lit and if you're looking along the row for tramps and jakies you're in the wrong place. There are butchers and brain surgeons. Junkies and chemists. Most members of AA, the general public would never believe were alcoholics at all. Even when they're performing. That's what they call drinking; performing. Performing: the very root of what it is to be an alcoholic.

Jamie B clink, clink, clinks a glass. The pre-meeting buzz dissipates.

—Hi yi. My name's Jamie and I'm an alcoholic. I'm honoured to be chairing the night at Christie's first birthday celebration.

Jamie, twenty-nine years sober, pauses for the clapping, lets it fade and continues. He will talk for fifteen minutes on what AA is and what it's not, then he'll pass it over to Devlin. For forty-five minutes Devlin will talk about what he was like before he drank, what he was like when he was drinking, how he stopped, and what he's like now.

In the Necropolis Sam flashes the light and a light flashes back. Footsteps always sound sinister in the dark and Sam is finding it hard to count how many people are coming over the gravel. But he's not as concerned as he would be if this was a rival gang. It's the Chief of Police. Since the rise of gun crime, Billy Pitt is under pressure to show results. The only results that matter to him are what's picked up by the media. He has to appear on the telly with piles of guns every now and then to appease public opinion. But no career criminal is going to give up his guns. When Devlin wants Pitt to turn a blind eye to an operation, like tonight's, he gives up a crush of guns. Everybody's happy.

Pitt's in full uniform. Two carrier bags secured with elastic bands cover his feet. Two plain clothes officers by his side.

—What's that? Some Masonic code? says Sam.

—Keeping my feet clean, says Pitt, —Bit of a polis do tonight.

Sam nods at the guns. Two beams of light sweep onto them. A prize haul.

—Two fifty calibre, tripod-mounted machine guns. Five machine pistols. A sawn off shotgun. A rocket launcher. Three grenades and the Chinkees gave us a load of hand-guns, Sam chants.

—The Chinese?

—By way of a gift to yourself. Christie arranged it.

Billy Pitt is doubly pleased. Good props for his media mission. And a conduit to the Chinese, who'll soon be running the city with Devlin.

—Christie's come up trumps this time.

—Aye a big clearout the night, says Sam.

—That should be good for the city. Less bosses, less trouble.

—Christie says to say thanks, Billy.

—So long as there's guns off the streets, son, I'm a happy bunny.

The cops, the guns and the shining torches make their way back through the graves.

Hamiltonhill sounds posh. It's not. It's part of Possil and even if they're knocking it all down, there's still dangerous people there. Brolly's one of them. He's dangerous but he knows Devlin's too powerful to fuck with. The deal Sholtz offers

Brolly is a fifty grand payment to hand over all his information. Who owes him what and where the violence needs to be
dished out. Then he'll work for Devlin with a drastically
reduced salary. He can refuse and leave Glasgow forever. Or
he can refuse and stay. Buried on one of Devlin's building sites.

Brolly takes the ASDA bag from Sholtz and looks in at the
money.

—Fifty?

—Count it.

—Naw. S'alright. Fair doos.

Brolly hands Sholtz his wee notebook.

—If there's anything ye don't understand, just geez a bell.

—Trying to say I can't fuckin read?

—Naw, man. Chill. I'm doin my best to help here.

Sholtz leaves Brolly's with a sneer.

Brolly sits down, sighs and begins counting the money.

The Clockwork Orange is what they call the Glasgow's Underground. The distant rumble of an approaching train catches
the crowd's attention in Buchanan Street Station. I Lo,
watched by Hung Kwan, makes his way towards a Jamaican.
This is I Lo's first test since he switched Triad gangs.

To anyone bold enough to stare it looks like a drugs
delivery. The Jamaican and I Lo exchange polite nods. The
Jamaican hands over the bag. The air pressure is popping ears.
The train can't be more than a hundred feet away. The rhythm
of the wheels is the rhythm of fear. The Jamaican sees evil in I
Lo's eyes. I Lo pushes him. He tips off the platform. Sticks his hand
out. The train smacks him. The thud is a sack of meat hitting
steel. He's stuck to the front like an awful swastika. The train
brakes. The Jamaican slides off. The station thrums with screams.

I Lo and Hung Kwan have already left.

In Springburn they used to make trains. Donnelly lives in a
building looking down towards the Sighthill flats where the
asylum seekers live. The stabbing, slashing, fighting and

peacemaking has collected media interest. But the Chinese came to the city many years before. They've gone about their business unnoticed. Now they are on the cusp of controlling Glasgow. If Tai Lo's plans run smoothly, they'll work with Devlin until they gather enough intelligence about his network. Then eliminate him.

Donnelly wants to know nothing about elimination. He's been losing his nerve recently, with the young team refusing to obey the rules of respect. Fifteen-year-olds packing guns. Where does that leave him? No power, that's where. But the way Devlin deals with opponents makes even the chaotic young team fear him. So Donnelly is secretly pleased with the offer of a job for life. He passes his book of contacts to Bonzo and Bonzo passes it to a Devlinite. Donnelly counts his fifty grand.

I Lo is eager to impress his new brothers-in-arms. This time it's an Indian restaurant in Sauchiehall Street. While Devlin expounds the virtues of sobriety at the AA meeting, I Lo, puffed with macho pride, is striding out of the restaurant. The owner teeters across the floor, his face rippling in strips.

Diners scurry out and stand on the street. It's cold. A cloud of terrified breath hangs above them. Some have stains where curries have fallen onto them. They can't look at the window. The owner's face slides down smearing blood on the lunchtime buffet menu. The glass acts as a brake on his skin, stretching it upwards. A thin line of red across his neck unzips into a gaping wound. He dies on the badly tiled window ledge gurgling in a half gallon of his own blood.

By the time anybody has the sense to look around for the Chinamen, I Lo and Hung Kwan are over the brow of the hill and into Chinatown.

The Oasis in Castlemilk is probably the most inappropriately named pub in Glasgow. The smoky air is acrid with adrenaline. Sholtz is handed a book by Riley, a man with no neck, bodybuilder's shoulders and piggy eyes. He speaks, the taste of fear on the back of his tongue.

—What would've happened if I told yees to get to fuck?

Sholtz answers with a grin. The Devlinite takes a step forward. Riley defuses the situation by leaning back into the upholstery.

—Fair doos my man, says Riley, —Fair doos.

In a Thai takeaway the queue of customers is leaving empty-handed, even though they've paid for their orders. Hung Kwan and I Lo have crashed in, I Lo swinging a cleaver over his head, yelling like a Red Indian attack. There's a worried eye in the gap of the slightly open kitchen door. I Lo clunks the cleaver flat on the counter and vaults it. While he's in mid-air, the kitchen door closes. The chef feels like he's walking through treacle. He's got to shut the hatch. The hatch is metal. If he can close and bolt it he can get out the back door, disappear into the night. But his arm takes a heavy blow from the cleaver. I Lo's face appears, smiling through the hatch. The Thai holds up a drum of oil for protection and steps back, but it's such a small kitchen I Lo slices a gaping silver wound in the tin. Yellow oil gushes out onto the floor. Now the Thai's desperately slipping and slithering towards the back door. I Lo's halfway though the hatch, trying to get some purchase. But he can't. He's balanced on his hip bone. Every time he swings the cleaver his feet move in an arc knocking over coke cans and bags of prawn crackers. He swings again and again. All Hung Kwan can see through the hatch is exploding crockery and slithers of oil.

—*Push me in. Push me in*, shouts I Lo, —*Hurry, hurry!*

He lands with a crash amongst the pots. The Thai has grabbed a cleaver of his own. The air fills with reverberative clangs. Then a cleaver clatters to the ground. A cleaver strikes flesh and bone. Smatterings of blood speed through the hatch like comets. I Lo is a man in a frenzy. A man with a lust for savagery. One slash is too many and a million are not enough.

The moans of the chef diminish and the thuds slow down. I

Lo's not slowing through pity or because the job is almost complete. No. He wants to see the chef's face at the moment terror turns to acceptance that he is, indeed, about to die. I Lo watches The Peace spread across the Thai's face then

CHUNK

he strikes. The chef is dead but I Lo strikes and he strikes and he laughs. Hung Kwan is worried about the amount of time they've been there.

—*I Lo*, he shouts.

Another crunch of the cleaver. I Lo slides back through the wood and metal vagina.

—*Congratulations Madam; it's a psychopath*, he says.

Hung Kwan looks through at the chopped up Thai. New man I Lo is very good to have on side. But needs to be controlled. That is what Hung Kwan will report to Tai Lo. I Lo takes his filthy jacket off. The only carry-out leaving tonight will be the chef. No more wee twists of heroin with the sweet and sours. Billy Pitt will subdue the investigation, make sure it comes to nothing, feed the papers a line about inter-gang rivalry. Orientals. So long as they're killing their own, that's okay. Chink on Chink violence.

At the AA meeting Devlin is spouting patter to the punters.

—I'm getting on really well, he's saying confidently. — Business is fine. I'm getting on great with my wife and daughter. In fact, I got on *really* great with my wife other day, if ye know what I mean. Music night.

He winks and the group laughs. An experienced AA punter could lift any one of Devlin's sentences, break open the clichés and watch the pain run out. Devlin spouts out more.

—It's all down to this fellowship I've found here. Life's never been better. When I came to AA a year ago fuckin rattling with the horrors, I thought yees were all loonies…

WARNING! Standard issue joke coming up

—Now I know yees're all loonies.

There's a ripple of laughter, though everyone knew that joke was coming.

—No, but serious, says Devlin, —AA's changed my life.

Cooney is a fifty-something Irishman. He's seated at the back of the hall, head tilted to the side, smoking. He isn't listening. He's watching the play of expressions on Devlin's face. Penetrating to the man underneath. Cooney knows AA doesn't change you into another person, but it can allow you to be the person you should've been in the first place.

Malky is a weedy coke-head with a penchant for young boys. *Eastenders* flickers around his Easterhouse living-room. Bonzo and Sam sit, staring at him. Malky thinks everything's just dandy. One line of coke too many. He says to tell Devlin he doesn't want to merge. He'd rather be self-employed, maybe downsize, if that's alright with Devlin. He knows he can't stop Devlin dealing in the East End but he doesn't want to join his gang. Bonzo steps up to Malky.

—That's alright then, Malky. If ye'd rather stay in business we'd be as well going then, eh Sam? Is that *Enders* that's on?

Malky is about to answer with a smile and a gentle push on Bonzo's back to get him out the door when

BOOSH!

the telly is burst by Bonzo's baseball bat. Glass drums on the couch. Clicks on the walls. Ticks on the window panes.

Silence.

Bonzo flings the bat to Sam who sets about smashing every breakable object. The glass doors on the wall unit. The bong on the mantelpiece. The Amstrad hi-fi. The three ceramic ducks on the window ledge.

Bonzo produces a sawn-off shotgun and pokes it in Malky's face.

—On the fuckin floor!

Malky lies on the floor.

—Bite the fuckin carpet!

He can hear his heart hammering through the floorboards.

—Shut they fuckin curtains, Sam, Bonzo says.

Sam swishes them shut.

That panics Malky. He's miscalculated. Total fuckin blunder. This is the day he's going to die. This is the day it all ends. The deal to work for Devlin now looks oh so much better.

—I'll take it, I'll take it, shouts Malky.

Bonzo grabs his hair and lifts his head up.

—Is that your final answer?

—Bonzo, leave me alone, I'll do what yees want.

Bonzo flips Malky onto his back and places the sawn-off shotgun on his forehead. Malky feels the cold and heavy dunt of the metal.

—Right, ya wee fuckin virus!

—Aw fuck! squeaks Malky.

A last splinter of glass topples from the telly and bounces on the carpet.

—Cushion, orders Bonzo.

Sam gets a cushion. They've done this so many times it's an art form. Sam covers Malky's face with the cushion. Bonzo reaches in his jacket and gets the sawn-off end of the shotgun barrels. Malky's pleas are muffled through the cushion.

—Please, Bonzo. I don't even need the money; yees could pocket that. I'll fuck off out of town. I'll do anything yees want me to do.

He's like a dreadful talking toy. Bonzo lifts up the cushion at Malky's chin. Up past his lips. He forces the sawn-off part of the gun into his mouth. Malky's silenced by the feeling in his groin at the taste of metal. He's crying. Bonzo points the *actual* shotgun at the floor next to Malky's head.

—Malky, you have been evicted. Please leave the Big Brother House.

BANG

Splinters of wood and bits of carpet fly up. Piss floods through Malky's quivering jeans. He thinks he's dead. Thinks there's life after death. Didn't feel a thing. He hears Bonzo's voice.

—Can anybody smell shite?

—Aye, what is that? echoes Sam.

—It's shite. Where's it coming from, Sam?

Malky's looking up at them. Even though he's shat his trousers and pissed himself, he's glad to be alive.

—Aw thanks, lads. Thanks. Jesus Christ, thanks.

Bonzo empties the fifty grand over Malky. The notes float down like confetti, celebrating his second chance at life.

Devlin's shared. One at a time the other punters say their piece. Jamie thanks Meat Market Ian.

—Thanks for that, Ian. Just remember, stay away from one drink for one day for one's self. If ye don't lift the first drink ye can't get drunk. It's as simple and complicated as that. Tony!

As Tony talks, Cooney continues to scrutinise Devlin's face.

—My name's Tony and I'm an arsehole. I mean that – a fuckin arsehole waiting to happen soon as I lift that first drink. Thanks for chairing the meeting, Jamie. Ye calm a room down just by being in it, so ye do. Thanks. And Christie, congratulations on your first birthday. A day's a long time for an alky, never mind a year. But one lousy fuckin drink and you're back where ye left off – and worse. Keep it up, big man.

Tony's the last punter to share. Jamie B thanks them all for coming and making it a good meeting, then hands over to Devlin for a few last comments. Devlin cracks his end-of-the-top-table-joke.

—There's these three nuns sitting on a wall. This guy comes up and flashes at them. Two of them have a stroke… the other one can't reach.

They all laugh and are about to rise to say the Serenity Prayer when the lights go out. Even though this happens at every birthday meeting, everybody acts surprised. The door opens and closes. Devlin's face is lit by flickering candles. Cooney is coming towards him carrying the cake. The AA punters sing.

♪♪ Happy Birthday to you. Happy Birthday to you. Happy Birthday dear Christie, Happy Birthday to you.

Cooney places the cake on the table. Devlin leans into the noise. Something falls onto the white raft of icing. Only Cooney notices it. A tear. Christie Devlin's tear. Cooney sees the tear fall onto the icing. Then

WHOOSH

Devlin blows the candles out in one go. Cooney knows he's ready.

Sholtz and a Devlinite stand in the arches of a derelict Saint Augustine's chapel in Dalmarnock. Sholtz is giving instructions. The Devlinite's young, eager to please, hungry for promotion.

—If ye hear anything, come in like Rooster Cockburn shooting from the hip.

—Who?

—John Wayne! says Sholtz.

Blank look.

Sholtz shakes his head.

—If ye hear any shouting or guns going off, come in shooting.

The demolished birthday cake lies with the blackened wicks like dead question marks. Punters mill about, talking.

Devlin's on his own in a corner. Cooney shouts him over.

—Christie, can I talk to ye for a minute?

Devlin ambles over thinking he's going to be congratu-lated for a year's continuous sobriety. But he's not.

—There's peace of mind to be had if ye'd only do what AA suggests, says Cooney.

—I've already got peace of mind, Devlin says.

Cooney looks down at Devlin's hands.

—Tell that to the polystyrene cup, Cooney says.

Devlin's torn the polystyrene cup into a big white flower.

Not so long ago Cooney's attitude would've met with a slap, a fist, a blade or a gun. But Devlin's always liked the life engraved in Cooney's face. He decides to give him that wee bit of scope.

—All AA's done for you is made ye better at being a gangster.

The rage that ignites in Devlin's eyes doesn't make Cooney flinch. Devlin explains to Cooney, beat for beat, how he's a legitimate business man.

—Don't try and kid the kid that kidded them all cos if ye try and kid the kid that kidded them all the kid that kidded them all'll kid you, Cooney says very fast. While Devlin fumbles for a sharp response he zooms in like a Zen master.

—A year I've watched you for and ye haven't changed one bit.

—What are you, a fuckin stalker?

—Ye haven't even *tried* to change.

One or two punters flick uneasy glances over.

—Are they all your own teeth?

Cooney ignores that.

—D'ye hear what I'm telling you?

Devlin decides to let the old bastard chunter on. No skin off his nose. Who needs to come back to this fuckin meeting anyhow? There's hundreds of meetings in Glasgow. He gestures for Cooney to carry on.

—A sponsor's what you need.

Devlin lowers his voice.

—And you need a good boot up the arse, ya cheeky oul cunt.

—The man that brung ye through these doors is the man that'll take ye back out, Christie!

Devlin walks away, Cooney's retort ringing in his ears.

Sholtz pads towards the confessionals, gun in one hand, ASDA bag in the other. He was brought up a Catholic and some reverence remains. He passes the altar with a deferential bow. There's nobody about, so he shouts.

—Garrett?

Garrett's voice comes from the confessional with Father Bradley's name on it.

—I'm in here.

Sholtz strides towards the door.

—Don't come in. I want to stay anonymous.

—How? Are ye a priest or something?

Sholtz and laughs out loud at his own patter.

—Ha ha. I just want to stay anonymous. I'm leaving Glasgow so there's no need to know who I am. Devlin can take over my patch. I just want the fifty grand.

Sholtz tries to open the confessional door but it's locked.

—Go in the penitent's booth. I'll give ye the details of all my business, says Garrett.

Sholtz shrugs and goes into the next booth. Sits the ASDA bag down and levels his gun at the shadow he can see through the grille.

—Bless me, Father, for I have sinned, says Sholtz.

—Can't help ye, mate. I'm a bit of a sinner myself, so I am, says Garrett.

—Good one. Like it. Okay. You give me the book and I'll give you the money?

—Shove it up your arse, says Garrett.

It's a joke too far. Sholtz pressures the trigger.

—What was that? he asks Garrett.

—Shove it up your fuckin arse.

BANG

Bullets burst through the confessional. One to the head. Garrett's shadowy figure topples back.

—In the name of the Father, says Sholtz.

One to the abdomen.

—And of the Son.

One to the left of his chest; one to the right.

—And of the Holy Spirit. Amen! Ya fuckin prick!

Sholtz leaps out. The big wooden Jesus is judging down on him.

—Sorry, Big Fellah!

He half means it. His childhood's only hiding. He kicks Father Bradley's confessional door, expecting Garrett's body. The moment he sees the red and white plaster body of the Sacred Heart of Jesus statue he drops to the floor. There's a plastic kitchen funnel attached to a length of hose pipe. Garrett's been speaking through the hose, into the funnel, into the confessional. Could be anywhere now, pointing a gun right at him. Sholtz flicks his head this way and that. Up and down. His mouth goes dry.

Garrett reaches in and takes the ASDA bag from the penitent's booth. Sholtz hears the rustle. The booth's empty. The money gone. But by fuck, Sholtz's not going to die easy.

—Fuck!

Footsteps at the altar. He fires a shot. Jesus, with his right arm missing, looks down from on high. Sholtz crawls along the floor checking under pews. A noise. He fires along the length of a pew. A crow flaps its wings and glares. He realises he's near the doors. Gets up. Bursts into the light. Looks left and right. Nothing. Grabs the Devlinite.

—I told ye to come in if you heard any fuckin shooting!

Sholtz is looking at the Devlinite but there's nobody home. A trickle of blood is making its way down the side of his neck.

—What's up with you? says Sholtz.

—Some guy thundered me on the head with a lump of wood.

Sholtz gawps down. The wooden right arm of Jesus lies on the ground. A shiver transmits up and down Sholtz's spine.

—Come on, let's get out of here.

They leave the chapel. Up above the doorway is a vast circle of stained glass. Garrett stares down from a missing panel. He could be part of the religious tableau. Until he grins.

I Lo arrives back in the Silver Seas from his bloody adventures. In the Mah Jong room there is a green door with red Chinese symbols that opens that into another massive hall. Students selected by Ming Fung perform esoteric movement with the grace that harnesses power. Swimming Dragon, Stroke the Pheasant's Tail, Pecking Rooster. Channelling the Chi Kung, the mysterious energy that, directed to a fist, can turn it into steel. Ming Fung has studied Tai Chi since she was five, merging that with Kung Fu from the age of ten.

None of the students look at I Lo, who is trying to catch Ming Fung's attention. The heroic soldier back from battle. The students copy her as she slides her front leg out into bow stance, then slowly transfers her weight to her back leg, pushing her palms into the air as if she was moving a mountain or a flapping dove. From a single chair in a corner, Tai Lo watches his daughter. Watching relaxes him as much as practising. Hung Kwan takes I Lo over. A skin of dried blood creases on I Lo's face like cherry tree branches scratching an ominous sunset.

—*I Lo worth a hundred soldier*, says Hung Kwan.

Tai Lo smiles and bows slightly towards I Lo. I Lo puts his feet together and bows long. Bows deep.

—*Go and get washed, soldier*, orders Tai Lo.

I Lo withdraws, swollen with Triad pride. Later Heung Chu hands out slips of red rice paper. Invites to the next Triad initiation ceremony. Summonses that must be obeyed.

The initiate is I Lo.

兒子
son

Do not remove a fly from your father's head with a hatchet.

THE STEEPLE OF St Theresa's dominates the Possil skyline. Devlin draws up outside a graffiti-covered close nearby. Through one of the windows he can see his father moving around. Devlin can tell what every nuance of his movements means.

He takes a big, fog-bound Possil breath. As he breathes out he looks up at the steeple. Has a memory he's not had for years.

He was ten, an altar boy, the picture of innocence with his blue eyes and fair hair, his red sultan and white surplice, an angel lost in Possil. He'd trained and practiced for two months and this was his first Mass. What he had to do was ring the bell three times during the celebration. Once when Father Brennan held up the Body of Christ. Once when he held up the Blood of Christ. Once when he genuflected. The other altar boys would do the wine and water and all the accoutrements of Mass. It was half-twelve Mass and St Theresa's was mobbed.

He came out of the vestry with the other altar boys. Out the side of his eye he could see his maw, his da and his twin sister Marie in the front pew. Marie and his maw were smiling but his da stared straight ahead.

The Mass went well. He rang the bell when he was supposed to. Now and then he'd catch the smile of his maw and a wee secret wave from Marie. He felt great. Important. People were looking at him. But towards the end he began to feel uneasy. Couldn't figure out why. He'd rang the bell three times at the right bits. There was nothing more to do but follow Father Brennan back into the vestry at the end of Mass. Then, turning to see if Marie was watching him, he caught sight of his da's face. It was thunder. It was no good when his da was angry. No good at all. When he had been kneeling at the side of the altar, his da had seen his boots sticking out. Big Doc Marten boots. The kind Neds wear on the corner. He seen his da say something to his maw.

—Has he not got a pair of shoes he can wear?

Devlin pushes the memory away and gets out his car.

Inside, he looks at Dan's latest painting of the Madonna with Child. He does Constables, Turners etc, but more than half his paintings were versions of the Madonna with Child. The room is dotted with sculptures carved from wood and stone. One is of Hercules and the Lion of Menos. Hercules is standing in muscular splendour with his right hand on the lion's head. In his left hand are two orbs the size of tennis balls. When Dan first carved it he told Devlin the orbs were the lion's balls. Hercules de-balled the lion and now it's under his command. That made perfect sense to Devlin. He decided to get a poster for his office and one for his wee room. He searched the internet and was surprised to find what he thought were the lion's balls were actually the lion's eyes. Hercules had blinded it.

That fact shot through Devlin.

He's looking at the blind lion when Dan comes into the room. Every time Devlin meets him Dan gets round to two things very quickly. One: how his good eye is starting to go. Two: violence.

The one blue eye flicks from Devlin to the painting. From the painting to Devlin. He picks out an area of sky and sweeps his palm.

—Ach, see that? My eye's getting worse. See that splodge there? That's just not me.

Devlin looks for the flaws. Dan bends down and comes back up with a glass of whisky sloshing in his hand.

—That's all I need, my only good eye fuckin up.

He takes a slug of the whisky, keeping his eye on Devlin. Holding him in his one-eyed gaze. Devlin changes the subject.

—How's things on the site?

Dan's a gaffer on one of Delvin's construction sites. Devlin likes to keep a watch over things and Dan could spot a three inch nail missing from a box of a thousand. With his bad eye.

—There's a new site agent starting, says Dan.

—Hope he knows the score.

—If he doesn't, you'll need to sort him out.

—Any bother, gimmi a phone and I'll come down and learn him.

Dan nods, downs what's left in the whisky glass and smacks his lips.

—Want a wee half?

—Nah.

—It's malt. Glenmorangie.

Devlin points at the painting to change the subject.

—That's no bad, that.

—Take a drink, man.

—I'm alright.

—There's Supers there. Crash one of them open.

—I'm a year sober the day.

Dan ignores that. Goes in close to inspect the blue on the eyes of the Madonna.

—It's like the real thing that, like a real artist done it, says Devlin.

—Only difference between they cunts and me is they're posh. Who wants a painting off a joiner from Possil? No cunt, that's who. Ah fuck!

—What's up?

Dan picks up a Super lager and opens it automatically.

—That eye's not right. Needs more blue. A wee touch of violet mibbi. Aye.

With a brush in one hand and the can in the other Dan skilfully touches up the eye. Dabs. And slugs. Leans back. Has he got the shape right? The transparency of the blue? He has. He takes another slug.

—Ahh! That's better.

Dan drops to the floor and rises up with a barbell, the paintbrush in his teeth. He performs the biceps curls at Devlin.

—I'm up to three sets of twenty. Fifty kilos. Feel they biceps.

Devlin wraps his hand round his da's biceps. Feels like iron.

—Fucksakes, Da, solid.

—Aye, they don't make Glaswegians like they used to.

Dan puts the barbell down and returns to the painting with microscopic concentration. When Devlin gives him the news of his impending grandfathership it's hard to tell if he doesn't turn round because he's so absorbed or for some other reason.

—Wendy's pregnant.

—Ye'd better hope it's not a boy. Sons bring ye trouble.

Devlin's caught in the whisper of the brushstrokes looking for a reason to leave. Thankfully his mobile goes. It's Sholtz reporting on the shambolic meeting with Garrett.

—Hello? Right. Right calm down. Meet me in half an hour at our Marie's.

On the mention of Marie, Dan stops painting. His one eye flicks like it's looking for something lost. The lion's eyes nestled in Hercules' hand are looking at Devlin. Staring.

—Have to go, Da. Business.

—Don't forget the site agent!

—Phone me.

And he leaves. Dan stares at the closed door a few seconds then pours another whisky. Devlin walks out, straight back into the memory of serving at half-twelve Mass.

By the time he got home he'd forgotten about his da's bitter stares. All that was in his mind was Marie's smiles and his maw's pride as he rang the bell. Three times he rang the bell. Three times. Perfect timing.

Christopher walked up Saracen Street with his sultan and surplice still on. He was to take it home and clean it. The other boys had theirs in bags but Christopher wanted to be seen. Women said hello to him. Was it his first Mass? They'd never have known, he was so good. Some of them even gave him money.

By the time he got home he was so puffed up with pride he skipped up the close and

f

   l

      o

         a

      t

    e

d

  into the house, catching a glimpse of himself in red and white as he passed the lobby mirror. He heard feet on the carpet and turned, expecting congratulations.

BANG!!!

A blinding flash of blue light. He was on the floor with his da bending over him and shouting. Couldn't hear for the zinging noise in his head. Through his da's legs he could see his maw shaking and Marie behind her.

BANG!!!

Dan's fist came down and he was lost again in blue light. Blue, blue light. When he came back his da had him stood upright against the wall. Still punching.

   —Dan! Dan! Leave him alone! You'll kill him! You'll kill him! his maw was screaming.

   —That's what I'm fuckin trying to do!

BANG!!!

A hook on the side of the head propelled him up the lobby. Dan had been beating him up since he could remember. And there always came the time when he dislocated from himself from the action. Became absent.

   Maw tried to pull Dan off but she was flung to the floor. The boots came in. And the slaps. And the punches.

   —Who the fuck do you think ye are, going up on that altar

with fuckin boots on? Eh? Up there like a ticket!

All the times he'd been beaten up by his da, Christopher's never cried. He'd stare at Dan as the blows came in. Dan thought it was defiance. Thought his son was thinking, when he was big enough he'd have his day. The retaliation. But Dan was wrong. Yes, Christopher had these thoughts. But the reason he would stare was simple. His emotions were frozen. Christopher's heart would take a long thawing out. A long thawing.

As Dan stepped forwards for the final assault, the door had opened and his cousin Gerald and Auntie Theresa came in. Gerald got behind his mother. Theresa placed a hand on Dan's shoulder and he stopped. Just like that. Where his maw had tried and failed so many times. Da and Auntie Theresa exchanged strange looks.

—I'm away to the fuckin pub, said Dan.

And he was gone.

姐妹
sister

Govern a family as you would cook a small fish: very gently.

WHEN YOU MEET a father and son you search for resemblances. You'd find a lot between Devlin and his da. When you meet father and daughter you'd expect similarities, but you wouldn't expect them both to have one eye. Marie's got an eye that doesn't move. She wears a patch when she's not at home. A genetic abnormality? How can it be, if Dan had his eye taken out in a pub?

Devlin's at Marie's window looking over the road at Dan's silhouette. Poverty hangs from Marie's curtains.

—What's happening? Anything good? asks Devlin.

—Aw, nothing much. Usual.

He places a wad of notes on the telly. Like he's done hundreds of times. This is Marie's and his ritual. She looks at the money and sighs.

—I don't want none of your fuckin dirty money.

Devlin knows sometime in the conversation the money will disappear. After a while, Marie limps over and picks the money up. He can see her in the dark glass.

—I've bought a big house in Galloway. I'm thinking about me and Wendy moving there. Retiring.

—Retiring? You?

—Aye. Wendy's pregnant.

—I'll believe that when I see it. Cow.

He ignores that.

—There's some cottages right on the sea. They're mine too. Ye can see the Lake District. And the Isle of Man. Ireland sometimes.

—Ireland? says Marie.

Her face lights up, showing how pretty she might have been, if only life had been different.

—The Mountains of Mourne! he says.

—The Mountains of Mourne? Ye can see them?

—Aye, when the weather's right.

Marie is on the edge of saying she wants to see the

cottages. Take a step away from Possil. A step he's been
wanting her to take for years.

David comes staggering in. Marie moves and meets him in
the doorway surreptitiously handing him some notes.

—David! Christie's here…

David spins and bolts.

—See ye later, crogagator! he shouts as he leaves.

Devlin shakes his head. Last time he seen David was six
months ago.

—When did he get out the jail?

—Couple of weeks ago.

—How did ye no tell me?

—So ye can give him the *My company financed you
though college and this is how ye repay me by dropping out
and becoming a junkie* lecture?

Devlin watches David meandering backwards down the
street, giving him the fingers. He turns, drops his pants, moons
and disappears into the yellow glow. David's never going to
leave Possil while he's still on the smack and Marie's never
going to leave David. A cottage in Galloway's as well being a
crater on the moon.

—D'ye want tea? says Marie.

—Ye could go down for the weekend. A week even. Try it
out. Get away from this place.

—I've no biscuits, she says, —I'll go to the shops. They're
doing *Wagon Wheels* two for one at the Co the now.

—I'm alright. Ye could take one of they cottages. Live
there. Take your pick. I've got photies. I'll bring them down.

—I can't leave Possil.

—How can ye not?

—I just can't.

—Know what's up with you?

—Apart from the limp and the useless eye, ye mean?

Her good eye is vibrating with anger.

—You're feart to leave here. That's what's up, he says.

—I'm frae Possil. I'm feart of nothing.

—You're feart of change.

—And you're feart cos you're powerless anywhere else.

Delvin says nothing.

—Eh? What've ye got to say about that? What's up? Cat got your tongue?

Devlin's saved by the toot-toot of Sholtz's Isuzu Trooper.

He goes down and Sholtz starts acting out what happened in the derelict chapel.

—He disappeared like a ghost.

—I thought you took somebody with ye?

—I did.

—And?

—I came out and he was walking about like a zombie. He's up in Casualty the now. Sixteen stitches and concussion.

Devlin paces up and down. Thinking.

—Not a word to the Chinkees, he says, —Far as they're concerned, Garrett's dead. Ye don't make mistakes when you're dealing with these cunts. Sam, find out where he stays. Bonzo, set it up. We'll pop this toe-rag soon as we get his address.

His men get into the Trooper. Sholtz hangs back.

—Boss, I'm sorry!

—Ach! says Devlin.

爸

father

Truth often hides in an ugly pool.

THE FOLLOWING SATURDAY in St Theresa's Devlin lies in wait for the Ned who's been robbing the collection boxes. The one who kicked Father Boyle in the balls. The chapel's empty except for a couple of old ladies finishing off a decade of the rosary in the back pews.

—How's your groin, Father? asks Devlin

—Fine, fine, he says with some embarrassment.

Boyle says a silent rosary. Devlin looks at the things in the church. The Sacred Heart statue. The crucifix. The Stations of the Cross.

—I used to be an altar boy, ye know.

Father Boyle's surprised by this.

—An altar boy. Where was that then?

—Here. Father Brennan was the priest.

—Father Brennan. Nice man.

The two women come out from the pews, genuflect and bless themselves. As they leave, the light outside floods in. When the doors close Devlin and Father Boyle are alone.

—Mibbi I should sit over there, behind that pillar, says Devlin, —So he'll not think I'm here with you if he sees me.

—Good idea.

Devlin stands. Father Boyle gets a pang of conscience and tugs him back.

—I only want him frightened, mind.

—No worries, Father.

—Just a wee fright, that's all.

Devlin puts his hand on Father Boyle's shoulder, winks and moves off to a pillar near the votive candles.

Twenty minutes pass. Devlin's lulled into calm by the smell of snuffing candles and the encaptured silence of the building. He jumps when the doors squeak open, then slides down out of sight. The Ned's walking around, turning in slow circles. The Ned radar locks on Father Boyle.

—Get out of here, says Father Boyle.

—Who the fuck're you talking to, ya child molester?

The Ned makes to go up the pew. Father Boyle scurries to the other end.

—Stop! shouts the Ned.

Father Boyle stops, the Ned pulls out a blade and unfolds it. He spins it in front of his menacing smile. Points it at Father Boyle.

—You, sit down and say fuck-all. Move, and I'll do more than boot your balls this time. I'll fuckin cut them off!

Father Boyle sits down.

Devlin's crawling under the pews towards the votive candles. As the Ned bursts open the collection box with a screwdriver he hears a noise and doesn't get the chance to turn before his head's smashed into the burning candles. He drops the knife.

—My hair – my hair's on fire!

—Burn, ya bastard, says Devlin.

The Ned's hands scrabble among the candles, trying to put them out. Burning skin. Devlin pulls him back. Thuds his head over and over into the votive candles. The short spikes puncture his forehead. He's pierced, pierced and pierced again. Devlin throws him against the pew. Lays in boot after boot. Punch after punch. Boyle tries to pull Devlin off. Can't. One punch is too many and a million are not enough.

—Attacking a priest, eh? Attacking a fuckin priest! What's it like to be on the receiving end? Eh? Can't hear ye – what was that?

The Ned would speak if he could, but he can't. Devlin punches him again.

—If I ever, ever, hear you're near this chapel again, you're a dead man. D'ye hear me?

It's only when Devlin sees two nuns that he stops, his fists still tight as oyster shells.

—He attacked me with a knife. I was lighting a candle for my mother and he attacked me with a knife. Get the polis, he rasps.

The nuns bend over the Ned.
—Have to go, says Devlin.

Monday morning. Half past eight. The Glasgow Tower turns, scanning the circumference of the city. But the sleet is heavy. The edges of Glasgow disappear.

The same sleet slithers down Devlin's windows. Nicole is nibbling at her Special K. Wendy's sipping coffee and marking jotters. Devlin's eating from a casserole dish overflowing with Sugar Puffs. Whenever he takes a spoonful some fall onto the table. Nicole grimaces each time he picks them up and pops them into his mouth. Wendy turns to Nicole.

—Father will drive you to school.
—No—o.
—I can't be late again. Father is taking you. Final!
—Well, ask him not to speak, Mum.

Nicole impersonates Devlin. He's listening.

—*Huv a nice week, hen. Geez a bell if ye need some dosh.*
He is so embarrassing. I tell my friends he's our gardener.

—He's your father.

Snort.

Devlin is driving through Possil to St Theresa's Secondary, where Wendy teaches English. Teenage gloom slumps in the back seat. On the pavement kids are straggling along, some soaked through.

—I wish I was in Galloway now, Wendy says.
—It'll be raining there too, Devlin replies.
—But it's away from this.

A fifteen-year-old girl rushes past, not even wearing a jacket. It's Kerry-Anne. Her mother's a junkie. Wendy shakes her head angrily and draws Devlin an unseen look.

A group of schoolgirls chatter under umbrellas. Their bodies perfectly balanced between youth and womanhood, Devlin can't help but notice. He eyes them as he approaches and in his wing mirror when he passes. Wendy digs him hard in the ribs.

—You're lucky if they're fifteen.

—What?

—Nicole's fifteen. Your own daughter.

—I'm sixteen, Nicole retorts.

—February, you're sixteen! Wendy tells her.

Devlin jumps to his own defence.

—I was looking in my wing mirror.

—Sad old man, offers Nicole.

—I was looking in my fuckin wing mirror.

By now he's parked outside St Theresa's. Wendy's opened
the door and has one leg out.

—Don't swear, she says, —Oh, and don't speak when you
drop Nicole off. She doesn't like it.

—So I heard!

Kerry-Anne sees Nicole.

—Nicole, hi yi! Haven't seen ye for ages.

—I've been busy.

—Phone iz!

Nicole nods, certain she's never going to phone. Kerry-
Anne takes Wendy's arm.

—Is Nicole leaving her posh school this year?

—I think she'll be staying on, Kerry-Anne.

Kerry-Anne's got nits and she's to go straight to the school
nurse. Wendy agrees to accompany her to take the edge off
the embarrassment.

The nurse takes one look and decides to take action. She
bends over the sink and runs the tap to the right temperature,
cupping the water and spreading it through Kerry-Anne's hair.

A voice comes from the ball of soap-suds.

—That's sore.

—It's for your own good, says the nurse briskly.

Kerry-Anne falls still. Lets things take their course. She's
used to letting things take their course. When her mother's
boyfriends slip into her bed at night she lets things take their
course.

—My mother used to drag me round the living-room by the

hair with one of they Derbac combs. Mind that lotion ye used to get that nipped your head? she asks Wendy.

—No, actually, I don't.

—No have nits in Manchester then?

The nurse winds Kerry-Anne's hair up in a towel and hands her a brand new outfit. Skirt, blouse, black jumper, underwear, shoes and socks.

—Away in there and get a shower, then get dressed.

—These for me?

—Well they're not for us.

Kerry-Anne turns the shower on and the nurse stuffs her old clothes into a bin bag. A shoe with a hole through the sole. She reaches inside and pulls out the cover of a book. *Of Mice and Men.*

—At least books are good for something.

—How do people get into such a state? says Wendy.

—Drugs. I can remember when there used to be gardens outside these closes. People sitting out in deckchairs in the summer. Then the drugs crept in. Blackhill, Garngad. Sighthill. Springburn. Possil. The polis turned a blind eye. It was as if they'd been told to let Glasgow die. The politicians too. Tory, Labour, the lot. Now everybody's paying for it. And there's worse to come. Mark my words. A lot worse.

Wendy's guilt's giving her the bends. She says nothing.

—They should give the dealers life.

—Life?

—Did I say life? No. Shoot them. Scum of the earth.

In the Wilderness a buzzard glides through torrential rain high above a single-track road. A Stag steps onto the road, hooves clicking as it moves this way and that. It's never been on tarmac before. Like rock, but softer. Like a river, but still. It's suddenly alert to a low whooshing noise. Vibrations on the black tarmac river. Close and deafening. Too close. Too close. Run. Too close. Jump. Its legs tremble and it springs into the forest where sound is swallowed by oceans of pine needles.

Devlin's Shogun zooms past, throwing up water. Nicole hasn't spoken for an hour. He's been wondering when the Chinese will spring their trap. What he'll do to prevent that.

Nicole finally cracks the silence.

—Did you notice the condition of Kerry-Anne?

—Eh?

—She looked like something from a Charles Dickens novel. A pauper.

—That's some way to talk about your pal.

—Ex pal.

—You should give her a phone.

—You must be kidding.

—What have I told you?

No answer.

—Nicole!

—Don't judge people by where they live.

—What else?

—Or how they speak.

—And don't forget it.

Nicole sees the Stag spring onto a rock in the distance where the road winds down the mountainside. It reminds her of a joke she heard at Eden Academy.

—Daddy, what would one call a deer with no eyes?

Devlin shrugs.

—No idea.

Devlin shakes his head. Nicole's on a roll.

—Right. Okay. Now listen carefully. What would one call a deer with no eyes and no legs?

—Don't know.

—Still no idea. Get it: *still* no idea.

—Who told you that?

—Gerry.

—Who the fuck is Gerry?

—My boyfriend.

Has that time arrived already? Only yesterday he rocked her in his arms and sang that Police song to her. *Every Breath*

You Take. Walking up and down the room as she cried. To give Wendy a break. That was when he decided there was no way she'd get the raw deal he'd had in life. She'd get every chance he didn't.

Now she's got a boyfriend.

—Why are you smiling, Daddy?

—Miracles never cease, he says.

—You're not angry I have a boyfriend?

—No. But the minute it interferes with your education, it's off.

They drive on a mile or so. He decides to try a couple of jokes on her.

—Hey, Christina Aguliera, what would *one* call a deer with no eyes and no legs lying at the side of the road?

—At the side of the road? I haven't the foggiest, Daddy.

—Still no idea, by the way.

Devlin sniggers. One generation away from him and she doesn't understand the patter. He goes for another joke.

—Is that a cake or a meringue?

—What cake?

Devlin grins. Nicole is puzzled.

screeeeeeeeeeeeeeeeeeeeeeeech

BANG!

Devlin's car punches into the Stag. It slumps to the ground, twitching in shock.

Devlin's wipers beat the sleet
side
to side.

The Stag's trying to get up. Its front right leg is shattered. Bone shows through a ragged wound.

—Great! We're going to be late. I'll be put on Pains and Penalties, says Nicole.

The Stag has stopped struggling. It stares in Devlin's eyes.

He's reminded of the Dragon in Chinatown.

—Drive round it! Nicole shouts.

—I can't. There's a drop.

—Run over the top of it then!

The Stag tucks its back hooves under its belly. Like an old man with a stick, it bends its good front leg. Pushes and strains. It's up, antlers quivering. And then, incredibly, it moves closer. Its long neck hovers over the bonnet. It looks directly at Devlin. The thump-thimp of the wipers does nothing to distract it.

Devlin sees himself reflected in its eyes.

—Come on, big fellah, says Devlin, —Move! Go!

The Stag lets out a cloudy snort, turns towards the forest, stumbles and falls. Devlin grimaces. It gets up. At the edge of the trees it falls again.

—Ah, fuck!

Devlin bundles out of the car and goes to the boot. The Stag moves into the forest on three legs. Devlin follows through barcodes of light and dark. In his hand is a baseball bat.

—What are you doing, Dad? Nicole shouts after him.

—Can't leave it like that, hen. Have to put it out its misery.

Devlin bounds after the Stag. Stops to listen. Silence. Has he lost it? Creeps forward into a clearing. There it is.

The whole forest holds its breath.

The Stag bellows. Knows its end has come. Devlin stands above the wounded beast, raises the bat high in the air…

Paris. In the Sacré Couer the sun blasts colour through a stained-glass window. Rows of nuns chant *Flos Regalia*. Candle smoke drifts up the vast cathedral. Sister Mary-Bridget's lips chant automatically but in her mind she sees Christie Devlin. Midway through his life. In a dark wood. Death raised above his head. And the way out of the forest almost lost.

The Mother Superior clap, clap claps her hands. The nuns stand up, Mary-Bridget a microsecond behind everyone else.

Mother Superior notices. As the nuns exit the chapel, she places her hand on Mary-Bridget's shoulder. She takes Mary-Bridget's hands, holding them in hers. They speak in French.

—*What is bothering you, Sister Mary-Bridget?*

—*I have to request permission to go to Scotland, Mother Superior.*

Pebbles of coloured light move over their faces.

In the Silver Seas Casino the roulette wheels send pebbles of light dancing over the faces of gamblers. At a small table Ming Fung is drinking green tea with her father. Hung Kwan is gambling at the Punto alongside I Lo.

Halfway along the Mah Jong room hangs a red and turquoise curtain printed with Chinese stencils. A Triad draws it back, revealing a black door emblazoned with Chinese text in gold leaf. Behind this door Heung Chu is setting up for I Lo's initiation ceremony. He sits contemplatively still. His internal world swirls with light and dark. Yin and Yang. He sees Christie Devlin. Midway through his life. In a dark wood. Death raised above his head. And the way out of the forest almost lost.

Devlin hurls the bat down

THUD

into the earth beside the Stag's head. He can't kill it.

Above the tree-tops a million birds rise.

Devlin lies on the mattress of pine needles, face to face with the Stag. Sees himself reflected in its eyes.

—Come on, big fellah, he whispers, —get up.

The Stag tries to rise.

—Come on!

The Stag suddenly twists and manages to stand.

—On ye go, big fellah! On ye fuckin go! Devlin shouts.

The forest closes on the Stag until it's an echo.

Devlin goes back to the Shogun. Throws the bat over

Nicole's head into the boot. Crunches into gear.
—Where's the antlers?
Now he's the one who doesn't want to speak.

Soon they reach Eden Academy. Devlin has selected this shrine to privilege carefully. Nothing less than the best for Nicole.
In the green spaces between the sandstone buildings, young things in light blue, V-neck pullovers are streaming towards church for morning assembly. Augustus waves to Nicole. He's also fifteen. A square-jawed handsomeness shows through his boyish features.
—Is that your boyfriend?
—Duuuh! Don't think so, says Nicole,—That's Augustus.
—Sorry!
Augustus likes Nicole. She's so hard-edged, has something even the daughters of Bosnian politicians lack. Nicole's inner diamond could light up your life. Or cut you to shreds.
She lugs her bags away. Augustus takes one from her. Devlin stands by the raised hatch.
—See ye at the weekend! he shouts.
She doesn't answer. Doesn't even turn round.
—Wee cunt, he says to himself. She needs embarrassing.
—Nicole! Hey, we'll get back down the Barras on Saturday, hen. Promise! Get ye some new clothes, BY THE WAY!
Soon all the kids are gone and it's only Devlin left. The crows in the trees look down. A shiver runs up and down his back
       and

BANG!

goes the tailgate.
       The crows jump and land. Devlin drives away.

Augustus came in with Nicole but now he can't see her anywhere. She must have sat at the back. Gorman, the

Headmaster, drones on.

—Here at Eden Academy we strive to develop the whole person. Every girl and boy here is expected to achieve their full potential and to show their mettle in the field of moral endeavour. As the future leaders of society, you will carry a great burden of responsibility...

Nicole is in the vestibule rifling through bags and jackets. She finds a credit card. Platinum. Puts it down her bra. Stopping to think, removes it and pushes it into her shoe. Sneaks back into assembly.

Jarkness stands on the Machair peninsula in Galloway. The house faces east, across to a five-fingered mountain range known as The Awful Hand. It's set in a sandy bay fringed with pebbles. The sand stretches for a mile when the tide's out. When it's in, the sea laps against the wall at the end of the garden. There are ten bedrooms. The old woman who used to live there used to hang her washing in the ballroom.

There are four ways into Jarkness. A single-track road from the west; Devlin plans to erect gates and cameras where it meets the main road. There's a way in from a small fishing village in the south, an hour's walk through coastal forest; Devlin will place cameras and infra-red sensors in the trees. There's a path from the north running through forest; that will get the same treatment. He's surrounding Jarkness with an ornate, ten-foot high fence. With cameras and guards.

The only other way in is from the sea.

A distant fishing boat chugs out of Wigtown Bay. Devlin, secluded in the trees, watches it glide past. Showers of snow gust over the low waves. This is the paradise Devlin promised Wendy. He's watching the deceased woman's family take the last of her belongings away in a truck. Then Jarkness will be his.

Perfect.

He hears a rustle.

Just beyond a giant spruce a heron rises into the sky. It could be China.

Nicole has gone to her room instead of class to call Gerry on her mobile.

—I've got a card.

—What kind?

—MasterCard. Platinum.

Gerry congratulates her. Asks if she's told her father about them yet. She says she has, on the way to school that morning. Gerry's pleased. He's hoping to meet him. But one step at a time. One step at a time.

Nicole's attention is drawn to the window.

—Have to go. Speak later. Mwah!

Gorman and a senior teacher are walking purposefully back towards the church. Buster Brown is with them.

Nicole takes off her shoe, removes the card, and reads it. Robert Brown. This time she peels back the inner sole and places the card there. Puts the shoe on and makes her way to Physics.

As Nicole struggles with the speed of light, Devlin drives through Galloway towards Glasgow.

All that empty space. Trees and moors and miles of sky. It's getting to him. Penetrating him. In a city there's never too much space to contend with. It's so much easier to control. But here there are no people in the endless landscape. How could he control it? The more he drives the more empty it becomes. It's making him nauseous. He clicks the radio on to take the mind off it.

Beat 106 pumps out the beat. Try for another station. The automatic search travels through the FM range unable to lock on. In the Wilderness sometimes all you get is radio silence. Then a religious channel bounces in, clear as day. Kris Kristofferson singing his AA song. That's a laugh. It reminds Devlin he's a year sober. He's amazed at his own willpower.

Joins in. But taking the piss. All these bible-bashers and holy rollers should be clubbed to death with their books. But sings anyway. Anything rather than face the space.

ONCOMING

LOG

LORRY

—Fuckin hell!

Devlin swerves.

Screeeeeeeeeeeeeeeeeeeeeeeeeeeeeeeeeech

squeals to a halt. The offending truck, laden with logs, rattles away towards Newton Stewart. Devlin's heart is pounding. But he's lived on adrenaline rushes. He smiles. In some ways fear is enjoyable. Fear is truth. He's elated.

Clicks the radio off. The mountains and moors stretch all around. The harder he concentrates, the more his adrenaline's quenched. The more it's quenched the calmer he gets. He's beginning to appreciate the peace. The glimmer of Tai Ping. Engine off. Window down. Fresh air like a new beginning. Closes his eyes. Sucks air in. Lets it out slowly. The mesh of sounds gradually separates. The river from the wind. The trees from the grass. Finches from curlews. The beats of his own heart. Never heard the beating of his own heart like this before. Not like in fights, in courts, in deals. Not just the blood in his ears. It's like an inner drum.

He steps out onto the moor. A man saturated with city, wearing an expensive suit, standing in a wilderness.

He turns. There's something behind him. Something behind him for sure. But there's not. Spins the other way. Nothing there either. Here you could be surrounded and know nothing. Surrounded so that you're part of it whether you like it or not.

Devlin's expression changes. He reaches up under the rear

of his jacket and produces a handgun from an upside down holster. For a reason he can't tell, he fires three shots into the peat, into the landscape, into the sound of the beating of his heart.

BANG

BANG

BANG

At St Theresa's Wendy's on dinner duty with Anne, another English teacher. Kerry-Anne lines up. Looks so good in her new clothes. Clunk, a ball of mashed potatoes lands on her plate. She nods for mince.

—Some of them, this is the only decent meal they get, says Anne.

—Or the only meal! says Wendy.

Kerry-Anne wolfs her dinner down and licks the plate, her eyes rising like two blue moons over a white planet. She spots Wendy and winks. Wendy smiles.

—Come on, hurry up, goes the boy beside her.

—Haud your horses, Michael, I'm going as fast as I can.

Kerry-Anne scoffs her custard and caramel cake. Michael gets up and waits outside. Restless.

—See you took her to the nurse today? Anne says. —Her mother used to be a decent lassie Now she's...

—I know, Wendy interrupts.

Anne claims she can spot the moment a kid's parents get taken by smack. She points over at a boy sitting alone with his eyes glazed over. For him, the only discipline is the school bell. Everything outside the school is dreadful. A mother he can't wake up, twenty-four hour telly and a father away some-where. He's thirteen. When puberty hits, the whole world will be his enemy. And the world better watch out. Anne points out some more.

—There's one. Him too. And her.

A pretty girl with dead eyes. Only on Friday they were bright and alive, but over the weekend the shutters have come down.

Here comes Kerry-Anne. She tries to slip past but Wendy grabs her arm.

—Don't disappear this afternoon!

—Mibbi my maw's needing me to cash her book.

Kerry-Anne's out the door.

—Dealers. I'd shoot them all, Anne whispers in Wendy's ear. Anne knows who Wendy is married to.

They stand in silence. Anne tries to be more friendly.

—This baby's doing wonders for you.

—Do you think so?

—All those hormones.

—You know, Christie's thinking about retiring.

—Retiring?

—We've bought a house in Galloway.

—Galloway?

—He's going to leave it all behind, says Wendy.

But Wendy doesn't really believe that herself.

兄弟
brother

Ceremony is the smoke of friendship.

TRIAD INITIATIONS ARE held on the twenty-fifth night of the Chinese month. In the Silver Seas Casino Triads file into the initiation room. Heung Chu, in spiritual master regalia, greets each man. Little strips of red rice paper are handed to him.

At the far end of the room is an altar, draped with a scarlet cloth. On an altar sits a wooden tub filled with raw rice. A sword made of peach and plum wood. A sandal made of straw. A yellow umbrella. A white paper fan. An abacus. A set of Chinese scales. An idol of Kwan Ti. Two brass, single-stem candle sticks. A brass Seven Stars lamp. A jug of wine and five wine cups. A pot of tea and three bowls. An incense bowl and a smaller incense pot. Eight bowls of fruit, nuts, flowers and diluted wine. A Triad handbook. A needle with red thread attached.

I Lo enters barefoot, his hair tousled and his coat open. Someone hands him five joss sticks. The smoke trails through the room. I Lo recites four ritual poems the last of which is this:

—I passed a corner and then another corner.
My family lives on Five Fingers Mountain.
I've come to look for the temple of the sisters-in-law.
It's on the third of the row whether you count from right or
left.

I Lo's name is announced. He's led to the First Gate. Shown the secret handshake. He performs a dance then steps through the gate to have his particulars entered into the records.

Another archway is formed from swords of copper, swords of steel. He walks underneath the Mountain of Knives. An old man steps from the shadows and hands him three red stones. Light from the candles flits across the stones. They become three dragon's eyes in the palm of his hand. I Lo pays his initiation fee and is led to the Hung Gate, which is guarded by two generals. I Lo kneels three times before them and they demand his name. From somewhere his name is called. The generals go through the gate, asking for Heung Chu's permission that the I Lo might enter. They return and lead him through to the Hall of Fidelity and Loyalty. Two more generals demand his name as he kneels to them four times.

I Lo is counselled on being true and loyal to his clan. The importance of being Chinese. He is warned what will happen if he breaks these bonds.

He's led through the Circle of Heaven and Earth, over an imaginary ditch, up to the East Gate of the City of Willows. Beyond lies the Hall of Universal Peace. Tai Ping. I Lo is led to another room where Tai Lo and Hung Kwan await him. A voice speaks.

—*We request permission that Tse Pong-hang, the fruit seller be allowed to enter Tai Ping Market.*

Once in Tai Ping Market I Lo is joined by Hung Kwan, who answers three hundred and thirty-three questions about the Triads on his behalf. At the end of this long process, Heung Chu asks I Lo if he still wishes to join. Say no at this point, and I Lo would never see dawn. He answers yes and a snip of his hair is taken. He is shaved. His hair is combed and his face washed to clean away any deceit or doubt. He is stripped and dressed in a long white robe. A red sash is tied around his head and a pair of straw sandals placed on his feet.

He is ready to take the thirty-six oaths.

1. After having entered the San Yee On gates I must treat the parents and relatives of my sworn brothers as my own kin. I shall suffer death by five thunderbolts if I do not keep this oath.
2. I shall assist my sworn brothers to bury their parents and brothers by offering financial or physical assistance. I shall be killed by five thunderbolts if I pretend to have no knowledge of their troubles.
3. When San Yee On brothers visit my house, I shall provide

them with board and lodging. I shall be killed by myriads of knives if I treat them as strangers.

4. I shall always acknowledge my San Yee On brothers when they identify themselves. If I ignore them I shall be killed by myriads of swords.

5. I shall not disclose the secrets of the San Yee On family, not even to my parents, brothers, or wife. I shall never disclose the secrets for money. I shall be killed by myriads of swords if I do so.

6. I shall never betray my sworn brothers. If, through a misunderstanding, I have caused the arrest of one of my brothers I must release him immediately. If I break this oath I shall be killed by five thunderbolts.

7. I shall offer financial assistance to sworn brothers who are in trouble in order that they may pay their passage fee, etc. If I break this oath I shall be killed by five thunderbolts.

8. I must never cause harm or bring trouble to my sworn brothers or Incense Master. If I do so I shall be killed by myriads of swords.

9. I must never commit any indecent assaults on the wives, sisters, or daughters, of my sworn brothers. I shall be killed by five thunderbolts if I break this oath.

10. I shall never embezzle cash or property from my sworn brothers. If I break this oath I shall be killed by myriads of swords.

11. I shall take good care of the wives or children of sworn brothers entrusted to my keeping. If I do not I shall be killed by five thunderbolts.

12. If I have supplied false particulars about myself for the purpose of joining the San Yee On family I shall be killed by five thunderbolts.

13. If I should change my mind and deny my membership of the San Yee On family I shall be killed by myriads of swords.

14. If I rob a sworn brother or assist an outsider to do so I shall be killed by five thunderbolts.

15. If I should take advantage of a sworn brother or force

unfair business deals upon him I shall be killed by myriads of swords.

16. If I knowingly convert my sworn brother's cash or property to my own use I shall be killed by five thunderbolts.

17. If I have wrongly taken a sworn brother's cash or property during a robbery I must return them to him. If I do not I shall be killed by five thunderbolts.

18. If I am arrested after committing an offence I must accept my punishment an not try to place blame on my sworn brothers. If I do so I shall be killed by five thunderbolts.

19. If any of my sworn brothers are killed, or arrested, or have departed to some other place, I shall assist their wives and children who may be in need. If I pretend to have no knowledge of their difficulties I shall be killed by five thunderbolts.

20. When any of my sworn brothers have been assaulted or blamed by others, I must come forward and help him if he is in the right or advise him to desist if he is wrong. If he has been repeatedly insulted by others I shall inform our other brothers and arrange to help him physically or financially. If I do not keep this oath I shall be killed by five thunderbolts.

21. If it comes to my knowledge that the Government is seeking any of my sworn brothers who has come from other provinces or from overseas, I shall immediately inform him in order that he may make his escape. If I break this oath I shall be killed by five thunderbolts.

22. I must not conspire with outsiders to cheat my sworn brothers at gambling. If I do so I shall be killed by myriads of swords.

23. I shall not cause discord amongst my sworn brothers by spreading false reports about any of them. If I do so I shall be killed by myriads of swords.

24. I shall not appoint myself as Incense Master without authority. After entering the San Yee On gates for three years the loyal and faithful ones may be promoted by the Incense Master with the support of his sworn brothers. I shall be killed

by five thunderbolts if I make any unauthorised promotions myself.

25. If my natural brothers are involved in a dispute or law suit with my sworn brothers I must not help either party against the other but must attempt to have the matter settled amicably. If I break this oath I shall be killed by five thunderbolts.

26. After entering the San Yee On gates I must forget any previous grudges I may have borne against my sworn brothers. If I do not do so I shall be killed by five thunderbolts.

27. I must not trespass upon the territory occupied by my sworn brothers. I shall be killed by five thunderbolts if I pretend to have no knowledge of my brothers' rights in such matters.

28. I must not covet or seek to share any property or cash obtained by my sworn brothers. If I have such ideas I shall be killed.

29. I must not disclose any address where my sworn brothers keep their wealth nor must I conspire to make wrong use of such knowledge. If I do so I shall be killed by myriads of swords.

30. I must not give support to outsiders if so doing is against the interests of any of my sworn brothers. If I do not keep this oath I shall be killed by myriads of swords.

31. I must not take advantage of the San Yee On brotherhood in order to oppress or take violent or unreasonable advantage of others. I must be content and honest. If I break this oath I shall be killed by five thunderbolts.

32. I shall be killed by five thunderbolts if I behave indecently towards small children of my sworn brothers' families.

33. If any of my sworn brothers has committed a big offence I must not inform upon them to the Government for the purposes of obtaining a reward. I shall be killed by five thunderbolts if I break this oath.

34. I must not take to myself the wives and concubines of my sworn brothers nor commit adultery with them. If I do so I shall be killed by myriads of swords.

35. I must never reveal San Yee On secrets or signs when

speaking to outsiders. If I do so I shall be killed by myriads of swords.

36. After entering the San Yee On gates I shall be loyal and faithful and shall endeavour to overthrow Ch'ing and restore Ming by coordinating my efforts with those of my sworn brethren even though my brethren and I may not be in the same professions. Our common aim is to avenge our Five Ancestors.

I Lo is taken through the West Gate of the City of Willows. The oath list is burned and rises in smoke to the Gods that they might bear witness.

Now Heung Chu approaches I Lo and asking
—*Where were you born?*
—*Under a peach tree.*
—*Do you have a mother?*
—*I have five.*
—*Don't you owe me money?*
—*I paid you, I recall.*
—*I don't recall that – where did you pay me?*
—*In the market in the City of Willows.*

In a Possil close-mouth a lone crisp bag scoops up the morning, lands and rocks itself still. The sound of nuns chanting *Flos Regalia* lingers over the discarded pizza boxes, kebab wraps shredded Rizla packets and empty Buckfast bottles.

To the lift and twitch of a crow's wing, the postman stops at Marie's door.

Devlin drops Wendy at St Theresa's. Anne and Cara go past. Wendy nods.

—Another day another dollar, says Anne.
—No rest for the wicked, says Cara, a Maths teacher.
Anne draws Devlin a look and swivels into the school. They wait until they're out of earshot.
—Bloody drug dealer's moll, says Anne.
—Shouldn't be allowed near children.

Devlin can't read their lips but knows exactly what they're talking about.

—I wish there was something we could do about her, says Anne.

—There is, says Cara.

They watch Wendy. But the hostility in Delvin's eyes turns them and walks them right into the school.

David picks up the letters, throwing them on the floor one at a time until he comes to the Giro. Stuffs it in his pocket. Senses something behind him. Turns with an insincere, junkie smile. Marie's staring at him.

—Couldn't sleep, he says.

—Me neither.

She doesn't move. She doesn't speak. She doesn't give anything away. This is the only retaliation she gets for the pain he causes her. Holding him in an indeterminable length of guilt. David cracks.

—Going out a walk.

Marie moves between him and the door.

—This time in the morning? says Marie.

He tries to get round her but she shifts. He goes the other way and she shifts again. He stares at the key in the lock. Marie moves to cover his view.

—I haven't got it! David says.

—We've no bread. No sugar. And I've got no fags.

—It didn't come.

She tries a different approach.

—I'll cash it.

—I haven't got it, I said!

—Right!

Marie turns the key. Pockets it. Folds her arms. Settles in for a long wait.

—Maw!

Amongst the junk mail there's a white envelope. The address is handwritten.

Marie Devlin
13 Fruin Street
Possilpark
Glasgow
Écosse

She hears her heart beating like Devlin did in the Wilderness. Looks at David. He knows who it's from. This is the second letter in six months.

—Gimmi it up.

—You get it.

If she bends down he'll go for her and try to get the key. How to get the letter and make sure David doesn't escape? She grabs him by the hand and bends down. But he pulls her onto all fours. She curls up so he can't get into her pocket for the key. David produces a key of his own.

—Aha! Got it made in the Savoy Centre soon as I got out the jail, ya fuckin daftie!

He fumbles in the lock. Marie rips open the letter. She can smell candles. She sniffs the letter and smiles. Sits back against the wall. David can't get the door open with his Savoy Centre key.

—Who's the fuckin daftie now?

—You've changed the locks again. Ya fly bastard, Maw! And he laughs, slumping down beside her.

—Two letters in six months. Is that not a bit strange? She nods as she reads.

—She's coming to Glasgow.

—After all these years. Is she fuckin mad?

—Here! She's coming here! Oh David, everything's going to be alright.

Marie gives David the new key. As he opens the door Marie speaks without looking up.

—Just make sure and get me fags.

David shoots off.

At four o'clock Devlin's outside the school waiting for Wendy.

Kids pour round about him. Some Neds try to impress him but he avoids eye contact. When the last few bullied kids emerge from nooks and crannies the teachers begin to come out.

Anne and Cara pass, nodding in his direction, then huddling like it's all a big secret. Devlin feels like asking who the fuck they think they are. Wendy appears with a pile of jotters crushed to her chest, head down. She gets in without speaking. They drive off.

—Who are they two fuckin weirdos?

—Anne and Cara.

—They were talking about me.

—They don't even know you.

—They were doing a good impersonation of people that do then.

—They don't know you Christie.

—Cunts!

They drive on lost in the hum of traffic and relentless radio banter. Devlin's thinking ahead. Tonight is The Burning of the Yellow Paper. He's apprehensive but he'd run through a building filled with fire to muscle into pole position in this city. To be untouchable. Wendy spots David pissing against a bus stop full of school kids and grannies.

—Look at the state of him.

—Fuckin waste of a working heart, says Devlin.

David wiggles his dick at Devlin. He slams the brakes on and is halfway out the door when Wendy grabs his arm.

—No violence, Christie. I can't take it anymore.

Devlin gives David a look that means I'll see you later and drives off. They're soon in leafy Bearsden avenues.

—Father Boyle was in my class today.

Devlin says nothing.

—Talking to the kids about morality.

—Makes a change from immortality, says Devlin.

Wendy is suddenly and unexpectedly angry.

—It took him almost two hours to scrub the blood off the altar railings and the votive candles.

—You wanted me to sort the Ned out. I sorted the Ned out. What did he want me to do? Go up and offer him a canoeing holiday?

—Father Boyle is a nervous wreck now. You did more damage to him than the Ned ever did.

—One minute you want me for my… my… qualities! Next thing you're disgusted by them. Make your fuckin mind up.

Wendy lets rip. The damage his drugs are doing to kids. He's tearing Glasgow apart.

—If it wasn't me it'd be somebody else! At least I've got standards. Morality! Like Father Boyle. A different sort of morality, maybe, but a morality all the same. There's some of these young bucks coming up now have none at all. All the old codes are breaking down. I'm holding this fuckin city together.

Wendy starts telling him about Kerry-Anne. How her life's as good as over. Her mother, ruined because of drugs. And where did those drugs come from?

—Aye, they might've came from me, says Devlin, —but ye've got to see it this way. Who takes them? They've all got a choice. Take it or leave it. It's getting rid of the weak. Maybe I'm doing the world a favour.

Wendy goes ballistic. Grabs him by the shoulder, pulling him in, pushing him away. She bloody held him together when he was drinking. When *he* was running to the bottle every time he had to face his responsibilities. He was a bigger waster than all the junkies put together.

—That's different.

—How? How is it different, Christie?

—It's alcoholism.

—It's the same bloody thing and if you don't understand that you're crazier than I thought you were.

—I've spent enough time in the horrors to know how bad it can be. But I pulled myself together. Used my willpower to get sober. That's what these junkie bastards should do instead of blame, blame, blame.

—Horrors? Horrors? Wendy says, —Come to my school and I'll show *you* some horrors.

—Come to my work, the place I make money to keep you in this lifestyle, and I'll show you some horrors!

They drive on in silence.

鬼子
demon

Man takes a drink. Drink takes a drink. Drink takes the man.

THE BURNING OF the Yellow Paper is normally conducted when two Triad gangs come together for a common purpose. Tonight Tai Lo and his Triad gang will merge with Devlin's gang. A Chinese-Scottish Burning of the Yellow Paper.

The ceremony is based on an ancient Chinese legal practice where each party would sign an agreement written on a piece of yellow parchment. The two papers were then burned before witnesses to make them binding. Even today in Hong Kong witnesses sometimes Burn the Yellow Paper before a trial.

Devlin, Bonzo, Sam and Sholtz line up alongside Tai Lo, Heung Chu, I Lo and Hung Kwan. Ming Fung is also present.

Devlin holds up one piece of burning yellow paper. Tai Lo holds up another. The words disappear. But now they exist in a much more powerful way. These are words you can't go back on.

Flames lick towards Devlin's finger and thumb. He squints at Tai Lo. He isn't budging. Devlin's hand is burning but he's not letting go. Not letting this wee Chinkee cunt show him up as weak. Then Heung Chu gives the signal to Tai Lo, who flips the burning paper into a bowl. Devlin copies. Heung Chu holds the bowl high in the air with three fingers of each hand. It reminds Devlin of when he was an altar boy.

—In The Burning of the Yellow Paper, we are bonded, brothers united for a single common purpose.

—We are bonded, brothers united for a single common purpose, say Devlin and his men.

Tai Lo shakes hands with Devlin. The Triads applaud.

Tai Lo hugs Devlin.

In the celebrations that follow, Bonzo keeps eyeing up Ming Fung. She's singing on the karaoke. Bonzo likes it. A lot.

I Lo watches Bonzo watch Ming Fung. Hung Kwan watches I Lo watch Bonzo. Hung Kwan nudges I Lo.

—You like her? Boss's daughter?

—*Yes.*

—*That Muppet seems to like her too.*

—*She'll be my woman soon enough. Watch this space.*

They avert their eyes because here's the boss coming. Behind him, Heung Chu with a tray of drinks.

Clap, clap, clap, goes Tai Lo and his men gather. He hands each a ceremonial glass of ornate crystal with dragons carved into them. They are ancient.

There is one left on the tray.

Tai Lo holds it out to Devlin.

—Tiger bone wine. Make you strong.

—I'm driving, says Devlin.

One drink is too many and a million are not enough. Tai Lo realises Devlin doesn't know the significance of this drink.

—It is tradition. To seal The Burning of the Yellow Paper.

Devlin and Tai Lo eye each other.

—Ach.

Devlin takes the glass. Swills the tiger bone wine round.

—Together, says Tai Lo.

—Together, says Devlin.

—Christie! warns Bonzo.

—I'm alright, says Devlin.

He clinks glasses with Tai Lo.

—Shit! says Bonzo.

The glass is tipped at Devlin's lips. Bonzo wants to say, to do something, any fuckin thing,

but he can't because

Devlin

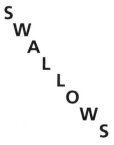

S
 W
  A
   L
    L
     O
      W
       S

The tiger bone wine goes down like golden flames. Devlin licks his lips. He wants more already. He slams the glass down on the Punto table. The Triads cheer.

The first time Devlin drank he was thirteen. He was going to the Tuesday night disco in St Theresa's. On the way he met some pals who had a stolen quarter bottles of whisky from somewhere. They gave one to him and he drank it in one go.

By the time he got to the disco he was rocking. Big Father Riley always made sure there were no fights. *See My Baby Jive* was playing and the dance floor was heaving. Christopher took off his Harrington bomber jacket and hung it over the back of an empty chair. So far, so normal. It's what he done next. Christopher walked backwards away from the chair. Sat directly opposite and stared at the jacket through the passing shadows of dancers and coloured disco lights. A few songs came and went. Then it was *Rubber Bullets* by 10CC. He was still staring at his jacket. Daring anybody to touch it.

Father Riley kept an eye on him for the next three songs, then went and got the jacket and took it over.

—Is this your jacket, Christopher?

—I'm not Christopher.

—Are ye not now? If you're not Christopher who are ye then?

—I'm the Devil!

Father Riley was about to laugh when Christopher jumped on him, wrapped his arms and legs round the priest and started biting his head shouting

—I'm the Devil!

And biting.

—I'm the Devil!

Father Riley got him by the scruff of the neck and the back of his trousers.

—I'll show ye what we do to the Devil round these parts.

He ran at the door and flung him out into the yard. Christopher looked back in through the doorway. The lights behind were the fires of hell. Father Riley leaned from the flames.

—See you on Judgement Day, Satan.

Devlin's on a table, swigging from a bottle of tiger bone wine, singing karaoke. Eddie and the Hot Rods. *Do Anything You Wanna Do.* The crowd's going wild.

♪♪ Goanna break out of this city, leave the people here behind, searching for adventure is the type of life you find. Tired of doing day jobs with no thanks for what I do, I'm sure there must be someone now I'm goanna find out who.

Devlin jumps high in the air like a goalkeeper, then lands on the crash of the next chord, points at the crowd:

♪♪ Why don't you ask them what they expect from you. Why don't you tell them what you are goanna do...

It's better than a rock concert. Sweat covers his face. Cheers and whistles. What a showman. In another life he might have been a pop star.

To I Lo's dismay, Hung Kwan puts an arm round Delvin's drunk neck and sings along, grunting sounds that approximate to the words. The Chinese go even wilder now that they have a man in on the act. On the sidelines Bonzo can't take his eyes off Ming Fung. I Lo sizes him up.

Morning. Devlin's face is glued to the bar. It peels from the surface like a balloon skin. He sees a glass half filled with whisky. Downs it. Forces himself not to be sick. Anchor Bar? Can't remember how he got there. He uses the Anchor to launder money.

This is how he used to find himself before AA. Lying in some bar. Maybe pissed his trousers, maybe not. He feels a pang? Remembers all the promises. But one thing's for sure: he can't stop now. Not even with a head full of AA. Benders have to take their course.

Sholtz, Bonzo and Sam are sleeping like babies on the cushioned seats, surrounded by coke cans and a scattered card game.

—Hey! Fuckin Babes in the Woods!

—Morning, boss, says Bonzo.

Sholtz opens a can of coke.

—Find fuckin Garrett, Devlin orders.

Bonzo's worried about him.

—What about leaving you here?

—Just find Garrett!

—Right, boss.

They lock the door behind them and push the keys back through. They fall with a crash.

Gerry has come to meet Nicole in the school grounds. She passes him some credit cards. He gives her a few grams of dope. She's seen something going on in the school and plans to muscle in on it. Gerry wants to know what, but she's not telling him till she's sorted it out.

Michael keeps watch outside a derelict Jehovah's hall. Inside the floor is covered in shards of glass and a film of icy water. A burst pipe hisses. A man with grey hair and missing teeth moans in ecstasy. Kerry-Anne's wanking him, trying to keep him the wrong side of orgasm to get more money. Once they've came that's it.

—D'ye want to see my tits?

The man moans. His cock throbs. She takes her hand away.

—Keep going, keep going, he says.

—Ye can see my tits for another tenner.

—No... I'm... I'm ahh...!

Too late. He comes. The hot viscosity spits onto her hands. His spunk shines like silver. He moans and collapses against the wall like his bones have been removed.

—Ya durty old bastard.

She pulls a tub of wipes from her bag. The man is off. He nearly bumps into Wendy, who's walking towards school filled with worries for Devlin. He must be back on the drink. She sees Kerry-Anne emerge from the derelict building.

The man.

Kerry-Anne.

Michael.

She puts it all together. Gets an answer she doesn't like.

—Kerry-Anne? What were you doing in there?

—Pish.

—In there?

—Was bursting.

—Who was that man?

—What man? I never seen any man.

Midnight. Devlin's in a corner on his own, his gun on the seat under a newspaper. He watches the barman let the last two customers out. The barman switches the main lights out.

—I can lock ye in, Christie?

—Put the keys through the letterbox.

Sunday morning and Devlin's snoring with his chin on his chest. Click! The door opens. Bonzo pads in, followed by Sholtz. They shut the door as if a baby was asleep. Bonzo removes the gun from under the paper. Stands well back and coughs. Devlin jolts upright, scrabbling where the gun used to be. His eyes just about focus.

—Christie! We've found him, says Bonzo.

Devlin's brain's not in gear.

—Who? Found who?

—That Garrett cunt, says Bonzo.

—D'ye want us to pop him? Sholtz asks.

—I'll do it. Gimmi my gun.

—Don't be daft, Christie, says Bonzo, —We'll do him. You sit on your fat arse and make plans. We do the dirties.

Devlin leaps out his seat and grabs Bonzo by the throat.

—I'll do it. Yees made an arse of it the last time.

—Right, right, okay. We're on your side, remember.

Devlin bends over panting with a mixture of alcohol, adrenaline and sudden effort.

Wendy feels the gap on the pew where Devlin should be. He's

been on the drink since Thursday.

—Say a prayer for your father, she whispers to Nicole.

—I thought you hated him?

—I was angry.

—Good. You should be.

—Don't you want him to be okay?

—I don't care, Mummy. He can drink himself to death.

Wendy looks up at the stained-glass windows. Sighs.

The Red Road flats are the highest domestic flats in Europe. They dominate the north Glasgow skyline. From the top floors you can see the whole city and miles beyond. On a clear day you can see into the Wilderness. Garrett watches the city from thirty-two storeys up.

He opens the window and pushes his head into the icy wind. There's a bit of concrete with the reinforcing bar protruding like a bone through flesh. Garrett ties mountaineering rope onto the bar and pulls the rope back in. Ties a clip on the end. He's wearing boxer shorts and a safety harness. He clips the rope onto the harness. Tests it by placing the soles of his feet on the sink unit and leaning back with full force. Fine. He unclips and dangles the rope back out the window, then heads back into the flat to get dressed.

Thirty-two stories below, Devlin and his men stand at the lifts. Bonzo and Sholtz have baseball bats. They're all wearing bulletproof vests.

—Let me see that again, says Devlin.

Sam hands him a hazy photo of Garrett. He got it from a waiter in the Silver Seas Casino. The lift opens and Bonzo tugs Sam in by the elbow. Sam unscrews the keyboard and commands the lift to stay on the ground with its door open. Now there are only two ways down for Garrett: the other lift or the stairwell. Devlin and Bonzo get in the other lift. Sam and Sholtz start the long climb up the stairwell. There's no way down for Garrett.

The lift moves up through the numbers in silence. Bonzo's

wondering if his boss's mood has changed when Devlin speaks.
—By the way, I've not got a fat arse.
Up the lift goes with Bonzo's smile. Stops at the tenth
floor. An enormously fat woman waddles in. Bonzo hides the
bat behind his back. Devlin's trying not to laugh.
—Fifteen, son, she says.
Bonzo presses fifteen. The lift stops. The door opens. The
woman gets out.
—Does my bum look big in this lift? says Devlin.
—Ya cheeky bastard, says the woman and flicks her cigarette at Devlin.
Bonzo and Devlin laugh. Their voices echo up and down
the shafts. When they get out at the second-top floor, Bonzo
jams the lift with his baseball bat. Now it's impossible for
anybody to get to the thirty-second floor except by the stair-
well. Garrett lives on thirty-two. The lifts only go to the second
top, the lifting gear being housed above. Devlin and Bonzo
take out their guns. Creep up one last flight. Wait for Sam and
Sholtz. It's ten minutes before they arrive. They pause to get
their breath back.
Sam points to Garrett's door.
—Trapped, he says.
Devlin's ready to take a run at it but Bonzo tries the handle.
Raised eyebrows time: it's open! There's music from the living-
room. Talking Heads. *Psycho Killer*.
Devlin takes pole position. They burst in, guns levelled. On
the couch, instead of a rogue drug dealer, is a woman. A
rather manly woman. A man in drag, wearing a long flowery
frock, crossed legs flashing black suspenders, a champagne
glass hanging between the fingers of her right hand. The rim
is bright with lipstick. Tugging the cigarette from her lips she
blows a line of smoke at Devlin.
—Hi, boys. I hope inside that rough exterior there's an
even rougher interior trying to get out.
—You Garrett? asks Bonzo.
—Aye. Are you fatboy poofy Devlin that likes it up the

arse? Give it to me, big boy.

There's a pause. They don't know what to do. Devlin has his gun pointed right at the head of this cross-dressing maniac. He or she glides the champagne glass down onto the table. Slips her long fingers from under its globe. Lifts her wrist slightly in the air then sends her hand downwards with grace. Into the space between the cushion and the couch. Devlin zooms in on the

        Hand going down the couch.

        Hand going down for something.

        Hand going down for gun.

BANG

CRACK

the bullet hits the drag queen forehead centre. Blood bone and body matter smack the back of the couch. A long sigh of air pressures from the nostrils as the body folds forwards.

—Did any yees know he was a poof?

Before anyone answers, there's a noise. Sam and Sholtz head into the hall. Devlin goes to the kitchen with Bonzo at his back.

Devlin's arm swings the gun to the moving curtain. The curtain hits a polystyrene cup.

It rolls

        along the worktop

               falls

                    off the edge

                            hits the floor.

Devlin squints at Bonzo. Bonzo can see he's nervous but that's okay, the boss is always nervous coming off the drink. Devlin closes the window. The city lights are spread below. Devlin's empire looks up for his inspection.

They meet Sholtz and Sam back in the living-room. Nothing's been found. Just a Monday Book and the parapher-nalia of poverty. Golden Virginia. Empty wine bottles. White socks. A bottle with twos and ones in it. A cheap CD player and some Talking Heads, Dire Straits, Rolling Stones and Oasis.

—Get his gun, says Devlin.

Sholtz stuffs his hand down the couch expecting metal but getting plastic. He pulls out the ASDA bag Sholtz lost in the chapel. The money intact. Devlin looks in the bag like he wants to be sick in it.

—He was going to give the money back!

Every man believes he's a good man and Devlin's no exception. He's got morals. He's got rules. The guy was only giving him the money back. The guy might not even be a poof. Might just be a good fuckin laugh. A guy with a sense of humour. And he's shot him. Right through the head. It's one thing when everybody's off the same starting blocks. When they've all got guns. But to shoot an unarmed man? Through the head? When he was surrendering?

—I thought it was a gun, says Devlin.

—Too late now, says Bonzo.

—It looked like he was going for a gun.

—Anybody would've thought it was a gun, Christie.

—Aw fuck!

Devlin takes out a half bottle of Black & White whisky and glugs. As he drinks he squints at the bloody head of his victim.

They drive away knowing if they were noticed coming out of the flat nobody's going to the police. Nobody's going witness against them when the body's found. And if they did? Billy Pitt would put a stop to any investigation. They'd put a stop to the witness. Devlin reopens the half bottle of Black & White. This is not the day to come off the drink.

From the thirty-second floor, Garrett, the mountaineering rope twisted round his arm, traces the route of the Shogun out into Royston towards Springburn.

—Arrivederci Erchie! Garrett says.

By nightfall Wendy's snuggled up, dreaming. It's a vivid dream. She's singing a lullaby to a laughing baby dressed in blue.

♪♪ Oh the summertime is coming…

She tucks the blankets to the baby's neck. Tiny face pink and glowing.

♪♪ And the trees are sweetly blooming…

Snuggles her nose in the nape of the baby's neck. Sniffs up the smell of contentment.

♪♪ And the wild mountain thyme...

But the contentment is gradually contaminated by the reality of her life. Of Devlin and his empire. The baby's dissolving. She tries to hold onto it. To keep it. Bring it out of the dream.

Wendy finds herself awake on the edge of her bed. In a dark room. In an empty house. She thinks of her husband out there drinking.

—Oh, Christie!

Her hand grabs at the sheets like she's trying to dig back into the dream, away from pain.

Dawn in the Wilderness. The Stag's alerted by distant footsteps and the cold bark of a dog. It smells the intruders through its shining nostrils. Takes another look at Devlin's face. Covered in a white film of frost, withdraws, limping into the forest. Devlin's body lies wrapped in two black bin bags. His face is visible through a ripped hole in the end of one bag. Another is pulled over his legs.

A hill walker strides down the track. His collie discovers the bin bags. The walker sees Devlin's white face. Is he breathing? Then his collie licks the face and Devlin wakes, as shocked to see the hill walker as he is to see him. Devlin produces out a cigarette.

—Ye got a light?

The hill walker rumbles in his pack. Lobs a box of matches. Devlin's shakes are making it difficult to light up.

—Looks like rain. Off up the Merrick? Devlin says.

—The Awful Hand. Sleep alright?

—Like a log. On the booze.

Devlin chucks the matches back.

—Well. Have to go. Come on Conner. We're away.

—See ye, mate. By the way, what day is it?

—Monday.

—Thanks for the matches.

The walker gives him the thumbs up. He sees a sprig of heather, the frost melting from it. Devlin picks it and looks closely. Then there's something hard in his bin bag sleeping bag. He fishes it out. His gun. In a flood he remembers. The drink. The Red Road flats. Garrett the drag queen. A poof. The hand down the side of the couch.

—Fuck, says Devlin, —Fuck, fuck, fuck!

His voice slices into the forest. The Stag, limping towards the Merrick, turns its head.

Devlin stops in his driveway. The giant black gate closes behind him. He stumbles towards the door. Looks up at the windows. He can feel Wendy watching, but from where he can't tell. Devlin's filling up with remorse and shame. He tries the door. Locked. His key! But there's a key at the other end blocking it. It's all back. Everything. As quickly as he's reverted back to how it was before, so has Wendy.

He rings the bell. Nothing. Shaking and sweating, he lifts the flap and listens. Presses the bridge of his nose against the edge of the flap.

—Wendy, let me in! he shouts. The silence doesn't care.

—I've got the fuckin horrors!

He puts his back to the door and wraps his arms around himself. He couldn't stop his shakes if he tried. The letterbox opens. Wendy's mouth appears. Red lips in a gold rectangle on the black glossy door.

—Go back to whatever Glasgow whore you've been with.

—I've been in the Anchor. Ye know it's just the drink with me.

The lips purse.

—I can't take this again, Christie, she shouts, —I'm not

going back to it.

—I had to drink. The Chinkees made me. It'll not happen again.

—If I had a pound for every time you have said that I would have eight hundred and ninety pounds.

Devlin's encouraged at the trace of humour.

—I'm going straight back to the meetings. Promise, hen. You've got to let me in. I'm rattling.

—Look, fuck off, Christie. Come back when you're sober.

The letterbox drops with a click. The horrors are closing in. He remembers the sprig of heather. Fishes it from his pocket, stands up and holds it through the letterbox.

He hears movement. When he's sure she's noticed the heather he tries to persuade her.

—I was thinking about you all the time. If I wasn't thinking about ye what did I pick that heather for? Eh?

WHACK!!!!!!!!!!

A brush handle hurtles through the letterbox battering him dead centre of the forehead. He topples back holding his head.

—Ah! Ya fuckin bastard. What did ye do that for?

The letterbox is a rectangular smirk. He takes one hand away from his forehead. There's blood.

—My head's bleeding now. See what you've done, ya mad…

—Morning, says the postman.

He hands Devlin his letters like it's normal for a customer to be lying drunk and dishevelled with blood on his forehead at his front door in the richest estate in Glasgow. Devlin watches him go out through the wee gate within the gate. Wendy must've opened it when she saw the postman coming. He's told her about that. Only open the gate when you're absolutely sure of identity. Identity identity identity identity identity identity identity identity identity identity identity. He's locked in the repetition of that word. Gets a rush of euphoria. Everything's abruptly beautiful. The black gate's a work of art. The winter flowers are supernovas. His hands have locked into fists. His forearms are rocks. He realises he's at the tail-end of a petit mal. Grand Mal to follow. Soon. The big alcoholic fit.

—Wendy! Help me!

And he's away. He falls. Great waves of electricity pass through his body until every muscle and sinew vibrates. His lips stretch back over his teeth as if someone has their fingers hooked into his mouth, pulling. Pulling hard.

Bump

       Bump bump

              Bump bump bump

bumpbumpbumpbumpbumpbumpbumpbumpbumpbumpbump

    Devlin's head knocks off the tiles. He's foaming and gnashing his teeth. The white foam is pink where blood and saliva have emulsified. A black moth flies about his head, an inquisitive satellite.

The letterbox opens. Wendy's eyes.

—Christie!

The door flies open.

He's come out his fit in the back seat of the Shogun as Wendy sped through the city. Accident and Emergency, Devlin sits hallucinating in an orange plastic chair. Shaking. His chin shines with a varnish of saliva. He's surrounded by the debris of Glasgow mornings. Slashings. Clubbings. Kickings. ODs. An old woman looking for sleeping pills. Assorted attention seekers. A drunk couple holding each other up. Devlin searches for Wendy up one corridor then the other. He can't see her.

—Where is she? Where's Wendy?

He panics.

—Wendy! Are ye there Wendy?

There's something not right. Something not right at all. His impulse is to flee. Get out. There's danger and he can't locate its source. He's about to run when Wendy appears. But relief falters when he sees two Dragons in her eyes.

—What's that in your eyes?

The Dragons sneer. Wendy pushes her palms into his hair and over the top of his head. Her fingers settle on the back of his neck.

—Shh. Everything's going to be alright.

—They're in your eyes.

—Right! says Wendy.

She marches away to find help. She's been here before. Devlin watches her travel at the speed of fear up the infinity of a corridor. His breathing is shallow and hard. Somebody's watching. Staring. He forces himself to look. Shit! Here comes the Dragon, dancing in slow motion. Nurses and doctors walk past like it doesn't exist. Devlin nudges a young woman with a cut hand.

—What's that? he says.

—Punched it through the chemist windie, she says, — Wouldn't gie me ma methadone.

—No. Not your hand. Can you see that Dragon, eh?

—What?

—That Dragon. Can ye see it?

She moves two seats away. Devlin senses another presence. His father comes at him. He's carrying something. It looks like rolled up carpet on fire. Nurses and doctors pass like Dan doesn't exist. Devlin turns to the young woman.

—Did you phone my da then?

She folds her whole body away from Devlin. Devlin turns. Here comes Tai Lo. Heung Chu in his incense master dress. I Lo with an oversized cleaver. Hung Kwan with a flick knife. Their blades glint in the clinical light. Wendy arrives back in the waiting area.

—Wendy, I'm fuckin scared!

The receptionist window's been closed since they arrived. Wendy pulls it open.

—Excuse me! Excuse me! My husband needs help.

—So do we all, hen.

Garrett, dressed in drag, comes at Devlin pointing a handgun. He pulls out a crisp bag and sniffs it like he's sniffing glue. Holds the bag up. Sparks a lighter. Lights the bag. It goes up in flames and a pall of black, black smoke. Devlin turns for help but Wendy is in full flow.

—I demand my husband be seen. Now! He needs bloody Hemanevveron!

The Dragon, the Triads, his father and Garrett.

—Wendy! he shouts.

Devlin slides down the chair. Tries to hide. He's crying. He draws his shoulders up to his ears. Garrett's big boots push out from under his flowery frock. He walks up to Devlin. Places a gun on his forehead and

BANG!!!

Devlin screams and runs, spinning a tramp round by the elbow.

—Hey, what's your game, ya mad bastard! the tramp shouts.

Outside, an ambulance screeches as Devlin darts in front of it. The driver watches him make for the trees, smash through them screaming —Fuck! Shit! Fuck!

The branches whip his face. He trips and gets back up. Behind he can see two boys coming at him sniffing glue. Accusing. He pulls himself through the trees. Jumps impossible heights over fallen trunks. Propels himself away from the two boys until he emerges on a knoll overlooking the city's massive sprawl. Terror as he looks out over his empire. He collapses to his knees, spreading his arms out like a soldier shot in the back. Looks up and prays for the first time since he was an altar boy.

—If there is a God, ye better fuckin help me!

In the port of Calais, a nun smiles.

麻煩
trouble

A weasel comes to say Happy New Year to the chickens.

WENDY'S COAXED DEVLIN back into Accident and Emergency. He can hear her voice faint, then audible. He can't tell if he's in paranoia or reality. He wants her. Needs her beside him. Inside him. To be part of him. Holding him up like steel in concrete.

—Wendy?

The clinks and echoes of a hospital.

—Wendy, are ye there?

A nurse appears. Where did she come from? She's got a knife. No, it's a thermometer. She takes Devlin's temperature without speaking. She examines the thin red line in the glass. Her face changes.

—A hundred and four! A hundred and four! Dearie, dearie me, a hundred and four.

Now he's on a trolley being wheeled along. He can see a drip swinging from its own wee pivot up in the squared-off cloudy sky of the hospital ceiling. He can hear Wendy but by now words mean nothing. Whatever's in the drip is working. He could die. Dying would be good. Up ahead all the sign-posts read

PEACE

SERENITY

—Oh My God, he's dying, he's dying. You were told never to drink again, weren't you? Weren't you, you stupid, stupid bastard!

Words are pointless. He's in chemical sleep now. She'll spend the day reading glossy magazines about actors and pop stars. She'll measure her night in cigarettes. She'll hum long-forgotten songs.

Devlin wakes naked on top of a white sheet. A fan blows cold air over his body. The window's open and through it he can see rows of corridor windows across the way. Something flits past one window, runs down the stairwell and appears at another. Then another. It's Garrett. In the flowery frock.

She follows Devlin's eyes.

—What is it? What do you see?

Devlin lifts a straight arm. Pointing.

—Garrett!

—There's nothing there, Christie.

But he points again.

—Garrett's in the windies!

—Shh, she says, —It's the middle of the night.

She settles him back on the pillow. He's vulnerable as the baby she dreamed of. Then she was angry. Now look at him. What good would anger do? There's a rush of the love she used to feel. She smiles and he smiles back.

—Have we moved to Jarkness? he asks.

—Aye, Christie, we've moved to Jarkness.

He sleeps. Wendy keeps vigil. Not that his life is in danger. But his sanity is. She needs to be there when he wakes.

Marie's leaning against the door. It's morning. Between wondering where David is and this, she hasn't slept.

—How 's he ended up back on the drink?

—He left the house sober. Came back days later.

—Bad sign that, staying away!

—Not coming home, Wendy corrects.

—Same thing.

—In Glasgow, perhaps.

—Perhaps. Per...haps. Been chewing a dictionary?

—No. I've been reading *Bella*. I kept it for you. Here!

She flings the *Bella* at Marie. But Marie doesn't move. The magazine hits her square on the chest. Falls to the ground.

Devlin wakes, panting with fear.

—I never knew he had a gun! he shouts.

Dan drank a bottle of whisky and went to bed at midnight. But now it's dawn and he's pacing about. Dan's tormented by one big secret. Four weeks before Devlin watched his Dragon in Sauchiehall Street, Dan was standing over a grave in Carstairs State Hospital for the Criminally Insane. There was a priest. A male nurse with big muscles. Two gravediggers. The priest prayed but Dan hardly listened. The burial was stirring up old memories and terrible emotions.

—Out of the depths I cry to Thee, O Lord!
Lord, hear my voice!
Let Thy ears be attentive to the voice of my supplications!
If Thou, O Lord, shouldst mark iniquities,
Lord, who could stand?
But there is forgiveness with Thee,
that Thou mayest be feared.
I wait for the Lord, my soul waits,
and in His Word I hope;
my soul waits for the Lord more
than watchmen for the morning,
more than watchmen for the morning.
O Israel, hope in the Lord!
For with the Lord there is steadfast love,
and with Him is plenteous redemption.
And He will redeem Israel from all His iniquities.

Dan held a cord, as did the priest, the nurse and the gravediggers. They lowered the coffin into the hole. Sleet was blowing off the moors through the chain-link fences and down through the gravestones. These corpses are lonely even in death. Imprisoned for all eternity behind forty-foot razor wire fences. At the end of the ceremony Dan lifted a pinch of earth and threw it onto the coffin. The nurse handed him a box of possessions. Words were useless. He never spoke to relatives. Words can gouge out souls.

Dawn comes from the trees and moves towards the sandstone buildings. Climbs to Nicole's room. Nicole is awake. Savouring power. Last night Augustus met pupils in ones and twos. She hid and watched. When he was alone she came out in front of him.

—Nicole! You startled me.

—And you surprised me.

—Pardon?

—I would never have taken you to be a drug dealer.

Thinking she was impressed, Augustus held some tablets out.

—Ecstasy. £10 for one, £25 for three.

Nicole handed him ten pounds. Selected one of the tablets. Inspected it closely.

—You must think I'm stupid, she said,—This isn't ecstasy.

—I've had no complaints.

—That's because they're all retards.

—This is ephedra – herbal ecstasy. Does the same job.

Nicole flicked the tablet into the trees. Stared at Augustus to unnerve him. Pulled him in close and whispered in his ear. The night-time forest suddenly filled with sex.

—I can access real drugs.

—Yeah! said Augustus, sarcastically.

Nicole bit his earlobe, pushing her nose into his ea, pressing against him to feel his erection. She pushed her palm against his cock.

—My new boyfriend's a real dealer.

She stepped back, leaving him too aware of his hard-on. Her eyes flitted to it as they spoke.

—I wasn't aware you had a boyfriend.

—There's quite a lot you don't know about me, Augustus.

Nicole produced a couple of grams from her sock and held it up to his nose.

—Smell!

Long breath in.

—What is that?

—Drugs. Do you want to go into business with me?

No answer. Dealing in herbal medicine is one thing, but real drugs? Instant expulsion.

Nicole moved in again. Wrapping her hand round his cock. Tugging slowly up. Pushing slowly back.

—Well?

Still no answer.

—Yes or no.

—Yes. Yes!

Zip down. A minute later Nicole wiped her hand on his pullover.

—Be seeing you soon, she said.

Augustus zipped himself up. She was gone.

And now it is dawn. Nicole looks out over the school. The place that will become her empire. With Gerry's help. She's horny thinking how she wanked Augustus off. Wants to call Gerry. Get him to talk dirty down the phone. Men like that.

Red Road flats. Strung-out junkies wander smackless. Devlin and the Triads have held back from supplying their own dealers to create a market. When the China White hits the streets it'll move like wildfire.

Garrett draws up in an old Citroën van. The junkies, happy at the distraction, watch him take out a concrete slab and carry it over, open the door and prop the slab against it. Back to the van. He gets another slab and takes it to the lift. Jams that open. When he gets back, two junkies are at his van. Garrett holds a pistol to the tallest one's balls.

—Fuck off.

They fuck off.

Garrett's inside the lift with the following items: six two-by-two concrete slabs, a giant tub of heat-resistant sealant, a set of metal tongs, a flexible stainless steel tube two inches in diameter, three bags of top quality coal, a roll of black plastic, box of firelighters, some sticks, a brand new Dyson vacuum cleaner, a cleaver and a chainsaw.

In his kitchen he arranges the slabs into a box, one flat on the floor and four standing around it. The last slab is the lid. He seals three of the corners with the sealant. Seals the last slab on top. The top slab holds the construction together. Garrett pulls the one unsealed slab forward like it's hinged. He puts in a box of firelighters, some sticks and a dozen handfuls of coal. Knocks the corner from the top slab and inserts the flexible stainless steel tube. Runs the tube through the sink under cold running water. Tapes the other end of the tube to the Dyson and switches it on. Lights the fire. Pushes the hinge slab up. Within seconds the inside of his furnace is white hot. Garrett rubs his hands together and spreads the black plastic sheet on the floor. He has a smoke then moves the Dyson to the open window. The filter is removed. The cold water on the steel tube keeps the Dyson cool enough to operate.

Two beautiful white feet. Spattered with droplets of blood. Tied with barbed wire. Hung from a hook above the bath.

The stocking feet have been ripped off so the wire doesn't slip. Sailing down the thigh is a perfect sheen. The suspenders, intact and black, disappear under the elastic of matching panties each side of the bulge of male genitalia. At the hips, the elasticised waist of the flowery frock. The hem has fallen down to the victim's neck. Below the neck a shadow has begun to appear on the chin. The teeth show through parted lips. The eyes are wide open. Above them is the hole Devlin's bullet made. The hair cascades into a pool of jellied blood on the bottom of the bath.

Garrett comes in, sharpening a boning knife. Swipes the throat open. Blood flows down the face. He turns on the hot tap. Garrett watches the warm water get between the blood and the bath enamel. Lift the blood. Break it. A clot blocks the drain. He stirs it with his finger.

He snips the barbed wire. The body bumps into the bath. He drags it to the kitchen in a pouch of black plastic. The acrid smell of hot concrete and metal permeates the flat. He lays the body spreadeagled. By now it's bloodless. He strips off the clothes. The flesh is extraordinarily white on the black plastic.

He starts up the chainsaw. Props an arm on a piece of timber. Cuts the hand off nicely. Next the forearm, off at the elbow. He holds a metal tea tray above the blade as he cuts. Below the buzz of the chainsaw he can hear the din of bone and flesh hitting the tray. The head comes off easier than he thought, the only resistance being the vertebrae. He sits the head to one side. Carries on. Sings his favourite song.

♪♪ Psycho Killer kiss coo say... fa fa fa faa fa...

He cuts the belly open, scooping the insides out with both hands. They must be burned first. With the lack of blood, the rest of the job'll be like burning a butcher's display.

Two hours pass. Half the body is incinerated. His mobile rings. There's only one person with the number. He leans his head into the living-room away from the racket.

—Hello?

—I'm missing you, Nicole says.

—Me too. Gimmi a second. I'm just putting something in the oven.

Using a set of metal tongs he puts a shin into the fire. Gets back to the mobile.

Hey, babe, d'you fancy going to the SECC next Wednesday? The Darkness are playing.

—I'd love to go, she says.

—Great stuff. Let's meet somewhere handy.

He picks up a hand. Flings it into the incinerator.

—How much marijuana can you get for me? Nicole asks.

—As much as you want.

—Guess where I am?

—School?

—In bed.

—No lessons today?

—I've skipped lessons, she says, —I'm on top of my bed.

—Mm mm!

—I've got my hand on my panties. Am I a naughty girl?

—Yes.

—Tell me I'm a naughty girl.

—You are a naughty girl.

—Ask me what colour they are.

—What colour are they?
—Your favourite. White.
—Lace?
—Silk. Are you doing what I think you're doing?
—I've got my hand on it now, says Garrett.
He has his hand on a severed foot.
—Tell me what to do next, she says.
He throws the foot into the white-hot furnace.
—Okay, pull your panties halfway down your thighs.
She does that.
—Run your fingers lightly over your fanny.
She doesn't like that word. She prefers pussy. Fanny is so…
common.
—Pussy, then, he says, —run your fingers over your pussy.
She does. Does he want her to do it again?
—Yes. Keep doing that till I tell you what to do next.
He places the head in the middle of the furnace. The
mascara runs down the cheeks. He picks up the phone again.
—Do you want me to push my fingers in? she asks.
—No. Not yet.
—What then? What will I do?
—Describe how you feel.
—No. I'm not describing that.
—But I want you to.
There's a pause.
—I feel really… randy! This is so sexy. Yes.
—Can you suck your own nipple?
—I've never tried to, she says.
She ripples her fingers over her nipple.
—Try for me.
—You have to ask me.
—Lean down and put your nipple in your mouth.
She lifts her breast out of her bra. Try as she might, she
can't get her nipple in her mouth. She tries. And she tries.
—Can you do it? asks Garrett.
—No, Gerry. My breasts aren't big enough yet, says Nicole.

Garrett smiles. Throws another foot on the incinerator. As he stares into the flames he sees pictures. A terrible film. A woman bursting into flames and coming at him. He's a boy. There's somebody else there too, running away from the burning woman. He can see the two boys shouting at each other. Arguing. Accusing. But he can't hear what they're saying. The crackle and hiss of the flames is drowning that out. There's a man. His hands are on fire. He holds them up like guilt. There's water. He can see water. The boy with Garrett dives into the water and stays under. When Garrett catches him he's going to kill him.

Garrett comes back to the present at the sound of Nicole over the phone.

—Oh! That was great, Gerry, she says. —Fantastic.

He arranges to meet her later after he's finished off getting rid of the rent boy.

Garrett gave him three grand to stay one week. Practice the scenario over and over until it was perfect. The scenario was that Garrett's pal liked to fantasise about being a big-time gangster. He also liked transvestites. On a certain night this pal would burst in demanding his money back. The rent boy has to answer to the name *Garrett*. Then bring him down with insults about his homosexuality. Once he's sufficiently angry, the rent boy has to reach down for the stash and give it back. At this point the 'gangster' inflicts the punishment by fucking him. Garrett will be in the kitchen the whole time. The rent boy's pretty convincing as a woman until he speaks. Takes up position on the couch. Garrett gives him the ASDA bag.

—There really is fifty grand in here, says the rent boy.

—If it's not authentic, he can't get a hard on.

Garrett leaves the room. Crashes back in.

—Gimmi the fucking money.

—Gimmi a fuckin blow job first.

—What!

—Swallow my glittering spunk.

—Grab him, men.

The rent boy throws himself round like a bad actor and pretends to be held over the couch.

—I'll teach you to steal money from my organisation.

Garrett lifts the transvestite's dress. Tugs his French knickers down and fucks him. Hard. By the end of three days the rent boy has the scenario off to a T.

The first drugs drop at Jarkness, and Devlin isn't there. Tai Lo is puzzled.

FRISHOOM!

A jet-ski, then another, then another, tear through the bay, leaving white trails of foam.

Two herons flap out from the trees and over the water.

Sholtz sees a fish, the light reflecting from its scales. Hung Kwan's nostrils dissect the layers of smell in the air. Seaweed, fresh and rotten. River water, sea water. A trace of pine. The forest floor. Carpets of snowdrops laid like fine lace over the winter mulch. A fishing boat blasts its klaxon.

Whooooo! Whoooooo!

The jet-skis rock, the sea is a chaos of waves. Hung Kwan pats his palm on his chest.

—I go beat, beat a beat.

They laugh their adrenaline away. The black fishing boat blasts again.

Whoooooo! Whoooooo!

Bonzo would swear he could see the sound coming like a gust of wind along the surface.

—Quick from ki – koo – bully, says I Lo.

—What? says Bonzo

—Ki – koo – bully. Three hours only.

They still don't understand. The boat's klaxon blasts again.

Whoooooo! Whoooooo!

—KI – KOO – BULLY, I Lo shouts.
Sholtz laughs. Finally, he gets it.
—What is it Sholtz? says Bonzo.
—Kirkcudbright, Bonzo. It's Kirkcudbright he's saying.
Bonzo looks across to the slab of estuary in the east that runs up to Kirkcudbright harbour. He laughs too.
—I'll give them that. Scottish cunts can't even say it, he says.

Whoooooo! Whoooooo!

—Tell them to shut fuckin up, Bonzo shouts.
Hung Kwan stands up, unsteady, cups his hands over his mouth and shouts in Cantonese.
—*Shut fuckin up!*
The boat shuts down its engines. The diesel drone is gone. The bay is still.
—Is good? I Lo asks Bonzo.
—Bet your bottom dollar is fuckin good.
The four men start their jet-skis and head towards the boat. Bonzo can see at least five Triads. One in the wheelhouse. One on the starboard side scanning the sea with binoculars. One lying on the port gunwales watching the sky, presumably for helicopters. Another two slashing open a white nylon sack.
As the sack opens, white queenie shells clatter onto the deck. Closer, Bonzo sees that the queenies surround slabs of dope. They slash another bag. Queenies clatter out along with three footballs.
—Balls? says Sholtz to Bonzo.
The Triads lower the slabs of dope to Hung Kwan and I Lo. They take two each. Sit on them so they can eject them into

the water if approached. Six footballs in two netting bags are lowered to I Lo and Hung Kwan. They tie a bag each to their jet-skis and make off back towards Jarkness. Bonzo and Sholtz follow.

Fifteen minutes later they've dragged their jet-skis onto the shingle beach.

No show without Smack. Smack was as happy as happy could be. Smack processed and turned to powder, given a power it didn't possess when it lived in the heads of purple poppies. Smack sealed into MADE IN CHINA footballs, made its waterproof and smellproof way across vast tracts of land and ocean. One day found itself on a fishing boat coming out of Kirkcudbright. In a house called Jarkness, Smack smiled and Chinese faces smiled back. It was good to be home. But Smack couldn't be further from home. Smack was cut with talcum powder, or glucose, or toilet cleaner or any other white powder. Sold on. And cut again. And again. Smack travelled throughout the city, out as far as Motherwell, Paisley, Coatbridge, Cumbernauld, Kirkintilloch and East Kilbride. Smack grinned in anticipation as it was mixed with water and heated and sucked up into the needle to say hello to the incoming blood and surge into another bloodstream.

And as every delivery went out to the dealers the Triads made note of the who, the where, and the when.

They're going to have Glasgow for themselves.

智慧
wisdom

A single conversation with a wise man is worth ten years of study.

MING FUNG TEACHES Kung Fu as her father speaks to Devlin's men. She can see there's something father is not pleased about.

CRASH!

she smashes a wooden board with a spinning kick. Two pieces revolve through the air. One lands with a rattle at Bonzo's feet. As Ming Fung comes gracefully out of the kick, she glances at Bonzo.

—What is wrong weeth Devlin? Tai Lo asks Bonzo.

—Told ye, he's sick.

—Ill. He's ill Mister Lo, says Sholtz.

—*Ill my arse*, says I Lo.

—What did he say? Tell him to talk Scottish, says Bonzo.

Tai Lo says nothing and Bonzo speaks to Sholtz and Sam in rapid Glaswegian.

—Sholtz, get ready to go right ahead. I'm gonni put the head right on this slanty-eyed wee cunt.

—What he say? says Tai Lo to Sam, —What say?

Bonzo dips his head. He's about to let loose when Sam steps between him and Tai Lo.

—Appendicitis! Sam shouts.

The whole room swivels. The kickers and Ming Fung. Bonzo, I Lo and Sholtz. Heung Chu and Hung Kwan. The birds on the roof. Spiders in their webs.

—He's in hospital, says Sam, —He's got appendicitis.

He holds onto his side, miming agony. The Triads get it. The bad atmosphere flows away, depressurising the room. It's all smiles. Except for I Lo.

In the hospital Devlin stares out of the window. Something moves in the glass. It's Cooney.

—What are you doin here, ya Irish cunt?

Cooney flashes a smile and rifles through the sweets on the bedside cabinet.

—I'm here for that boot up the arse ye were going to give me.

He scoffs some Maltesers and pours two Irn-Brus into plastic cups. Devlin sits on the bed and Cooney hands him a cup. Drops some Maltesers into his huge hand. Cooney sits in the bedside chair saying nothing. Sipping Irn-Bru and flinging Maltesers up one at a time and catching them in his mouth. Forcing Devlin to break the silence.

—If you're to here to spout AA pish, ye can fuck off.

Cooney launches another Malteser. Devlin can hear bubbles of carbon dioxide bursting in the cup. Cracking like fire.

—You're here to gloat. AA cunts always gloat when somebody goes back on the drink.

—What happened? Cooney asks, —Tell me what happened.

It's a soothing voice. Non-judgemental. Devlin relents.

—I was doing a business merger with these Chinkees. They've got this big traditional ceremony. The Burning of the Yellow Paper.

—The what?

—A big ceremony for business mergers. Anyway, part of this ceremony's drinking tiger bone wine. If I never done it I'd probably be Devlin Sweet and Sour Hong Kong style the now. I took the drink and...

—Ye took the first drink? says Cooney.

It's not an accusation. More an observation. Devlin tries to remember what happened after he took the first drink.

—I thought I could get away with it. It was only a drink to cement the deal. Take that and take no more. That's what I was thinking…

—If ye go into the barbers you'll come out with a haircut, says Cooney.

Devlin knows he's broke the number one rule.

Don't lift the first drink

—Ye want to've seen the state of me! says Devlin.

—I could be doing with a laugh, so I could. Tell me.

—Up on the tables. Singing! I was like that – spinning my shirt round my head.

—Man after my own heart, says Cooney.

—Thank you, kind sir.

—Was it a good song? I hope ye didn't come across like an excuse for an alky or we'll have to sack ye, ye know!

—*Do Anything You Wanna Do.*

Cooney knits his eyebrows like he doesn't know it. He does. But he wants Devlin to sing himself upwards.

♪♪ Goanna break out of this city, leave the people here behind...

Aha! Cooney knows it now. Eddie and the Hot Rods. Sure, did he not used to sing that one himself. It was out in the Seventies when he first got sober.

—I gave it laldy, says Devlin, —They loved it. Even the Chinkees joined in.

—Good man! Never let the side down. Great choice.

—I thought so.

Cooney takes it one tiny step further.

—Oh, another thing.

He gives a quick tilt up with the chin and pushes his tongue into his bottom lip.

—Nnnnnngh, he says.

—Ah ya bastard! says Devlin, —I knew ye were here to gloat.

—If ye want to stay sane ye need to stay sober.

—You want me to ask ye to be my sponsor, don't ye!

—No. I'm just here to see you're alright.

—Well I am alright. But if you're wanting me to ask you to be my sponsor, ye can fuck off back to AAsville.

Cooney makes a calculated move to open Devlin up. In battle, sometimes God will send an Angel.

—I seen the tear that fell on the cake, he says.

—What?

—At your birthday meeting… I seen the tear that fell on the cake!

Vulnerability. Cooney waits a bit then asks a question.

—Did you have the DTs?

—Aye.

—What was it like?

Devlin sighs and recounts his DTs.

—My Auntie Theresa that died in a fire. She's burning up and there's me and my cousin running away. And something about my da… his hands are on fire… flames coming out his hands. He's coming at me like he's gonni put these burning hands round my throat. Choke and burn me at the same time. Next thing I dive under water to keep the flames away. I can hardly breathe. I look up. The whole surface is red and yellow flames. I can't go up or I'll burn and I can't stay under or I'll drown. Then my da and my maw and me're all underwater, and our Marie. My da's eyes turn to fire and explode and these flames shoot out and frazzle my maw. Then he turns to get Marie and I'm on his back biting him, trying to stop him killing her.

Devlin stops, locked in the horrific procession of images. Nightmares or memories? Cooney wants in there.

—Why is your da chasing you and your cousin?

Devlin speaks like a man under hypnosis.

—He wants to fuckin kill us!

—Why does he want to kill yees?

—He wants to kill us.

—Why?

—He just wants to kill us.

—Why does he want to kill yees?

—He wants to kill us because he wants to kill us.

—But why?

—How the fuck do I know?

Cooney changes tack.

—Why did your maw leave?

—Not long after my Auntie Theresa died in the fire, my

maw disappeared. Here today, gone tomorrow. Nobody's
heard from her since.

Cooney scrutinises Devlin.

—There's something else. Ain't there?

It's somehow alright to tell him.

—There's this guy I had to, you know...

He mimes putting a gun to his head.

—He keeps haunting me. Appearing and coming at me
with a gun. Bumping me off. In my dreams and my DTs.

—When did ye...? Cooney holds an imaginary gun to his
own head.

—When I was on the drink. Days ago. But I don't think he's
dead. There's this... feeling... that he's still about. Ach, you've
went off me now. I can see it. It's too heavy for ye!

—What do you know about me?

—Nothing.

Devlin hears something.

—Shht, he says, —Say nothing.

Sholtz, Bonzo and Sam march in. Seeing Cooney, Sam
whispers in Devlin's ear.

—Appendicitis? he shouts, —Fuckin appendicitis! What the
fuck did ye tell him that for?

Cooney leaves them to it.

幸存者
survivor

Suspect a man, don't employ him, employ him, don't suspect him.

A BUNCH OF distorted Chinese faces framed in a silver rectangle. It's a cleaver and it's rising up. Hung Kwan and a Forty-Nine hold a terrified Afghani's hand on a beech tree cut at chest level. I Lo can smell garlic from his breath and shampoo from his tight curly hair. He smiles, the man smiles back expecting late leniency. But

down

the

cleaver

comes

and

CHOP!

The heavy blade crunches through his little finger. The pinkie rolls sideways onto its knuckle, rocks a few times and is still. Blood spurts out against the other side of the cleaver, runs along where the blade meets the chopping board, searching for a way back to the severed finger.

There's a prayer flag stuffed in the man's mouth. Two Forty-Nines hold him up to stop him from fainting. I Lo pulls the ribbon of prayer flag out like a long silk white tongue. The Afghan moans and gasps. His legs become steadier. The Forty-Nines move away. I Lo asks the question for the first time. The Afghan had been prepared to tell them anything. He offered to tell them but they slapped him.

—Where are they selling?

They are a gang of young Pakistanis with no respect for

the old ways. Fuck Devlin and fuck the Chinks. They all have guns. High on drugs, they're ready to go to war. They've been dealing freely on the streets. I Lo splashes a drink into the Afghan's face and asks him again.

—Where are they selling?

The cleaver is poised. The victim finds his voice. He blurts it out to save his other finger.

—Next Wednesday. The SECC. At a rock concert. The Darkness.

The Afghan could swear Hung Kwan and the Forty-Nine loosen their grip.

down

the

cleaver

comes

and

CHOP!

Another finger rolls over twitching beside its dead companion. I Lo waits until the screaming has stopped. He raises the cleaver and asks him another question.

—Are you sure?

—They will all be there.

—Everybody?

—The whole gang.

—What are they driving?

—Two red BMWs.

I Lo raises the cleaver again.

—Please!

But I Lo pushes his elbow up and to the side bringing the

cleaver downwards with such reckless force that Hung Kwan and the Forty-Nine let go. The Afghan's eyes are closed.

down

the

cleaver

comes

and

BLOCK!

Heung Chu grabs I Lo's arm. The cleaver vibrates.

—*Enough*, Heung Chu says.

The man collapses, weeping. Hung Kwan whispers to two Forty-Nines. They take the Afghan to the back door of the casino, pop his fingers in his pocket and push him out to wander in shock along the banks of the Clyde.

Later, the room scoured and cleaned of blood, rattles again with Mah Jong. Tai Lo has arranged a surprise for the Pakistani Gang on Wednesday night at the SECC. I Lo bows lightly.

—*That's the Pakis dealt with. Now let's deal with Devlin's appendicitis.*

—*You think Devlin is lying?* asks Tai Lo.

—*There is, with respect, boss, one way to find that out.*

—*And that is?*

I Lo lifts up his shirt revealing a scar down his side.

—*If Devlin has appendicitis he will have a scar like this.*

The Triads stare at I Lo's appendix scar.

Half a mile down river from the Silver Seas is a massive building site. Leisure, business and residential. The new Glasgow. A sign

displays the contractor's name. CLYDE DEVELOPMENT. Listed
among the subcontractors is DEVLIN CONSTRUCTION & DEMO-
LITION.

Among concrete slabs and columns reinforced with steel,
Dan Devlin works at the bottom of a steep slope, shoring up a
shutter for the base slab. A multi-storey tower block goes up
slab – columns – slab – columns, the same materials and
measurements repeated floor by floor.

Devlin employs five extra men for every ten on the books.
Ghosts. A site like this could have fifty ghosts. At five hundred
pounds a week per man. Clyde Development pays Devlin
Construction, Devlin Construction pays the men.

The new site agent doesn't know the score. He looks at his
clipboard and thinks he might have made a mistake. Goes to
count them again.

When he comes back the Jaeger is pumping liquid concrete into the matrix of steel. Four men screed the concrete to
a rough level. The concrete just keeps on coming. Once the
Pour starts to go off it has to be polished with massive hori-
zontal metal propellers until the floor is smooth and flat and
shining. It can take forty-eight hours non-stop. The site agent
shouts down through the racket.

—Mister Devlin. Can I have a word?
—After. I'm busy.
—No! Now!
—Can ye not see we've got a Pour on here?
—I want to see you up here now!
—Who the fuck're you talking to?
Here we go. All the workers watch.
—I'm talking to you.
—Talking to me?
Dan's about to snap. What the site agent says next doesn't
help.
—Don't have me coming down there.
—Away and fuck yourself!
Critical mass. Anything could happen. Dan turns away. It's

not worth the hassle when the Pour is on. Next thing the site agent's a ball of fury careering down sand and rubble. The whole site watches.

Dan whips his hammer out, spins it like a six-gun and holds it out to the side of his body.

—What ye going to do now you're down here, ya fat cunt?

The site agent hands Dan the clipboard.

—Aye? Dan asks. —What's up?

—There's fifty men on the books who're not on site.

—And?

—Where are they?

—They're the ghosts.

—Ghosts?

Obviously he's not done the lesson on ghosts in site agent school.

—What are ghosts?

—Don't tell me you don't know?

—No. Explain it to me.

—You'll have to get my son to explain.

—Your son... and where's he?

—How the fuck do I know?

—He's never on site.

—I'll get him to come and see you.

—You do that.

—I will.

—Good.

—Great!

The site agent scrambles back up the slope. When Dan gets back to the slab his men are powering in.

—Cunt! Dan says.

He takes out his mobile phone.

Devlin's signed himself out the hospital against doctor's orders. He could suffer DTs any time, without warning. But he's got a bunch of crazy Triads believing he's got appendicitis. They'll want proof.

Bonzo drives the Shogun through Glasgow, filling Devlin in

on everything that's happened.

—The Chinkees love Jarkness. Love it. We've distributed the new smack, so we're in business.

Bonzo presses the button and the black gates swing open. Devlin's phone goes. It's Dan.

—Gimmi a minute, Da. Check the gates, Bonzo.

—Right y'are, Christie.

Dan tells Devlin about the site agent.

—Right, Da. I'll sort it.

—When?

—I don't know, do I?

He tells Dan he's got other problems right now. Dan rants on. Devlin hangs up.

He goes inside and straight up to his wee room where he spends an hour listening to Fauré. Readjusting. Thinking about nothing. Looking out at the monkey-puzzle tree. There's a space appeared in his mind he can't remember being there before. If his mind was a house, someone's bolted on another room.

He goes down and calls his men together in the kitchen to discuss the way forward. They have to rebuild trust with the Triads. Why the fuck did they tell them he had appendicitis?

—Sorry, boss, says Sam.

Devlin waves him away.

—It's done now. What we need to be looking at is the solution. Any ideas?

Bonzo pipes up first.

—So what, ye had appendicitis! Everybody gets sick now and then.

—If they think I'm not up to the job they'll team up with some other Glasgow mob.

—We'll wipe out any competition, says Sholtz.

—If the Chinkees don't wipe us out first! Devlin says.

—They're hardly going to contact the hospital to see if you were sick are they? asks Sam.

—They already did. I checked, Devlin says.

That brings a whole new atmosphere.

—What did the hospital say? asks Sam.

—What I told them to say. Appendicitis. I persuaded them.

—There ye go then boss, says Bonzo, —They checked. You were in. You had appendicitis. Case closed.

Devlin opens his shirt.

—What d'ye see there?

—Your belly, says Sam.

—Exactly, says Devlin. —Phone Quack Quack.

Bonzo turns to Sholtz, —Phone Quack Quack.

—Who're you talking to? You're not the boss! shouts Sholtz.

—Just shut the fuck up and phone him, says Devlin.

When Sholtz's finished setting up a meeting with Quack Quack Devlin has a quiet word with him.

—Sholtz. See from now on, get this. I'm the boss. He's second in command. You take orders from him.

—Right, boss. Sorry boss.

Devlin signals for them to be quiet. He calls Tai Lo.

—Tai Lo? Christie Devlin. No, I'm out. Fine. I'm fine. It's not that big an operation, no. Aye, they told me. It's a good place Jarkness, is it not? I knew you'd like it. Listen, sorry I wasn't there on the first day. I just doubled up and they rushed me to hospital. Hey, let me apologise by treating you and your men to some real Glasgow hospitality. There's a Celtic and Rangers game coming up. Great. I'll arrange it. Quite sore. I Lo? Has he? Now there's a coincidence. *Tsoi kin.*

Devlin hangs up and turns to his men. His hand is on his belly where his scar should be.

—Could ye not have said a heart attack?

—Sorry, boss, says Sam.

—Fuckin pricks, so yees are.

In the edgy silence Devlin whips round, paranoid. Looks at the window. He's seen something move past.

—They gates're locked, int they?

—I'll check if ye want, says Bonzo.

—No, I'm alright. Must be these drugs.

But Bonzo's not leaving it. He orders Sam and Sholtz to check the grounds. Make sure everything's secure. Ask the men in the gardens if they've seen anything different this morning. A leaf turned over. A blade of grass bent the wrong way. Once they're gone, Bonzo puts his hand on Devlin's shoulder.

—What's up, Christie?

Devlin looks at him with anxious eyes.

—Has there been anything in the papers about that Garrett cunt we popped?

—Not seen nothing.

—What about the radio?

—Diddley.

Bonzo's worried. He's not seen this before. Fear. Even in the jail when they were up against it together, it was Devlin who'd walk up to the biggest ugliest con and set about him. That's how they ruled the jail. That's where they learned violence pays dividends. Where they had the idea to take over Glasgow. And now that dream's coming true Bonzo thinks Devlin might be losing it. He's about to delve further when Sam appears.

—Nothing there.

—See what information ye can pick up on the internet, Sam. Devlin says. —About that Garrett guy we popped... any reports of a body. Anything at all.

—On it, boss.

Sam presses a key on the laptop. Sholtz comes back in.

—Nothing.

—No Sam, in fact, find me Cooney's address, says Devlin, — The AA guy.

Eden Academy. Nicole and Augustus have converted some of their chums, Lucy, Catherine and Steven, to marijuana. On lunch break they shared a badly made joint and now it's afternoon. They're in English. Giggling. There are only eight in the class. That's what you pay for.

Mister Neville asks them to concentrate on the text. They fall quiet. But the marijuana snorts a little laugh and sets them off again.

—Lucy! Stand up.

Lucy holds the book close to her face.

—Thou art too like the spirit of Banquo. Down!

She takes a fit of giggles.

—Augustus.

Augustus is totally lost. Mister Neville puts his finger bluntly on the line. Augustus focuses.

—Thy crown does sear mine eyeballs...

He erupts. His behaviour will also be going on his report. Catherine's turn next.

—...thou other gold-bound brow, is like the first. A third is like the former.

But she breaks down, giggling. Mister Neville orders Nicole to continue.

—...like the former. Filthy hags...

The five descend into hysterics.

Wendy's teaching third years. They're a disruptive class but when you get them working they almost seem glad of the peace. She looks at the clock and there's half an hour to go. Her bladder feels like it's going to explode.

If the teacher leaves the classroom, anything could happen. And it usually does. Wendy sneaks to the door as the kids scribble. When she's sure none are watching, she slips into the next classroom.

—Could you watch my class, Anne. I have to go to the loo.

Anne refuses.

Wendy's class start murmuring. But she has to go to the toilet. As her footsteps echo into the belly of the school, Anne sends a kid to Miss Newell with a note sealed in an envelope.

Cooney lives in a cul-de-sac in Lambhill. Devlin pulls up, looks about for any lurking danger, and gets out. Cooney sees him from the living-room. He's not surprised. As Devlin reaches out to ring the bell, Cooney swings the door open, giving him a fright.

—I'm not that ugly, am I? says Cooney. —Come in.

He takes Devlin into the kitchen. Devlin expected the house to be filled with AA stuff. There's a glass Serenity Prayer on the wall. That's all. Cooney bumps down a mug of tea.

—Two sugars and no milk?

The mugs have shamrocks on them. Cooney produces a plate of Custard Creams.

Devlin nibbles. Cooney sips his tea. Sleet comes down outside.

—Why did you come here, Christie?

—Just for the crack... Jack.

Cooney stares Devlin out. Devlin looks into his mug as if he's trying to see the bottom, then looks up.

—The para's ripping right out me.

—Seeing things?

—Imagining. I'm imagining things.

Cooney's not letting him off the hook.

—If ye want to stay sane, ye need to stay sober. If you want to stay sober you have to stay away from the first drink. If ye want to stay away from the first drink ye have to get to meetings and get a sponsor.

—That's why I'm here, to ask ye to be my sponsor!

—Ask me then.

—I just did.

—No, you said you were here to ask me.

Devlin is a stranger to humility. But he tries.

—Okay, I'm asking.

—Asking what?

—Will you be my sponsor?

—Will I fuck, says Cooney.

Devlin's fists curl. Just as the fury is about to spew, Cooney flips the tone.

—Only kidding. Aye, I'll be your sponsor.

—Ya cunt, ye!

—Some way to address your sponsor! They laugh. —In a spiritual journey, humour is the balancing rod we use to walk the razor's edge, says Cooney.

—On ye go then. Start, Devlin challenges, —Do some sponsory stuff.

—Like what?

—Well, what does a sponsor do?

Cooney explains. The difference between an AA sponsor and a psychotherapist is that the sponsor's been through the same mental, spiritual, emotional and physical traumas.

—Are ye sure you're not staying sober to be a better gangster?

—I'm a businessman.

Devlin directs his blue psychotic eyes at Cooney. But Cooney flinches not one bit.

—Are ye sure you're not staying sober to be a better businessman then?

—What's up with that?

Devlin's not allowing Cooney in, so Cooney tries a trick he learned from his own sponsor. He lays a hand on Devlin's shoulder. Smiles a benign smile.

—What kind of childhood did ye have?

The simple words are a depth charge. Devlin weeps. Cooney lets him cry.

Christie's reliving early memories. Early and bad. Cooney prompts him. Get it out. Don't lock it all in.

—When I was wee I used to read a lot of books. I liked fairy-tales mostly. Especially the one where the woodcutter gets three wishes and wishes for a black pudding. His wife is raging that he wasted a wish on a black pudding, or a sausage I think it might've been, and she wishes it would stick to his nose. So it does. It sticks to his fuckin nose like that. So they've got to use the last wish to get the sausage off. I used to sit and wonder for years how they could've been so daft, to waste three wishes like that. On a daft sausage. But now I think I see what that meant.

Cooney reacts not one jot. Devlin changes stories.

—Anyway, that's not what I was going to tell you. I was going to tell you about *Pinocchio*. This time I was in my room and I'd got *Pinocchio* out the library. It was quite a long book with pictures. About a hunner pages, with a lot of writing. But I decided I was going to read it in a oner. I was always doing stuff like that. Like I'd take a notion to run out to the city limits and back and off I'd go. In the rain or whatever. Testing my limits, that's what I was doing. So anyway, I decides to read this book in one go. Our Marie was sick in bed. She's my twin. Did ye know that? I think I might've said at the meetings. So I goes into her room and read it to our Marie without stopping, except to get her a drink of water halfway though. It was a great book. Me and her loved it, so we did. Took me hours to read it. The wee cunt getting took in by a pair of right chancers and his da wandering the earth looking for him. And he was trapped in thon whale.

Anyway, when I'd finished Marie had fell asleep. I pulled the covers up to her chin. My maw still lived there. This was before she disappeared. I pulled the covers up to Marie's chin and laid the book down open at the page where I thought she must've fell asleep, so that she could read it herself when she woke up. I went out and closed the door, quiet as mouse. I mind the shadow sliding over her face. I went into the scullery for a drink of water and maybe a piece on jam if there was nobody about. My maw was in the living-room in the dark, just sitting. She done that a lot. Sometimes she just sat and sometimes she said a million decades of the rosary, mumbling like a nun. But when I go in the scullery there's my da at the table with a can of beer. Ye can tell they've had an argument. And another thing, there was a big red mark on his neck. I thought he'd been in a fight but years later it came to me that it must've been lipstick.

He looked at me and I froze. Used to... he could make me

freeze with just a look. He goes, were you sleeping? I was reading a book, I says. You're a fuckin liar, he went. And I goes, I was reading *Pinocchio* to our Marie. You're a fuckin wee liar. He reaches out and grabs me by the jumper and flings me on the floor. I mind my head cracked off the edge of cooker. In comes my maw. She stops in the doorway and stares. Just stares. My da starts laying in. Tell the truth. Tell the truth an I'll stop. I hate a fuckin liar! he was shouting. I was reading a book, I kept saying, but the more I says it the more he punches me. The blows were getting harder and faster. He started kicking. Kicking me round the place. Dan, Dan, you'll kill him, you'll kill him, my maw was screaming. That just made him worse. Our Marie appeared, white as a ghost, in the door. My da shouts to her, Was he reading you a book? I nodded to our Marie to say no. I knew he'd do her in an all if she agreed with me. I can remember the tears running down her cheeks as she shook her head that I never read her a book. See! shouts my da. See! I knew ye were a fuckin liar. A chair came crashing down on my back. Maw and Marie screamed. I must've blacked out. There's not a lot of weans been knocked unconscious for reading *Pinocchio*.

—Jees Christie, what age were ye? Cooney says.

—Twenty-eight.

Cooney sprays his tea all over the place. Laughing. Devlin laughs. Tears stream down his face.

—C'mere.

Cooney hugs Devlin. Apart from Wendy, Devlin's never been hugged since he last seen his mother. It feels good. Progress has been made. Once they stop laughing. Stop crying. Devlin steps back.

—I was ten, he says, —Ten. She always tried to pull him off but he was too strong.

—What happened to your maw?

—Disappeared. Said she was away to the shops. She said to me, now you mind and look after your sister when I'm away. Don't you let anything bad happen to your sister. She was crying. Her eyes were black and blue. I mind thinking, imagine crying just cos you've got to go down the shops for the messages. But I never seen her again. What's your advice on that oh great sponsory one?

  —What have they got to say about it?

  —Who?

  —Your da and your twin.

  —My da and Marie? I've brung it up couple of times but they don't want to know.

  —You've got to approach them.

  —What for? They'll just blank me.

  —Bring up again. Start a dialogue.

  Devlin leaves Cooney's. As he drives away he feels a lightness of heart. He decides to go straight to his da's.

Light falls on a misty copy of Madonna and Child. With a six-gun held up in front of the painting, Dan spins the chamber. It falls and hits the floor with a thump beside the cardboard box and wrapping.

  —Fuckin thing.

  Dan picks up the chamber, greases it and replaces it. He greases the barrel and slides it into the holster. Squares up to the wall like the gunslinger he always wanted to be.

  —Okay, you son of a doubt picking Possil jakey, draw!

  Dan draws. The wall doesn't even get its gun out.

  —Not quick enough, says Dan.

  —What the fuck are ye doing?

  Devlin's been there since Dan greased the barrel. Dan's embarrassed.

  —I'm just… is all he can say.

  Devlin flings down a wad of cash.

  —The men's wages, he says.

  Dan counts the money. Devlin looks at the painting thinking how to bring up the past. He wasn't due to deliver the money until tomorrow. How do you start a dialogue about why your father beat you up when you were young? This is how difficult getting sober is.

—When ye going to come round and sort out this new site agent?

—Set a meeting up, says Devlin,—I'll talk to him.

Dan waits , sure Devlin's going to say something else. But he just stares out of the window.

—Ye alright?

Devlin's realised the enormity of his task. He needs more of whatever it takes to broach the past. He'll try again another time. Anyway, he's got a meeting with Quack Quack.

—Aye, my head was away there. Listen I'm Joe the Toff. Phone me when you've set up a meeting with the cunt.

Dan lifts his hat with the tip of the barrel.

—Yes sirree!

Once his son has gone Dan gets himself reflected in the window so he can see his full Cowboy glory.

—You looking at me? Hey, Railroad Jack! I said, are you looking at me? Hoy, fuck-features, d'ye want your eyes back? On your feet!

Dan draws and fires at his own reflection with an ineffective click.

—Get a box. Take him home.

Devlin lays the wad of notes on the telly.

—What you wanting? Marie says.

—I was thinking about my maw the day.

—Eh? What brung that up?

Devlin shrugs. Marie lines a row of chips on a slice of bread.

—Want a piece on chips?

He doesn't. He wants to talk about the past. Marie munches away, turning the volume up on the telly by increments. Eventually Devlin switches it off.

You're not going to sit there and tell me ye don't remember nothing!

—I don't want to talk about it.

—But just before she left, can ye remember that?

—No.

—Something happened!

—Did it?

—Aye! What was it?

Marie stares at him. For a second he thinks she's going to open up.

—I've got enough problems without waking any dragons.

The words drops into him like stones.

—Why this all of a sudden? Have ye heard something? Has she made contact with ye or something?

—I'm just trying to get a handle on what it was like before... Get my mind straightened up. It's AA.

—AA?

—Kind of philosophy.

—Philosophy. Ha! D'ye know the philosophy I've got by on since I got this limp and this useless eye? Fuck before, fuck theday and fuck themorra, that's my philosophy.

He's about to reply when David comes in.

—Alright, fatty, David says.

Marie sees the flash of anger in Devlin's eyes.

—Don't hit him!

—Don't want to catch lazy bastard disease, Devlin says.

David flops onto the floor smiling.

—I've had enough of that from your snobby wife, Marie says.

—Don't start all that again.

—Well, no wonder.

—Marie, leave it!

—She talks to me like I'm a school wean!

—It's you that riles her up.

—Oh aye, stick up for the English cow.

—You'd get on better if ye left people alone, says Devlin.

BOOSH

Marie explodes her plate of chips off the wall. The chips slide down leaving a trail of sauce, David sees giant slugs eating the faded wallpaper flowers.

—I should leave people alone? I should fuckin leave people alone?

—Your maw's a nun, David squeaks.

Devlin uses all his control to stop from stamping David in the ribs.

—David, shut it! Marie says.

But he doesn't shut it. He's laughing and doesn't care.

—Your maw's a nun! Two bags of smack please.

Marie glowers.

—Sorry, Maw.

David shuts his mouth with his thumbs and index fingers like a cartoon duck. That makes him laugh all the more and he rolls about the carpet expecting a kicking any second.

—He should be shot like a dog, Devlin says, —Fuckin junkie scum!

—I'm coming off it, fatso, David snorts, —I'm cleaning up, so fuck you!

—Cleaning up? You'll never clean up. You're a dirty, no-good junkie.

Marie gets between her son and her brother.

—And you're the same lying, cheating, conniving bastard you've always been, Christopher Devlin.

—Character reference, Maw! says David.

—Shut that bag of bones up, says Devlin, —or I'll throw him out the windie.

—Touch one hair on his head and you'll not set foot in this house again!

Devlin walks away. David follows making monkey noises. Marie lifts the wad of notes and goes to the window. Devlin strides towards his car. Marie snaps the elastic band and hurls the notes one, two and three at a time, down at Devlin.

—You'll never change, she shouts, —You're better off on the drink.

Devlin's having trouble unlocking his car. Electromagnetic

waves of rage are interfering with the electronic lock. He tries the key and it still won't open.

—Look, Marie shouts, —Even your car hates ye. Pick your dirty money up ya bastard! I'd rather live on a Monday book.

The door beeps and unlocks on its own. Devlin gets in and drives off. David's underneath his mother's window now grabbing the falling notes. Manna from heaven. He sings Pink Floyd.

♪♪ So, so you think you can tell heaven from hell, blue skies from pain, How I wish...

Dan's at his window. He sees Marie and Marie sees him.

David sings and other junkies join in.

♪♪ How I wish you were here. We're just two lost souls swimming in a fish bowl year after year. Running over the same ground. What have we found? The same old fears. Wish you were here.

Dan tries a smile. Marie gives him the fingers.

—I hope your good eye gets pecked out with big black crows, ya oul bastard!

Devlin is on Saracen Street, driving south. His mind's not right. He heads past St Theresa's and the Possil Bar, down by Speirs Wharf and round onto the M8.

Midnight on just another street in Easterhouse. Long streets with rows of three- and four-high sandy coloured council flats. Now and then Housing Association buildings brighten the place up. Number 1342 is nondescript. Top right flat. Inside there's the wide screen television. Microwave, fan assisted oven, enormous American fridge that dispenses ice. Nothing amiss in Quack Quack's house. Until you unlock the back room. There the windows have blinds on the outside but are bricked up on the inside. You couldn't see into that room with x-ray eyes. The door is similar to those used by middle-range drug dealers who live and serve in the schemes of Glasgow. The Malkys and Brollys of this world.

But Quack Quack's no drug dealer. He's a surgeon. Struck

of after a baby died during a routine heart operation. He was found to be under the influence of Pethadine. Quack Quack likes his smack. Now he makes his living fixing up stab wounds and gunshot wounds. There's a state of the art operating theatre in this back room.

Devlin lies naked and unconscious on the table. Quack Quack knows if anything goes wrong, for whatever reason, Bonzo has orders to perform a wee operation on him. Quack Quack draws the scalpel down Devlin's skin. It slices along making a sound like cutting paper, the blade glinting at the head of a tail of blood. With the Triads you can't leave anything to chance. They might even demand a scan.

As Devlin lies on the table, Sister Mary-Bridget stands on the deck of a cross-channel ferry. She meditates on the flicks of white against the night sky – gulls flying over the sea and disappearing against the foam. Spirits going back to the One. Continually going in and continually coming out. Being born and returning. Returning and being born.

The day she left Glasgow comes into her mind. The dread that any second somebody would come and drag her off the bus. Beat her up. But nobody came. She watched people on the platform fold their waves and walk back into their lives. She watched faces in the next bus slide past one by one and wondered if they were running too. And what from? The pangs she felt for those she'd left behind… like God plucking her ribs, playing notes of sorrow.

Her world disappeared behind her.

She had no money. At the first service station she saw a purse left lying on the table. She slid it along towards her. No one noticed. It was heavy. Heavy with money, heavy with guilt.

In the toilet she flushed the cistern as she clicked it open. One hundred and fifty six pounds. A small fortune.

She re-boarded the bus. When she got to London she could afford to book into somewhere. She hoped her black eyes would fade some more by morning.

謙恭
humility

Gems can't be polished without friction, nor a man without trials.

THE TRIADS SEND a man to Devlin with details of the drugs operation at The Darkness Concert. The Celtic and Rangers game is the same night. The Triads want Devlin to invite Pitt to the game. While the drugs bust goes on, Pitt's men will pass on the information and Pitt will relay it to the Triads. The Triads are making moves to bring him under their umbrella. Devlin, on the back foot, has agreed to their suggestions. Devlin meets Pitt.

—Drugs deal at the SECC. Pakis. Wednesday night.

—How did you get that info?

—Our friends the Chinks.

—They're keeping their end of the bargain then.

—Aye. Billy, ye couldn't do me favour, could ye? Check if there's been any reports of bodies... shootings, whatever... in the north of the city. The Red Road flats especially.

Pitt taps the side of his nose.

—What's up with your side? he asks.

—Nothing.

Devlin goes to Cooney's house and shows him the scar. All Cooney seems to be interested in is where Devlin's headed. If he doesn't change his thinking now, he never will. He reads out the first three steps and asks Devlin his thoughts. Devlin hasn't given them much thought at all.

—How many times have you promised not to drink and drank? For example important occasions?

Devlin's always known whenever he takes one drink, a wee man runs in and nails his feet to the floor. Cooney reminds him of what happened at the Burning of the Yellow Paper. What happens if he lifts that first drink. Cooney reads step 2: came to believe that a power greater than ourselves can restore us to sanity. Devlin stops him.

—Are you saying I'm a loony?

—No.

—Good job.

—AA's saying you're a loony.

Cooney goes over what Devlin's heard at hundreds of meetings. Alcoholism is a physical, mental and spiritual illness. If he accepts it's a mental illness he has to accept the alcoholic needs restored to sanity. Devlin's not convinced. Cooney tries a parable he's used before.

—Supposing ye went into the Paki's this Friday and said, Tin of corned beef, please. Ye open it up outside. Eat it with your fingers. Go back in and buy another three tins and eat them. Then another three to take home. Ye stagger up the road kicking cats and dogs and shouting abuse. Ye get home and wreck the house. Batter lumps out the wife and chase the weans to their beds. That night, ye're out in the garden firing bricks through the neighbours' windows. The cops come. Ye're lifted. Spend the weekend in the cells. Appear in court on Monday. Get a hefty fine. Ye spend the next few days fixing the broken furniture and avoiding the neighbours. By Thursday the wife's talking to you again and the kids have brightened up. Then this thought comes on ye – wouldn't it be nice to have a wee tin of corned beef? So off ye go to the Paki's. Tin of corned beef please, Karim, ye say. Did you not go mental last week after you ate this? he says. Never mind, it'll be different this time, ye tell him. So he sells ye the corned beef. Ye go outside and eat it with your fingers. Ye go back and buy another five. Ye wake up in the cells next morning. The judge gives ye a last chance. By the next Friday ye fancy a tin of corned beef again. Karim says corned beef makes ye go crazy, but ye convince him you've got it under control, this time it's going to be different. He sells ye it. Ye do the same thing all over again. This time ye get three months. When ye come out the jail, the first thing ye do is head to Karim's for a tin of corned beef. But ye ended up in jail the last time, he says. Ye convince him three months in the jail has changed ye. You're a different man. He sells ye the corned beef. Ye're back in court, having wrecked the house and battered the wife again. The judge wants to know why ye keep eating corned beef when it makes ye go crazy. Ye promise never to eat it again and he takes the unusual step of setting you free, provided you undergo psychiatric treatment. Ye last a couple of weeks, and guess what? Ye fancy a wee tin of corned beef. Karim refuses to serve ye, so ye grab a few tins. You're arrested three hours later. In jail all ye think about is how great it would be to have just one wee tin of corned beef. Christie, the insanity of the alcoholic is to keep on drinking, believing this time things're going to be different. But if ye keep doing what you're doing, ye'll keep getting what you're getting.

—I'm not too sure about this God bit.

—It doesn't need to be God.

—What then? The Force? *You can't kill me, Luke. I'm your father!* Devlin starts doing asthmatic Darth Vader breathing.

Cooney wants to know if he's ever had an experience that he can't explain, where he felt forces outside him were working for his good. Devlin's about to say no when…

—What is it? What is it you see? asks Cooney.

He tells Cooney about the Stag in the Wilderness. How he lay down in the forest and looked in its eyes. At the time he couldn't find words for how he felt.

—There ye go, big man! says Cooney.

Cooney's got what he needs. To complete the first three steps Devlin has to turn his will and his life over to that power. That Power Greater Than Himself. Is he willing to do that?

—I'll do anything.

—Okay, kneel down.

Devlin scrapes his chair back and kneels on the scullery floor. Cooney hands him the *Big Book of Alcoholics Anonymous*. Cooney kneels.

—Read this prayer with me. God I offer myself to thee…

Devlin says nothing. Cooney starts again.

—God I offer myself to thee, Cooney says.

Devlin has his head bowed looking into the book.

—I can't, he says.

—This time, Christie. God I offer myself to thee...
—God I offer myself to thee, stumbles Devlin.

Cooney joins in. They say the prayer to the end. Devlin feels white light fill his body from the knees up through his stitched-up side and out though the crown of his head.

—To build with me and to do with me as thou wilt. Relieve me of the bondage of self, that I may better do thy will. Take away my difficulties that victory over them may bear witness to those I would help of Thy power, Thy love and Thy way of life. May I do Thy will always.

Praying in a London convent, Sister Mary-Bridget feels Devlin's brush with spirituality. She bows and meditates on the task ahead.

Heung Chu, seated at his altar in deep contemplation lights another incense stick. Life works on many levels.

Devlin remains on the floor after the prayer. These are not the same tears as when he told Cooney about *Pinocchio*. If you look inside these tears, there's a white light like a star in each one. A tiny voice.

—Christie, it whispers, that light is you.

危機
crisis

To understand your parents' love you must raise children yourself.

BY WEDNESDAY, DEVLIN'S recovered enough to move about without discomfort, except if pressure is put on the wound. Since meeting Cooney, a tranquil haze has come over him. Until this argument with Nicole. She wants to go to a concert. He'd normally be alright with that. But not this time. Not The Darkness concert. Pitt has set up a major bust. Armed response unit. Back-up from outside Glasgow. There's going to be trouble.

—I'm sixteen, Nicole screams.

—Not yet you're not.

He wants to grab her neck and hurl her across the room. But he's promised himself he will never strike his daughter.

—Christie! Wendy says, —Leave it!

Nicole looks to her mother for support.

—Why do you let him control our lives? It's not as if he's the epitome of taste and style.

Devlin mishears and bursts back in. He wants to know what she said. But all he gets is a backwards wave from Nicole. He spins her round.

—What did you say?

—Later Frankenstein.

Devlin asks Wendy, —Did she say she pitied me?

—Epitome she said.

—Aw, right, well listen you here to me hen, keep your posh words for your posh pals and your posh school. When you're talking to me, talk Scottish!

Nicole makes for the door but he gets there first. She insults him in her best movie trailer voice.

—And the control freakazoid prepares to control the planet by ruling his own dining room.

—If I find you a within a mile of the SECC I'll ground you for a year. And see that new boyfriend of yours – what's he called? Gerry? I'll kick the shit out him.

Devlin stalks out. Once he's gone Nicole hangs her sorry head trying to elicit sympathy. Wendy hugs her. It seems recently there's been nothing but stress in their lives.

—He doesn't fit in here, In a house like this. With people like us.

Wendy pushes fifty pounds into Nicole's hand.

—Oh Mummy! You are a dream!

—It's every teenage girl's right to sneak off and meet boys her parents don't approve of, whispers Wendy.

—Thanks!

—For what?

—The money.

—What money?

—Gothcha! Like, excellent, says Nicole.

—Can I meet him? asks Wendy.

Devlin's gone out driving. The thought of Garrett has been eating at him.

Garrett's door is unlocked. He opens it with his gun out, ready to pump bullets into anything that moves.

Nothing in the hall. He swings into the bedroom. Nothing in there either. Nothing in the toilet. He jumps into the living-room. Empty. The whole place has been cleared. The walls have been painted white and the floor red gloss. Bright red gloss. He can see the fuzzy outline of his reflection in it. Feels dizzy. Sick. The floorboards seem to buckle and bend.

He feels a presence.

There's only one room left. The kitchen.

Devlin kicks the door open. It's also painted white with a red gloss floor. But there's something in the middle of the floor. A dark rectangle. It's a scorch mark. He's puzzling that out when he feels the chill kiss of a gun on the back of his neck.

—Move, an inch and your brains are porridge.

Devlin stays stock still.

—Remember me?

—Who are ye?

—I was wearing a flowery frock when ye shot me. Name's Garrett.

Devlin smiles. He knows what this is. He realises what all the white paint and red paint is.

—I'm hallucinating, he says.

Garrett cracks him one, sending a blue flash through his head.

—Argh, ya cunt ye, says Devlin.

He falls onto on all fours, then twists to see Garrett. But Garrett keeps out of sight. He points the gun at Delvin's head.

—Some hallucination, eh! Sit up, please.

Devlin sits up.

—Thank you!

This is no hallucination. Devlin is worried for his life.

—Who the fuck are ye?

—Oh, you know who I am.

—No I don't. Who the fuck are ye?

—Oh, you know who I am.

—What do you want?

Garrett snorts a laugh.

—What do I want? Let me see now. I want to destroy ye spiritually, emotionally and mentally before I destroy ye physically. I'll have ye on your knees begging like an Anderston hoor to be shot.

—I'll be on my knees for no man.

CRACK!

Devlin wakes half an hour later and blinks. The flat's empty. It's still white and red but nobody's there. His gun's on the floor, still loaded. Was it a hallucination? He searches himself for bullet holes. Feels his head. His fingers come back smeared in blood. Maybe he tripped and hit his head on the door. Aye, that's what it might have been. He makes his nervous way out. He has a sense that everything is going terribly wrong. He has to find Cooney.

The meeting's started. Cooney welcomes him with a wink, registers his agitation.

Jamie B's at the top table, talking about the DTs.

—The worst horrors I ever had, man. I'm trying to talk but it's like my tongue's a page out a book and the wind's shaking the words off. I see them screw their way into ma pal's ears. Words like blood.

Something at the end of the row grabs Devlin's attention. It's Garrett, wearing the flowery dress! There's a small, round hole in the front of his head. He turns to show Devlin the gaping wound in the back. Nobody else seems to notice. Maggie All Meetings thinks Devlin's looking at her and smiles. Devlin closes his eyes. This must be a hallucination. When he opens them again, Garrett is gone.

After the meeting Cooney takes Devlin into a corner.

—What's up?

Devlin whispers hammer and tongs.

—How did I not see him?

—I don't know, do I?

—That chair's been empty all night. Nobody sits beside Maggie All Meetings. She'd talk the hind legs off a fuckin donkey, her.

—I think I might be losing my mind here.

—That's what the DTs do. Did ye not listen to Jamie B?

—That fuckin nutcase. He's sick.

—Made plenty sense to me.

—He's a rocket!

—A rocket that was talking about the DTs. I'd say your Higher Power brought ye here the night.

—You saying I'm as mad as that dipstick?

—Madder. And he's got a PhD, by the way.

—What in? Cartoons?

Devlin puts Cooney's hand to a lump on the side of his head.

—Feel that.

—A lump.

—He fucking whacked me on the head. See, there's blood.

—In here? During the meeting?

Cooney laughs. Devlin tells him about the white walls and the red gloss floor. The gun. The promise to destroy him physically, mentally, emotionally and spiritually.

—How do you know you didn't fall?

—He banged me on the head, twice. How d'ye explain that?

—Maybe you fell twice.

—What about the red paint?

—Maybe you went to the wrong flat.

—It was the right flat.

But doubt has set in. Cooney convinces him he's suffering recurrent DTs. Drink again and he could go into the DTs and never come back. Wet brain.

Cooney asks him if he's ready to go through the fourth step: Made a searching and fearless moral inventory of ourselves.

Garrett's waiting for Nicole in Sarti's. She comes in with her mother. Garrett looks Wendy up and down.

—Hi Nicole. And… this must be your sister.

—You're very kind, says Wendy.

He kisses her politely on the cheek.

—Mum – Gerry. Gerry – Mum, says Nicole.

—Call me Wendy.

—And your husband?

—Oh, he doesn't approve of you two.

—I'm sure we can win him round, says Garrett.

—I'm sure.

—Mum, Gerry can take me back to school tonight.

—Thanks. That would save me explaining to her father where I've been.

Garrett hands her the menu.

—Have you decided what you want? she asks.

—Yes, I have, says Garrett.

That night in Eden Nicole lies naked on her bed blowing

smoke out the window. As the smoke clears the stars appear.

—What are the stars? she says.

Garrett's head is clamped between her legs. She starts to moan in the early throes of orgasm. As she comes she grabs Garrett's hair. When she relaxes he rises up and kisses her.

—Did you like that?

—Mmm.

She stares out at the stars again. Garrett slides an ounce of dope from his pocket and squeezes it in behind the radiator.

Next day. Wendy's got two free periods before lunch. She piles jotters on her desk and pretends to be marking, in case Miss Newell comes in. She sees Kerry-Anne sneaking off with Michael and rises to follow. But Miss Newell is just outside her door.

—May I speak to you in private?

Miss Newell takes her elbow and walks her back to her desk.

—Rumour is your husband is involved in the drugs trade.

—Is that right?

—It could prove to be detrimental to your teaching career.

—Rumours are only rumours.

—I'm sure you are aware that if you bring the profession into disrepute you will be reported to the General Teaching Council.

—Is this an official warning?

—No, no. Advice.

—Advice to do what, exactly?

—Just advice.

As soon as Miss Newell leaves, Wendy goes over to the window. She can see a man talking to Michael outside the old Jehovah's Hall.

Wendy sneaks out of school. No sign of Michael. She goes into the hall and stands at the back. The floor is covered with water and ice. She can see Kerry-Anne and Michael in the reflection of a broken mirror. Michael lights a joint and hands it to Kerry-Anne. Then he starts making a tiny tin-foil bowl. Next thing, Kerry-Anne's school pullover lands near to Wendy.

—What d'ye do that for? asks Michael.

—Fuckin jumper was covered in spunk.

She puts her jacket back on.

—I said to buy johnnies, but you said no! he says.

—We'll use them from now on. I'm not chucking a jumper away every time I gie some old pervert a wank.

Michael holds the tin-foil bowl up.

—Chasing the dragon or...

He produces a needle.

—There's no way I'm jagging up, says Kerry-Anne.

Michael holds the lighter under the bowl. Kerry-Anne makes an O with her mouth and sucks the smoke in. Her world mists out.

Wendy leaves without intervening.

A bubble flops from the mouth of a golden fish and pops on the surface of the pond. Garrett sit together watching the giant carp. Both are breathing heavily. They've just run from The Darkness concert, across Bell's Bridge into the Science Centre. Garrett lights a joint, takes a long, head-tilted-to-the-sky puff.

She dangles her bare feet in the pond. The freezing water between her toes chills her whole body. She likes it.

—Watch you don't catch your death of cold, Garrett says.

—Teach me again, she says.

He repeats what he's repeated a hundreds times before.

—A wrap of speed. Charlie. Blow. Smack. E. Acid.

Nicole repeats,—Wrap of speed. Charlie. Blow. Sash.

Garrett corrects her, —Smack – heroin.

—Smack. E.

He likes how her lips move to the words. Over at the SECC there's activity. Cop cars everywhere. Plain-clothes cops with guns leaning over walls, fences and cars surrounding a red BMW with its doors flung open.

—Looks like a raid, Garrett says.

Suddenly two Pakistani men burst through the crowd and run for the cars. Shots ring out. Three. Bam bam bam. The crowd ducks. Police crawl about, shoving fans to the ground.

—Stay down. Stay down, they're shouting.

A loudhailer announces, Hold fire!

An immense silence falls. A cough could draw gunfire. Nicole is excited.

—Whoo, that could have been us, Gerry.

—Why d'you think we left early and I made you run over here?

—You knew?

Garrett nods. Nicole's impressed.

—You're bullshitting me, she says.

She gives him a little push. Her feet lift out of the water. Droplets plip into the pond. The fish think it might be food and make their way towards Nicole's toes.

—There's a lot of things I know, says Gerry.

She's going to kiss him. But there's a nip at her toes.

—This guy I know, says Garrett, —He gets his kicks sometimes from flinging piranha in public ponds. Sits and waits to see who's first to get their fingertips chewed off. It's usually children.

Nicole's horrified. She'd be even more horrified if she knew he was talking about himself.

—Sure you're tough enough to start your own business? he goes on.

—Of course I am, she says.

The Pakistanis are spreadeagled over the bonnets of cars, being searched.

—Could you handle that?

—I could handle anything.

—Anything?

—Anything!

He grins. She can't decipher what that means. She puts her socks and shoes back on. Cops push handcuffed men into cars.

Twenty arrests. That'll be the end of that gang. Gerry scans back towards the SECC door. But he's taken by a small group of men. Scans back. It's Heung Chu. With him is the Afghan, I Lo, three Forty-Nines and a high ranking plain-clothes cop speaking into a radio, relaying information the Afghan is giving him.

—There's another BMW. The gang members are lying on the floor, he's saying.

Garrett calculates. Devlin. The cops. The Triads. He smiles and glances at Nicole. She's watching two Pakistanis emerging from the other red BMW, hands on their heads. Everywhere they look, the barrel of a gun stares back. A cop pulls two bags from the boot. Bingo! They'd got good weights from the first red Beamer, but here's the big haul. A cop stands on top of a car overseeing everything. Landressy. Pitt's right-hand man. He's on his mobile. Probably to Pitt. Devlin can't be far away. Garrett places an ounce of dope in Nicole's hand.

—Wrap your fingers round that!

—What is it?

—You know what it is.

—An ounce!

—Good girl. Now tell me how you're going to sell it.

—Five pounds a gram. Seven if I'm lying on it.

He corrects her, —Laying it on.

—Seven for that. What do I cut it with?

—That's powder. Smack. Charlie. You don't cut this with anything.

—What I mean is, how do I saw this into grams?

He hands her a Stanley blade.

Meanwhile the Rangers and Celtic game is in full flow. Pitt gives the thumbs up to Devlin and Tai Lo, who's standing in a bunch of Chinese wearing Celtic scarves.

Tai Lo tells his men, —*The Pakistani gang is gone. Now we must find out if Devlin really did have an operation on his appendix.*

Tai Lo smiles at Devlin. Devlin smiles back. The Rangers fans sing.

♪♪ Hello! Hello!
We are the Billy Boys.
Hello! Hello!
You'll know us by our noise.
We're up our knees in Fenian Blood
Surrender or you'll die
We are the Billy, Billy boys.
Tai Lo is mesmerised. Celtic get a free kick on the edge of
Rangers' penalty box. The Rangers fans diminish and the Celtic
fans rise.

♪♪ Against the famine and the crown
I rebelled they cut
me down
Now you must raise our child with dignity.
Low lie the fields of Athenry...
Tai Lo likes the passion of it all. He tugs at Devlin.
—What it all mean?
Devlin tries to formulate an explanation.
—Years ago, he says, —In Ireland...
But the blank faces of the Triads stop him. How do you
explain THAT in three or four shouted lines above the racket
of an Old Firm game?
—Fuck it, Devlin says, —Sing after me.
♪♪ Hail! Hail! The Celts are here.
The Triads sing,
♪♪ Hail! Hail! The Celts are here...
They're a group of mad Chinamen out to experience the
cauldron of an Old Firm game. But there's something else. A
determination.
Pitt is a diehard Rangers fan, but today it suits him to be a
Celtic fan. Devlin's putting him under pressure to scour calls
and reports to see if there's anything, anything at all on
Garrett.
—Nothing so far, Christie.
—No mention?
—Not a whisper.

Devlin's worried. If he wasn't hallucinating, the flat's been cleared, cleaned and bizarrely painted by somebody. Somebody who knows what happened to the body.

—Is everything alright? Pitt asks.

Devlin nods and joins in the singing. The Triads have got into the spirit of things. Amid the roars, Tai Lo gives the signal to I Lo. Out comes his hand. It squeezes Devlin's side, quick and hard. Holds on like a bird's claw. Devlin doubles up with pain. He grabs I Lo.

—What's your game, ya wee cunt?

Tai Lo steps forwards and bows.

—Sorry Mister Devlin. We had be sure you tell truth.

Devlin shoves I Lo back so that only the crowd keep him up.

—Well, now ye know.

Tai Lo bows again.

—I am sorry.

Devlin's glowing inside. He has just jumped what could have been an insurmountable hurdle.

Home from the game and happy at how things went, Devlin watches satellite telly. Couples *Who Wants to be a Millionaire*.

—Drummer crab? You are thick as fuck, hen! Hornblower whelk? Are ye mad? Fifty–fifty and I bet they don't leave fuckin drummer crab or hooter shrimp. It's a fiddler crab. Go for it, ya fuckin diddies. What ye smiling for, a monkey would've knew that. Throw them off, Chris! Get them to fuck.

Wendy comes in. She's not in a good mood.

—Ye want to have seen that bonehead on the telly there – fuckin drummer lobster they said the answer was... what's up?

—Where do you want me to start? I'm pregnant. Everything's going wrong at school. You said you'd stopped drinking.

Devlin moves in to hug her.

—Darling!

—Don't you bloody darling me. You promised me a new life. Where is it?

—I'll take ye there the morra. The house just needs tidied up.
Wendy impersonates his Glasgow accent.

—I've got a deal with the Chinkees. Everything's going to
be alright, doll. You don't give a fig for me, or Nicole, or this
new baby. You're a selfish bastard!

—I'm a selfish bastard? Who do you think I'm doing all this
for?

—Yourself, that's who! Your own bloody ego.

Chris Tarrant chunters to two new contestants. Nicole
comes in.

—How's she not at Eden? says Devlin.

—Gerry picked me up.

—Picked ye up for what?

Nicole walks past with grace and attitude. He stands in her
way.

—Wait a fuckin minute, were you at that concert? Were
you at the SE fuckin CC?

—Gerry took me.

—Gerry? Gerry! I'll punch him that hard I'll kill his whole
family.

Nicole stands defiant. He wants her to say something.
Anything. She doesn't.

—Who the fuck is this Gerry?

She folds her arms and inspects the toe of her shoe. Inside
she's got tornadoes turning.

Devlin takes Nicole by the shoulders.

—What did we tell you?

Nicole looks at Wendy. Devlin pushes her.

—What did we tell ye?

She looks back at her shoe.

—I warned you not to go to the SECC, says Devlin, —
Wendy, talk to her.

—I told her she could go.

Devlin's stunned.

—What?

—I gave her permission to go.

—Great! says Devlin, —Fuckin great. Nicole, you're grounded!

He turns on Wendy. —And you're a fuckin idiot.

—It was only The Darkness concert, says Nicole, —Oh, you are such a silly fool.

Delvin's fists are clenched.

—It was a drugs bust! They busted a gang of crazy Pakis!

—How do you know? Nicole asks.

—It was on the telly.

Her face is still puzzled.

—How could it have been on the telly so quickly?

Devlin ignores that.

—You could've got fuckin lifted.

—Lifted?

—Fuckin arrested… don't come that posh shite with me, hen!

She curtseys.

—Sorry, your eloquence.

Devlin turns to Wendy.

—She could've got fuckin shot.

—You're over-reacting.

—Over-reacting? Rapid response, fuckin guns, marksmen. Trigger-happy, teenage Pakis. Anything could've happened.

—But it didn't, says Nicole.

—It could've. Were you there when the cops arrived?

—We left early.

She thinks that'll calm him slightly.

—Where have you been since then?

—None of your business.

He's about to tell her she is his business when he sees the Stanley knife in her bag. He grabs it.

—What the fuck're ye doing with that?

Nicole stays outwardly cool.

—School work.

She takes it from Devlin, retracts the blade, and drops it in her bag. Keeps her hand in her bag.

—We're taking you back to school in the morning Little Bo fuckin Peep.

Nicole smiles. In her bag is the ounce of dope.

Next morning. Devlin sits in the Shogun. Wendy kisses Nicole on the cheek. He watches her join her schoolmates for assembly. Watches her talk to Augustus with great animation. Wendy's crunching her way back over the gravel. Just then, Devlin's hairs stand up so intense they feel like creaking trees. He can't take his gun out here. He can't. He can't. He reaches up his back, whips his gun out, ducks and turns the muzzle onto the empty back seats.

He puts it away. Maybe Cooney was right. Maybe this is another flashback. The DTs. Maybe the last encounter with Garrett was a hallucination. Maybe he dreamed it all. Maybe…

—What's up with you? says Wendy.

—Nothing. Heartburn.

He watches the schoolkids disappear. Wendy nudges him.

—Well?

—Well what?

—I thought you were taking me to see our new house?

He nods and drives off. Wendy called the school secretary at eight and told her a domestic problem had cropped up. She wonders what Miss Newell will do when she realises she's taken the day off. To take her mind off it she looks out at the view. The snowdrops are up in the fields and under the roadside trees she can see blue and white crocuses.

Christie's eyes are on the road, his mind miles away. She places a hand on his knee.

—Slow down.

He eases off.

—I can't help it. Everything's saying run.

—Run? Run from what?

He's holding the steering wheel so tight muscles are bulging in his wrists.

—I thought you went to see Cooney?

—That bam! He wants me to write a book about all the bad things I've done. Fuckin write it all down and then tell some cunt about it! Is he mad?

—You've stopped, says Wendy.

—What?

—You've stopped.

The car's stopped.

They're being watched from the woods. The Stag. Devlin makes eye contact.

He speaks without taking his eyes off it.

—Is that real?

—What?

—In the trees. That there!

Wendy spots the Stag.

—Yes, that Stag is real.

Devlin gives her a kiss.

—What was that for?

—Wendy, look. Has it got a limp?

—What?

—A limp. Can you see if it's got a limp?

She thinks it's moving strangely but can't be sure. If she had to guess, she's say yes. Devlin opens the door and is about to get out. She stops him. What about the house? By the time he's looked at Wendy and back, the Stag's gone. He's sure that was his Stag. Even if it's not, it's a sign. A good omen. Sent by... sent by his Higher Power!

—What are you smiling at now?

—God.

—Aw Christie, don't go all born-again on me.

He drives off towards Jarkness.

Miss Newell has noted Wendy absent. Again. She's ripped the note up and told the secretary to forget about it. She makes sure there's no one available to cover. Wendy's third and fourth years are told to contact their parents and go home. Parents phone the school. Threaten to take their complaint further. Fine, thinks Miss Newell, standing smug at her window.

When Wendy sees Jarkness she bursts into tears. She clicks the car door open and steps out. Devlin parks behind the boat shed and follows her onto the beach. He can smell her happiness.

She's overcome. The bay windows. The views over the estuary. The garden. The woodland paths north and south along the shore. It's enchanted. At last he's getting out of that awful business. She kisses him. Everything's going right today. Even the foot she pivots on turns easily, the sole of her shoe turning on the dome of a pebble. As their lips part, she is perfectly balanced on the absolute grace of being.

—C'mon, wait till you see the inside, says Devlin.

The key in the lock brings an intricacy of clicking metal, followed by a sense of space. The door opens in an arc so beautiful it could be faultless mathematics. And the house? The house is like religion. Too many doors. Too many doors. Devlin steers her into the living-room.

Wendy walks up and down the living-room, her steps echoing into the future. Annihilating the past. Right here, the future starts. A fishing boat drifts into view.

—Oh look at that, she says, —It's beautiful.

The boat passes out of sight behind a peninsula.

—All ours, Devlin says, —Every brick, every tree, every inch of shoreline.

Ripples from the boat arrive on the shore. The sea has crept over the sand and is moving among the pebbles. Coming closer.

—There's a great feeling in this house, says Wendy.

Devlin massages her shoulders.

—Serenity, he says.

He nuzzles at her neck. She tilts her head backwards, taking a breath. Devlin turns her and they kiss, pressing hard. He can feel her breasts pushing into his chest. Her groin moves over his. Her hands go down and she undoes his trousers. Fingers his cock out. Starts wanking him, looking directly in his eyes. She sinks to her knees and kisses his cock. She wraps her mouth round the tip, tugs his trousers and boxers down in one heave.

—What the fuck is that?

In the blue light Devlin's scar shows up well against his white skin. He'd forgotten she didn't know about it.

—A scar.

His hard-on drains.

—I know it's a fucking scar, Christie, but what's it doing there?

—They must've done it at the hospital.

—You didn't get that at the hospital. They'd've fucking told me.

Devlin decides to tell the truth. That he got it to appease the Chinese, in order to keep the deal going. To get the money. To buy the house. To get out. He done it all for her.

—For me? Thanks a million!

—I'm trying to stay alive here, so you can get your fuckin dreams.

—They're not my dreams, Christie, they're ours!

—Ours then! Look, don't worry.

—Don't worry? I've got a husband who comes home slashed and sewn up and he tells me not to worry.

There's a noise. Devlin whips his gun out and points it at the door. He's almost squeezed the trigger when he registers Bonzo and Hung Kwan. He lowers the gun. They lower their eyes to his dick. His trousers and boxers at his ankles. Wendy kneeling.

They've got bags of the China White.

—What the fuck are they doing here? Wendy says.

Devlin doesn't answer. He zips up his trousers. Bonzo hands him a set of keys. Wendy sees what's going on. Jarkness was only bought to bring drugs ashore under cover. Devlin isn't getting out. She moves to the window. The fishing boat is heading out to sea on the turn of the tide, waves from the stern obliterating the calm sheen of the water.

—Great! Bloody great!

She bumps past Bonzo and Hung Kwan as she leaves.

—There goes my blow job, says Devlin.

The three men laugh. But the laughter is hollow and false.

Outside, Wendy marches to the car.

Garrett watches from the trees.

自豪
pride

Once on a tiger's back, it is hard to alight

IT'S THE MIDDLE of the night. Devlin's in his room listening to
Fauré's Requiem. Thinking about making the leap. About
getting out. Will he lose Wendy before the time's right? Will
he lose his mind? Should he go and see Cooney about the
fourth step? Will Garrett get him?

If he's real?

Wendy's downstairs drinking, playing the message from
her school over and over on the answering machine. The more
she plays the worse it sounds.

Eventually she falls asleep on the couch, face wet with
tears. Dreams crazy dreams. Wakes with a start. She can't lay
her eyes on one innocent object. Everything takes her back to
Christie. And that scar. And her kneeling on the floor like a
slut. But something new has coming into her life. She can feel
it. She can feel it like the tide on Jarkness beach bleeding
through the pebbles.

Nicole's spiked running shoes picking up old leaves as she runs
through the trees. She stops under a chestnut and pulls a bin
bag over her upper body. Crouches down, and squeezes
through the dark apex at the roots of the hollow tree. She
braces her back into one side and digs the spikes into the
other. Climbs ten or twelve feet. Locates her stash and stuffs it
into her top. Creeping back to the dormitory, her breath
plumes out in ghost fog. She keeps to the shadows.

Inside, Gorman's prowling too. As he approaches Nicole's
door she appears at the end of the corridor. Sensing something, Gorman turns. Nicole's ducked behind a pillar. Hears
him moving towards her. Spots a coke can. Picks it up with
such delicacy there's not a dink. Leans out of Gorman's line of
vision. Launches it in a high parabola over his head. The clang
rotates him. He sprints towards the noise.

Nicole slips down the corridor and sneaks into her room,
hides the drugs in her underwear drawer, strips, and jumps

into bed. Gorman comes in and hovers. She moans and rolls onto her side. He leaves.

Devlin's turned up at Cooney's flat in the middle of the night. He wants to write his fourth step. When dawn comes he's been writing for three hours.

Step 4. Made a searching and fearless moral inventory of ourselves.

Cooney picks up a crumpled piece of paper. Flattens it out and reads. Devlin watches like a schoolboy. Cooney laughs.

—What?

—The fourth step's not just a list of all the bad things you've done in your life.

—That's what you said.

—A *moral* inventory.

—Aye!

—You write down all the people you resent and ask why you resent them.

—That's what I've done.

—No, you've wrote down what you've done to all the people you resented.

Cooney explains the fourth step again. You write down the names of people you resent. You write down what they done to make you resent them. You ask what actions of yours might have caused them to act in this way. Your own patterns of behaviour start to show.

You resent a guy. When you ask yourself why, your first answer might be, he's cocky. Look harder and you find it's because he's good with women. Look harder still, and you see you're scared he'll take your woman. He's a threat to your pride.

—The first he knows about it is you've smashed his head in, says Cooney. —When I was a teenager in Belfast I got into a fight with this bar owner. He knocked me out. I couldn't live it down. Used to tell people there was three of them, but there was only one guy and there was only one punch. My pride was hurt bad. Pride, Christie! Five years later. Five years, mind. I'm

married and kinda staying off the drink. Benders now and
then. But pretty successful at staying off it. My wife comes in
this day and tells me she's pregnant. Now listen closely how
this thinking goes here. She tells me I'm going to be a Da. I
goes out and gets a bottle of whisky. After one drink I'm
dreaming about me and my new son – oh aye, I had decided it
was a boy – me and my son fishing and walking up the mountains and camping. After another drink I start to get uneasy.
By the time the bottle's half-finished, I'm wondering what my
son's going to think when he hears his da's a coward. When he
hears that I got knocked out with one punch and done nothing about it. Left it. Never went back and stood up like man.
Ran out the pub with a bust lip. Five years after the event,
Christie, and it's still in me. Cutting me deep. I can't admit that
I was beaten fair and square by a man with a faster, stronger
punch. That I wasn't the best fighter in Belfast. D'you know
what I done?

—What?

—I go out to the car. No son of mine is getting brought up
thinking his da's a coward. She's just trying to pull me back,
the wife. I take the hose off the carburettor. Turn on the
ignition. Fill a milk bottle with petrol. Put some sugar in it.
Stuffed a rag in the top. And all the time she was screaming,
Don't, Larry. Please don't. But I keep going. I'm foaming at the
mouth, heading for the bar. Five years after I got knocked out,
I'm heading for the same bar. That crazy thinking. Here we go.
I'm snarling like a dog and driving through West Belfast like a
demon. When I get there I light the rag and fling the bottle in.
As I drove away men were running out with their clothes on
fire. I could've killed them.

—Is that why you went to AA?

—No. It was another ten years before I went. And a lot
worse things than that happened.

Devlin stares at him.

—I never knew you had weans.

—I don't. She miscarried the next day. That was the end of

us. My pride almost had me killing a pub full of men. Lost me my baby. Lost me a woman I loved. That's what the fourth step showed me. If I'd done the fourth step then I'd've said I resent the bar man. Why do I resent him? He knocked me out. Why could I not accept that? Cos I was a hard man. Why did I think I was a hard man? Pride. Excessive pride. I could've seen the pride for what it was. There would've been no petrol bomb. No miscarriage. No divorce. And! And I'd be able to keep a watch for that pride and arrogance in the future.

Devlin starts writing.

Wendy's feeling better. She's going back to school in the morning. She's sent a sick line in. Depression. They won't believe that. But, oh, if depression was her only problem. Today she's hanging about with Devlin. He's gone up to see Marie and waiting in the Shogun she sees Kerry-Anne and Michael. They nip the joint they're sharing and come up to the car.

—Hi yi, Miss!

Wendy presses the button and the window rolls down.

—How's your mother Kerry-Anne?

—Out her head, Miss. There's some good smack about. Great. The best stuff ever.

The more Kerry-Anne praises the smack, the more guilt Wendy feels.

—She was sparkled this morning an all, Miss. I could've plugged her in and she'd not've moved. N'at right?

—She was lying on the floor like a starfish, Miss, says Michael.

Wendy's worried about how skinny Kerry-Anne looks. Is she injecting? No, not Kerry-Anne. Saint Gallus.

—Are ye alright, Miss? asks Kerry-Anne.

Wendy snaps back to the moment.

—Have you had your breakfast?

Kerry-Anne laughs.

—I'm lucky to see my maw, never mind get a breakfast. She's a hoor.

—Don't call your mother that.

Kerry-Anne realises she's picked her up wrong.

—No, Miss. She *is* a hoor. That's her job. Works at Park Circus. Out all night. Out her head all day.

Wendy knows she's out of her depth.

—Here. Ten pounds. Get both of you something to eat.

Kerry-Anne's embarrassed for Wendy. She's got a hundred pounds in her pocket. But she takes the tenner. She and Michael disappear into a close. They're going to chase the dragon. Wendy sees Dan leaning out of his window. He waves and Wendy waves back. It seems this whole place is crowding in on her. She looks at her watch. What's keeping Christie?

Inside, Marie picks a dout from the ashtray, straightens it and lights it. As she smokes, she notices the letter from Sister Mary-Bridget on the telly. She folds it into her pocket. Devlin's going on about seeing David pissing up against a bus stop.

—And a line of oul women watching. D'ye think that's alright an all?

—He's a man. He can do what he wants.

—He's lucky I didn't break his back.

—I don't want to talk about it any more.

Devlin sees she's actually smiling.

—What you doing smiling when there's been no plane crashes?

—What, is it an offence to smile like?

—You, in a good mood? Should I throw a party?

—Why not? You've threw everything else in your time.

Devlin goes to the window as he talks, trying to get it out of her.

—Right, he says, —David's done the Giro in. He's floating about Saracen out his face on smack. Probably pishing over old women and flashing at motors. And you're *happy*?

—I've got no control over David, you know that better than anybody.

—And what's that ye stuck in your pocket earlier?

—When?

—The letter that was on the telly.

—What letter?

—The one ye never wanted me to see?

Marie clamps her hand on her pocket. Devlin takes a step towards her, but she leaves the room, closing the door behind her, and runs up the hall. By the time he opens the door she could've planked it anywhere.

Wendy tries to catch his attention by flashing the lights. But Devlin's still asking about the letter.

—Knowledge is power, Christie, eh?

—Aye, but it's not intelligence, he says.

—Look, ye can question me all ye want, Einstein. I'm not one of your... soldiers.

Marie sees Wendy looking up impatiently. Decides to keep Devlin as long as she can.

—D'ye want a mug of tea and an outsider on jam?

There's nothing he likes better than a big outsider on jam and a mug of tea. Ten minutes later he's munching into the piece. Marie gives Wendy a little wave. Kerry-Anne and Michael roll another joint. The phone rings. Marie picks it up and listens for a couple of seconds.

—No, sorry, she says, —I don't want any double glazing today thank you.

She hangs up.

—Who was that? asks Devlin.

—Double fuckin glazing.

The phone rings again.

—Hello? No... no gypsies thank you. Goodbye.

She hangs up. It rings again immediately. She picks it up.

—Yes, he is here.

—Put him on the phone.

—He says you're spoiling his meal.

—Oh, does he? Tell him to get out here now or there's going to be trouble.

—What trouble can you cause, like?

—Plenty.

—Well ye better watch out, ya English hoor, cos I can cause plenty an all.

—Oh can you now? Maybe you'd be better controlling that junkie son of yours.

Wendy screams as Marie drags her out of the car. Kerry-Anne and Michael run over, nipping the joint. Wendy's on the ground dazed. Marie grabs her by the hair and starts laying punches into her head.

—Fuck sakes! says Kerry-Anne.

Marie strikes and strikes, shouting about Wendy being a snobby English bastard. Wendy's bag has been dragged out the car. She reaches in, takes out a can of hairspray. Kssht! into Marie's face. Marie whips her hands to her eye.

—What've ye done? What've ye done?

Blinded, she throws wild kicks and punches. Punches the car with a klang to the laughter of the gathering crowd. Wendy gets to her feet. Screams. Grabs Marie by the hair. Jerks her head down and bangs it off her knee.

—On ye go, shouts Kerry-Anne.

Marie sinks to the ground.

—Kill her Miss Devlin! shouts Kerry-Anne.

Wendy pushes Marie onto her back, sits astride her, takes off her thick heeled shoe and lays into her head, grunting a mantra of hate.

—Who's a snobby cow now?

Smack. A bruised forehead.

—Eh? Who's a snobby cow now?

Smack! The bruise bursts open.

—What's that? I can't hear anything.

Smack! The heel splashes into the blood.

—Louder! What's that? Your son's a junkie? Pardon?

—Miss, here's your man! says Kerry-Anne.

Devlin, with the outsider on jam stuck in his mouth, grabs Wendy and pulls her back. Dan arrives with his Cowboy gear on. Marie recognises the foggy shape of her da.

—Get your fuckin hands off me! she shouts.

The crowd disperses.

—Fuck sake, Devlin says, —What yees playing at?

—She sprayed hairspray in my eyes, says Marie.

—After you beat me up, shouts Wendy.

She climbs back in the car. Marie shrugs Devlin off and makes her way to the close.

The Millennium Tower watches over the city. Devlin's Shogun moves towards Bearsden. Wendy's started an argument about what drugs are doing to the kids in her school.

—Every bloody one of them almost, she shouts.

—Weans are like that. They tell lies.

—They weren't lying.

—They copy each other.

—That's what I'm worried about, Christie. They copy their parents and on we go downhill.

—And I'm responsible for that?

—In a fucking word, yes!

—Ye make your choices in life. They choose to be junkies.

—And you chose not to?

—Exactly.

—It's easier to choose a route from the top of a mountain, Christie.

—Who are you… Jesus? Fuck off with the parables.

Devlin leans over and squeezes her breast twice.

—Beep beep! he says.

—Take your fucking hands off me!

—I'm trying to cheer ye up. It's not my fault you're a nervous wreck.

She stares at him.

—I'll have a word with Marie.

—Marie! What's a couple of bruises and a black eye? It's your fault I'm a nervous wreck.

—I stopped the fight!

—Pull over.

He keeps going. Wendy grabs the steering wheel. The

Shogun veers and comes to rest at the side of the road to the horn-tooting disapproval of a Volvo. Devlin leans out of the window.

—I'll rip your fuckin head off!

Off goes the Volvo.

—I never know what the next day's going to bring, says Wendy, —living with gangsters.

—Business man.

—You're a gangster, Christie.

—I'm a business man.

—A gangster. You prey on other people's lives. Make money from their pain and fear.

—They choose...

—They choose what you present to them. Why do you keep doing it? You've got everything. There's nothing else to get.

—I'm not listening to any more of this.

Devlin starts singing to drown her out.

♪♪ Frosty the snowman...

—It's all going wrong, Christie! I don't know where to turn.

Wendy jumps out the car.

—Where the fuck're you going?

—A walk. Among normal people.

—Get in the car, ya maddie.

Wendy walks away.

An hour later she's at the sink in the small downstairs bathroom, cleaning her cuts. Devlin comes up behind her, gets a piece of cotton wool and tries to dab her swollen bottom lip. She pushes him back with her hip.

—Get away from me.

He leaves. Wendy looks at the state of her face. Her right eye's swollen up. It's going to be black. Her bottom lip's cut. Her forehead's bruised and her cheekbones are both swollen. What'll she look like at school tomorrow? And she has to go in. She's told Newell she'd be back. As she holds onto the sink she hears Christie's voice. He's on the phone. She turns the tap off. Puts her ear to the door.

—I just phoned to see if ye were alright. I know it was her fault. Ye know what she's like. No, don't. Marie? Marie? Fuckin women.

Devlin puts the phone down. Wendy turns the tap up full pressure watching the water spinning furiously in the bowl. She takes some Ibuprofen. Sleeps on top of the duvet. Devlin's out all night. Business with the Chinese or talking to that AA nutter. Or drinking? So what if he's drinking? She hopes he drinks himself to death. He's useless. Their life's useless. A bloody dead end.

In the morning the damage confronts her. She can cover some with make-up but that'll look like she's trying to hide it. In the end she decides to go in without make-up.

Kerry-Anne's old busted trainers splash through the thin ice on a puddle. She sees Wendy and catches up. A first year notices Wendy's swollen mouth and shouts for her mammy. One by one kids and parents turn. Wendy's running a gauntlet of gasps and whispers. She faces a group near the door.

—There! Is that what you wanted to see?

—Who done that – Mike Tyson? someone shouts back.

—Ignore them, Miss, says Kerry-Anne. The registration bell rings.

—Go to your class, Kerry-Anne.

—I'm going nowhere. I'm staying here to make sure you're alright.

Wendy sets up her first lesson. She's doing the First World War poets with the fourth years. As she writes on the board, Kerry-Anne chats away.

—Ye were no bad, Miss. At first I thought ye were going to get your cunt kicked...

—Kerry-Anne!

A shoal of pain under her skin.

—Sorry, Miss. But ye were. I never knew teachers could fight.

—Everyone's got to fight sometimes.

—And some people's got to fight all the time.

Wendy pauses, holding the chalk towards the ceiling at an angle. Kerry-Anne's message is simple.

—Miss, listen! says Kerry-Anne.

—Fighting in the street? says a teacher in the corridor.

—On the ground. Rolling about, says a kid.

—And you watched this?

Wendy recognises Anne's voice.

—Yes, Miss. From my window, Miss.

—What did your mother say?

The girl falls silent.

—Well?

—Can't tell you.

—Yes you can.

There's a pause.

—Tell me, orders Anne, —Tell me now!

—Rip her tits off! That's what she said, Miss.

Wendy and Kerry-Anne make an O with their mouths and laugh silently. The rumble of approaching kids precedes the bell for the end of registration. Kerry-Anne stays put. The class fills with kids trying to look like they're not looking at her face. Wendy acts like there's nothing wrong. Kerry-Anne hands out the poetry books. Wendy tunes in to Johnny Shields retelling the fight to four boys. Wendy lets him go on.

—Miss Devlin got on top of her and took her shoe off and started welding into her head with it. Like this...

Johnny hammers insanely on the desk, grunting. A skinny girl with lank blonde hair pleads to Wendy.

—Miss, I'm scared.

Wendy goes over and whispers in Johnny's ear.

—Shut your fucking mouth!

He does. Wendy claps her hands.

—Come on. Settle down. Quiet please. Quiet now! Quiet!

Near the end of the lesson Wendy plays *Waltzing Matilda*. The version about the Australians who fought in the First World War in Gallipoli. She asks the kids to put their heads on the desk and simply listen to the words of the song.

—When its finished, write down any images that passed thought your head: the weirder the better.

The song plays.

Near the end the singer sings low and quiet.

♪♪ For I'll go no more Waltzing Matilda all around the green bush far and near, for to hump tent and pegs a man needs both legs, no more Waltzing Matilda for me.

Crushed dreams. Wendy struggles to hold back her tears.

Kerry-Anne whispers, —There, Miss. It's going to be alright.

—Thanks. You're very wise, Kerry-Anne.

—You're as wise as your life's hard, my granny used to say.

Wendy apologises for crying.

—My maw cries all the time when there's no drugs.

A boy sticks his hand up.

—So does mine, when there's no money for drugs.

A girls sticks her hand up.

—And mine, when my da got put in the jail. He's in for shoplifting for drugs.

Three-quarters of the class have their hands up.

—There's new drugs, the China White.

The class all nod. Wendy's head's spinning. The bell goes.

—D'ye want me to stay, Miss? asks Kerry-Anne.

—No, just you go.

But as she's opening the door Wendy says her name. Kerry-Anne turns. Wendy's unable to speak. Kerry-Anne reads every nuance.

—I'll be alright. I'm as tough as fuck! she says, winks, and leaves.

In the site agent's hut Devlin flicks though piles of newspapers, searching for any mention of Garrett. A body. A shooting. A hospitalisation. A report of gunfire. But there's nothing. He comes across a photo of Pitt standing over a pile of guns.

GUN AMNESTY GOES WELL

He phones Pitt and arranges lunch. Sees Dan and the site agent coming. Leans back in the chair. Puts his feet on the desk right on the site drawings and folds his hands behind his head. Dan discretely locks the door and stands in the corner.

The site agent's not pleased at all. He removes the drawings from under Devlin's boots.

—Can I help you? he says.

—Ye can help yourself, says Devlin

He takes out a notebook and pen.

—How's that?

—I've been getting paid for ghosts with Clyde Development site agents for years.

—Ghosts?

—It's a simple operation. You pay me for men that don't exist and get your cut.

—Is that a bribe?

—No. It's a threat!

Devlin's click clicking away at the pen in his hand. Dan's thinks he's going to stab the site agent in the eye. The site agent assesses the situation. Wrongly.

—Fuck off.

—You're new so here's one last chance to reconsider, Devlin says.

—The only thing I'm considering is the police.

The site agent sits down. Lifts the phone.

Devlin drops his pen.

—Oops!

He fumbles under the desk. The site agent listens to the ring tones. There's an almighty

BANG

from under the table. Louder than a gun. The site agent screams and stands upright. Tries to move back but he can't. Looks down. His left foot's nailed to the floor with a Hilti nail. As he tries to get away the leather on his boot stretches and oozes blood. The site agent collapses into the chair.

—Oh God! Oh God! Oh God! Oh God!

Devlin dunts the Hilti on the table. Leans towards the site agent.

—I'll come back when you've got less on your mind.

Dan opens the door. He notices Devlin holding onto his side as he is leaving.

—Ye alright?

—Constipation.

—Prunes, says Dan, —They're great.

Devlin leaves.

Dan approaches with a crowbar. The site agent cowers but Dan leans down, sets a block of wood beside the blood-stained boot and levers the nail out.

Dan drives the site agent to the Royal Infirmary.

Devlin and Pitt finish their lunch. Pitt puffs on a cigar: media star. Devlin's been at him all through the meal. Any reports of shootings? Anything at all? Gunfire? A body? Hospital admissions? Pitt's shook his head to them all.

—There's been nothing. Not a jot.

—Surely somebody's heard something?

—Mibbi your men didn't do the job.

Devlin stares at him.

—I popped him myself.

—Allegedly, says Pitt.

He checks about for anybody listening,

—Watch what you're saying, Christie!

—I *allegedly* put one right through his fuckin skull.

—No shootings, no murders, no hospital admissions, no bodies, Pitt tells Devlin again.

Devlin thinks. Hard. He's doubting his own sanity. Did he do it? Was he there? Of course he did. His men were there too. But when he went back and got a pistol-whipping? What was all that?

Pitt interrupts, puffing on his cigar like pride.

—Hey, have ye seen me on the telly?

—What for?

—The gun amnesty. It's going great guns, he says, knocked out by his joke.

As Pitt laughs, Devlin gets a text message. Has to go. Business to take care of. If Pitt hears anything he's to call right away. Be good if Pitt could put some men on finding out who this Garrett is.

Pitt draws on his cigar. The red glow seems to be just for Devlin.

—Will co! he says.

Soon Devlin's back at the building site. The site agent limps in with Dan, his foot in a plaster. Dan locks the door.

—Have a seat, says Devlin.

—I'd rather stand, thank you.

—Understandable. Did you think about our offer?

—Great business opportunity.

—Good to hear it, says Devlin.

He reaches across to shake hands. The site agent nearly refuses but thinks better of it, offering Devlin a limp fish.

—Make arrangements with my da here, says Devlin.

Classes are over for the day at Eden Academy. From the edge of the woods Nicole watches a girl approach Augustus. One of the ultra-rich bunch. Goth by night. Perfect pupil by day.

—Are you Augustus?

—Yes, I am.

—I heard…

—You heard correctly.

She gets as close as she can.

—Can I have some marijuana please?

—Five pounds, says Augustus.

She gives him the money.

—Want some ecstasy?

She does. Augustus giver her four Es. Tells her to bring twenty pounds when she can. Augustus winks over at Nicole.

They meet in her room and share a joint. Nicole gets her diary and writes. They've to be paid for twenty Es. Get another ounce of dope from Gerry. Perhaps they should order two? What does he think? He thinks they should get some amphetamine sulphate. Nicole laughs.

—Speed. Don't call it amphetamine sulphate in front of Gerry if you ever meet him.

—Sorry, speed. Let's get ten wraparounds of speed.

Nicole laughs again.

—Wraps. Ten wraps of speed.

They'll ask for two ounce of dope. And what about some acid? Yes they should get some acid. Nicole takes the joint and flops back onto the bed taking a big tug. Star blazers burn her school shirt.

—Shit!

She wipes them off, handing the joint back to Augustus. Takes off her shirt and sits in her bra to his squint-away shyness.

—Inhale Augustus!

He does and his face drains of colour. He coughs and splutters. Nicole gets on the mobile.

—Hi. It's me. Oh, that's just Augustus coughing. He's helping me. No. He would never do that.

Augustus asks, Do what? with his face.

—You'd never grass. He'd never grass, Gerry. Two ounces? Yes. It's gone. Honest. We're not as naïve as we look, you know. It's not only slum-dwellers who know how to party. And another twenty E. Speed. Okay, text me and I'll let you in. Mwah! Mwah!

She comes off the phone filled with Gangsta pride.

—Can he get it? asks Augustus.

—Of course he can. He's connected. Now go and collect all the money we're owed. None of this pay me when you can. We have to pay Gerry when he comes. Augustus gives her back the joint and leaves.

Later that night they meet in the usual spot.

Augustus gives her a wad of notes.

—You've collected it all?

—I'm paying some from my own account.

As she counts, they become aware they're being watched.

—There's somebody out there, Nicole whispers.

She grabs Augustus and pretends to snog him, peering over his shoulder into the trees. Someone's coming towards them.

—Hello? says Nicole. —Who's there?

The Stag steps out of the trees, snorts and limps back into the forest.

—Gosh. I thought it was the DS, says Nicole.

—What's the DS?

—Drugs Squad.

—When's Gerry coming with the next consignment?

That's for her to know. Augustus better not be hanging around like a lost puppy. Nicole's underworld contacts don't like strangers. Fear glimmers on Augustus's face.

—Are you sure you can cope with the pressure? Nicole asks.

—I could rule this school. When I see an opportunity, I grasp it.

—Okay. I'll text you when he comes.

At ten o'clock, Nicole gets a text: Couldn't come up. School being watched by the Headmaster. Message in tree. Nicole tries to call back but Gerry's mobile's on voicemail. She sneaks out to the tree and retrieves a plastic bag. Back in her room she texts Augustus to meet in the girls toilets. They lock themselves in a cubicle. Nicole lifts up her skirt and shoves her hand down her knickers.

—What are you doing?

—You wish, says Nicole.

She produces the stash.

—That's a lot of drugs, he says.

Nicole holds up two ounces of dope.

—That's eighty grams.

—There are only 28.3495 grams in an ounce.

—Dhuu! I know that. Cut less, sell for more. You sell it, keep your profit, and give me my hundred and fifty pounds.

Augustus knows he's placing his future in jeopardy for someone who doesn't care one iota for him.

—If my father found out, he would procedure me.

—That's what makes it so exciting, isn't it?

Nicole hands him the Stanley knife.

—Use this to cut it.

—Shh!

Footsteps in the toilet. It can only be a teacher. Tap tap goes the door.

—Yes? says Nicole.

—Nicole Devlin? says Gorman.

—Yes?

—Why are you not in your room?

—I have diarrhoea, says Nicole.

She smiles at Augustus. But Augustus isn't smiling back.

—Oh, I'm not well, sir, she moans.

—Ahem! Go straight back to your room and if you still feel ill in the morning, make sure you see the nurse.

—I will, sir. I'm going to be sick.

Nicole's retching rings around the toilets. They hear Gorman's footsteps fade down the corridor.

—Count to a hundred and leave, orders Nicole before she goes.

The Kung Fu class is coming to an end. Bonzo's being taught the Drunk Style. Ming Fung staggers about. This way... oops, nearly falls. Forwards – she stamps her foot to stop herself falling flat on her face. Bonzo copies her every move. She falls over to the side so that the palm of her left hand has to touch the floor. She thrusts herself up, bringing her right fist round in a hook. A punch like that can kill. Bonzo copies. He was a boxer in his younger days and his perfect hook brings admiring glances. Especially from Ming Fung.

She claps the class back into rows. Bonzo joins in. Now he's had a few lessons he doesn't feel as out of place. And if he's allowed any Guanxi, he's just earned some from Ming Fung.

She fancies him and he knows it. And I Lo knows it too. He keeps a fixed stare on Bonzo as Ming Fung teaches reverse-turning kick.

—*The back foot seventy degrees to the front. Move the weight onto the ball of the front foot and whip the leg round landing where you started. This blow is delivered with the heel. Be careful. It is deadly.*

Bonzo's waiting for her to demonstrate when she asks him to step forward. Gets him to hold a wooden board at head height. It's two hundred millimetres square and twenty five millimetres thick. He holds it with a tight fist.

—Like this?

—Finger and thumb, she says.

She shows him how to hang it from his index finger and thumb. A gust of wind could rock it, but it won't drop.

—Very light or I will break your hand, she says.

She reaches her front hand out and almost, but not quite, touches the edge of the board. A quick breath. Spins. When her head's turned through three hundred and sixty degrees and her right heel is a foot from the board, she checks Bonzo's screwed up face. Her heel

CRACKS

the board at full speed. It halves and spins away. Ming Fung lands in her previous stance.

—Fuck me! says Bonzo.

—I don't think so, she says.

—Bonzo! Sholtz shouts.

He taps his watch. Devlin will be here soon for the meeting. Bonzo hangs back and tries some Chinese on Ming Fung.

—*M Koi!*

Ming Fung smiles and bows.

—*M Koi!* she says.

Bonzo bows. He and Sholtz make their way into the Mah Jong room with a group of Triads.

—We are hungry, yes? asks Tai Lo.

—I could eat a scabby hoor in a folded over mattress! says Sholtz.

Tai Lo puzzles for a bit, then laughs.

—*What did he say?* asks I Lo.

—*I could eat a scabby hoor in a folded over mattress!* Tai Lo says.

The Triads fall into fits of laughter. The joke makes its Chinese way thought the rattling Mah Jong tiles out into the Casino. As Devlin enters, the blackjack table at the door is filled with Chinese bobbing in laughter. For a minute he thinks they're laughing at him.

He meets Tai Lo and both sets of men round a table in the Mah Jong room. They eat and discuss glitches here and there in the set-up. Otherwise everything's going fine. What does Devlin think? He's well pleased. Once the next week's consignment is planned they retire into the casino.

The karaoke is out. Ming Fung sings. Bonzo's riveted. I Lo prays malice to the Gods.

Her song is lost in the rattle revolving roulette wheels and the perpetual thunder from the Mah Jong room. The Triads look very happy. Devlin tries to push his luck. He suggests that now the Pakis are dealt with and Glasgow is theirs, why don't they expand? Edinburgh, Dundee, Aberdeen? Tai Lo answers with a downwards sweeping, softly-softly hand.

—Not to move too hurry.

—Suggestion, that's all, says Devlin.

Tai Lo understands Devlin's ambition.

—Other cities can wait. We need trust each other first.

Devlin's thumbs up to that, then he's off to the toilet. Tai Lo looks over to where Ming Fung stands with an arm over Bonzo's shoulder. She's laughing.

Tai Lo gets I Lo's attention and nods for him to follow Devlin into the toilet. Take two Forty-Nines with him. Tai Lo follows seconds later with Hung Kwan and Heung Chu. Sholtz and Sam are on a Triad-induced winning spree at the roulette and Ming

Fung is doing her job. A job Tai Lo sees she likes too much.
Devlin finishes his piss. I Lo's hand squeezes Delvin's side.
Hard.

—Argh! For fuck sake, what d'ye think you're doin?
He breaks free from I Lo's Kung Fu grip.
—Get your fuckin hands off me, ya mincing poof!
—Scaa! demands I Lo.
—What?
—Scaa!
The two Forty-Nines move in. Devlin pulls a fast blade and
has the point at I Lo's throat before anyone can act.
—I'll scar you, ya slanty eyed sewer rat. Call off your dogs.
He pushes enough to draw blood. I Lo signals the Forty-
Nines down. Tai Lo and his entourage arrive. No Bonzo. No
Sam. No Sholtz. I Lo feels the cold sting of the blade.
Tai Lo's calm voice seems out of place in the high voltage
situation.
—We have to see scaa. Keep all happy faces. Trust.
—You think I've been kidding about my operation? Devlin
asks,—Ye don't trust me?
—We trust, but see scaa!
—Get to fuck!
Heung Chu tries with Devlin.
—It would bring serenity.
—Get Bruce Lee back then.
I Lo's pulled away. Devlin lowers the knife, undoes his shirt
and shows them the bloody bandage.
—There! Satisfied?
But I Lo isn't satisfied.
—Underneath, he says, —Underneath bandage.
Devlin directs his questions at Tai Lo.
—Happy? Are you happy?
—Yes. I happy, says Tai Lo.
I Lo kicks the bin in frustration. When it's stopped rolling
Devlin has his gun levelled at Tai Lo.
—I want *you* to teach *them* some respect!

Tai Lo bounces and side kicks I Lo into a cubicle. As I Lo lies humiliated Tai Lo bows at Devlin. Devlin bows back. Bonzo, Sam and Sholtz crash into the toilet with their guns out.

—It's cool. Put them away, says Devlin, —Everything's sorted.

正直
integrity

If you must play, decide the rules, the stakes, and the quitting time.

NEXT NIGHT IN Nicole's room, the window wide open, her gang pass joints and take photos of each other on their mobiles, impersonating their teachers.

—Right. That is half an hour. You will stay here until this infernal giggling has stopped and one of you recites the required passage, says Augustus, —Lucy! Stand up.

Lucy stands up.

—Recite, bitch!

—Filthy hags!

They all burst out laughing.

—Anyone care for an E?

Everybody does. She writes her customers' names in her diary. Gives them an E each. Two hours later the party is still swinging. They're all out of their heads. Augustus tries to kiss Nicole but she pushes him back.

—I think the boys should do a Full Monty for the girls, says Nicole.

—And I think the girls should strip for the boys, says Augustus.

In a corridor not far off, Gorman is on the prowl.

In Nicole's room a row of girls in their knickers and bras shout to a row of designer boxer shorts.

—Off! Off! Off! Off!

Lucy notices Augustus is getting a hard-on.

—Look, Augustus is bulging!

The girls laugh.

—Off! Off! Off! Off!

Gorman crashes into the room. Three other teachers stand behind him. Nicole swallows the last of the dope. But there's no escape. Augustus has a joint in his hand. It's confiscated and the culprits are led away. In the mayhem Nicole notices the way Gorman looks at her. They're ordered to dress. Escorted to their rooms. Their rooms searched. Nothing is found.

Later, Nicole calls Gerry. Tells him they had a raid. Her parents are being informed. He wants to know if they searched her room.

—They did but there was nothing there to find.

—They found nothing?

—Just the joint Augustus had. What will I do, Gerry?

—Lie, lie and lie again, he says. Blame that Augustus guy.

Gerry says he has to go.

In the middle of the night Gorman gets a call on his private line.

—Who is this?

—Search behind the radiator if you want to find drugs.

—What radiator?

—The one in Nicole Devlin's room.

—Hello? Hello?

Nicole wakes when he comes in.

—Stay where you are, he says.

She sits up in bed. Why is he squeezing his hand down behind the radiator? He finds the ounce of dope.

—What's this?

—Where did that come from? says Nicole.

—Smells like marijuana.

—That's not mine.

—It's in your room.

—Someone must've put that there. Augustus… it must be his.

She's out of bed. Gorman stares at her. She drops her pyjama top off.

—I'll let you do anything. You can do anything you want. Don't tell my parents.

There's a moment before he speaks.

—Put your shirt back on.

But she doesn't. To distract himself he searches the room again. The first drawer he opens is her lingerie drawer.

—Do you like my knickers, sir?

She locks the door.

—I won't have anyone breaking the law in my school, he says.

But she's topless, next to him. Their breath mingles.

—Anything you want, she says.

Gorman buries his face in her breasts.

—Do you like them sir?

—Yes.

She places a nipple in his mouth. He's sucking on it. She springs back, covering herself.

—Now who's broken the law, sir?

—Give me the phone.

—HELP!

—Shht. Give me the phone.

She clamps it between her legs.

—I'll scream rape!

He sits on the edge of the bed, defeated.

—I'll give you the phone once we've come to an arrangement, she promises.

Next morning Gorman plucks Augustus from a line of pupils filing into a classroom.

—You! You, boy! Come here!

Gorman holds the lump of dope. Nicole cries and blabbers. Devlin and Wendy listen intently.

—You're a brave girl, says Gorman.

—He's been bringing drugs in for months. He asked me to help sell them. Threatened me.

Devlin can't get his finger through the handle of the china cup.

—If I had my way it would be the death sentence for drug dealers, says Gorman, —We need a name, Nicole.

Nicole confesses on cue.

—Augustus.

—Augustus Macmillan? says a suitably surprised Gorman.

Nicole nods. Wendy holds her. Gorman pats her on the back. In the midst of all this, Nicole slides the mobile phone onto his desk. He sweeps it into his drawer.

—Where are the toilets? asks Devlin.

—End of the corridor.

He leaves Wendy to work something out. Gorman is inclined to be lenient. To make the news public and tarnish the school's reputation would do no one any good. He deletes the images. Devlin picks up a pair of pliers lying on a window-ledge. Might come in handy. He finds Augustus's room, crashes in and grabs him.

—Who's giving you the gear?

—Gear?

Devlin punches him.

—Who?

—I can't tell you.

—They're mighty posh gnashers you've got there, son…

Devlin takes out the pliers, grabs Augustus by the face and forces open his jaw.

—How come posh people have always got nice teeth? We were born with our teeth falling out.

He grips a shiny white tooth and twists.

—A name!

Augustus shakes his head.

—Who?

Augustus shakes his head.

Devlin snaps the tooth off. Shoves a pillow into Augustus's face to muffle any noise.

—Who?

—I'll tell, Augustus splutters, spitting blood.

Devlin removes the pliers.

—Nicole.

Devlin clicks the pliers twice in front of Augustus's face.

—Nicole? My Nicole?

—Yes, sir. Nicole.

Devlin's tortured enough people to know this boy's telling the truth.

—You fell and broke your tooth on a rock.

—I broke it on a rock.

When Devlin gets back to Gorman's office, everything's been

sorted out. Wendy's happy. In the car park, he studies Nicole's face as they watch Augustus being driven away from the school. Expelled. Wendy tells Nicole how lucky she is to still be there. She'd better keep a close eye on her behaviour from now on. Gorman has promised to keep the drugs a secret. All they have to do is never, ever mention it again. Nicole agrees. Kisses her parents goodbye. Devlin doesn't speak all the way home.

That night he goes to Cooney.

—How's the scar?

—Killing me.

He tells Cooney about the Triads asking to see it. Cooney gets the kettle on. Lets him ramble on. Devlin thinks Garrett might be his cousin. The one he has nightmares about. The one who tries to drown him in his dreams. His Aunt Theresa's son, Gerald. He's not seen him since they were kids. Last night he had the usual dream where Gerald tries to drown him. But then it was Garrett. Then Gerald. Then he was both of them at the same time. Cooney sits the tea down.

—What happened to this cousin? What's his name... Gerald?

—Dunno. It's that long ago, I can't remember. There's big bit missing out my memory.

—Who's likely to know?

—Can't think.

—What about your da?

—Suppose he's as likely to know as anybody.

—Let's go see him then. Then you can at least eliminate your cousin.

Devlin parks at Harry Ramsden's and they walk together over to The Grand Ole Oprey. On top of the building at the cross, there's an angel watching over them. Cooney nudges Devlin and they look up.

—I knew ye had a guardian angel.

As they approach the Oprey, Devlin stops and stares into the dark alley at the side.

—What is it? asks Cooney.

—There's something in there.

Devlin takes out his gun.

—Aw fuck, put that away, says Cooney.

Devlin holds the gun close to his body and makes his way to the end of the blind alley. Pushes his left hand into the shadows. It's cold.

—Christie, shouts Cooney, —come on!

Once Devlin and Cooney's silhouettes have gone, Garrett springs up from the dark corner. Makes his way over the wall. Squirms in through a window so small you'd think it impossible. Sydney Devine's singing in the main auditorium.

Cooney gives Devlin a what-the-fuck've-ye-brung-me-in-here-for? look. Cowboys, Indians, Whores and Cowgirls dance a crazy line dance, thumping their feet in unison. There's a bowl of fruit on each table.

The band has five resident musicians, but any competent musician can join in. A fiddler climbs up and works into the song, scratching like the Devil. The energy lifts. Bodies turn and twist and spin, cigarettes tracing red arcs in the dancer's hands. Ma Kettle watches Devlin and Cooney come in, eejits in their civvy gear among all these Wild West heroes.

—Three pounds each, please.

—What?

—Six quid. It's three each to get in.

Cooney pays Ma Kettle. But she's concentrating on Devlin. His face is white.

—What's up son? Seen a ghost?

—Looking for my da.

—So's half Glasgow, on account of the Child Support Agency, says Ma Kettle.

—Good crack, says Cooney.

He repeats the line to memorise it.

—Dan Devlin? asks Devlin.

Ma Kettle doesn't know him. Devlin closes his eye.

—Wee guy with one eye.

—Ah! You mean Dead-eye Dan! He's up there!

—Cheers.

Devlin walks away. Ma Kettle reaches out of her booth and pulls him back.

—D'yees not want to buy a Stetson? Yees would look great.

—Ye mad? We'd look like a pair of pricks, says Devlin.

He changes his mind when Cooney tugs him to look round the hall. They are the only two without hats.

—One each, says Cooney, —He's paying.

The fiddler digs his bow into the strings. He's wearing a Stetson too, and if Devlin could see under the rim he'd see Garrett. Garrett's eyes follow them through the dancers and watch Devlin putting his hand on his da's shoulder.

—What's the crack, Jack? he says.

Dan spins and draws his gun. When he sees who it is, he flips it back in its holster.

—Christie! I thought ye were Railroad Jack there. What d'ye want?

—Just popped in.

—Nobody just pops in here.

—He wants to ask you a question, says Cooney.

—Who's he?

—Never mind, says Devlin, —Remember Theresa's laddie, Gerald?

Dan looks in Devlin's eyes. Cooney feels reverberations.

—What happened to him after she died? Devlin asks.

—In the *fire* ye mean? Dan barks.

Cooney sees below this ice is a deep sea, and at the bottom a volcano ready to blow.

Dan won't talk. The music's stopped. Sydney's asking the band what to play next. Cowboys and Whores wait on the dance floor hoping it'll be something to keep them riding the happy waves.

Garrett plays a few notes.

♪♪ Da daa da da da.

They all recognise the tune.

♪♪ Da daa da da da.

The audience cheers.

♪♪ Da daa da da da.

Sydney coughs into the microphone. One, two, three, and he starts singing When You and I Were Young, Maggie.

Dan's eyes fill with tears.

—Ye want a drink, Da? Devlin asks.

Dan nods aye, his lips tight pressing his emotions back. On the way to the bar Cooney suggests they get Dan drunk. See if that'll bleed anything out of him.

They do.

They don't.

On the way home all Dan can talk about is what a great woman Theresa was.

—She shouldn't've died. No she shouldn't've. No fuckin need for it. Where was God that day? Eh? Don't give me your God patter. A daft fire. A stupid fuckin fire!

They help Dan to his close.

—Naw, naw, I'm alright, leave me go.

He squirms free, slaps the close door with his back. Lights the cigarette that was behind his ear.

—Right, what d'ye want to know? he says right out of the blue.

Devlin steps in.

—Gerald. Theresa's laddie…

—I know who's fuckin laddie he is!

The threat of violence swings like a pendulum.

—Do you know what became of him? asks Cooney.

Dan likes his Irish lilt.

—Last I heard he was in Bar-L.

—When? When was that? asks Devlin.

—Fifteen year ago. Hic!

Fifteen years ago! How are they going to trace him with that? Cooney agrees to contact the jails. He's got a lot of contacts in the jails doing good work.

—Are yees goanni tell me what it's all about?

—It's nothin, says Devlin.

—Nothin? Hic!

—Call it nostalgia.

Dan snorts. Talks to himself incoherently for a few seconds and goes into the close.

Devlin and Cooney walk to the car.

A somewhat sobered up Dan stands behind the close door. Why is Christie asking about Gerald after all these years? Why is he pretending he doesn't know? Or has he forgot?

Just as Devlin reaches to open the car door he's thumped by an almighty blow. I Lo's side-kicked him into the door panel. At the same time, a Forty-Nine pistol-whips Cooney to the ground and points the gun at Devlin.

—Scaa! demands I Lo.

—Fuck off!

The Forty-Nine presses the gun to Devlin's temple.

—No move, says I Lo.

He opens the buttons on Devlin's jacket and flings it back.

—I'll do you for this ya wee cunt, says Devlin.

I Lo opens Devlin's shirt and is about to rip the bandage off when a gun is placed to his head.

—Reach for the sky, hombre, says Dan.

I Lo's hands creep skywards.

—Alright, Da! says Devlin.

Dan has the six-shooter at I Lo's head. The Forty-Nine has the pistol at Devlin's. It's a stand-off. Devlin's first to speak.

—Tell him to drop the gun.

—You no gun first, I Lo says to Dan.

—Drop fuck-all gun, Da, says Devlin, —Shoot him.

Dan pulls the hammer back.

I Lo shouts to the Forty-Nine —*If he shoots me you shoot him.*

Cooney is standing up, still groggy. He sees the guns.

—What's the... Whoaa!

Dan slips him a weapon.

—Keep him still, says Dan.

Cooney presses the tip of his weapon into I Lo's back. Dan swings his gun on the Forty-Nine. Now it's two for one. As I Lo and the Forty-Nine compute the situation, Devlin ducks, grabbing the Forty-Nine's gun

BANG

Devlin punches I Lo in the face. I Lo staggers back. Sees Cooney's gun is actually a banana!

—Aye, a fuckin banana, ya eejit, laughs Cooney.

I Lo smiles and shakes his head.

Garrett, hiding in a close, smiles too.

—Come on! Devlin challenges I Lo to fight.

I Lo corkscrews from the ground with a whipping motion and launches a barrage of kicks and punches. Devlin staggers sideways protecting his head with his arms and takes a pounding for about a minute. Cooney's going to move in but Dan stops him. If there's one thing he's passed onto his son, it's this: You never give in. I Lo steps back, panting.

—Is that it? Is that all you've got, ya slanty-eyed wee runt?

I Lo goes at him again, slower this time. Devlin grabs a punch with his big, meaty hand and pulls I Lo close. Bear-hugs the breath out of him. Props him against the Shogun and lays in. Brutal hooks to the head and the body. I Lo sinks to the ground.

—Shove him in the motor, says Devlin.

As they lift him into the car, Cooney pulls Dan.

—What's your game, throwing me a banana?

Dan laughs. Cooney shakes his head. Devlin shoves the Forty-Nine face down on the floor.

Tai Lo is questioning Ming Fung about Bonzo. She admits she likes him. A lot. Tai Lo's not worried that he's white. But what if the partnership goes wrong? She hopes it won't. But what will she do, come the day they move to take over

Devlin's empire? Does she think Bonzo will shift sides?

She shrugs. Maybe that time won't come.

—*Daughter, daughter. We always take over. Triads only can work with Triads. Working with Devlin is only a means to an end. You should finish the relationship.*

—*I can't, Father. I ask for your blessing.*

Tai Lo knows how difficult it is for her to trust men. He owes her a chance at happiness. He agrees to sanction the relationship so long as things stay as they are. But he warns her there will come a time when Bonzo will have to choose between her and Devlin.

Five minutes after Ming Fung leaves, the casino doors burst open. I Lo crumples onto the floor at Tai Lo's feet, his face a bloody mess. The Forty-Nine is flung down beside him.

—Here's your man, says Devlin.

The Silver Seas grinds to a halt. Watching.

—What going on? asks Tai Lo.

—We're partners or we're enemies! says Devlin.

—What you mean?

Devlin asks what he's doing ordering I Lo to find out if he has an appendix scar.

—I order nothing.

Devlin looks at I Lo for confirmation. I Lo drops his head.

—*Is this true?* Heung Chu asks.

—*Yes. I acted alone.*

Devlin turns to Dan and Cooney.

—Lower your guns.

He tells Tai Lo what he wants.

—Allow any these cunts near me again, I'll kill them.

—Cunts. What ees cunts?

Devlin grabs his own crotch by way of explanation.

—Fannies, he says, —fuckin fannies.

—I apologise, says Tai Lo, bowing lower than the Silver Seas has ever seen. In return Devlin lifts his shirt and removes the bandage.

—Scarred for life – no compensation!

I Lo is in big trouble.

Tai Lo clicks his fingers three times and leads them into a room off the Mah Jong hall. Secured to the middle of the floor is the trunk of a beech tree cut at chest level. Seven cleavers hang on the wall.

Two Forty-Nines hold I Lo's hand on the chopping block. He doesn't resist. Tai Lo selects a cleaver and hands it to Devlin.

—You choppy.

—Whoaa! Fuckin mental man! Dan whispers to Cooney.

But Cooney's seen violence like this before. Ritualistic IRA tortures. Taken part in them.

Devlin brings the cleaver sweetly down to thump through flesh and bone. I Lo's pinkie rolls away from his hand. Blood pumps onto the wood. He doesn't move his hand. Stares in Devlin's eyes.

He turns towards Tai Lo, holding his dripping hand in the air.

—*I am here to serve and obey, he affirms. —You are my master.*

I Lo bows. Tai Lo bows back.

Devlin, Cooney and Dan spill out onto the cold Glasgow street.

變化
changes

If you wish to know the mind of a woman listen to her words.

WENDY IS AT her desk. The class is watching *Kes*. Rough third-years love *Kes*. The tornado that started spinning when Devlin took that first drink has sucked in every part of her life. Wendy feels as if the floor's cracking beneath her feet. Her break-down has started.

Panic. Her eyes dart about the classroom.

She has to go.

She has to go.

She has to go

The kids barely notice her leave. In the corridor she leans on the wall, gasping for breath. The fire door's slightly open.

She has to go.

She has to go.

She has to go

—Where are you going?

Miss Newell.

Wendy can only stare at the vertical strip of freedom.

—There's a family crisis.

—What sort of crisis?

—I can't discuss it.

They stand locked in mutual antagonism.

—Alright, you can go… if you can find someone to cover for you.

Wendy knows that's impossible and, feeling defeated, returns to her class.

When she gets home after school, she's overwhelmed by the feeling that there's no meaning in anything any more. What she's tried to nurture, Christie's killing off. She stands looking into space. In total despair. After what might have been a minute or an hour, she becomes aware of a pin-point of light moving out, moving away from her.

She has to do something.

She has to do something.

She has to do something
She has to take action.
She's dying spiritually.
She decides that, whatever Christie does, she has to contact someone who can help.

—Is this your first meeting?
Wendy nods yes and bursts out crying. Nobody else takes any notice. The meeting's listening to the top table. The woman gets Wendy a cup of tea.
—Just listen with an open mind. That's all we're asked to do.
Someone's describing how her man had her pinned to the fireplace with a knife at her throat.
—And if I thought *he* was sick, what about me, later that night, when he was sleeping? I laid into him with a Buckfast bottle and put him in a coma for three months. And I didn't drink at all. That's how sick living with an alky makes ye. I thought once Jake stopped drinking, everything would be alright, but his behaviour was still bizarre and so was mine. He was three years sober before I realised I needed help an all. Coming to Al-Anon's the best move I've ever made. Jake and me's brilliant now.
Punters share one by one. Wendy listens with horror.
After the meeting's over, the woman who talked to her when she first came in introduces herself. Alyth's a surgeon in the Glasgow Southern General. She says there is a way to be free from Devlin's alcoholic behaviour.
—Have you ever tried to control a man like that?
Alyth laughs.
—That's your illness, trying to control him. His alcoholism's made you ill.
—Will you be my sponsor? Wendy blurts out. She likes the fact Alyth's a professional.
—I'm afraid not. But a good friend of mine might be just the person. Her name's Jet Set Jane.

Wendy agrees. Alyth makes a phone call. Gets a result.
—Jet Set's willing to meet you. Saturday afternoon alright?
Wendy can't wait.

Devlin's spent the day working with the Triads, showing them
how the smack gets to the dealers, making changes in route
every delivery. His instinct detects something brewing. It might
only be paranoia.

He noticed something different about Wendy. He's suspicious at her niceness, all smiles and touchy feely.
—Are you on Prozac or something?
—No. But I went to Al-Anon.
—The Sisters of Perpetual Revenge! He starts speaking in a
take-off of a woman's voice. —My name's Mary and I'm
powerless over alcohol and powerless over my Tam. He'd come
in pished and boot me right on the head. Then he'd drag me
in the scullery and put me through the mincer and leave me in
wee ASDA bags all over the living-room. I'm not going to take
that treatment anymore. I'm going to be strong. Next time he
puts me though the mincer there's no way I'm letting him
stuff me in they ASDA bags.

Instead of making Wendy angry, he's made her laugh.
There's a second when they remember what they used be like.
—Oh that's funny, Christie. That's just like the woman who
was speaking.
—Rest my fuckin case.
—I've got a sponsor.
—A sponsor? I was at AA a year before I even thought
about a sponsor, ya fuckin doughball.

Wendy composes herself so that no matter how hard he
tries, he can't provoke a reaction. Eventually he goes to his
den. Wendy is cocooned in hope.
—I will not be affected by other people's moods, she
repeats to herself under her breath.

At the appointed time, Wendy's on the top floor of Princes

Square, positioned where she can see everyone coming up the escalator.

What will Jet Set Jane look like? She's late.

Wendy notices a *Big Issue* seller. Takes in the busted Reebok trainers, the man's kilt, the pink jumper, the roll-up hanging from the lips, the face criss-crossed with broken veins. What a state! Wendy's surprised they let her in the place. The beautiful ones walk around this blemish in their perfect, botoxed world.

Wendy's been staring. The *Big Issue* seller starts to come towards her.

—Sorry, I don't buy that, says Wendy. —Can you go away now, please. I'm waiting for someone.

—Are you Wendy?

—Pardon?

—Is your name Wendy?

—Yes! And you are?

—Jet Set Jane. Pleased to meet you.

Jet Set shakes Wendy's astonished hand.

—I expected someone…

—What, fatter? Ach! I've been on a diet. Come on, let's get out of here. Gives me the fuckin creeps.

Wendy follows her down the escalators and out into Buchanan Street. Jane's already in full flood, describing how her man drove her mad.

—Kept me in the house for ten years, so he did. Only let me out to get the messages. He'd go with me. Once I was safely home he'd go drinking. Never knew when he was going to be back. If I wasn't in, he'd batter me black and blue when he found me. I used to stand at the sink, so I did, and watch the aeroplanes coming in over the Sleeping Giant and wonder what it was like to be going somewhere. Anywhere. To be jet set. I swore that before I died I'd be up in one of them things. High above Glasgow, leaving that bastard behind.

—What was the turning point? Wendy's interested, in spite of herself.

—A twelve-inch steak knife.

—What?

—I was at the sink and in he came. Punched me on the back of the head. Grabbed my hair and span me round. Next thing he was on the floor with the knife through his heart. D'you know what his last words were? —I'll get ye for this, ya ugly bastard. And he died.

Jet Set sighs.

—Got ten years, done six. Started Al-Anon in jail. Now I've been twenty years on the programme.

By now they're heading across St Enoch's Square towards the city morgue. Alongside old railway arches there's a raggle-taggle collection of traders, selling anything from odd rolls of wallpaper to first generation computers. Here in Paddy's Market, if you can imagine it you can buy it. And if you can't imagine it, you can still buy it. In the lane the traders are the poorest of the poor, their wares strewn on dirty blankets. Inside the thirteen curving railway arches are two rows of stalls, running up the middle of each arc back-to-back, and cafés the likes of which haven't been seen since the fall of Communism.

Jane's stopping to chat to everyone. They all know she's an Al-Anon punter. When she introduces Wendy as a New Pal they say things like, —Never you bother your arse, hen, you're in good hands now, so ye are.

Wendy's mortified.

Jet Set disappears into one of the arches.

The smell has Wendy gagging. This is where Jet Set has stall selling Our Lady Statues, Bibles, Crucifixes, Serenity Prayers, Footprints, Desiderata.

Clasping a tin mug of Jet Set special tea, Wendy decides she'll trust the situation, bizarre as it seems, and see where it goes. Jet Set has been through uncannily similar experiences and emotions.

Wendy explains how she's finding it harder to cope with Devlin since he lifted that first drink a few weeks ago. He might be losing his mind. Imagining things. Even slashed himself and swore he'd had an operation. Jet Set gives some simple advice. Wendy has to stop trying to change things she has no power over. Has to do things for herself. If she's not right nothing's right. Get a good foundation of self. Then tackle the world. Jane hands Wendy a wee Serenity Prayer card. As Wendy reads it, Jet Set recites.

—God, grant me the serenity to accept the things I cannot change, courage to change the things I can, and the wisdom to know the difference.

An old Bay City Rollers tramp starts singing *I Only Wanna Be With You*. Jane tells Wendy she's powerless over everything except herself.

—Ye might think it's the philosophy of a simpleton, but to put that prayer into action ye need the personality of a saint.

Wendy's read some AA stuff and thought they were a bit religious.

—Just take the word God out. The Steps aren't the only path to sanity, but they've worked for millions of people. First you have to admit that you're powerless over alcohol and that your life has become unmanageable.

Wendy sees the logic. She's powerless over Devlin, so she's powerless over alcohol. She's got no problem admitting that her life's unmanageable. It's unbearable, in fact.

Step two's a bit more difficult for her.

—Came to believe that a Power greater than ourselves could restore us to sanity, recites Jet Set.

—That's where it starts to sound like Bible thumping. says Wendy.

—You've got rosary beads there.

—Where?

—I saw them in your bag. D'you go to chapel?

—Yes, but...

—Well, you're halfway there.

Wendy'd never thought of any practical use for God before.

—Did you ever get away on a plane?

—No. I was too scared. Booked a ticket and couldn't get on.

Their laughter echoes round the caverns of Paddy's Market.

Devlin's been summonsed to the casino. He knows he's on top but takes Bonzo and Sholtz tooled up, just in case. He's still uneasy.

Tai Lo indicates to sit. When they're settled, in come six Forty-Nines. Each place two deals of smack on the table. Tai Lo chucks a bag over to Devlin.

—How much cost this, you think?

Bonzo and Sholtz shrug.

—Dunno. Is it ten we're charging? says Devlin.

—Five, says Tai Lo.

—When did we agree to sell for five?

—We never agree, says I Lo.

Devlin can't help but notice blood seeping through the bandage on I Lo's finger.

Tai Lo asks, —Do you know where it come from?

—Nope. Haven't got a clue.

—We thinking you took care of every dealer in Glasgow.

—And me thinking you took care of the ethnics!

—What you suggest, Mister Devlin?

Devlin's knows this just has to be Garrett.

—Don't worry. Whoever it is, he's as good as dead.

Tai Lo thinks Devlin might be selling his own smack as well as the China White. Devlin explains the economics. Where would he benefit from selling substandard smack for cheaper, in a city where he can get twice the price for it? Tai Lo suggests maybe he's keeping his old supplies open in case he wants to renege on their deal. Devlin laughs. He's in it for the money. Where can he make so much in such a short space of time with a guaranteed supply of top quality gear? He promises he'll find out where this stuff's coming from and who's selling it.

—Somebody might've got out the jail and not knew about

our changes. Or somebody from another city. It might blow over once they hear the word.

Devlin realises what was happening yesterday. The Forty-Nines were out buying bags of smack from junkie dealers.

—Who did they buy it off? he asks.

—Many junkie, says Tai Lo, —They not know where it come from. Mobile phone ring. Offer to sell. They accept. Sometimes bag in a tree. Sometimes old car. Sometimes cigarette packet on ground.

—We torture them, says I Lo, smiling.

Where were they dealing?

There's a big Triad pause. The answer goes through Devlin like a cleaver.

—Chinatown!

—Right, I'll sort it out.

Devlin rises, his head swimming.

—Do you need any help?

—No. Thanks but.

To accept help would be to admit he's not in control of Glasgow. That could turn the Triads on him. Thin, thin ice. When they leave, Devlin orders his men to find out who the fuck is selling this gear and wipe them out. But inside he knows who it is. Garrett.

It's dark at seven on Saturday morning. The streets are dusted with frost. A spectral Glasgow watches a bus pull into Buchanan Street Bus Station. Sister Mary-Bridget gets off and waits for the driver to get her bag. Breathes in Glasgow.

—Here's your bag, sister. Hey, what's the Pope's hobby?

—I don't know. What is the Pope's hobby?

—He's none.

She smiles politely and rumbles her bag over the concourse to the automatic doors. Compared to the Glasgow she left, this is the Brave New World. As she tries to fix her bearings, she sees the start of Sauchiehall Street. The city grid clicks into place. As she heads for Hill Street convent, she recites the

Desiderata to herself.

—Go placidly amidst the noise and haste and remember what peace there may be in silence...

Her breath steams into the cold dawn.

Less than a mile away, Marie jolts up, sweating, in bed. Her breathing is quick. A presence. There's a presence. Yellow street light filters through the curtains. She knows there's something there. She's scared, but when she does turn, her fear is washed away. In the corner is a woman in blue, a heavenly light emanating from her centre. Is it Our Blessed Lady? The woman hovers above the floor gaze fixed on Marie. She's filled with calm when the Lady smiles. Gets out of bed and walks to the vision. The Lady reaches her arms out. Marie puts hers out. But when she closes her arms round the vision it vanishes. The diesel engine of a bus drills up from Saracen Street. It's morning. But this morning is different. Marie is happy. She makes her way into David's room. He's curled up on the bed with his clothes on. His works beside him. She shakes him.

—David. David, wake up!

He comes to, but hardly moves. Notes the beaming smile on her face.

—What the fuck's up with you?

—It's Sister Mary-Bridget, shouts Marie, —She's in Glasgow!

—I'm not going, he says.

Dan watches Marie leave her close. Her step is unusually confident. She stops twenty feet down the street and waits. David opens the window and leans out.

—Maw, did you plank my stash?

Marie pulls out two wee bags of smack and waves them.

—What ye plying at? Get back up here with them right now!

Marie walks away.

—Where the fuck're ye going, ya maniac?

She holds the bags out to the side and behind her. Clicks

three times like she's clicking to a dog.

—Come on. You can be my wee donkey for the day!

She walks on, laughing. In seconds he's out the close, giving Dan the fingers as he runs past.

—Maw! Maw! Stop!

By the time they get to Chinatown she's got him under control with the promise of a bag if he behaves himself. David's as strung out as he's been in a long time. The early rise and the weird happy maw and walking into town. He stops outside a Chinese poultry shop. Lights a fag and looks in the window at the hanging chickens, ducks, pheasants and a massive upside-down turkey.

—Come on, hurry up, says Marie.

—I'm having a fag.

—Smoke and walk!

David exhales against the glass. Through the clearing smoke – BING! The turkey's eyes open. David chokes. Down the street Marie waits with folded arms. She wants to pull the bags of smack out, but not here. David looks at the turkey's eyes. Are they moving? A Chinaman leans in, takes the turkey from its hook. The wings give a little flap and the neck curls in desperation. Even after all he's seen in his life, this horrifies David.

He takes it out on Marie.

—Fuck off, Maw. I don't want to meet some daft nun.

—I don't care. You're coming, and that's that. She's came here special for you.

—Oooh Sister Mary-Bridget, can I kiss your frock, Sister Mary-Bridget!

In the gloom beyond the window display, the turkey's laid out on a marble slab.

—David, stop it, please!

—Gimmi my other bag. I'm fuckin strung out here, Maw!

—You'll get it when we get there.

Slam! The turkey's chopped. Blood seeps onto the white marble.

—I'm not moving.

—Fine, says Marie.

She walks away. David looks in the window again. The turkey is hung back up, blood dripping from its neck. He catches a movement out the side of his eye and turns, following the arc of the turkey head as it's flung into the street. It bounces like rubber. Is its mouth moving? The beak? Opening and shutting? It is. It's fuckin moving! Wider it gets. Wider. David wants to run but he's rooted. Wants to look away but he's transfixed. Closes his eyes.

He opens his eyes. The turkey head's singing to him. A small fog of breath's coming from its beak.

David looks about. Chinatown goes about its morning business. David is in panic. He inches away with his back to the window. The eye blinks. A slither of blue skin slides down the eyeball and up again. David runs. Behind the rumble of his footsteps the turkey taunts him.

♪♪ So, so you think you can tell heaven from hell?

Garrett watches David zig-zag through Chinatown and catch up with Marie.

Marie knocks on the convent door.

—I'm not going in there. Gimmi the bags – I'm Joe the Toff.

He's thinking about wrestling the smack from Marie when a nun opens the door. Marie's bursting with excitement.

—I'm here to see Sister Mary-Bridget.

—Come in, says the nun.

They go in. The door closes. Garrett crosses and stops beside the convent door. A few flakes of snow have begun to fall. He reaches out and lets one melt on his hand.

Marie and David are in a large room with small high windows. Marie sits on the edge of a huge leather couch, her feet together and her hands tight between her legs. David paces, his mind half on smack, half on what's to steal. The door opens. Sister Mary-Bridget comes in. Marie gets up. Opens her arms. She wants. She's a wee girl. Out comes

THE WORD

—MUM!

Mary-Bridget holds her daughter. Tight. Marie caves. Sobs uncontrollably. A tear scratches down David's cheek. A tear filled with the ache for smack. Filled with gimmi, gimmi, gimmi.

—I think I'm gonni faint, says Marie, —I need to sit down.

Mary-Bridget guides her to the couch.

—Sit down here. You'll be fine, you'll be fine.

Marie touches her mother's face.

—I can't believe I'm touching ye. I never thought we'd be this close again.

Mary-Bridget nods over at David.

—How is he?

—He's… he's…

David interrupts.

—A junkie, Sister Mary-Bridget. Junkie aka scum. Thought I'd tell her and save ye the embarrassment, Maw.

The two women are so absorbed in each other they don't notice him pick up Marie's bag.

—I got your letter, says Marie, —Couldn't believe it that they were letting ye come. What did ye tell them?

—That I had a vision. That I had to come to Glasgow.

Marie had a vision herself this morning. That's how she knew her mother was back. She only just arrived.

—Did you make my vision happen, Mum?

—No, the Manager probably.

—Manager?

Mary-Bridget points to a golden crucifix.

—Works in mysterious ways.

David likes the golden crucifix. As he figures how get it off the wall Mary-Bridget tells Marie she's ready to bring David into the convent. They'll do everything in their power to clean him up.

—Thanks, Mum. Thanks. This means everything to me.

Mary-Bridget squeezes her hand and looks into her eyes so fiercely Marie's scared.

—Has anything happened strange recently, Marie?

—Just the usual. Can't think of anything special.

—I'm talking about big changes.

Marie can't think of anything. Except Christie went back on the drink after a year off it.

—Is Christopher drinking?

—But he stopped again.

—That's good. He's in my prayers. As are you all.

Mary-Bridget blesses Marie. Prays over her. David can't take any more.

—Pray I can get a wee bag of smack Sister Mary-Bridget, he says, —I'm rattling here.

—I'm sure we can do something for you David.

Mary-Bridget raises an eyebrow at Marie. Marie takes the smack and David's works from inside her pullover. Hands it to him.

—The toilet's through that door there, says Sister Mary-Bridget.

—Top of the Pops, Sister Mary-Bridget.

Once he's gone Mary-Bridget is serious again.

—How's your dad?

Marie ignores her.

—Danny, is he alright? You never write about that bastard.

—I don't want to talk about him!

—But is he alright?

Marie relents.

—He's alright. If anything had happened to him I'd've wrote to tell you... Mum.

In the toilet, a tear of blood runs down David's arm. He plunges the needle home and flops back onto the cistern. His feet stretch out and clunk against the door. His elbow accidentally flushes the toilet. He loses himself in the sound of the water.

He's in the wooden womb of the convent toilet floating on opiates. A piece of tin foil rocks on its own arc on the floor. The lighter lies beside it. The needle hangs from his arm. He knows he has to remove it. And he will when the rush goes. But that beautiful needle. Oh that gorgeous needle, tugging at his skin. The muffled voices of his mother and his grandmother. Here it is! A little piece of heaven. Oh, that it could last forever, a timeless hit of comfort and painless joy.

Bliss.

He comes out half an hour later.

—Hello, says Marie.

—How are you? says Mary-Bridget.

They're drinking tea. There's cakes on fancy china plates.

—Do you want one?

—No. I want my other bag of smack!

—You'll get it when you've had a shower and you're in your room, says Marie, —Half tonight, half in the morning.

—Let me see the bag, says Mary-Bridget.

She looks in the bag like she's trying to ascertain how good the gear is. But she's making her way towards the toilet. She's in and flushed it away before David realises. Out she comes. Looks him in the eye.

—We're getting you clean. The more you give us the more we can give you. There's methadone. You'll get that when I say.

He falls into the chair.

—Promise me you'll try.

David says nothing.

—That's all we ask.

Mary-Bridget places a hand on his shoulder.

—You need to make a big space in your life for God.

—Why the fuck would I want to do that?

—Because God has made a big space for you.

David weeps. If it's the hand on the shoulder, or the words, or even God, he can't tell.

—Promise me, for your mother, just try, that's all!

David promises by shaking his head. He has to go to the

toilet again. He trudges off, the torn bottoms of his jeans sliding over the floor.

David's outside the pawnshop. He takes the gold crucifix from his jacket and goes in. David feels he's being watched. He turns. It's only a man looking in at the watches.

Only a man. Only Garrett.

David comes out a hundred pounds richer. Looks up and down the street for junkies. A shark can smell one drop of blood in ten miles of sea, like people who've been abused as children can spot each other on a crowded street. David blinks. There's a junkie. By his body language David surmises he's selling smack to keep his own habit going. David crosses over.

—Anything happening, mate?

Garrett is the nervous junkie.

—No. I've just got my personal.

—Ye can sell us a bag surely!

—Can't do it, man.

—Come on, I'm rattling.

—The squints are coming down heavy on anybody selling.

—How're they going to know?

—They've got dealers all over the city now.

David thinks about taking the smack. He girds up for violence but a voice deep inside tells him no. Don't. He shows Garrett the wad of notes.

—Just a bag man. I'll pay double.

Garrett holds up his fingers.

—See these? I want to keep them. And if you want to keep yours, ye better fuck off.

—How?

—Any one of these Chinks could be a Triad. One wrong look and you're dead.

—At least gimmi a fix then. Come on. Ye know what it's like mate! Brothers-in-arms and all that.

Garrett gives in. Slips David a bag. That's all he can do for him. But if he's here tonight he can get him a few bags of the really good gear that's going about. The China White. Garrett moves off.

David heads back to the convent and climbs in the toilet window. He shoots up. In the rush he's free from all pain. The women are talking about him but he doesn't care.

—He's been an awful long time, says Marie, —D'you think he's alright?

The toilet door opens. David stands in the doorway, unable to take that step forwards.

—Cream ring, dear?

He can't answer. His eyes are stuck on the gold crucifix back up on the wall. Mary-Bridget smiles.

—What's going on? he shouts, —What's the score, man!

He passes out. When he comes round, he's in a sparse clean room. Crisp sheets, a votive candle burning in the corner. His hit is wearing off. He needs more. He gets up and looks out the door. A long corridor. He sneaks away through the back door of the kitchen and he's already hit the streets of Chinatown when Marie comes into his room with a glass of Irn-Bru and a Mars Bar. At the sight of the empty bed she starts crying.

David buys five bags from Garrett.

—Got to go.

Garrett leaves suddenly. David doesn't know Devlin's entered the street. He's moving down in his Shogun watching every person. Bonzo and Sholtz concentrate from the back seats. Zooming in on every hand. They've been told they'll find a rogue dealer on that corner tonight. Devlin expects it to be Garrett. This time he's going to make sure he's dead. Wait a minute? Is that David he's just passed? Can't be David. What the fuck would David be doing in Chinatown? He turns and passes again. It is. It fuckin is him! He pulls over, gets out and sneaks up. Grabs David by the hair, pushing him into a doorway. Sholtz and Bonzo stand each side, keeping watch.

—What's the crack, Jack? says Devlin.

David sees the menacing smile.

—Let go of my hair, ya gorilla.

—I'll rip your head right off.

—Fuckin try it!

—What're you doing here?

—Waiting on my maw.

—Hang about a lot in Chinatown, does she?

No answer.

—Turn your pockets out.

—Fuck off.

Bang! Devlin brings his fist down on David's head. His legs give way but Devlin holds him up. He hangs like a rag doll as Devlin goes through his pockets. Finds nothing.

—Socks, barks Devlin.

David's recovered his senses enough to run. Sholtz stops him.

—Lift him, orders Devlin.

Sholtz and Bonzo turn him upside down. Devlin pulls off his trainers. David starts shouting. He doesn't want to lose his smack.

—Phone the polis! Somebody phone the polis! I'm getting fuckin mugged here!

Passing Chinese chatter. They've got to hurry before the Triads turn up. Devlin rips off one sock. Nothing but the smell of junkie's feet.

—Aw for fuck sakes! Take his other sock off, Sholtz.

Five bags of smack fall out. Devlin cocks his gun and holds it to David's head.

—See you've took up dealing, ya wee cunt.

—It's all personal, screams David.

Devlin cracks him with the pistol. Sholtz slams him into the door and Bonzo lays the punches in.

—Where did ye get it? asks Devlin.

—A guy. I got it off a guy.

—What guy?

—A junkie.

—What fuckin junkie?

—I donno. I've never seen him before.

Devlin hooks him three times to the ribs.

—Christie… Christie! warns Bonzo.

But it's too late. Marie's in the doorway.

—What the fuck's going on?

David sinks to the ground, apparently exhausted. But not too exhausted to pick up one of the bags.

—What the fuck are you up to? Marie asks.

—No. What the fuck are you up to? And your junkie son? What're yees doing in Chinatown? demands Devlin.

—None of your fuckin business, she says.

—My twin sister's running about Chinatown, her junkie son's standing on a corner with five bags down his socks and it's none of my business?

—That's right. It's none of your business. Come on, David.

David ducks into his mothers arms.

—Cheerio, Laurel an Hardy! Cheerio, Uncle Drug Dealer!

Marie takes a right turn downhill, away from the convent, aiming to double back later. Devlin's left on the street with two men, four bags of his own smack and a head filled with puzzles. Does Garrett exist? Did Garrett give David the smack? If he did, does David know him? If he does, does Marie know Garrett? A hundred yards away, his own mother waits for Marie to return. Mary-Bridget senses Devlin is near. The end is coming. The Final Battle.

—There's only four bags here, boss, says Sholtz.

—Is it our stuff? Is it the China White?

—Aye, says Bonzo, —It is.

Devlin pockets the bags and they get in the car.

—Where d'yees want dropped off?

—Take me home, says Bonzo.

—Drop me off at the hoors, says Sholtz.

When Devlin gets back home he flushes the heroin. He has to keep this wee escapade secret from the Triads.

As soon as Devlin drove away Bonzo made his way back to

Chinatown to meet Ming Fung. She's invited him to her flat.
It's in an ultra-modern apartment block, on the top floor,
looking north.

Ming Fung's already had a few drinks before he arrived.
She wants to have sex with him. Bonzo kisses her, pushes
forwards until she's on the couch with him on top. He can feel
her breasts on his chest and her pubic bone against his thigh.
He bites and kisses her shoulders. Her hands run up and down
his back. But when he opens a button on her blouse she stops
him.

—Give me a minute, she says, and leaves the room.

He lets out a long sigh. Tonight's the night.

Ming Fung comes back in. Short skirt. High heels. Under her
white blouse Bonzo can see a scarlet bra. She lifts the skirt,
revealing red knickers. She says nothing, leads him by the
hand to the dining alcove, where there's a massive glass table.

—You go underneath, she says.

Ming Fung lies face down on the table.

—Underneath, she says.

This time it's an order. The little girl who left the room has
come back like a hot hoor from a movie. Bonzo gets under the
table. He can see her face as the mist clears on the glass…
then clouds… then clears.

She opens the blouse and tugs down the cup of her bra.
Presses her breast into the glass.

—You like?

—I like.

She lifts the skirt, gyrating her hips. The flesh at the top of
her thighs turns white against the glass.

—Order me.

—What?

—Order me to do things.

Bonzo, game for anything and experienced enough, has
seen all sorts of foreplay. But not this. He gives it a go. Once
he's into it he quite likes it.

—Lift your skirt.

—A bit.

—A bit more.

—More.

—Stop there.

—Open your legs a bit.

—Open the blouse.

—You masturbate, she says.

He does.

—Slip your other nipple out.

Ming Fung masturbates. They get more and more worked up. Giving and taking orders. Revealing more. Wanking. They come, their breath clouding both sides of the glass.

—Weird as fuck! says Bonzo.

Laughing, he takes her hand and leads her over to the couch. He's so horny, his hard-on hasn't disappeared. It's filled with blood. Throbbing. He didn't notice, but when he touched her hand she transformed back into the little girl. He gets on top of her. Pushes himself in. Lifts her up to go deeper. Starts thrusting. Watching her face for flickers of eroticism. But she screams and throws him off.

—No. No. No, she says.

She crawls into a corner and starts crying. He touches her shoulder but she shrugs him off. Any other woman, and Bonzo would've left. But now he covers her with the throw from the couch. Gets dressed and waits.

For an hour she doesn't move.

When she does come round she thanks him for not leaving. He hugs her and makes her a coffee. Being a hard man doesn't necessarily make you hard. There are aspects that bring out the humanity in you. Like in jail. A good cellmate can connect in ways you'll never connect with another human being. Most people know how to love in fair weather. Others know how to love when it matters.

—Feel better?

—Yes.

All night they sit. Ming Fung tells how her father's brother used to come into her room and do things to her. Raped her from she was six until she was fifteen. Then one Chinese New Year a family argument broke out. An innocuous argument about how duck should be cooked. Some were for roasted and other for boiled. Ming Fung got involved and her uncle kept putting her down. At the height of the argument, Ming Fung stood up, pointed at the uncle and screamed.

—That bastard has been raping me for ten years!

The uncle's face convinced Tai Lo of his guilt. He was dragged into the bathroom. Ming Fung could hear the thumps of the cleaver. The next day there was a spot of blood on a tile near the ceiling. She didn't have the courage to wipe it off. When she was having a shower she'd imagine the spot of blood was watching her naked body. She's not had penetrative sex since. Only when she's in control and there's no physical contact can she have sexual relations. Even becoming a Kung Fu master is a result of nights when she'd lie in bed terrified, praying her uncle wouldn't come.

—I'll understand if you don't want to see me again.

Bonzo does.

She kisses the back of his neck. He arrived infatuated. Now he's in love.

謀殺
murder

Shed no tears until seeing the coffin.

GARRETT'S ON A shopping trip. First stop, Halfords. He bumps a heavy-duty car battery on the counter. The assistant scans it.

—Anything else?

—These.

Three trolleys filled with the shop's entire stock of heavy-duty batteries.

—What's that? A Lego set? she says.

—Can never be too prepared for a Glasgow winter.

He takes the thirty batteries, one trolley at a time, to a hired van. He logs the look the assistant gave him. She likes him. Might come in useful later. Might not. With a psychopath, nothing's wasted. Everything has potential. The world is yours.

Bonzo makes his way to meet Ming Fung for breakfast in the town. He passes John Lewis's. Garrett is in the kitchen section checking out the pots. He steps up and down stroking his chin like a man in an art gallery.

—Can I help you, sir? asks an assistant.

Garrett points to the soup pots.

—What's the biggest pot you've got?

The assistant shows him. Not big enough. He's looking for something bigger. Much bigger. Ah! What he needs is the catering department. In the basement another assistant shows him a pot the size of half a barrel.

—That's our best big pot there. We do lot of these to soup kitchens and the Sally Ann.

A beautiful pot. Garrett falls in love instantly. Exactly what he's been looking for.

—I'll take it.

—Certainly, sir.

—Can I see your selection of ladles?

He leaves the store with the pot, a thermometer, a large ladle and a brass funnel.

Bonzo's in Princes Square with Ming Fung. Coffee and laughs. One night together and there's no separating them now. She wants to know how he's going to tell Devlin. Bonzo doesn't know. How's she going to tell Tai Lo? Ming Fung shrugs. Doesn't tell Bonzo of the conversation she's already had with her father.

Devlin's under the monkey-puzzle tree puzzling how last night's events relate to the Garrett mystery. Are David and Garrett connected? Could Gerald, if that's who Garrett is, have got back in touch with the family?

Sister Mary-Bridget administers her grandson's methadone.

Wendy's in her classroom, numbed by life.

Dan paints a giant Stag in the Wilderness. He doesn't know why.

Garrett, in a plush penthouse flat in the city, empties the contents of the last two car batteries into the soup pot. He turns the hob on, opens the window and goes through to the living-room to read his favourite book: *The Private Memoirs and Confessions of a Justified Sinner*. When the battery acid has boiled into dust he mixes it with a large consignment of China White.

There's no quiet like a convent in the middle of the night.

♪♪ Protect us while we are asleep.

David stirs and Garrett whispers to meet him in the chapel. He's gone when David fully wakes. Curious, he gets up and shuffles along to the chapel. Was there somebody there or did he imagine it? Silhouetted against the candles, Garrett sits on a pew. David approaches.

—How did ye get in?

—Toilet window. Same as you got out the last time. Want gear?

—You broke in here to sell me gear?

—I'm new. I'm trying to build up a customer base.

—I'm brassic man. They took my money away.

—I'll lay it on ye.

David's suspicious. He thinks Sister Mary-Bridget's setting him up. A test.

—What would ye want to lay it on me for?

Garrett's going to go up against the big dealers. He's assembling a network. David could be one of his dealers. He'll set him up in a flat. All he has to do is sell bags to whoever comes along.

—Sounds good, but I don't want to let ma maw down. She's set this recovery programme up for me.

Garrett's willing to keep David supplied while he's in here. Help him fool the nuns into thinking he's recovered. Then, when he's convinced them he's cured, the world's his oyster.

—Just think of your future laid out there in front of you, promises Garrett, —I can give you anything you want.

David's methadone has worn off. He eyes Garrett's bag of smack.

—Look, says Garrett, —I'll give ye this anyway. No pressure with the dealing. If ye don't want to deal, next time tell me to fuck off.

David figures he can take one last bag of smack. Get back on the methadone in the morning. Who's going to know? Then he can ignore this junkie if he ever comes back.

—Have you got the works there?

Has Garrett got the works? Has he not just! Spoon! Fills it from the font. Sprinkles the contaminated heroin into the water. Heats it over an almost extinguished candle. The candle Marie lit before she went to bed. Lit for David's recovery. As the last grains of powder melt, Mary-Bridget bolts awake. Visions of flames. Visions of hell. She runs to David's room. Bursts into the empty cell.

Garrett inserts the needle in David's arm.

—Ready?

David nods. Garrett pushes the needle. Mary-Bridget shakes Marie awake. The smack floods into David's veins.

Surprise.

Puzzlement.

Fear.

Horror.

Pain.

Agony.

Garrett savours each change of expression like a connoisseur of fine wines.

—Maw! Help me Maw! screams David.

When Marie and Mary-Bridget get to the chapel David's writhing around on the floor.

—What is it son?

—The Devil set me on fire.

—The Devil? What d'ye mean the Devil?

—All inside me's on fire. The Devil done it!

Sister Mary-Bridget prays.

Marie is screaming. —What ye praying for? Get a doctor, get a fuckin doctor.

But it's no use. David's foaming at the mouth and nose. Blood seeps from his tear ducts. He stops thrashing. Lies still except for the occasional twitch, breathing fast and shallow, his eyes wide and staring.

—My wean, my fuckin wean. The nuns pray.

—Out of the depths I cry to Thee, O Lord!

Lord, hear my voice!

To save Marie the horror of an autopsy and the holding back of a funeral, Devlin gets a doctor to cite the cause of death as heart failure. But not before finding out exactly what the cause was. When he gets the news that the smack was contaminated by battery acid, he knows Garrett's to blame. He draws his men together.

—When this funeral's over we're going to find Garrett. When we do I'll personally slice him into strips. Hang him bit by bit on a tree.

Devlin's been back and forth to Garrett's flat many times and found nothing. Just red and white. And he's got spies reporting who comes and goes. So far, only the other neighbours.

Wendy's taking time off because there's been a death in the

family. Miss Newell calls a meeting. How can they allow a teacher to continue in their school when her lifestyle is supported by drugs?

The wake makes its way from Marie's house, up Fruin Street and onto Saracen Street. The wheels of the hearse crunch through snow, followed by the crinch crinch of hundreds of slow pairs of feet. Black on white. Devlin and his men walk directly behind the hearse. A strange fog hangs above them. The streets are lined with mourners. Some just love a good junkie funeral, some always turn out for funerals associated with gangsters.

A reporter approaches Devlin holding a microphone. It's all caught on the high camera scaffold of the BBC.

In the Silver Seas, Tai Lo and his men watch Devlin lose his cool. They are losing faith in him.

Ming Fung meets Bonzo and tells him I Lo and Hung Kwan are pressing to move against Devlin.

Bonzo takes Ming Fung up onto the hill at Ruchill Park and they make a snowman. They could be any couple. But freedom is a dream for them.

In the chapel Marie and Mary-Bridget keep vigil over David's body.

Dan comes in at three in the morning, drunk and crying. Mary-Bridget asks Marie if she knows who's sitting at the back.

—I can't stop him coming to a chapel, can I? says Marie.

—He would understand your pain better than anyone.

Marie goes to the coffin, puts her ear to it like she's listening for her son's heartbeat, and lets out a long moan.

Next morning, lines of people file into the chapel, nodding and offering condolences to Devlin, Marie and Dan. Marie resents the attention Devlin's getting. Cooney stands to the side, smoking. Nicole's waiting for Gerry. Where is he? He said he'd be there at quarter to ten.

—Nicole, hurry up! Devlin shouts.

—In a minute.

—It's starting.

—Right. In a minute!

Nicole is soon alone. She hears footsteps and turns, expecting Gerry, but it's a news-hound. He pushes a microphone at her.

—How does it feel to be the daughter of Glasgow's most notorious gangster?

She tilts back a few inches. Screws her face up.

—Come again?

—Being the daughter of Glasgow's most notorious gangster. How does it feel?

She shakes her head.

—Didn't you know your father was a gangster?

—No comment!

She strides into the chapel. The words ring in her head.

A figure in black appears at the far end of the car park. Garrett. This morning, Bonzo picked up another consignment of China White. Garrett opens Bonzo's car and gets in, closing the door quietly. He lies on the floor and swaps the clean bag of smack for his contaminated bag. Later today, the consignment will be separated into smaller packages and delivered to the dealers all over the city. They'll make deal bags and sell it to Glasgow's junkies. Glasgow's junkies will fill their veins with fire. Garrett slips out and locks the car. He changes his body language to Gerry.

Nicole's down the front. She steals the odd glance at Devlin, having come to the full realisation of who he is.

Father Boyle's started. Garrett's the picture of embarrassed humility coming down the aisle.

Gerry sits and holds Nicole's hand. She's bursting to tell him she's the daughter of Glasgow's most notorious gangster. When the service is over, cars and buses ferry mourners to the graveyard. Nicole whispers her secret to Gerry.

—Guess who my father is?

Garrett shrugs. Indicates to her to have some respect. But she's got to tell him.

—I didn't tell you in case I frightened you away.

—Who?

—The number one gangster in Glasgow. Not so naïve now, am I?

She gives his balls a squeeze. Father Boyle sprinkles the coffin with holy water. In the freezing air, the droplets turn to ice and click off the wood. It's time to lower David's body. Devlin, Sam, Sholtz, Bonzo and Dan are given a chord each. They look about for another man. Wendy pushes Garrett forward. The gravedigger hands him the final chord. Devlin's angry this stranger's lowering his nephew's coffin alongside the family but there's nothing he can do. Nothing he can say. Father Boyle prays as it bumps downwards. Devlin throws a handful of dust and slides over to comfort Marie. But her anger breaks free.

—You can shrivel up and die, the same way you've made this whole scheme shrivel up and die, ya bastard! You've got all the kids hooked on smack. You've corrupted them. You're worse than a fuckin paedophile. That should be your baby going down that hole.

As he tries to hold her off, she bites his hands. Father Boyle gets between them until they're separated. Marie spits in Devlin's face.

—I hate you. You're a curse!

—I'm a curse? Who was it that done five years for you, eh? Answer me that, ya ungrateful cow!

—Ye never done five years for me.

—No? Who did I do it for then?

—Ye done it cos ye hate my da, that's how ye done it.

Dan bows his head.

—I fuckin done it cos of what he done to you! shouts Devlin.

—No, says Marie, —Ye used that as an excuse to take revenge on him!

She marches off. Soon Devlin finds himself alone at the grave.

There's a hand on his shoulder. It's Cooney.

—Everybody's under pressure.

—Larry! Am I glad to see you.

—C'mon back in my car.

Cooney runs Devlin to the club where a meal is being served for two hundred mourners. Marie glares at them and they sit at the other end of the table beside Nicole and Garrett. Devlin's choking for a drink.

—Whisky or vodka for the toast? asks the waitress.

—Two cans of coke here, says Cooney.

Devlin eyes Nicole's boyfriend. He's much older than he thought. Devlin lifts his top lip, baring his teeth.

—What age are you?

Garrett says nothing. Devlin grabs Nicole's wrist.

—What age is he?

Nicole flicks her hair back and makes sure she's got the attention of the table before she retaliates.

—I didn't know you were a drug dealer, Daddy.

Devlin glares and lets rip.

—D'you think I don't know about you in Eden?

—What?

—Eden!

—What about Eden?

—It was you that was dealing.

—Don't know what you're talking about!

—Augustus told me.

Devlin leans forwards with menace meant for Garrett.

—After I cracked one of his fuckin teeth out.

Nicole tries to speak but can't.

—That fuckin shut ye up, says Devlin.

He turns on her boyfriend.

—What've you got to say about it?

Garrett puts his hands up in submission.

—Family. I'm staying out of it.

—See if I find out you've been giving her dope, I'll kill ye with my bare hands.

Nicole turns on her father.

—Leave him alone, you animal!

Now the whole hall's listening.

—Animal, is it? says Devlin, —Aye, mibbi. I ripped and tore my way to the top so that you wouldn't need to. I fuckin sacrificed my life for you so that you'd be on easy fuckin street. An this is how ye repay me.

His nose is an inch from hers.

—That's right, go on, hit me you moron! she screams.

He's dumb with rage. She pushes so their noses press together. She challenges him again.

—Come on big tough gangster!

BANG

Devlin slaps her. The room is shocked. Garrett jumps up. Devlin grabs him round the windpipe.

—An what the FUCK!! are you going to do?

Nicole pulls Devlin's arm away. Cooney tugs him into his seat. A red bruise grows on Nicole's cheekbone. She grabs Garrett and makes her way to the door. Turns and shouts back at Devlin.

—I'll not be fucking back.

Nicole leaves. There's a blow on the back of Devlin's head. Wendy's laying into him with a can of coke. Cooney wraps both arms round Wendy and tells Devlin to get out.

Wendy's decided to go in to school and ask for time off to search for Nicole. When she arrives, she's told she's to go up in front of the General Teaching Council on the charge of bringing the profession into disrepute and is therefore suspended.

She leaves feeling desperate. Where can she turn to for help?

Jet Set Jane.

They meet at Paddy's Market. Jet Set can't see there's any case against her. It's all hearsay.

—They don't need bloody proof. Just enough gossip.

—There's no mountain that can't be climbed, hen, says Jet Set.

News is, somebody's been spotted in Garrett's flat. Devlin and his men burst in, bristling with guns. Devlin's stunned. The flat's furnished exactly the way it was when they shot Garrett in drag. Gone are the white washed walls. The carpets are back on the floors. Furniture all in place.

—What's up, boss? says Bonzo.

—It all... changed. Different.

—Eh?

—All this stuff wasn't here.

—You been on the sauce again?

Devlin's lifts a corner of carpet.

—That was red gloss, the whole floor!

Bonzo hasn't got a clue what he's on about.

Sam shouts for them from another room. They rush to see what he's found. Inside, the car batteries are arranged in the shape of a letter

G

There's a tin of Evo Stick, a cheap lighter and a half-burned crisp bag sat on top. Bonzo, Sholtz and Sam don't see any significance in these. Devlin zooms in on the Evo Stick. Zooms in on the batteries. Topples the closest battery with his foot. No liquid comes out. He punches a few holes in the walls.

Gerald's come back to haunt him. And there's something else. It wouldn't take the contents of so many batteries to kill one person.

Across the city in another penthouse flat Garrett looks over the dark waters of the Clyde. The Silver Seas shimmers on the cold water. Here and there the river has frozen over. His flat is minimalist, with state-of-the-art furniture and hi-fi. The air is laced with sexy jazz. Nicole's sprawled on the mezzanine bed in her new underwear. One of her arms is flung out and her fingertips stroke the beech panel wall. Garrett's making up a syringe of smack and telling her his life story. Father was married to another woman. Two kids of his own. Didn't want him. Didn't fuckin want him. His mother died. He got put in a home. Ran away. Caught. Ran away again. Caught. They put him in another home. Kept running away. Stuck him in St Mary's secure unit. At sixteen they said he was unredeemable. Unfixable.

—How did your mother die?

—In a fire.

—That is so sad. Come here.

She hands Garrett the joint and hugs him as he smokes. He lays the joint down in the ashtray and lifts a syringe full of smack.

—Ready?

—Are you sure it's good, Gerry?

—Like sex, times a million.

He runs his fingertip down her arm. Stops at a nice young vein. Nicole gasps as she's penetrated by the needle. Her eye widen as Garrett injects her.

Devlin's called Cooney. Told him he thinks Garrett's contaminated a whole batch of smack. Cooney tells him he has to stop that smack hitting the streets. Get it off the streets if it's already there. Devlin sends all his men out to retrieve the smack.

—Tell them not to sell it. Not to use it. Get a list of everybody that bought it. From a hundred deals down to a single deal.

Cooney drives Devlin to see the Triads. Waits in the car while he goes in. A few heads turn as Devlin passes the roulette and blackjack tables. He's on his own. Anything could happen. He gets to Tai Lo and blurts it all out.

—Listen, there's a guy called Garrett and he's still alive but fuck knows how and he's contaminated the smack. We've got to get it off the streets.

—Who are you? asks Tai Lo.

—Eh?

—Who are you?

Devlin repeats his rant. The Triads pretend they don't know him. Ask each other if they've ever seen this man before. Decide they haven't. Devlin's desperate.

—I'm asking yees for help here. We have to get the gear back in.

No answer.

—I gave yees everything yees needed.

They continue with their Mah Jong. Ignoring him. Devlin moves closer until he's shouting in Tai Lo's ear. In the background there's a tear in Ming Fung's eye. She knew it would go wrong. It had to.

—Yees would have nothing if it wasn't for me!

They ignore him.

—Great. Fuckin great!

Devlin overturns the Mah Jong table. The Triads sit staring at the tiles in their hands as if the table's still there. Devlin leaves. Garrett steps out of the shadows, rights the upturned table and pulls up a seat.

—Deal me in, Tai Lo.

As they play, they talk. Garrett tells Tai Lo that when Devlin came to kill him he had begged for mercy. Crying. He admits he was crying. Devlin promised to spare him. But he'd owe him a favour. A big favour.

—And this favour? asks Tai Lo.

—Like I told you. He asked me to contaminate a bag of smack and distribute it. I pretended to go along with it. Contaminated a couple of kilo. It all backfired when his nephew David got hold of some.

—How did he get it?

—Probably knew where his uncle stored it.

—Why Devlin contaminate his own smack? Why jeopardise his business? asks Tai Lo.

Garrett's ready with an answer to that.

—He's not jeopardising his business at all. He's consolidating it.

They don't see at first. Garrett spells it out.

—This smack's Chinese. Far as the cops know, only you guys can get hold of it. Devlin and Pitt are planning a drugs scare the likes of which Glasgow's never seen. The Triads'll take the blame. They're going to fabricate an inter-Triad war. You'll be burst apart. Devlin'll rule the city. That's his plan.

The Triads speak low in Chinese. Then Heung Chu sees a flaw.

—Why would Devlin come in accusing you of trying to spread contaminated drugs throughout the city? Why warn us if he is trying to incriminate us?

—He had a witness outside in the car. Look at your CCTV tapes.

A Forty-Nine comes back from the TV monitor room confirming Devlin drove away with another man in the car. Garrett goes on.

—That man's Cooney. Contacts from the lowest of the low to High Court Judges. He's as *bone fide* as witnesses come. Devlin will pretend he came to persuade you not to flood the city with contaminated smack. He'll say David bought the hit that killed him from your men and when you made out you knew nothing about it he left in a rage, throwing tables over. Look at all the witnesses.

The Triads look at the Gwai Los in the casino who have seen Devlin's outburst.

—And you can't kill them all, says Garrett.

The Triads talk amongst themselves again.

—Aye, says Garrett, —He's a clever man, Devlin.

—Why would we contaminate or own heroin? says I Lo.

—You wouldn't. That's what I'm saying. But another Triad gang wanting to move into Glasgow would. Devlin's got an ex-member of the Wu Su willing to tell the cops he witnessed the acid going into the smack.

The Triads have one final question.

—Why you telling all this? What do you want?

—I know Devlin's whole network of dealers. I could run that side of the business instead of him.

The Triads will consider it. But for now, can he find the contaminated smack before it hits the streets?

—I hope so. Junkies are the scum of the earth. But I don't want to see anybody dying like that.

Tai Lo shakes Garrett's hand.

火
fire

You can't put out a fire on a cart-load of wood with a cup of water.

THE DRUGS ARE already out there. Smack laced with battery acid, seeking revenge.

Smack grins in anticipation as it's mixed and heated with water and sucked gurgling up a nice new needle. Or an old needle. Smack says hello to the incoming blood as the junkie checks for blood before injecting. Smack takes a deep breath as the plunger shoves down. Smack surges into the blood-stream of its victim.

Cooney and Devlin sit in the car by the Clyde waiting for news. Cooney reads out a passage from the *Big Book*.

—You are going to know a new freedom and a new happiness.

Somewhere a junkie injects and freezes with shock.

—You will not regret the past nor shut the door on it.

Somewhere a junkie twists in pain.

—You will comprehend the word serenity and you will know peace.

Somewhere a junkie screams in agony.

—No matter how far down the scale you have gone, you will see how your experience can benefit others.

—Somewhere a junkie squirms in death throes.

—That feeling of uselessness and self-pity will disappear.

Somewhere a dead junkie lies on her living-room floor. Saliva and blood drip from the corner of her mouth. Her three-year-old shakes her.

—Mammy – up! Up, Mammy!

Devlin's phone goes. It's Bonzo.

—Did ye get it in? Is it bad gear? Is it…

—Boss, ye'd better get over here quick. Pitt's here.

It's the first time he's seen Pitt unafraid of Devlin. He rages and rants. Ten dead. The papers onto it already. If they connect him to Devlin, it'll all be over. They have to get the smack back in.

—What the fuck d'ye think I'm doing?

—How are people still dying then?

—The dealers out there don't even know half the people that's bought their deals, that's how!

—We have to go to the media, says Pitt.

—What?

—Have you got a better suggestion?

—You want me to say, my smack's contaminated by the way, can you tell the junkies not to take it.

—No. You can't. But I can!

Devlin slides a book over to Pitt. Pitt slides it back.

—We know all the addresses, Christie. We're not as daft as you think. Everybody plays their own game.

Pitt calls in. Gives the go-ahead.

—Now stay well away from me till this is all over.

By the time Pitt's back at the station, reporters have gathered outside Devlin's house. He drives at such a speed they have to jump, but the cameras are on him and the flashes explode.

Wendy meets him in the hall.

—I hope you're fucking happy. This is like being in jail. But then you know all about that, don't you! You make me sick. I can't stay in here with you. I can't get out for those serpents.

—There's some heavy shit going on. I'm trying my best here.

—Well your best ain't fucking good enough! What are these vultures doing here?

—Turn on the telly, he says.

She does. Devlin's face is in a little square at the top right-hand corner. The reporter is listing the dead.

KLUNK!

Wendy cracks Devlin on the side of the head with the iron and lay lay lays into him. He fends her off from the floor.

—Bastard! Bastard! Bastard! You right rotten fucking bastard.

He grabs the iron and flings it across the room.

—What the fuck're ye trying to do?

—Something I should've done long ago. Get you out of my life. You're a cancer! And what about Nicole? I've no idea where she is and her mobile's switched off. I've got to find her.

Wendy packs a bag and storms out through flashbulbs and questions.

From an upstairs window Devlin, bruised and bloody, watches the blitzkrieg of lights move along the street after her.

—I need a fuckin drink!

In the kitchen he finds a bottle of cooking sherry. Screws the lid off. Sniffs. Licks his lips. Puts the bottle to his mouth.

—The man takes a drink. Then the drink takes a drink. Then the drink takes the man.

It's Cooney. Devlin puts the bottle down.

—How did ye get in?

Cooney doesn't answer.

Garrett traces his finger around Nicole's black eye and asks if she wants another hit. He aims to feed her from the good bag of China White he took from Bonzo's car. Keep her stoned. Push her to seek revenge on her father.

—How can he love you? He gave you a black eye. That doesn't sound like love to me.

—He's never hit me before.

—Look, it's obvious to anyone else, he doesn't care for you, not at all.

—He's paid for my education. To make sure I get a chance in life.

—Nicole, he sent you to a private school to get you out the way.

Nicole snorts a line of coke and leans back to welcome the rush.

—I can't believe he's treating me like this, Gerry.

—There's a badness in him. I can see it in his eyes.

—He's an angry man, says Nicole.

—Angry? He's more than that!

Gerry switches on the telly. Watches Nicole as she recognises her father and hear what he's being blamed for. She's shocked to her core.

—Oh God, he's evil.

Nicole points at the screen.

—That's my house!

A reporter is relaying an urgent warning.

—Repeat: do not inject. Hand the heroin in at your nearest police station. You will be given methadone in return. The death toll now stands at twenty-four. This is the biggest drugs crisis Glasgow has ever seen. It is believed the drugs were deliberately contaminated.

—There's your father for you, says Garrett.

The same broadcast is being watched in the Silver Seas Casino. I Lo wants to move on Devlin now, kill his whole gang, obliterate any connection back to the Triads.

Ming Fung keeps listening to the news.

—At about midnight, acting on an anonymous call, police found a teenage girl in St Theresa's school in Possil. Paramedics are trying to revive her.

But it's in vain. On camera, the paramedics roll the body onto a stretcher.

Watching with Garrett, Nicole is riveted. Wendy is walking towards the school entrance. She's been driving all night looking for Nicole. Miss Newell grabs her arm and frogmarches her off the premises.

—I have to ask you to leave the premises, Mrs Devlin.

Just then, Kerry-Anne is wheeled past. Dead. Nicole sees the body being loaded into the ambulance, hears her mother's screams being broadcast to the nation.

—Your father's even killed Kerry-Anne, says Garrett.

In her drugged state Nicole finds it difficult to make sense of it all.

—I hate him hate him hate him.

—So what are you going to do about it?

—Fucking destroy the evil bastard.

Hill Street convent. Wendy sits in the chapel, at the very spot where David died, though she doesn't know it. She has to talk to somebody. She'd phoned Jet Set. No answer. Marie's her only option. It's hard when the only person you can talk to hates you.

Wendy takes one look at Marie and bursts into tears. Where there had been a tough and angry woman, there's a wasted shell. The women cling to each other. After a while, their sobbing subsides.

Marie moves over to the votive candles and lights a joint she found among David's belongings. She was keeping it as a keepsake. A memory of her son. Marie takes a long puff, and hands it to Wendy. Neither woman's ever smoked dope before. Their eyes follow the smoke trailing into the upper atmosphere. Wendy speaks.

—I'm pregnant.

Marie holds the joint away from her lip.

—A baby? A wee fuckin baby! Christie said that but I thought he was full of shite as usual.

—Nearly four months.

Marie gets up, hands Wendy the joint and shouts back as she's leaving.

—You stay here. I'll go and tell Sister Mary-Bridget. She'll be well chuffed.

Wendy takes another draw and starts to feel detached.

She looks up at the stained-glass window. The Stag is magnificent. The colours! It could jump down and run up the aisle like a fragmented rainbow. She turns. Marie's back, with a nun. She does the introductions.

—I understand you're looking for somewhere to stay?

Sister Mary-Bridget says Wendy can stay in the convent for as long as she needs to. Wendy's grateful. Mary-Bridget takes the joint and passes it to Marie.

—Sorry, says Marie, —I gave her it.

Marie puts the joint out and lifts Wendy's bag.

Mary-Bridget is staring up at the stained-glass window at the Stag. Her face is white. Tormented.

—Christopher, she says.

—Christie? says Wendy.

—Should we tell her? asks Mary-Bridget.

—Up to you, says Marie.

—Tell me what? asks Wendy.

—He's my son, Mary-Bridget says, —I'm Christopher's mother.

Marie nods soft easy nods that don't look like they're going to stop. Wendy closes her eyes. If this is a nightmare, now's a good time to wake up. When she opens her eyes Marie and Mary-Bridget have their arms around about her. That's when Wendy realises she's on the floor. She's never wept like this before.

—God is good. God is good, Mary-Bridget is murmuring.

An owl hoots in the Wilderness. A camp fire lights the fringes of pine trees. Devlin, in his suit, cooks a sausage on a stick.

—How can you be certain? says Cooney.

—It's my cousin Gerald. The batteries. The crisp bag. The lighter. Every sinew of me knows it's him.

Devlin holds out a sausage on a stick.

—Want one?

Cooney nods, Devlin flips another slice of bread on a stone. Puts another sausage on a stick. They stare into the flames.

—You're not telling me everything, are you? says Cooney.

Devlin stares in the flames.

—How can I help ye if you're holding back?

—I killed his maw. I killed Gerald's maw.

—I thought ye said he done it?

—What d'ye expect me to say? For years I've blocked it out. But now it's back to haunt me.

—Tell me what happened.

—Me and Gerald were in my Auntie Theresa's house. In

the bedroom. She was on the bed, gouched from smack. Smack was just coming into Possil then. We never knew hardly nothing about it. She used to call it her medicine and all we knew was it made her sleep. Gerald was sniffing a bag of glue. He'd started sniffing the glue about a year before that. I mind staring at the bag coming at my face and getting sucked back. In and out it was going. Cheese and onion. Cheese and onion. That's what it was saying. Cheese and onion. Next thing Gerald hands me the poke. You do it, he said. I was scared. D'ye know that? Terrified of my own cousin. I looked at Theresa hoping she'd mibbi wake up and tell him to stop fuckin sniffing glue. But she was well gone. I've got the bag in my hand and he's leaning right in my face with this fuckin mad grin. He's all teeth and big wide eyes so he is. So I put it to my lips and take a few sucks. That's it, that's it, he's going, egging me on. Delighted he was. I kept sniffing. First I felt my feet disappearing then this light feeling rose up my body till my head felt like a balloon. Next thing there was this helicopter noise. The bag's going up so that I can't see nothing and then down again and there's his big laughing face. Gerald's. I started laughing an all. Next thing I remembers is us two laughing and rolling about. Laughing our heads off at nothing.

Then... Then... I've got this lighter off the bedside cabinet. I'm sparking it and we're amazed at the flames. The two of us are amazed at the flames. We put the light out. Every time I flicked the lighter, the sparks make a fireworks display and the flame's a blowtorch. I thought I heard my Auntie Theresa laughing. Then Gerald screams. Christopher! he shouts. Christopher! The glue poke's caught fire. I'm like that, trying to flick it from my hand. But it's stuck. It's a ball of flame and it's stuck to my hand. I manage to fire it across the room. It lands under the bed. Time...time... must've passed, cos next thing the room's up in flames. There's black smoke everywhere. Gerald's trying to drag his maw across the floor. I can only see him for a second then he's gone in the smoke. Then back again. HELP ME! HELP ME! he's shouting. But I was that feart. I was at the door. I wanted to go back in and help him but I couldn't. I couldn't go back in that room. I ran. Last thing I hears is Gerald slapping at his maw to try to get her to wake up. When I got out the back close I heard footsteps. It was him running after me. The back close went right onto the canal. It was covered with ice. The fire was blazing. I couldn't turn round. Neither could Gerald. He kept on saying, It's the glue int it, Christopher? It's the glue that's done it. Everything's gonni be alright when it wears off, eh? Aye, when it wears off it'll be fine, I said. But there was running feet and shouting in the street behind us. The glue had wore off enough to tell me it was all real. Gerald was coming round to the reality of it an all. Next thing... next thing my da comes out the back close. His arms are on fire. Then I sees that he's got something in his arms. I remember thinking, what's he doing bothering with that old carpet? But it wasn't a burning carpet. It was my Auntie Theresa. Gerald's maw. My da ran past us and threw her on the ice an her body was hissing as the flames hit the ice an the ice cracked and gave way. My da's right in there, he keeps pushing her under the water to douse the flames. He pulls her back out and holds her dead body. Theresa! Theresa! he's howling. Don't leave me don't leave me don't leave me. He laid her down on the bank and turned his head round slow. Next thing, Gerald throws me in the canal. My da does nothing. Sits on the bank. Greeting. He's gave up. Gerald gets my head under the water. Drown, ya bastard, he's going. Ye killed my maw. Drown. I struggled at first. Then I mind thinking it was me. I did kill his maw. It was my fault. I mind giving up. I pissed myself. The warm piss around my legs. It even felt nice. I gave out a long line of air and then somebody pulled me out. It was the polis.

Next thing we were being questioned.

I said... I said it was Gerald that done it. I told the polis he was sniffing glue and lit the bag deliberately and flung it under the bed. He kept denying it. Saying it was me. But he was a known glue-sniffer and the polis had lifted him a few times. They carted him off. The last thing I saw of Gerald was the look he gave me as they led him away. That's how I hate grasses. I'm a fuckin grass myself.

Devlin awaits judgement from Cooney, but none comes. Only this.

—I killed a twelve year old girl. A bomb. I was a terrorist. I see her dead body every minute of the day. And all night long in my dreams. There are some things you should never forgive yourself for.

They stare into the embers, two men linked forever by shared secrets.

Devlin sees something moving in the distance.

It's the Stag.

—Look! There it's there. That's fuckin weird how we've just shared all that stuff and then… there he is. That's got to be my Stag! Come on!

Devlin runs towards the Stag but it doesn't move. He stops. And lucky for him. In the moonlight he suddenly sees a deep gorge between him and the Stag.

—That's water down there! says Cooney.

—I've got to know if it's the same Stag.

—You're scared of water!

—I've got to know if it's the same one!

Devlin takes a few steps back.

—Fuck it, he says.

He runs forward and makes a massive leap.

—Geronimo!

He falls down the chasm, crashing through trees into the tumbling water and is whisked away. Cooney runs along the side of the gorge. The Stag keeps up on the other side.

—Christie, aw fuck, says Cooney, —Christie can ye hear me?

—They could hear ye at George Square, ya cunt!

—Are ye alright?

—Aye.

He slips down a small waterfall on his back.

—It's quite good, in fact!

Cooney hears a rumble. He peers up ahead. Shit! In the moonlight he can see the white roaring foam of a great waterfall.

—There's a waterfall up ahead!

—Good, says Devlin.

—Good?

Devlin stretches his arms out.

—God, I offer myself to Thee, to build with me and to do with me as Thou wilt. Relieve me of the bondage of self, that I may better do Thy will. Take away my difficulties, that victory over them may bear witness to those I would help of Thy Power, Thy Love, and Thy Way of life. May I do Thy will alwaaaaaaaaaaaaaaaaaaaays

Over

he

goes

sucked helpless into the turbulence. A minute later Devlin surfaces, gasping He looks up at the Stag high above. It looks straight at him, then it starts limping off.

—Yeeehaa. Yeeehaa! That's it! That's the fuckin one.

Cooney clambers down the rocks towards Devlin.

Among the things Nicole's told Garrett about the movements of Devlin's men is that every morning Sam drives to a shop in Maryhill Road to get well-fired rolls. He likes them fresh. He'd only said it in passing, but wee bits of information can be dangerous.

Sam's driving back to his flat on the outskirts of Chinatown. He's singing along to Talking Heads. *On the Road to Paradise.*

Garrett puts a gun to his head from the back seat. Sam immediately and deliberately smashes the car into a bridge stanchion. His head crashes into the windscreen. Stunned, he looks about the wrecked car. Garrett isn't there. But the door opens and Garrett drags him out.

—Clunk click every trip, my man. Always wear a seat-belt.
A car slows to see what's happening. Garrett points the
gun and it speeds away.

Garrett cracks Sam on the head with the gun then jabs it
into his side and leads him to an old Ford Escort. There's a box
of cable ties on the back seat. He pushes Sam in on his belly and
binds his hands and feet behind him. When the cops get to
Sam's car the engine's still running. The witness can't remember
what anybody looked like. Or if there was another car. But that
other car's stopped outside the Silver Seas. Garrett slides a box
under Tai Lo's black Mercedes. Drives across the bridge and
parks. Takes out his mobile phone and dials.

BOOM

The Mercedes explodes. Tai Lo and his men run out into the
settling debris and smoke.

—Devlin! says I Lo.

Ming Fung warns Bonzo first chance she gets.

Nicole's still sleeping when Garrett brings Sam in, gagged
and blindfolded. Garrett gave her enough smack to keep her
sleeping all morning. He takes Sam to a small room. Ties him
to a bed frame using the straps normally used to secure items
on a roof rack. Tightened by ratchets. He ties Sam's arms at the
wrist and on the forearms and biceps. Ties his forehead and
his neck. His ankles, below the knee and mid thigh. The hips.
Sam's completely immobilised. All he can move is his eyes and
his mouth.

—In space, no one can hear you scream, says Garrett, —I
liked that movie, did you?

Garrett turns the hi-fi on. Loud. Sam's eyes follow him. He
opens a shoe box revealing a hundred pre-loaded needles.

—Like smack?

—Fuck off! You're a dead man.

—On the contrary, says Garrett.

Garrett presses lightly on the plunger. A tear of liquid

squeezes out and rolls down the needle.

—If you like smack, you'll love this, he says.

He inserts it into a vein. Sam feels the prick of the needle. The steel sliding into the vein. And something else. A burning sensation. Like a lighted cigarette against his skin.

—What the fuck is that?

But as he asks, he realises what it is. Garrett inserts another needle in Sam's left arm. That begins to burn.

—I know you don't want me to press the plunger, says Garrett, —But by the time I'm finished you'll be begging me to press one of them.

Garrett inserts needle after needle until Sam's in agony. Every tendon and muscle strains to break free. But he can't move. Every inch of his skin's on fire. He tells Garrett all he needs to know at the fiftieth needle. But Garrett doesn't stop. He wants a hundred acid-laced syringes in Sam's veins. He thinks it would be beautiful. A work of art. By seventy, Sam's begging to be killed.

—I told you you'd be begging, but would you listen? No.

He inserts the hundredth needle between Sam's toes and stands back to admire his handiwork. Sam's still conscious as Garrett goes round the needles, touching each one light as a cat's paw. Sam strains like a man in the electric chair. But a man in the chair dies only once.

Garrett's disappointed when Sam is finally gone. He's been enjoying himself. A good morning's work. He's made sure there'll be full-scale war between the Triads and Devlin. That will distract Devlin from what Garrett's real work of art is going to be.

An hour later I Lo unzips a black bag full of automatic guns. Hung Kwan tosses them to his men. Garrett describes the architecture of Devlin's house to Tai Lo, pointing out the security, passing on the information he tortured out of Sam.

—His room's on the top floor. There are cameras here, here and here.

—You know much about Devlin.

—Some people will tell you anything for smack.

In Devlin's office, Bonzo hands out guns. Devlin rushes in with Cooney. If Cooney's alarmed by the weaponry he doesn't show it. Devlin looks about.

—Where's Sam?

Nicole wanders over the laminate flooring in a pair of Garrett's socks. She'd woken abruptly in a panic. Thought there was someone in the flat.

—Gerry? Gerry, are you there?

She hears dripping. Down she goes into the toilet. None of the taps are dripping. She can still hear it. Drip, drip, drip.

—Gerry? She opens a door. —Gerry is that...

Sam's lying naked, crucified on the bed-frame with a hundred needles coming out of his body. Every inch of vein has a syringe hanging from it. The acid has burned through the flesh. Blood and pus run from every puncture. Nicole sinks to the floor. Hyperventilates for a full hour before coming to her senses. She wanted to teach Daddy a lesson, but when she said destroy him she only meant hurt him enough to let him see how he's hurt her. This is beyond beyond. The needles filled with acid. She'd overheard it in the house as Mummy fought with Daddy about it. When David died. She realises Gerry murdered David.

She puts her clothes on. She's got to get out before Gerry comes back. Runs to the door. It's locked. So are the windows. She lifts the telephone. It doesn't work. Her mobile! She gets it from her bag. Battery low. Dials.

—Sorry, your call cannot be taken at the moment. Please leave a message after the tone.

—Mum. It's me. Nicole. Help me.

Devlin's giving out instructions to his men.

—Two together at all times. Shoot first, ask questions later. We're moving in on the Silver Seas soon as it's dark. But don't assume the Chinks are going to wait till dark. They could come through that door right now.

His mobile rings. He sees it's Nicole. Okay, he wants his daughter back but she couldn't have phoned at a worse time. He's about to go to war and she'll be wanting him to come and take her home from wherever she is. He's in two minds to take the call. But he does.

—Nicole?

She starts blabbering.

—Dad, Sam's… Sam's… it's horrible.

—What about Sam?

—He's dead. Gerry's a maniac. He's injected him with acid.

—Where are you?

—Somewhere in the city centre.

—Is there a phone?

—Yes…

—Phone me from that and I'll have it traced.

—He's cut it off.

—What can you see from the window?

—The river.

—Anything else?

Garrett's keys rattle at the door.

—Have to go.

—Nicole!

Garrett comes in. Nicole stands terrified in the middle of the room. He locks the door.

—See you've met the lodger.

—What?

—The lodger.

—What lodger?

—Sam. In there. I see you've met him.

She doesn't answer. She feels heavy. Her legs are weak. She bends and vomits on the floor.

—There are worse ways to die, says Garrett.

Devlin's cleared the room so that it's only him and Cooney. He tells Cooney Garrett has his daughter. Fuck the war with the Triads. He has to find and kill Garrett. Devlin wants to buy whisky. Get himself fired up. Cooney convinces him he'll be more efficient sober. He'll be in control.

—How can I tell Wendy?

—D'ye not think it'd be better if you found Nicole first?

—But how the fuck can I do that?

—What did she say?

—She can see the Clyde. How many flats can ye see the Clyde from?

—Did ye hear anything? The motorway? A train? Any distinctive noise?

Devlin shakes his head. A dead end.

—Did you not say he's in with the Triads? says Cooney.

—The wee Chinkee bird, Ming Fung. She phoned Bonzo. Says Garrett's in there mixing it up. Trying to take over.

—Go to the Triads then.

—We're just about to go to war with them! Or did you not notice?

Suddenly Cooney sees a way they can kill two birds with the one stone. Find Nicole and avert a war.

—I'm listening, says Devlin.

Garrett's told Nicole Sam tried to kill him. That he brought him back to extract information because the more they know about Devlin the safer they'll be.

—I'm fed up running, says Garrett, —We have to stop and fight.

Nicole pretends to empathise.

—I love you, Garrett says.

—I know you do.

—I find the love of my life and she turns out to be the daughter of the man who ruined my life.

—Dad ruined your life? I don't understand.

Garrett pours out his life story.

—Sometimes I'm here in this luxury flat. Sometimes down

Paisley Road West in a flea pit. It's perfect for me, a flea pit. An anonymous bedsit. Not even a change of clothes. That's how I move about this city. A room with no clock. No telly. No radio. Just one plastic watch keeping perfect time. One bed. One cupboard: empty. A sink. A window with the blind pulled down. A lampshade full of dead flies. A blessing after the clinical whiteness of Carstairs, those dead flies. Even death can substitute for life sometimes. I had a plan. And a long time to execute it. Since before you were born, Nicole.

One day I'm a waiter. Next a *Big Issue* seller. When my clothes get dirty, I buy more. From second-hand shops. Dead men's shirts. I can be anybody I want. Money? I've got as much as I want. Or none. I can be at the front of a crowd and you'd never notice me. I could be in the crowd and you'd mistake me for somebody else. I can be anywhere and nowhere. I could leave the room and you'd think I was still there. I've been in your school before you met me. Looking at you sleeping in your bed. If I wanted to harm you, I could've slit your throat as you slept. But I thought... think you are beautiful. I had to have you.

Nicole feels sick. Garrett goes on.

—When I'm not with you, I spend a couple of days here, take care of business. Then on to another location. Nobody knows when I come or go. Possessions mean nothing to me. You can't spend your life locked up and stay attached to material objects. It's all going on in there. In your head. The world outside your head shrinks and the one inside grows. But you want *things*. Or you think you want them. What you really want is the feeling they give you. And the ultimate feeling is power. And the degree another human being can make you afraid is the measure of how much power they have over you. I learned that when they put me in a home and forgot about me. I decided to eradicate fear from my life. And the only way to eradicate fear is to stay unattached to anything. Even life itself. That's the way to power.

I learned a lot in my white room in Carstairs. One bed. One

blanket. One book at a time. Strict obs. I took my mind to places you could never imagine.

Your hard-man daddy's nothing compared to me. He's got too many attachments. If he was anybody else, I'd just kill him. But he's not just anybody else, is he? So? So, I'm a cat with a mouse. No... that's not what I am. He's a cat. I'm a scorpion. I'll let him play with me all he wants, thinking he's lining me up for the kill. And at the end of the day, the sting. And I'm gone.

I've ground him right down. He's got the fear and it was me who put it there. Me! I put that darkness over his life. Power is no use if you're not using it. When he's defeated, I'll take the whole city. Not that I really want it. I bet you're wondering, so why bother?

Has he ever mentioned a cousin called Gerald? No, I don't suppose he has. We were sniffing glue when we were kids. He set fire to the house. Killed my mother. Blamed me and I spent the rest of my life in institutions. Do you know how that felt?

Nicole hugs him.

—I don't care about the past. Lets get out of here Gerry. You've got the money. We could go to Spain. Tonight.

—I promised myself I'd destroy him spiritually, emotionally and mentally before I destroy him physically.

—We could live on a beach! Both of us. In peace. What reason have we got to stay here?

—Tomorrow is a special anniversary, Nicole. I want you to share it with me.

Garrett kisses her deep and hard. All night long she fucks to save her life.

The Golden Moon's open all night long. Bonzo has phoned Ming Fung and asked if they could meet.

—I can't. Father said not to step outside Chinatown.

—I'll come and meet you then.

—In Chinatown?

—The Golden Moon.

—Are you crazy?

—Aye. About you!

—You'd be in danger.

—Don't care. I love you.

—No.

—Ming Fung, that's the last place they'll be looking for the likes of me.

—I don't know.

—I've wrote ye a wee poem. In Cantonese. I want to read it to ye.

—Read it over the phone.

—I want to read it to ye in person. In case anything happens. There's silence. He knows he's nearly persuaded her.

—Who knows, by tomorrow night I might be dead. She's not got time to make up her mind.

—Golden Moon. An hour's time.

When Ming Fung gets to the Golden Moon there are two Forty-Nines in the corner. They know her but they're too far down the chain to know there's an imminent war with Devlin. They've been told to get themselves ready. For what, they don't know. There are six Scottish couples. The men are wearing black suits with flowers in their lapels. The women are dressed for what was probably a wedding. Ming Fung feels safer now that there are so many white faces. Sometimes Gwai Los can be useful. One white face sticks out more than a dozen. She orders some green tea and sits not listening to the chatter of late night diners.

When Bonzo comes in he's nervous. But that's only natural. There's a Triad gang nearby who'd cut him to pieces. She admires him all the more. He can offer the protection she's craved since childhood. Since she was raped.

He gives her a bunch of flowers and two candles. They light the candles and set them into two foil ashtrays.

—You eaten?

He doesn't want to eat. Only wants to be with her. They share green tea from one cup and gaze. She's deep in love now. She can see he is, too. Only there's something in there. A reticence to let go with his love. Is that what it is? She's not sure.

—This poem?

—Soon.

—My father will know we're here in minutes. I've seen the chef on the telephone. He kept looking over when you came in.

Bonzo takes out a bit of paper, moves close to Ming Fung and reads in Cantonese,

—*Little girl, you have placed a basket of flowers in my heart. I love you, White Swan. My eyes are your eyes.*

She leans over to kiss him. He pulls away.

—I'm sorry, he says.

A gun is placed at her head from behind. It's Devlin.

—You're coming with us.

The Forty-Nines flinch but every white male diner has already drawn a gun. Their female partners leave. The white men disarm the Forty-Nines and back out of the Golden Moon with their guns trained on the Chinese. Devlin and Cooney take Ming Fung into a white van waiting with back doors open.

—Thanks Bonzo, says Devlin.

—Don't you harm a hair on her head, Christie!

In seconds they're speeding out of Chinatown.

When Tai Lo hears the news he's quiet. He goes to a corner and thinks. And thinks. Tries to put all the pieces together. He knows Devlin doesn't want a war. He's kidnapped Ming Fung to stop a war. There's a call.

It's Devlin.

Tai Lo takes the call on his own. Devlin does want to avert the war. He promises Ming Fung will not be harmed. Okay. Devlin wants Nicole back. Tai Lo doesn't know what he's talking bout.

—What I do know about your daughter?

—You're dealing with Garrett!

—Perhaps.

—He's kidnapped my daughter.

—I have knew nothing of this.

Devlin says if he gets Nicole back safe and well, he'll hand over his business to Tai Lo.

—You mean?

—Aye – do mean. With all my fuckin heart I mean! I'll keep Jarkness. You can take the rest.

—You can give me no guarantee, says Tai Lo.

—Tell you what, I'll come into the Silver Seas on my own, unarmed. You can take me hostage. Once you've found Garrett and Nicole is free, I'll order Ming Fung to be released. You can even kill me then, if you want.

—I call you back, says Tai Lo.

Ten minutes later, Heung Chu and Tai Lo are discussing the situation when the door opens. In comes Devlin. He's wearing a T-shirt. He walks through the casino, turning, his hands in the air.

—You brave Gwai Lo, says Tai Lo.

—I want my daughter.

—Me too.

—You'll get her says Devlin.

—We talk.

They sit in a corner of the Mah Jong room. Heung Chu listens to the conversation. A pot of green tea is set down. Two cups. I Lo and Hung Kwan are across the room playing tiles. Watching.

—She'll not be harmed, says Devlin.

Devlin's still thinks Tai Lo is in cahoots with Garrett. That he knows where Nicole is.

—If Ming Fung harm. Big trouble.

Devlin knows that. He repeats his offer. Give him Nicole. Tai Lo can have the whole city.

—I only want my daughter back, says Devlin.

—How can I trust you to release Ming Fung, says Tai Lo.

—Trust? Here's trust, says Devlin, —I'll show ye fuckin trust.

He lifts his T-shirt showing Tai Lo the appendix scar. Across the room I Lo becomes very interested.

—This is false. I done it myself, says Devlin.

—Done yourself?

He mimics cutting a scar with a scalpel.

—It was me. I never had appendicitis.

Tai Lo screams. Jumps across the table. Devlin's chair topples back. Head thumps on the wooden floor. The room is swimming. A hundred Chinese faces above him. Feels a searing pain in his hand. Tai Lo is trying to bite off his pinkie. Trying to exact repayment for I Lo's finger chopping. He gets his hand on Tai Lo's chin and jerks his head round. There's a crack and a yell of pain as Tai Lo opens his mouth. Devlin jumps to his feet shaking his bleeding finger about.

—Ooh ya bastard! That's sore as fuck.

I Lo slides a cleaver from his jacket. Devlin lifts a chair. He knows he's dead but he's taking I Lo with him.

—*Stop!* Tai Lo shouts.

They stop. Devlin keeps talking. Persuades Tai Lo that Garrett's trouble. Tells him that Garrett is his cousin. That he's out for revenge. They should stick together and eliminate him.

—But why I not employ Garrett and get rid of you? asks Tai Lo.

—Employ a man who's blew up your car? Put battery acid in your smack? Caused a war between you and your business partner? Brought about the kidnap your daughter? Go ahead if you want.

Tai Lo consults Heung Chu.

—Garrett doesn't care about money or power, says Devlin, —all he cares about's mayhem.

—Okay. Okay. We get rid of Garrett. And you will give me your business?

—Take it! Find Nicole and it's all yours. Except Jarkness. I'm moving there with my family.

—Yes. You leave Glasgow. Plenty money we give you. We look after your men.

—How do I know you'll not pop the lot of us?

—You have to trust.

Devlin raises his eyebrows. Trusting is not enough. Heung Chu coughs and Tai Lo goes to him. The Triads watch as Tai Lo's nods get more frequent. He turns to Devlin with a big smile and flings out arms.

—They will be safe.

—How do I know?

—Because, my friend, they would become part of the Brotherhood.

—Brotherhood?

—I would make them Triads!

—Triads! Sam and Sholtz and Bonzo?

—And you.

—Protected for life, says Heung Chu.

I Lo's fury convinces Devlin this is the truth. He was ready to slice Devlin to death. Now they're to be brothers-in-arms.

—And my family? asks Devlin.

Tai Lo smiles, —A Triad's family is protected by the Brother-hood.

—Right. You're on, says Devlin, —It's a deal.

He reaches out to shake. Tai Lo looks at Devlin's hand.

—One thing we must first do.

Tai Lo gives the signal. Everybody moves into the room with the trunk of a beech tree secured to the floor.

The door is closed and a grave hush descends. Devlin sees what's happening now. Ach well! A finger's a small price to pay to get the Triads searching for Nicole.

I Lo takes the cleaver. Devlin spreads his fingers. I Lo lifts the cleaver high in the air. Looks Devlin in the eye. The cleaver comes down thumping through flesh and bone. There's not a flicker of pain on Devlin's face as his pinkie rolls away from his hand. Blood pumps onto the wood. He keeps staring in I Lo's eyes.

—*Bandage*! says Heung Chu.

Devlin holds his dripping hand up and faces Tai Lo.

—Trust!

Devlin bows. Tai Lo bows back.

—So, says Devlin, —Where the fuck is Garrett?

—Where the fuck is Ming Fung? says Tai Lo.

—Come on, says Devlin.

The Triads meet Devlin's men near Garrett's penthouse flat. Sholtz and Cooney release Ming Fung from a doorway. She runs towards her father. But she stops when she's almost there. Goes back to Bonzo. He thinks she's going to kiss him. But she kicks him hard in the balls. The Triads laugh. He crumples to the ground. Ming Fung hugs her father.

—Devlin, come, says Tai Lo.

Sam's needle-punctured body is spread out on the floor. There are signs of Nicole everywhere. And signs of sex, drugs, madness. Devlin is at an all-time low.

Cooney puts an arm over Devlin's shoulder and leads him out onto the landing. Triads come and go removing things from the flat. Tai Lo comes up to Devlin.

—Sorry. We do our best. All our men look. We find. I keep promise.

He slaps Devlin's back and leaves.

—What the fuck am I going to do? says Devlin.

—You have to tell Wendy now, says Cooney.

An hour later, they meet Marie in the convent chapel.

—Where's Wendy?

—How, so's ye can wreck her fuckin life?

—Where is she?

—Here, says Wendy.

She's kneeling underneath the Sacred Heart statue. Praying. Devlin tries to take her hand but she draws back.

—Have you found Nicole?

—Listen…

—Have you found her?

—There's been a maniac stalking me.

—All you you you. Have-you-found-Nicole?

—He's caused all the trouble, the battery acid in the gear that killed Kerry-Anne and all they dead junkies.

Wendy stands up and faces him. He can feel her breath on his face.

—He killed David, says Devlin, —And now he's killed Sam.

Wendy half-knows where this is going.

—Where is she?

—Garrett's got her.

—Who the fuck is Garrett?

—Nicole's boyfriend. You've met him.

—Gerry!

—He calls himself Garrett but he's Gerald, my cousin.

A voice behind Devlin stops him in his tracks.

—Christopher!

He doesn't turn.

—Maw?

His eyes well with tears.

Mary-Bridget comes over and hugs him. He hangs in her arms, looking up at the stained-glass window through his tears. The Stag stares down.

Has his mother been here in this convent all the time? What do Wendy and Marie know about it? Has he gone mad?

—I thought ye were dead, he says.

She holds him tight.

—I thought ye had died, he says.

Wendy's wailing at the top of her voice. Her daughter is as good as dead. She might be dead already. Marie comforts her. Cooney kneels and prays. Prays for Devlin. For Wendy. For Nicole. For insight or inspiration.

—I thought ye were dead, says Devlin.

His mother places a hand on each cheek and tilts his head up to hers. Looks into Devlin's eyes.

—Have you actually seen Gerald?

—Aye.

—Did he say anything to you?

Devlin nods yes.

—Think. What exactly did he say?

—He said... he said... I want to destroy you spiritually,

emotionally and mentally before I destroy ye physically.

—Listen carefully, Christopher. Gerald is not your cousin.

—He's my cousin.

—No. He isn't.

—He's my cousin.

—He's not. He's your brother. Your dad and Theresa… they were lovers.

—Garrett's my brother?

Devlin's vibrating in confusion. He never had shakes like this on the drink.

—What the fuck's going on?

Cooney steps forward.

—Answers and explanations can wait, Christie. First, you have to find Nicole.

—Aw aye? And where do we fuckin start?

—Your father, says Mary-Bridget, —Start with your father.

—Come on, says Cooney.

He drags Devlin out of the convent. It's dawn when they reach Possil. Cooney waits in the car while Devlin goes in to see Dan.

Dan has a wreath in his hand. He's going over the painting of an emaciated Madonna and Child. The Madonna is Theresa. The child is Gerald.

—Alright? says Dan, —What happened to your finger?

Devlin grabs him by the throat and throws him against the wall.

—Where is he?

—Where's who?

—Answer me.

—How the fuck can I answer if I don't even know what the question means!

Devlin swipes a palate knife and presses it up to Dan's eye.

—I know he's my fuckin brother!

—That's right, take my other eye out, ya evil bastard.

—Gerald's in Glasgow calling himself Garrett. Gerald and Garrett's the same guy, ain't he?

—No.

—He's the same fuckin guy, ain't he!?

—He can't be the same guy, ya daft cunt.

—No?

—No. It's not possible.

—How? How not?

—Let me up.

Devlin steps back, letting Dan up. Dan rumbles in the cupboard. Brings out a wooden box with Gerald's name printed on the top, and a number. Like a prison number.

—He changed his name to mine. Long time ago, says Dan.

Devlin opens the box. There's a photo of Dan when he was younger. Another Polaroid of Gerald with Devlin at Largs. Devlin was about seven. They're in the water and Gerald's splashing Devlin. Devlin's standing with his eyes shut and his head down as Gerald swings his arm round in a big sweep. The water's cascading into Devlin's face. There's a Bible. Some letters. A small plastic transistor radio. And that's all.

—Possessions, says Dan.

Dan thinks that explains it all. But he sees Devlin doesn't understand. Dan digs out a white card from the bottom of the box. Gerald Devlin. Carstairs State Hospital 82628.

—There's your fuckin brother.

—Where is he?

—He's dead, ya prick.

—How's he dead? He can't be dead. I've seen him.

—I was at his funeral two months ago.

Devlin spits on the painting and storms out. As the cold sun comes up, Triads spread out through Glasgow like a web, seeking any morsel of information.

母親節快樂

happy mother's day

Butcher the donkey after it finishes his job on the mill.

DAWN. IT'S THE 31st of January. The temperature today is expected to fall to minus ten. Cooney drives fast on winding roads.

—Faster, says Devlin.

He has to get there. He has to find out. Devlin's pulled a favour. Card, Gerald's psychiatrist, has agreed to see him. Seemingly he's got some very strange sexual habits which he sates in a knocking shop owned by Devlin. The windscreen wipers beat side to side flinging off sheets of snow. Carstairs appears in the early morning light.

Once they're through the high-security procedure they're driven to Kelvin Ward by van. The van draws up. The back doors open into the ward. Card, anxious that Devlin and Cooney shouldn't talk to anyone else, leads them straight to his office. He closes the door.

—Take a seat, gentlemen.

—We're not gentlemen and we don't want a seat.

—What do you want?

Devlin moves menacingly close. But Card's well-versed in that behaviour. Deals with it daily. Shows no signs of fear or distress.

—Gerald Devlin, says Devlin.

—Yes?

—Is he here?

—I'm sorry. I can't give out information about patients.

BANG

Devlin floors him. He crashes between the filing cabinet and the window. Blood trickles down his nose. He's not had a punch on the nose before and he's surprised at two things.

1. How it didn't hurt.

2. How much it disorientates.

—Is he here? asks Devlin.

—No!

BANG

—Is he here?
—Yes and no.
—What kind of fucking answer's that?

BANG

—Is he here?

Devlin puts his boot on Card's neck and presses. Card is choking.

In St George's Cross, Garrett is a junkie. He's got Nicole dressed the same too. They're heading north towards Possil. It's bitterly cold and it looks like they're huddled for warmth. But he's holding onto her. Tight. On a cold day like this, nobody looks at each other in a city. They get the head down and walk to their destination. To warmth and shelter. A lone Triad passes slowly in a car. Doesn't even glance their way. All the time, Nicole's searching for an escape route. She could run into the underground and along the tunnel. But he's fit and fast, Garrett. She could yell for help. Would he kill her in front of so many witnesses? He probably would.

—What do you think of the question of death and everlasting life? asks Garrett.

—I've never really thought about it, Gerry.

—No?

He grabs her hand. Runs across Maryhill Road heading for the canal bridge into Possil. Nicole senses imminent catastrophe.

—Let's go to Spain, Gerry.

—But the rain always falls on the plain in Spain and that's no good, is it?

—I could go first.

—Would the plain not be lonely in the rain without me?

Under the bridge Nicole feels the full weight of the canal pressing down. The menace of the hanging icicles. Flurries of snow are blown in with every passing car. Nicole suggests she could go to Spain and he could follow once he's finished his – business. But her voice is trembling. Garrett grabs her throat. Shoves her through a hole in the fence.

—Game's over, he says.

He drags her up the embankment onto the canal towpath. Ties her arm to his with a cable tie and makes his way towards Possil. A duck comes in for landing and skids along the thin ice.

—I called Daddy, Nicole says, —He'll be looking for us.

Garrett puts an open razor to her throat and snorts.

—When you called daddy, that's exactly what I wanted you to do, ya wee hoor.

—Please. I've not even sat my Highers yet.

—I've not even sat my Highers yet, he mimics.

—I'm only fifteen.

—Fifteen. Fuckin fifteen? I was a long time in jail by that age. Sit down.

He forces her to sit on the bank and sits down beside her. Garrett reaches into his pocket and takes out a tiny black velvet bag tied with yellow string. He opens it and shows her a tiny bit of charred wood.

—D'ye know what that is?

—Wood?

—Wood? Fuckin wood? Are ye mad. Look again.

—I don't know!

—You're not very good. You're off my quiz team. It's a lock of my maw's hair. I broke it off when she got burned to a lump of wood.

He laughs like that was a good joke. Gazes over the canal. A dust of snow covers the ice. Near the edge where ice hasn't formed there's a huddle of ducks.

—D'ye know what day this is, Nicole?

—Tuesday?

—Aye, it's that. But it's the thirty-first of January.

Nicole searches for the significance of that.

—The anniversary of my mother's murder.

Nicole's terrified. Why didn't she run when she had the chance to? Garrett stands, pulling her up with him.

—D'ye want to see where it happened? Where your daddy murdered my mother? And then blamed me for it? I loved my mother!

He brings down a swiping blow on her face. A trickle of blood comes from the corner of her mouth. Garrett licks the blood away with his tongue.

—Come on. I'll show you. I'm sure you'll love it.

He drags her towards a distant row of houses on the canal.

In Carstairs, a spade slices into the soil. They've covered the grave with a white incident tent. Card digs towards Garrett's coffin. Devlin stands above and Cooney's outside in case anybody shoves their nose where it's not wanted.

—Faster, or it's your own grave, shouts Devlin.

Cooney pokes his head in.

—Calm down, Christie. You've got what ye want.

CLUNK

The spade hits wood. Devlin throws a rope down. Card wraps it around the coffin and climbs out. Devlin hauls the coffin out on his own. Card notes his strength. It's a long time since he's been on the wrong end of a psycho. Devlin flips the coffin on its side. Jams the spade between the lid and the box. Stamps the lug. The spade slides into the coffin. Devlin levers the lid open a few inches. Works his way round breaking bolts and bending nails. One last twist and the lid falls off. The three men stare into the coffin in disbelief at… the skeleton of a goat.

Devlin leaves Carstairs a beaten man. Somehow, Garrett has duped the State Mental Hospital into thinking he's dead. Somehow, he's got them to bury a goat instead of him.

Cooney starts the engine. Wipers clear away the thick snow as they drive away over a pristine white road. The more Carstairs recedes, the more Devlin cries. Cooney says nothing. Lets the man cry. There's nothing they can do now but wait and pray. The only lead they had to Nicole is dead. Ten minutes later, on a remote stretch of road,

—Stop the car, Larry, eh?

Cooney stops. Devlin gets out and closes the door. Snow breaks free and slides down the panels. He crinches towards a frozen stream. Stops and listens for something. Anything. Then he cries at the top of his voice.

—Nicole!

He pulls out a handgun and fires three shots into the snow. Into the Wilderness. Into the sound of his aching heart. When the reverberations have stopped he sinks to his knees. His head bobs up and down as he sobs. Cooney goes over.

—Come on, let's go back to the car.

As Devlin shuffles back, Cooney kneels in the snow, raises his arms and prays.

—God grant me the serenity, to accept the things I cannot change, the courage to change the things I can, and the wisdom to know the difference. Amen. We need some fuckin help here, Big Man! Gimmi something. Anything!

He waits. His eyes are turned up to the sky. There's nothing. He bends his head down. Tries to meditate. Snowflakes whiten his shoulders and hair. When he's calm he opens his eyes slightly. He feels compelled to go down to the frozen water. But there's no revelation. He crouches, looking closer. Still nothing. But his heart beats faster. He takes a deep breath, holds it for a few seconds letting it out slowly through his nose. He runs his fingertips over the ice. It's an electric shock. A jolt up Cooney's arm. He falls back into he snow. Has to reach out to steady himself. He bounds up the slope shouting.

—Start the engine. Start the fuckin engine.

Devlin star the engine, Cooney jumps in.

—Drive!

—What is it?

—Drive, shouts Cooney, —Glasgow!

A wee spark of hope lights in Devlin. Cooney slaps both palms on the dashboard. The wipers attack the snow.

—He wants you to be on his tail, says Cooney, —That's why he let Nicole call you.

The car fires across the moor. Devlin throws Cooney a puzzled glance.

—Right, Cooney explains, —What was the exact date of the fire?

—How the fuck do I know?

—Ye said it was January.

—Did I?

—Aye and ye said there was ice on the canal!

Devlin thinks. January. This is January. Ice on the canal. Theresa's death. An image appears in his head.

—Fuck!

—What? asks Cooney, —What is it?

—My da. He had a fuckin wreath in his hand the day.

—Phone him. Ask him if this is the anniversary of Theresa's death!

Devlin calls Dan, who confirms it is the anniversary of Theresa's death.

—Where exactly on the canal did he try to drown ye? asks Cooney.

The light is low. Coming to the brow of the hill on the M8 at Chapelhall they see Glasgow immersed in fog, its lights struggling against the winter fog.

—Go! Speed up! says Cooney.

Devlin stretches over, pressing the accelerator to the floor. Along the M8 they go, hazard lights on and headlights flashing from dipped to full beam. Full beam to dipped. Every now and then Cooney hits the horn. In three minutes they pass into the city boundary.

From the canal, Garrett shows Nicole where he used to live.

—I've done alright for myself, coming from this, he says.
He laughs. Takes her into an abandoned building. Lights a
few candles. He cable-ties her at the ankles and wrists. Sits her
on an upturned ASDA trolley. Looks at his watch. He steps
outside and looks along the canal, to left and right.

—He was always a daft cunt, your daddy. What've I got to
do, send him a postcard? I've got the right date. Thirty-first of
January. I've got the right place. Mibbi I should phone him.
D'ye think I should phone him, honey pie? Don't answer me or
nothing!

Nicole's legs are blue with cold. Garrett goes over and
takes off her warm jacket. He rips her dress open at the top.
Lifts her breasts out of the cups of her bra.

—My my, whose nipples are standing to attention?
He kisses one nipple, then the other.

—Never mind little puppies, soon be all over!
He pushes two supermarket trolleys outside.

—Come on, Nicole. The weather's lovely.
She obeys, shuffling as fast as her bonds will allow. Her
breasts are blue.

Devlin's left the M8 and is speeding towards the canal.
Screaming on the phone to Bonzo.

—Just get there. Fuckin now!
Cooney's on his phone guiding the Triads to the spot they
believe Garrett has Nicole.

He's got her bent forwards over a trolley and he's fucking
her.

—Ooh, I love ya baby. Ooh, you're so good!
Nicole's neck pulsates with pain as Garrett wrenches her
back by her hair.

—Look, here's Daddy!
Devlin's sprinting down the tow-path with his gun out.
Can't fire for fear of hitting Nicole. Garrett comes, his body
straining up into the freezing day. He withdraws.

—Thanks, babe.
Nicole's hopeless eyes are fixed on Devlin as Garrett slides

the security chain from one trolley between the cable ties on her ankles and clicks it into the other trolley. Wherever the trolleys go, Nicole will go too.

—Nicole, you are the weakest link. Goodbye!

Garrett pushes the trolleys into the canal. They break through the ice and submerge. Nicole struggles to stay afloat but she sinks thrashing under the ice. Devlin runs, jumps, and dives through the ice.

—Fuck sakes, he's supposed to be terrified of water, says Garrett.

The cold engulfs Devlin. He can hardly see in the dirty water. He swims one way, then the other. Searching. Garrett sees Cooney, Sholtz, Bonzo and some Triads arrive.

—Adios amigos, he says.

Garrett runs, bullets whizzing past. They give chase. Ahead, four Triads are marching along the tow-path. One pulls a gun. Garrett dive-bombs through the ice. As they fire into the water, black holes appear on the ice.

Under the surface, Devlin's found Nicole. He pulls her to the surface. His head comes through the ice but hers stops just beneath the surface. He tugs and pulls but can't move her. Only succeeds in pulling himself under. Takes a deep breath and dives again. In the murky waters he sees the trolley chain through the cable tie on her legs, locked into the other trolley. He tries to snap the chain. He can't. Tries to snap the cables. They cut into her leg. Diluted blood encircles her feet. He kisses her and swims up. Surfaces, gasping for air.

—Pound coin! he screams, —Any cunt got a pound coin?

Cooney is about to ask why.

—Just gimmi a fuckin pound coin!

Cooney fumbles in his pockets.

—Come on!

Cooney throws it. It misses and slices into the water. Devlin gulps and dives. His slow underwater hand reaches out and swipes it. He swims down. Finds the round hole with his fingers. Slots the coin in. Bangs it home.

Makes for the surface with Nicole.
Nicole crashes upwards with water and bits of ice falling
off her. Takes a choking breath. Devlin's arms rise out of the
water holding her waist. He surfaces and takes a rasping
breath. Nicole glues herself to him weeping and shivering.
—I'm sorry, Daddy, I'm sorry!
—I know, hen. I know. Get her fuckin out of here, Bonzo.
In the car. Get the heaters on.
Cooney and Bonzo drag her out by the arms and lead her
along the tow-path. Tai Lo helps Devlin out the water. When
he's gained some composure, Tai Lo pats him on the back.
—Glasgow Dragon. That your new name.
Movement in the water.
—He's under the ice, boss, shouts Bonzo.
—Kill the cunt! shouts Devlin.
They all open fire. The ice is riddled with holes. Under-
neath, Garrett breast strokes through whirling holy statues,
Buckfast bottles and syringes. Bullets surge past like underwa-
ter comets. He comes to a Zanussi washing machine. Rips the
lid off, rubbing his wrist off the ragged edge. Blood floats to
the surface where it's spotted by I Lo and Bonzo.
—Look, says Bonzo, —We've got the cunt!
A shivering Devlin stares at the blood staining the ice. His
men wait for instructions. He eventually speaks.
—Line the canal, both sides. He's not dead.
Garrett has pulled a hose from the washing machine. He
swims off, turning belly-up now and then to puncture the ice
and breathe through the hose. A hundred yards up the canal
he surfaces in reeds beside a congregation of ducks. As the
ducks skid away on the ice, Garrett watches Devlin's entourage move away. Triads and Devlinites walk up and down the
banks, guns at the ready. They've seen the commotion of
ducks and are heading in his direction. He sinks. Swims away.

Devlin, Wendy, Nicole and Marie spend the night in the
convent. The street is guarded by inconspicuous Triads. At

midnight Wendy's asleep with Nicole, wrapped around each other. Devlin's sitting on the side of his bed thinking when Sister Mary-Bridget comes in.

—How are you son?

—Mum!

—Come with me.

She takes him to the chapel where a priest is preparing for Mass. Devlin makes a confession to the monk. This is effectively his fifth step. The monk absolves Devlin of his sins. Mary-Bridget sits beside her son throughout Mass. The communion is for Devlin alone.

—Body of Christ.

—Amen! says Devlin.

He takes the wafer on his tongue. The monk holds up a chalice of wine to Devlin's lips.

—Blood of Christ, he says.

Devlin leans back to catch his mother's eye. She nods to drink and he does. The wine brightens up his mouth and warms his throat all the way into his belly, heating his insides. Devlin senses he's being watched. Up in the window The Stag stares at him. When he gets to his seat he wonders if that one drink will have him craving for another. AA teaches that once an alcoholic has taken a drink nothing can stop him from going on a binge. There are alcoholics who will drink wine from the chalice. But they firmly believe in transubstantiation, that the wine has been transformed into the blood of Christ. But Devlin doesn't. His mother whispers.

—I believe it enough for us both.

Devlin wonders if he was speaking out loud.

寬恕

forgiveness

Enjoy yourself. It is later than you think.

THE SEVENTH OF February. Winter still has Glasgow in its grip.
Wendy, Marie, Nicole and Bridget are at Jarkness. The whole
area is guarded by Triads. Devlin's in Glasgow waiting for news
of Garrett.

Cooney's taken him to an AA meeting. The meeting's over.
AA punters chat. Devlin drinks tea with Cooney. Cooney's
certain Garrett must be dead. When the ice melts his body will
be found. Devlin's not so sure. Cooney asks Devlin to read a
section from the *Big Book*. Devlin scans it but keeps checking
the clock. His mind hasn't been on the meeting at all tonight.

—In a hurry?

—Mibbi.

—Read it again.

—Fuck off, says Devlin, —With all these cunts here?

—Okay, keep your fucked-up mind then.

—You're telling me this shite can fix my problems?

—I've seen it fix a lot worse than you, and I've seen it fail.
Read it again.

Devlin reads.

—You are going to know a new freedom and a new
happiness. You will not regret the past nor shut the door on it.
You will comprehend the word serenity and you will know
peace…

Devlin stops, sighs and looks at Cooney.

—It's like an instruction manual for a Salvation Army
trumpet, Devlin says.

—Don't go backwards, Christie.

—I'm not. I'm getting initiated the night. Into the Triads.

—Appeal to your ego, does it?

—Aye! It does. And protection for my family appeals even
more.

—Do you want to rely on the Triads or God for protection?

—A wise man would take both.

Cooney smiles. An hour later Devlin, enters the ceremonial

room, barefoot, with his hair tousled and his coat open. I Lo hands him five joss sticks. The smoke makes its way up through the room. Devlin recites four ritual poems the last of which is this:

—I passed a corner and then another corner.
My family lives on five fingers mountain.
I've come to look for the temple of the sisters-in-law.
It's on the third of the row, whether you count from right or left.

When the poems have been recited and the thirty-six oaths taken, Devlin is led through the West Gate of the City of Willows. The oath list is burned. It rises in smoke to the Gods so that they might bear witness. Heung Chu approaches Devlin.

—Where were you born?
—Under a peach tree.
—Do you have a mother?
—I have five.
—Don't you owe me money?
—I paid you, I recall.
—I don't recall that. Where did you pay me?
—In the market in the City of Willows.

Tai Lo steps up to Devlin and hugs him.

—Welcome to the Brotherhood, Glasgow Dragon.

Tai Lo snaps his fingers. Bonzo and Sholtz step into the City of Willows.

—Where were you born?
—Under a peach tree, they answer...

Devlin leaves his men with the Triads and makes his way to Jarkness. He arrives in the middle of the night and sleeps for a few hours. Gets up early and walks along the shoreline. Jarkness is no longer used for drug deliveries. The Triads have bought another house down the coast.

When Devlin arrives back he sees Marie and Wendy to-gether in the garden. Watches them for a while. He'd never thought these two could speak, never mind be close. Wendy's hand touches Marie as they talk. Reconciliation. Devlin steps back into the trees. Who's that walking on the shore? It's Dan. How did he get there? Must have been Wendy. Or the Triads even. Protecting the whole family. Get everybody in the one spot until they're certain of the fate of Garrett. Over near the house Nicole chats up two Triads. He hears a noise and spins whipping out his gun. Heung Chu stands with one arm behind his back and another held out. In the palm of his hand: a tortoise.

—For you.

Devlin takes the tortoise. Turns it up and down. The wee head comes out to greet him and retreats back into its shell.

Heung Chu sweeps his arm over Jarkness.

—Tai Ping, he says.

—Tai Ping, says Devlin, still looking at the tortoise.

—Give a man a fish he eat for a day. Teach him to fish and he eat for life, says Heung Chu.

—Aye.

He was puzzled by the gift. Now he's puzzled by the Zen. You can't give a man Tai Ping? Is that it? You can give a man peace of mind for a day but in order to gain lasting peace you have to show him how to get it for himself. Devlin looks back along the Garlieston path. Heung Chu is gone. He steps out of the trees onto the shore. Dan's sitting on a rock. Looking out to sea.

—Da, did you see a Chinaman coming out of the woods?

—No. Did you see a nun?

Devlin hadn't thought of that. Sister Mary-Bridget must be at Jarkness too. His da thinks he's looking for a nun. What happens when he meets her? Devlin has an instinct to say something. To tell Dan. But the Serenity Prayer comes into his head. Accept the things I cannot change. It's someone else's problem.

—A nun? Nope.

Devlin sees Nicole hanging all over a laughing Triad.

—See ye after, Da, says Devlin.

—Aye son. Right.

Devlin leaves Dan flicking pebbles into the water.

—Nicole!

Nicole turns deliberately, hand on her hip. Pouting.

—Papa! she shouts.

Devlin drags her away from the Triads. Tells her to stay away. But her time with Garrett's attuned her to danger. Sex and dangerous men. Devlin wants her to concentrate on her studies from now on. Go to Eden. Forget everything that's happened.

—And especially don't talk any more to these Chinese.

—They're only assets of the business.

—Business?

—Yes, business.

—What business?

—Our business.

—Listen you here to me, we've not got a business, and even if we did, it would be *my* business.

—I quite like the idea of being part of a criminal family. It's made me realise how dull my life had been.

She's already had an interview at Glasgow University. She's going to study Law. In her opinion, Devlin needs a good lawyer.

—It'll be just like *The Godfather*, Dad! You were born for this sort of life. You won't be able to leave it. A few weeks rest and you'll be back.

Devlin puts his arm round her and walks her to the house. Will he be able to give it up? He's thrived on it his whole life? He's sure he can.

He will. He will. He will.

Marie stands at the end of a rocky peninsula. She's got an old Nike training shoe of David's. She smells it. The smell of her son. She's been sleeping with that shoe every night. Now she has to let it go. Sister Mary-Bridget thinks it best to let it go. If we don't let them go, they can't leave. They get stuck

3316

316

—Eternal Rest grant unto them, oh Lord.

She takes one last smell and throws it out to sea. It lands with a silent splash, steadies and floats away. She watches it drift until she's not sure if it's the shoe or the top of a wave. Dan places his hand on her shoulder.

—Marie...

Marie flings his hand away. She notices the burns are still on his hands.

—Can I talk to ye?

Marie tap taps her nail on her eye patch then slaps him hard. He hangs his head.

—Slap me. Slap me again, he says, —I deserve it.

Marie walks away. Dan looks out to sea.

When Devlin was sixteen he was passing his da's room and there, beside the bed was a bottle of Buckfast. Unopened. Devlin sneaked in, cracked the lid open and took a long slug. He screwed the lid back on and placed the bottle exactly where it had been.

An hour later Dan shouted him into the living-room. When he got in, Marie was standing with her head swung low. Her face was red and there was a slight cut on her lip. Dan had been slapping her about. When Devlin saw the Buckfast on the mantlepiece, he knew why. Dan held the Buckfast up and punched Devlin square on the nose. Devlin toppled backwards but managed to stay up by getting one hand against the wall behind him.

—Did you open that?

—No.

—Aye ye fuckin did, said Dan and kicked Devlin in the stomach.

—Leave him, Da, leave him, Marie shouted, —You'll kill him.

That only reminded Devlin of Maw who had left years ago. Dan was high on violence now. He held the bottle up like a holy chalice.

—Well if it wasn't you and it wasn't her, who the fuck was it?

No answer.

—Eh?

He punched Marie again.

—Who the fuck opened it and took a slug?

He punched Devlin.

—I hate liars.

Punched Marie.

—Tell me who drank it, an I'll stop. That's all I want, for every cunt to stop telling me lies in here!

Devlin looked at the blood on Marie's forehead. He was about to confess when Marie stepped forwards.

—It was me, Da! I opened it, she said, —I drunk it.

At least that'll be that all over, Devlin was thinking. He was flooding with guilt when Dan's face took on a new rage.

—Oh was it now!? said Dan.

He placed the Buckfast on the mantelpiece. Crashed a backhander into Marie's face. She fell against the wall looking up in terror with her chin in her chest. Dan kicked at her in a frenzy. On the head. Always on the head. Devlin tried to get him away but Dan was too strong. He was still a boy and every time he tried to stop his da he was propelled against the wall. And Dan kept kicking. Kept on kicking. He only stopped when Marie's eye was bulging from the shattered socket. He took one step back, looked at the eye, looked at Devlin curled into the corner like a kicked dog.

—Phone an ambulance. And remember, she came in like that.

He grabbed Marie by the hair.

—You came in like that. If they ask questions, you got attacked on the way home.

Marie nodded. That stuck in Devlin's head. That she could hear her da and still nod. That was the moment he saw the power of terror. Dan left flinging a handful of coins at Devlin on the way out.

—That's for the phone.

When Devlin was helping Marie into the ambulance a cop

asked him what happened. Devlin shrugged his shoulders. The cops knew there was nothing coming out of this kid. Devlin stayed with Marie until the surgeon told him she was going to be alright.

—Do you know who did this terrible thing?

Devlin shrugged the shrug.

—It's just that a young girl like that, losing her eye…

—Her eye?

—Yes, I'm sorry, it was so badly damaged.

The thought of his twin sister with only one eye sent Devlin racing along the corridor.

And into the street.

And back to Possil.

And into the Brothers Bar.

Devlin shoved through the crowds of men. Straight to the barman who had already decided not to serve him. Not because he was under age. No. He could see the badness in him.

—Seen my da? Says Devlin.

The barman nodded to a group of men playing cards and laughing in the corner. Devlin spotted his da. Over he went. Dan spoke without hardly turning his head.

—Are the polis snooping about?

—Outside! Now! said Devlin.

Dan's mates laughed. A silence spread through the bar until everybody was watching. Dan burst into loud laughter. Shook his head dismissing Devlin. But Devlin stood his ground.

—I said, outside, cunt!

—Aw, it's so funny, said Dan,—hilarious. But away home before ye get hurted. Come back when you've learned how to fight!

The men resumed their cards. The bar-room buzz went back to normal. Nobody seen Devlin pick up a thick pint tumbler. But when he stepped forward holding it like a weapon the place fell silent.

—What ye going to do with that? laughed Dan.

Devlin looked round the waiting faces.
—Fuckin bastard!

SMASH

Devlin crushed the beer glass into his father's face.
—How does that feel? Eh?
He twisted a shard of glass into Dan's eye. Dan sounded
like a pig squealing. His legs were caught under the table,
jerking up to get some purchase. But he couldn't get any.
Devlin had him pressed into the upholstery of the chair. He
finally pushed the shard in behind the eye.
—An eye for a fuckin eye!
With a flick he took the eye out. Dan's body juddered. He
passed out. Some men tried to pull Devlin off but he slashed
and gouged at them with the glass.
—Get back. Get fuckin back!
They cleared and Devlin walked out.
Devlin truly didn't give a fuck. From then on, violence
rewarded him. He was addicted.
Now he stands at his security gates watching Bonzo, I Lo,
Hung Kwan and Sholtz drive off to pick up the gear. They're
using his Bearsden house as a base now. The gates close.
Devlin's as well being in prison until they find Garrett.

The next day Garrett's inside Devlin's Bearsden garden. He
feeds a sausage to a ridgeback. It gobbles it up. Sits waiting
for more.
—Shht, Scooby.
The black gates open. In comes the Shogun. Bonzo, Hung
Kwan and I Lo get out and make sure the gates close behind
them. Sholtz drives to the automatic garage. It normally detects
Devlin's car and opens. But this time it doesn't. Sholtz opens the
glove compartment and rumbles about for the clicker.
—Yees go in. I'll park this, he says.
Bonzo, Hung Kwan and I Lo go in the house. Sholtz tries to

open the garage door. Click-click. Nothing. Click-click. Nothing. He gets out to open it manually. The only sound in the garden is the drill of the diesel engine. As Sholtz steps onto the gravel, Garrett steps onto the gravel at the passenger side. As Sholtz slams the driver door, Garrett opens the passenger door and pushes the ridgeback in. As Sholtz turns the handle on the garage door, Garrett flips the automatic lever into drive. Sholtz hears something, turns and screams. The car shunt-shunts him against the door, cracking both his legs. Pinning him. His legs are being broken over and over. The engine running and the car pressing against his legs. Garrett feeds the dog another sausage. As it eats, he stabs it three times in the arse and slams the door. The dog lets out an almighty howl and starts ripping the interior to shreds.

Garrett goes up and inspects the pain on Sholtz's face.

—Tell Devlin I want to meet him. Dawn tomorrow. Alone.

Garrett writes the coordinates on the bonnet of the car: 855 427.

Bonzo, I Lo and Hung Kwan run out with guns drawn but Garrett's gone. Bonzo rushes to open the car but the dog crushes its face against the window, growling. Its mouth's all bloody where it's been licking its wounds.

—Fuck me! says Bonzo jumping back, —How did that get in there?

—I was that Garrett cunt! screams Sholtz, —He wants to meet Christie. He's got fuckin coordinates!

Hung Kwan points his gun at the dog and fires. The bullet ricochets off the window. All the men duck. Even Sholtz.

—What the fuck're ye doing? says Bonzo, —That's bullet-proof, that glass.

They don't know what to do. Sholtz is in agony. Then I Lo slips under the car and pulls the diesel pipe off. A few moments, and the car shudders to a stop.

They bounce it back and Sholtz passes out. He spends the night in hospital surrounded by Triad guards.

That same night, Devlin pores over a map of the Wilderness,

—What d'ye want?

—You know what I want.

—No. I don't.

—That's funny, cos I know what you want.

—You dead, says Devlin.

—No, says Garrett, —That's what ye think ye want.

—Aw aye? What do I want then?

—Ye want me to forgive ye.

Devlin takes a step back. Can't believe he's listening to this.

—Would it not be better if that knot in your belly – the thing that's been bothering ye your whole life – was gone, and then I was dead? Now that would be a lovely world for Christopher Devlin.

Garrett steps forwards. Devlin takes out a gun.

—What, protests Garrett, —I was only going to hug my brother.

Garrett steps forwards with his arms open for a hug. Devlin fires.

BANG

Garrett whumphs down in the snow, his arms and legs twisted. The shot echoes round the mountains.

The Stag limps slowly, stepping up the icy incline.

Devlin inches towards Garrett. There's some fog coming out of his nostrils but that might be normal. It's minus twenty up here. Garrett's forehead. Devlin aims the gun and is leaning in to make sure he doesn't miss when a powder of sharp snow blinds him. Garrett grabs the gun. Devlin stands, blinded. He's surprised at how peaceful acceptance of death is. Accept that, you can accept everything. A lesson too late. When his eyes clear, Garrett throws the gun down the cliff face and opens up his jacket showing Devlin a bulletproof vest.

—I knew ye'd try to shoot me right away so... look, I've had my fun. I've tortured ye enough. Let's call it quits. I'd've done the same. We were wee boys. The only reason I got the rap is that you got in there and grassed first.

Is he serious? Aye, he is. He means this. He wouldn't have chucked the gun away if he wasn't. Maybe he's learned a lesson. Devlin's beginning to consider Garrett. What it might have been like for him. Garrett sees a small spark of empathy light up in Devlin's eyes.

—See! Told ye! says Garrett, —Ye didn't think it affected ye but an inch of forgiveness goes a long way.

—I didn't say it hasn't bothered me.

—Bothered ye! Ha! Understatement of your life. It's made ye what ye, are. Just like you've made me what I am. You're Frankenstein. I'm your monster!

—D'ye not think I've thought about it? There's not a day went by when I haven't felt the guilt.

—Some people are punished by society, Christopher. Others carry their punishment with them. I understand.

Garrett takes a step. Devlin steps back. They move as they speak, towards a five hundred foot drop. Garrett shows his palms.

—Christopher! I'm here to forgive you. Ask and ye shall receive.

Devlin's aware of the change in temperature. Warmer air from the ground far below. He sees the cliff out the side of his eye.

—Ask, then it's all over, says Garrett.

Devlin tries to move away from the edge in case Garrett plans to push him off. Probably wouldn't care if he went over too. Keep him talking. Keep him talking and move away from the edge.

Think. Think. Think.

—Okay, I'm asking.

—The Lord be praised, says Garrett, —He's asking. But oh, a wee bit of humility, please!

—I'm asking ye to forgive me.

—Forgive me. Say that.

—Forgive me.

—No. Say, forgive me, brother.

—Forgive me, brother!

—Certainly, brother, says Garrett.

He lunges and stabs Devlin with a blade.

—Ya fucker! Ya fucker! shouts Devlin, scrabbling as far away from the edge as he can.

Garrett lands on him with two hands on the ten-inch commando knife. Devlin has his wrists. Pushes him away. Garrett keeps downward pressure on the blade. Down, down it goes.

Devlin can't keep him off.

—By the way your daughter's a good ride, sneers Garrett, —and later today I'm going to find out if your wife's a good ride too.

The tip of the blade is into Devlin's neck a half inch. He can feel the thrum of the vibration from their locked muscles.

Footsteps behind them.

Garrett eyes flick to the side. In that microsecond Devlin rolls and kicks him off. Springs to his feet. Before Garrett can get up, Devlin drops kicks him. Two feet on the bulletproof vest send Garrett sliding downhill over the rock and ice.

Using the knife as an ice axe, he manages to stop his fall.

The Stag stands on the summit looking at Devlin.

—Cheers, big fellah.

Devlin goes over to Garrett. The knife's jammed in ice at the edge of the cliff. Garrett's legs hang into dead space.

—What ye doing hanging about up here? says Devlin.

The knife's six inches into ice. Garrett's body is pivoted at the chest, his abdomen and legs swinging under an overhang, out into air, back under the overhang. One light push and he'd fall into the sea of snow and rock.

Garrett played enough games with him. Now it's time for Devlin to play a little game with Garrett.

—How much do you hate me, cousin? asks Devlin.

—I'm sorry but I forgot my hateometer. And I'm your brother, not your cousin.

Devlin lies on his back in the snow, pushing himself towards the edge until his head is level with Garrett's. Devlin's upside down head chats to Garrett.

—Hi, he says.

Garrett spits.

—Ooh! Who's a naughty cousin, then?

—I'm your brother. We're brothers.

Devlin exposes his neck to Garrett.

—Here's the deal. I know you like wee games. So here's mine. You can hang there till your strength runs out and fall to your death. Or you can try to take me with you.

Garrett's eyes light up.

—If you pulled the knife out yourself, you'd have a microsecond as you slip down. You might be able to cut my throat.

Garrett stares.

Thinking about it.

—Come on, goads Devlin, —Push with your left hand, take the knife out with your right, slice my throat before you fall.

Garrett does nothing.

—So much for you destroying me. What was it again – mentally, emotionally and spiritually, then physically.

Garrett bursts into manic laughter.

—I've gave my business to the Chinkees and I'm out. When I go down this mountain I'm going to Jarkness and I'll live there with Wendy, Nicole and our new baby.

Garrett's laughing so much tears are running down his cheeks, turning into ice as they make the long drop. His hand grips the blade even harder. It looks like he's going to try.

—Did I tell you Wendy was pregnant? asks Devlin, —No!? Oh, what an oversight. Looks like happy ever after for me!

The slice and ring of the blade as it rises from the ice. It pauses a microbeat over Devlin's throat and then

Garrett tumbles

out

into

the abyss.

Devlin rolls over in time to see the body thumping into the rocks below, smudging the snow with blood. He lifts his jacket and pats his own bulletproof vest. The cold has coagulated the blood on his neck. He's had worse wounds in pub fights.

The Stag bellows.

—Looks like I'll live big fellah.

The Stag comes close, so close Devlin can see himself reflected in its eyes. He holds it by the head and kisses it smack on the wet nose. The edges of the world disappear into mist. There's no telling where it all ends.

Smoke rises from the chimneys at Jarkness. Wendy, Nicole, Marie and Dan sit by the fire, waiting for Devlin's call. For the first time in years they are together in the same room. Then Mary-Bridget walks in. Everybody registers Dan's shock.

—Is that you? says Dan.

—It is.

—Is that you?

—It is me.

—I thought ye were dead.

The phone goes. Wendy picks it up.

—Darling, it's me. It's done.

—Are you okay?

—Just a scratch. I'm alright. Everything's going to be fine.

—Is he…?

—Stone dead!

—Are you sure?

—Without a shadow of a doubt this time.

The release is incredible.

—I'll be home in under an hour. Get the dinner on, hen. I love you.

Devlin hangs up. And drives. His face is normal. Until he weeps and cries. The wipers flick left and right. Everything's going to be fine. It's a winter fairy-tale with only Devlin's Shogun moving through it. The car drives up over the mellow curve of a snow covered hill and

BOOM

It explodes.

永恆

eternity

Some other books published by **Luath Press**

Me and Ma Gal
Des Dillon
1 84282 054 0 PB £5.99

Winner of the World Book Day *We Are What We Read* poll.

If you never had to get married an that I really think that me an Gal'd be pals for ever. That's not to say that we never fought. Man we had some great fights so we did.

Me an Gal showed each other what to do all the time, we were good pals that way an all. We shared everthin. You'd think we would never be parted.

A story of boyhood friendship and irrepressible vitality told with the speed of trains and the understanding of the awkwardness, significance and fragility of that time. This is a day in the life of two boys as told by one of them 'Derruck Danyul Riley'.

Dillon captures the essence of childhood and evokes memories of long summers with your best friend. He explores the themes of lost innocence, fear and death; writing with subtlety and empathy.

Quite simply, spot on.
BIG ISSUE IN SCOTLAND

Reminded me of Twain and Kerouac... a story told with wonderful verve, immediacy and warmth.
EDWIN MORGAN

Ripe with humour and poignant vignettes of boyhood, this is an endearing and distinctive novel.
SCOTLAND ON SUNDAY

A brilliant debut filled with ironic revelation.
THE TIMES

The authenticity, brutality, humour and most of all the humanity of the characters and the reality of the world they inhabit in Des Dillon's stories, are never in question. Neither is the talent that allows us to share a window on that world.
LESLEY BENZIE

Des Dillon's exuberant mastery of language energises everything he writes.
JANET PAISLEY

...a classic account of childhood and a vividly imagined story of innocence and vulnerability...
BBC NEWS

A talented writer, deployed to great effect the traditional cheeky patter of urban Scottish kids.
THE SCOTSMAN

...to spend an hour in Dillon's company and listen to his quick-fire verbal delivery is to sample the undiluted language of the man that is the raw-material used in the crafting of his writing... BRIAN WHITTINGHAM

Six Black Candles
Des Dillon
1 84282 053 2 PB £6.99

"Where's Stacie Gracie's head?"
… sharing space with the sweetcorn and two-for-one lemon meringue pies… in the freezer.

Caroline's husband abandons her (bad move) for Stacie Gracie, his assistant at the meat counter, and incurs more wrath than he anticipated.

Caroline, her five sisters, mother and granny, all with a penchant for witchery, invoke the lethal spell of the Six Black Candles.

A natural reaction to the break up of a marriage?

The spell does kill. You only have to look at the evidence. Mess with these sisters, or Maw or Oul Mary and they might do the Six Black Candles on you.

But will Caroline's home ever be at peace for long enough to do the spell and will Caroline really let them do it?

Set in present day Irish Catholic Coatbridge, *Six Black Candles* is bound together by the power of traditional storytelling and the strength of female familial relationships.

Bubbling under the cauldron of superstition, witchcraft and religion is the heat of revenge; and the love and venom of sisterhood.

A darkly humorous and satanic fictional brew… with punchy directness and enormous brio.
SCOTLAND ON SUNDAY

Hilarious.
THE MIRROR

The author's humanity and the sense of real hardship are what make the novel… An exciting, entertaining read. It's farcically funny, it's sad, it's more than a little mad . . . just buy it.
THE BIG ISSUE

… thanks to writers like Des Dillon… Scotland is getting to know itself better every day. And in looking so deeply and sharply at ourselves, we of course learn more about those great undercurrents of 21st century life that go far beyond Scotland.
THE SCOTSMAN

Dillon clearly understands the mechanics of human interaction, particularly where the family is concerned…
THE INDEPENDENT

Picking Brambles
Des Dillon
1 84282 021 4 PB £6.99

Combining both the personal and the political in *Picking Brambles*, Dillon's trademark openness and humanity allows him to address serious topics along with the more light-hearted, allowing an accessibility for all readers that is rare and refreshing. Focusing on life's realities, on the joy and pain inherent in life, he allows us to share a window into each of the poem's worlds, to laugh and cry with easy humour and stubborn authenticity shining through. A collection that will definitely take you on a journey not to be easily forgotten, *Picking Brambles* is confessional poetry in a very modern context.

I always considered myself to be first and foremost, a poet. Unfortunately nobody else did. The further away from poetry I moved the more successful I became as a writer.

This collection for me is the pinnacle of my writing career. Simply because it is my belief that poetry is at the cutting edge of language. Out there breaking new ground in the creation of meaning.
DES DILLON

Each [poem] is well observed with that extra touch of insight... that turns a merely well-written poem into *something of greater weight and sensitivity ... Poem after poem captures a fleeting scene... these are poems that draw our attention to everyday life and show us how special it can often be. Most of them are short and ranging from the serious to the light-hearted, are very accessible...*
SUNDAY HERALD

A superb collection which easily matches his award winning novels for quality.
JIM CRAIG

These poems will draw many folk back to poetry. I loved them.
ANNE MACLEOD

Both sensual and spiritual, this is a seductive collection.
JANET PAISLEY

This is a collection which beats with a full, tough heart, and thrums like good music.
ALAN BISSETT

Through his poetic soul a big, big heart and a soft underbelly.
LESLEY BENZIE

Driftnet
Lin Anderson
I 84282 034 6 PB £9.99

Introducing forensic scientist Dr Rhona MacLeod...

A teenager is found strangled and mutilated in a Glasgow flat.

Torch
Lin Anderson
I 84282 042 7 PB £9.99

Arson-probably the easiest crime to commit and the most difficult to solve.

Leaving her warm bed and lover in the middle of the night to take forensic samples from the body, Rhona MacLeod immediately pervceives a likeness between herself and the dead boy and is tortured by the thought that he might be the son she gave up for adoption seventeen years before.

Amidst the turmoil of her own love life and consumed by guilt from her past, Rhona sets out to find both the boy's killer and her own son. But the powerful men who use the Internet to trawl for vulnerable boys have nothing to lose and everything to gain by Rhona MacLeod's death.

A strong player on the crime novel scene, Lin Anderson skilfully interweaves themes of betrayal, violence and guilt. In forensic investigator Rhona MacLeod she has created a complex character who will have readers coming back for more.

Lin Anderson has a rare gift. She is one of the few able to convey urban and rural Scotland with equal truth... Compelling, vivid stuff. I couldn't put it put it down. ANNE MACLEOD, author of *The Dark Ship*

When a young homeless girl dies in an arson attack on an empty building on Edinburgh's famous Princes Street, forensic scientist Rhona MacLeod is called over from Glasgow to help find the arsonist. Severino MacRae, half Scottish/ half Italian and all misogynist, has other ideas. As Chief Fire Investigator, this is his baby and he doesn't want help – especially from a woman. Sparks fly when Rhona and Severino meet, but Severino's reluctance to involve Rhona may be more about her safety than his prejudice. As Hogmany approaches, Rhona and Severino play cat and mouse with an arsonist who will stop at nothing to gain his biggest thrill yet.

The second novel in the Dr Rhona MacLeod series finds this ill-matched pair's investigation take them deep into Edinburgh's sewers – but who are they up against? As the clock counts down to midnight, will they find out in time?

I just couldn't put it down once I started. It's a real page-turner, a nail-biter – and that marvellous dialogue only a script-writer could produce. The plot, the Edinburgh atmosphere was spot on – hope that Rhona and Severino are to meet again – the sparks really fly there. ALANNA KNIGHT

The Road Dance
John MacKay
1 84282 040 0 PB £6.99

Why would a young woman, dreaming of a new life in America, sacrifice all and commit an act so terrible that she severs all hope of happiness again?

Life in the Scottish Hebrides can be harsh – 'The Edge of the World' some call it. For the beautiful Kirsty MacLeod, the love of Murdo and their dream of America promise an escape from the scrape of the land, the repression of the church and the inevitability of the path their lives would take. But the Great War looms and Murdo is conscripted. The village holds a grand Road Dance to send their young men off to battle.

As the dancers swirl and sup, the wheels of tragedy are set in motion.

[MacKay] has captured time, place and atmosphere superbly... a very good debut.
MEG HENDERSON

Powerful, shocking, heartbreaking...
DAILY MAIL

With a gripping plot that subtly twists and turns, vivid characterisation and a real sense of time and tradition, this is an absorbing, powerful first novel. The impression it made on me will remain for some time.
THE SCOTS MAGAZINE

Heartland
John MacKay
1 84282 059 1 PB £9.99

This was his land. He had sprung from it and would return surely to it. Its pure air refreshed him, the .big skies inspired him and the pounding seas were the rhythm of his heart. It was his touchstone. Here he renourished his soul.

A man tries to build for his future by reconnecting with his past, leaving behind the ruins of the life he has lived. Iain Martin hopes that by returning to his Hebridean roots and embarking on a quest to reconstruct the ancient family home, he might find new purpose.

But as Iain begins working on the old blackhouse, he uncovers a secret from the past, which forces him to question everything he ever thought to be true.

Who can he turn to without betraying those to whom he is closest? His ailing mother, his childhood friend and his former love are both the building – and stumbling – blocks to his new life.

Where do you seek sanctuary when home has changed and will never be the same again?

Heartland will hopefully keep readers turning the pages. It is built on an exploration of the ties to people and place, and of knowing who you are.
JOHN MACKAY

The Great Melnikov
Hugh MacLachlan
0 946487 42 1 PB £7.95

A well crafted, gripping novel, written in a style reminiscent of John Buchan, and set in London and the Scottish Highlands during the First World War, *The Great Melnikov* is a dark tale of double-cross and deception.

We first meet Melnikov, one-time star of the German circus, languishing as a down-and-out in Trafalgar Square. He soon finds himself drawn into a tortuous web of intrigue.

He is a complex man whose personal struggle with alcoholism is an inner drama which parallels the tense twists and turns as a spy mystery unfolds.

Melnikov's options are narrowing. The circle of threat is closing.

Will Melnikov outwit the sinister enemy spy network? Can he summon the will and the wit to survive?

Hugh MacLachlan, in his first full length novel, demonstrates an undoubted ability to tell a good story well.

His earlier stories have been broadcast on Radio Scotland, and he has the rare distinction of being shortlisted for the Macallan/*Scotland on Sunday* Short Story Competition two years in succession.

Short, sharp and to the point... racing along to a suitably cinematic ending, richly descriptive, yet clear and lean.
THE SCOTSMAN

Milk Treading
Nick Smith
1 84282 037 0 PB £6.99

Life isn't easy for Julius Kyle, a jaded crime hack with the *Post*. When he wakes up on a sand barge with his head full of grit he knows things have to change. But how fast they'll change he doesn't guess until his best friend Mick jumps to his death off a fifty foot bridge outside the *Post*'s window. Worst of all, he's a cat. That means keeping himself scrupulously clean, defending his territory and battling an addiction to milk. He lives in Bast, a sprawling city of alleyways and claw-shaped towers... join Julius as he prowls deep into the crooked underworld of Bast, contending with political intrigue, territorial disputes and dog-burglars, murder, mystery and mayhem.

This is certainly the only cat-centred political thriller that I've read and it has a weird charm, not to mention considerable humour... AL KENNEDY

A trip into a surreal and richly-realized feline-canine world. ELLEN GALFORD

Milk Treading *is equal parts* Watership Down, Animal Farm *and* The Big Sleep. *A novel of class struggle, political intrigue and good old-fashioned murder and intrigue. And, oh yeah, all the characters are either cats, or dogs.* TOD GOLDBERG, LAS VEGAS MERCURY

Smith writes with wit and energy creating a memorable brood of characters...
ALAN RADCLIFFE, THE LIST

But n Ben A-Go-Go
Matthew Fitt
1 84282 041 1 PB £6.99

The year is 2090. Global flooding has left most of Scotland under water. The descendants of those who survived God's Flood live in a community of floating island parishes, known collectively as Port. Port's citizens live in mortal fear of Senga, a supervirus whose victims are kept in a giant hospital warehouse in sealed capsules called Kists. Paolo Broon is a low-ranking cyberjanny. His life-partner, Nadia, lies forgotten and alone in Omega Kist 624 in the Rigo Imbeki Medical Center. When he receives an unexpected message from his radge criminal father to meet him at But n Ben A-Go-Go, Paolo's life is changed forever. Set in a distinctly unbonnie future-Scotland, the novel's dangerous atmosphere and psychologically-malkied characters weave a tale that both chills and intrigues. In *But n Ben A-Go-Go* Matthew Fitt takes the allegedly dead language of Scots and energises it with a narrative that crackles and fizzes with life.

I recommend an entertaining and groundbreaking book. EDWIN MORGAN

Be prepared to boldly go...
ELLIE MCDONALD

Easier to read than Shakespeare, and twice the fun. DES DILLON

Bursting with sly humour, staggeringly imaginative, exploding with Uzi-blazing action. GREGOR STEELE,
TIMES EDUCATIONAL SUPPLEMENT

The Fundamentals of New Caledonia
David Nicol
0 946487 93 6 HB £16.99

'David Nicol takes one of the great 'what if?' moments of Scottish history, the disastrous Darien venture, and pulls the reader into this bungling, back-stabbing episode through the experiences of a time-travelling Edinburgh lad press-ganged into the service of the Scots Trading Company.

The time-travel element, together with a sophisticated linguistic interaction between contemporary and late 17th-century Scots, signals that this is no simple reconstruction of a historical incident.

The economic and social problems faced by the citizens of 'New Caledonia', battered by powerful international forces and plagued by conflict between public need and private greed, are still around 300 years on.
JAMES ROBERTSON, author *The Fanatic* and *Joseph Knight*

A breathtaking book, sublimely streaming with adrenalin and inventiveness... Incidentally, in a work of remarkable intellectual and imaginative scope, David Nicol has achieved some of the most deliciously erotic sequences ever written in Scots.
SCOTTISH BOOK COLLECTOR

The Strange Case of RL Stevenson

Richard Woodhead

0 946487 86 3 HB £16.99

A consultant physician for twenty-two years with a strong interest in Robert Louis Stevenson's life and work, Richard Woodhead was intrigued by the questions raised by the references to his symptoms.

The assumption that he suffered from consumption (tuberculosis) – the diagnosis of the day – is challenged in *The Strange Case of RL Stevenson*. Dr Woodhead examines how Stevenson's life was affected by his illness and his perception of it. This fictional work puts words into the mouths of five doctors who treated RLS at different periods of his adult life. Though these doctors existed in real-life, little is documented of their private conversations with RLS. However, everything Dr Woodhead postulates could have occurred within the known framework of RLS's life. RLS's writing continues to compel readers today. The fact that he did much of his writing while confined to his sick-bed is fascinating. What illness could have contributed to his creativity?

This pleasantly unassuming book describes the medical history of Robert Louis Stevenson through a series of fictional reminiscences... I thoroughly enjoyed it. This would make a charming gift for any enthusiastic fan of RLS. MEDICAL HISTORY JOURNAL

RLS himself is very much a real figure, as is Fanny, his wife, while his parents are sympathetically and touchingly portrayed. SCOTS MAGAZINE

The Golden Menagerie

Allan Cameron

1 84282 057 5 PB £9.99

His fateful meeting with a mirth-seeking sect plunges Lucian Heatherington-Jones, an adolescent from Croydon, into a nightmarish series of metamorphoses from which he can only be saved by the wise and magnanimous Fotis. Drawing on mythology, eschewing the expected and engaging the reader, *The Golden Menagerie* defies our concept of the novel – and entertains.

... consistently fascinating and readable, the work of a writer... who has a stylish way with words. ERIC HOBSBAWM

Allan Cameron writes beautifully, sometimes with easy economy, at other times with a startling sharp pinprick of humour. This novel is, however, so pungently itself, with an unmistakable and singular voice, that it will appeal across a spectrum of taste. Like Yann Martel's Life of Pi, *its originality might well mark it out from the pack...* ALISTAIR MOFFATT

... involving, funny and stimulating, with a central character who manages to be both flawed and likable. MIKE ALEXANDER

FICTION

The Tar Factory
Alan Kelly
1 84282 050 8 PB £9.99

Outlandish Affairs: An Anthology of Amorous Encounters
Edited and introduced by Evan Rosenthal and Amanda Robinson
1 84282 055 9 PB £9.99

POETRY

Tartan and Turban
Bashabi Fraser
1 84282 044 3 PB £8.99

Drink the Green Fairy
Brian Whittingham
1 84282 045 1 PB £8.99

The Ruba'iyat of Omar Khayyam, in Scots
Rab Wilson
1 84282 046 X PB £8.99 (book)
1 84282 070 2 £9.99 (audio CD)

Kate o Shanter's Tale and other poems
Matthew Fitt
1 84282 028 1 PB £6.99 (book)
1 84282 043 5 £9.99 (audio CD)

Talking with Tongues
Brian Finch
1 84282 006 0 PB £8.99

Immortal Memories
John Cairney
1 84282 009 5 PB £20.00

Men and Beasts: Wild Men and Tame Animals
Valerie Gillies and Rebecca Marr
0 946487 928 PB £15.00

Madame Fifi's Farewell and other poems
Gerry Cambridge
1 84282 005 2 PB £8.99

Scots Poems to be Read Aloud
Introduced by Stuart McHardy
0 946487 81 2 PB £5.00

Poems to be Read Aloud
Introduced by Tom Atkinson
0 946487 006 PB £5.00

Bad Ass Raindrop
Kokumo Rocks
1 84292 018 4 PB £6.99

Sex, Death & Football
Alistair Findlay
1 84282 022 2 PB £6.99

THE QUEST FOR

The Quest for Charles Rennie Mackintosh
John Cairney
1 84282 058 3 HB £16.99

The Quest for Robert Louis Stevenson
John Cairney
0 946487 87 1 HB £16.99

The Quest for the Nine Maidens
Stuart McHardy
0 946487 66 9 HB £16.99

The Quest for the Original Horse Whisperers
Russell Lyon
1 84282 020 6 HB £16.99

The Quest for the Celtic Key
Karen Ralls-MacLeod and Ian Robertson
1 84282 031 1 PB £8.99

The Quest for Arthur
Stuart McHardy
1 84282 012 5 HB £16.99

FOLKLORE

The Supernatural Highlands
Francis Thompson
0 946487 31 6 PB £8.99

Tall Tales from an Island
Peter Mcnab
0 946487 07 3 PB £8.99

Luath Storyteller: Highland Myths &
Legends
George W MacPherson
1 84282 003 6 PB £5.00

Scotland: Myth, Legend & Folklore
Stuart McHardy
0 946487 69 3 PB £7.99

Tales from the North Coast
Alan Temperley
0 946487 18 9 PB £8.99

HISTORY

Scots in Canada
Jenni Calder
1 84282 038 9 PB £7.99

Plaids & Bandanas: Highland Drover to
Wild West Cowboy
Rob Gibson
0 946487 88 X PB £7.99

A Passion for Scotland
David R Ross
1 84282 019 2 PB £5.99

Civil Warrior
Robin Bell
184282 013 3 HB £10.99

Reportage Scotland: History in the
Making
Louise Yeoman
1 84282 051 6 PB £6.99

SOCIAL HISTORY

Pumpherston: the story of a shale oil
village
Sybil Cavanagh
1 84282 011 7 HB £17.99
1 84282 015 X PB £10.99

Crofting Years
Francis Thompson
0 946487 06 5 PB £6.95

Shale Voices
Alistair Findlay
0 946487 78 2 HB £17.99
0 946487 48 0 PB £10.99

ON THE TRAIL OF

On the Trail of William Wallace
David R Ross
0 946487 47 2 PB £7.99

On the Trail of Bonnie Prince Charlie
David R Ross
0 946487 68 5 PB £7.99

On the Trail of Robert the Bruce
David R Ross
0 946487 52 9 PB £7.99

On the Trail of Mary Queen of Scots
J Keith Cheetham
0 946487 50 2 PB £7.99

On the Trail of Robert Burns
John Cairney
0 946487 51 0 PB £7.99

On the Trail of the Pilgrim Fathers
J Keith Cheetham
0 946487 83 9 PB £7.99

On the Trail of John Muir
Cherry Good
0 946487 62 6 PB £7.99

On the Trail of Queen Victoria in the
Highlands
Ian R Mitchell
0 946487 79 0 PB £7.99

On the Trail of Robert Service
G Wallace Lockhart
0 946487 24 3 PB £7.99

BIOGRAPHY

Tobermory Teuchter
Peter Macnab
0 946487 41 3 PB £7.99

Bare Feet and Tackety Boots
Archie Cameron
0 946487 17 0 PB £7.95

The Last Lighthouse
Sharma Krauskopf
0 946487 96 0 PB £7.99

ISLANDS

Easdale, Belnahua Luing & Seil: The Islands that Roofed the World
Mary Withall
0 946487 76 6 PB £4.99

Rum: Nature's Island
Magnus Magnusson
0 946487 32 4 PB £7.95

TRAVEL & LEISURE

Die kleine Schottlandfibel [Scotland Guide in German]
Hans-Walter Arends
0 946487 89 8 PB £8.99

Let's Explore Edinburgh Old Town
Anne Bruce English
0 946487 98 7 PB £4.99

Edinburgh's Historic Mile
Duncan Priddle
0 946487 97 9 PB £2.99

Pilgrims in the Rough: St Andrews beyond the 19th hole
Michael Tobert
0 946487 74 X PB £7.99

FOOD & DRINK

The Whisky Muse: Scotch Whisky in Poem and Song
Introduced by Robin Laing
1 84282 041 9 PB £7.99

Edinburgh and Leith Pub Guide
Stuart McHardy
0 946487 80 4 PB £4.95

WALK WITH LUATH

Walks in the Cairngorms
Ernest Cross
0 946487 09 X PB £4.95

Short Walks in the Cairngorms
Ernest Cross
0 946487 23 5 PB £4.95

The Joy of Hillwalking
Ralph Storer
0 946487 28 6 PB £7.50

Scotland's Mountains before the Mountaineers
Ian Mitchell
0 946487 39 1 PB £9.99

Mountain Days and Bothy Nights
Dave Brown/Ian Mitchell
0 946487 15 4 PB £7.50

LUATH GUIDES TO SCOTLAND

The North West Highlands: Roads to the Isles
Tom Atkinson
0 946487 54 5 PB £4.95

Mull and Iona: Highways and Byways
Peter Macnab
0 946487 58 8 PB £4.95

The Northern Highlands: The Empty Lands
Tom Atkinson
0 946487 55 3 PB £4.95

The West Highlands: The Lonely Lands
Tom Atkinson
0 946487 56 1 PB £4.95

South West Scotland
Tom Atkinson
0 946487 04 9 PB £4.95

Details of these and other Luath Press titles are to be found at www.luath.co.uk

Luath Press Limited

committed to publishing well written books worth reading

LUATH PRESS takes its name from Robert Burns, whose little collie Luath (*Gael.*, swift or nimble) tripped up Jean Armour at a wedding and gave him the chance to speak to the woman who was to be his wife and the abiding love of his life. Burns called one of *The Twa Dogs* Luath after Cuchullin's hunting dog in *Ossian's Fingal*.

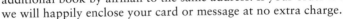

Luath Press was established in 1981 in the heart of Burns country, and is now based a few steps up the road from Burns' first lodgings on Edinburgh's Royal Mile. Luath offers you distinctive writing with a hint of unexpected pleasures.

Most bookshops in the UK, the US, Canada, Australia, New Zealand and parts of Europe, either carry our books in stock or can order them for you. To order direct from us, please send a £sterling cheque, postal order, international money order or your credit card details (number, address of cardholder and expiry date) to us at the address below. Please add post and packing as follows: UK – £1.00 per delivery address; overseas surface mail – £2.50 per delivery address; overseas airmail – £3.50 for the first book to each delivery address, plus £1.00 for each additional book by airmail to the same address. If your order is a gift, we will happily enclose your card or message at no extra charge.

Luath Press Limited
543/2 Castlehill
The Royal Mile
Edinburgh EH1 2ND
Scotland
Telephone: 0131 225 4326 (24 hours)
Fax: 0131 225 4324
email: gavin.macdougall@luath. co.uk
Website: www. luath.co.uk